GOOD GIRL
BAD GIRL
MICHAEL
ROBOTHAM

sphere

SPHERE

First published in Great Britain in 2019 by Sphere
This paperback edition published by Sphere in 2020

1 3 5 7 9 10 8 6 4 2

A CIP catalogue record for this book
is available from the British Library.

ISBN 978-0-7515-7343-5

Typeset in Bembo Std by Palimpsest Book Production Ltd, Falkirk, Stirlingshire
Printed and bound in Great Britain by Clays Ltd, Elcograf S.p.A.

Papers used by Sphere are from well-managed forests
and other responsible sources.

MIX
Paper from
responsible sources
FSC® C104740

Sphere
An imprint of
Little, Brown Book Group
Carmelite House
50 Victoria Embankment
London EC4Y 0DZ

An Hachette UK Company
www.hachette.co.uk

www.littlebrown.co.uk

Before becoming a novelist, Michael Robotham was an investigative journalist working across America, Australia and Britain. As a journalist and writer he has investigated notorious cases such as the serial killer couple Fred and Rosemary West. He has worked with clinical and forensic psychologists as they helped police investigate complex, psychologically driven crimes.

Michael's 2004 debut thriller, *The Suspect*, sold more than 1 million copies around the world. It is the first of eight novels featuring clinical psychologist Joe O'Loughlin, who faces his own increasing battle with a potentially debilitating disease. Michael has also written four standalone thrillers. In 2015 he won the UK's prestigious Crime Writers' Association Gold Dagger Award with his standalone thriller *Life or Death*. He lives in Sydney.

Also by Author

Joe O'Loughlin series
The Suspect
The Drowning Man (aka Lost)
The Night Ferry
Shatter
Bleed for Me
The Wreckage
Say You're Sorry
Watching You
Close Your Eyes
The Other Wife

Other fiction
Bombproof
Life or Death
The Secrets She Keeps

The book is for Jonathan Margolis.

For want of a toy
A child was lost.

TOM WAITS,
'MISERY IS THE RIVER OF THE WORLD'

1

'Which one is she?' I ask, leaning closer to the observation window.

'Blonde. Baggy sweater. Sitting on her own.'

'And you're not going to tell me why I'm here?'

'I don't want to influence your decision.'

'What am I deciding?'

'Just watch her.'

I look again at the group of teenagers, girls and boys. Most are wearing jeans and long tops with the sleeves pulled down to hide whatever self-inflicted damage has been done. Some are cutters, some are burners, or scratchers, or bulimics, or anorexics, or obsessive compulsives, or pyromaniacs, or sociopaths, or narcissists, or suffering from ADHD. Some abuse food or drugs, others swallow foreign objects, or run into walls on purpose, or take outrageous risks.

Evie Cormac has her knees drawn up, almost as though she doesn't trust the floor. Sullen mouthed and pretty, she could be eighteen or she could be fourteen. Not quite a woman or a girl about to bid goodbye to childhood, yet there is something ageless and changeless about her, as if she has seen the worst and survived it. With brown eyes framed by thickened eyelashes and bleached hair cut in a ragged bob, she's holding the sleeves of her sweater in her bunched fists, stretching the neckline, revealing a pattern of red blotches below her jawline that could be love-bites or fingermarks.

Adam Guthrie is standing alongside me, regarding Evie like she is the latest arrival at Twycross Zoo.

'Why is she here?' I ask.

'Her current index office is for aggravated assault. She broke someone's jaw with a half-brick.'

'Her *current* offence?'

'She's had a few.'

'How many?'

'Too few to mention.'

He's attempting to be funny or deliberately obtuse. We're at Langford Hall, a secure children's home in Nottingham, where Guthrie is a resident social worker. He's dressed in baggy jeans, combat boots and a rugby jumper, trying too hard to look like 'one of them'; someone who can relate to teenage delinquency and strife rather than an underpaid, low-level public servant with a wife, a mortgage and two kids. He and I were at university together and lived in the same college. I wouldn't say we were friends, more like passing acquaintances, although I went to his wedding a few years ago and slept with one of the bridesmaids. I didn't know she was Guthrie's youngest sister. Would it have made a difference? I'm not sure. He hasn't held it against me.

'You ready?'

I nod.

We enter the room and take two chairs, joining the circle or teenagers, who watch us with a mixture of suspicion and boredom.

'We have a visitor today,' says Guthrie. 'This is Cyrus Haven.'

'Who is he?' asks one of the girls.

'I'm a psychologist,' I reply.

'Another one!' says the same girl, screwing up her face.

'Cyrus is here to observe.'

'Us or you?'

'Both.'

I look for Evie's reaction. She's watching me blankly.

Guthrie crosses his legs, revealing a hairless pale ankle where his trouser cuff has ridden up his shin. He's a jolly, fat sort of bloke who rubs his hands together at the start of something, presupposing the fun that awaits.

'Let's begin with some introductions, shall we? I want you to each tell Cyrus your name, where you're from and why you're here. Who wants to go first?'

Nobody answers.

'How about you, Alana?'

She shakes her head. I'm sitting directly opposite Evie. She knows I'm looking at her.

'Holly?' asks Guthrie.

'Nah.'

'Evie?'

She doesn't respond.

'It's nice to see you're wearing more clothes today,' says Guthrie. 'You, too, Holly.'

Evie snorts.

'That was a legitimate protest,' argues Holly, growing more animated. 'We were protesting against the outdated assumptions of class and gender inherent in this white-male dominated gulag.'

'Thank you, comrade,' says Guthrie sarcastically. 'Will you get us started, Nathan?'

'Don't call me Nathan,' says a beanpole of a boy with pimples on his forehead.

'What should I call you?'

'Nat.'

'You mean like a bug?' asks Evie.

He spells it out: 'N . . . A . . . T.'

Guthrie takes a small knitted teddy bear from his pocket and tosses it to Nat. 'You're up first. Remember, whoever has the bear has the right to speak. Nobody else can interrupt.'

Nat bounces the teddy bear on his thigh.

'I'm from Sheffield and I'm here cos I took a dump in my neighbour's VW when he left it unlocked.'

Titters all round. Evie doesn't join in.

'Why did you do that?' asks Guthrie.

Nat shrugs nonchalantly. 'It were a laugh.'

'On the driver's seat?' asks Holly.

'Yeah. Course. Where else? The dickhead complained to the police so me and my mates gave him a kicking.'

'Do you feel bad about that?' asks Guthrie.

'Not really.'

'He had to have metal plates put in his head.'

'Yeah, but he had insurance and he got compensation. My ma had to pay a fine. Way I see it, the dickhead *made* money.'

Guthrie starts to argue but changes his mind, perhaps recognising the futility.

The teddy bear is passed on to Reebah from Nottingham, who is painfully thin and who sewed her lips together because her father tried to make her eat.

'What did he make you eat?' asks another of the girls, who is so fat that her thighs are forcing her knees apart.

'Food.'

'What sort of food?'

'Birthday cake.'

'You're an idiot.'

Guthrie interrupts. 'Please don't make critical comments, Cordelia. You can only speak if you have the bear.'

'Give it to me then,' she says, snatching the bear from Reebah's lap.

'Hey! I wasn't finished.'

The girls wrestle for a moment until Guthrie intervenes, but Reebah has forgotten what she wanted to say.

The bear is in a new lap. 'My name is Cordelia and I'm from Leeds and when someone pisses me off, I fight them, you know. I make 'em pay.'

'You get angry?' asks Guthrie.

'Yeah.'

'What sort of things make you angry?'

'When people call me fat.'

'You are fat,' says Evie.

'Shut the fuck up!' yells Cordelia, jumping to her feet. She's twice Evie's size. 'Say that again and I'll fuckin' batter you.'

Guthrie has put himself between them. 'Apologise, Evie.'

Evie smiles sweetly. 'I'm sorry for calling you *fat*, Cordelia. I think you've lost weight. You look positively svelte.'

'What's that mean?' she asks.

'Skinny.'

'Fuck off!'

'OK, let's all settle down,' says Guthrie. 'Cordelia, why are you here?'

'I grew up too soon,' she replies. 'I lost my virginity at, like, eleven. I slept with guys and slept with girls and smoked a lot of pot. I tried heroin at twelve and ice when I was thirteen.'

Evie rolls her eyes.

Cordelia glares at her. 'My mum called the police on me, so I tried to poison her with floor cleaner.'

'To punish her?' asks Guthrie.

'Maybe,' says Cordelia. 'It was like an experiment, you know. I wanted to, like, see what would happen.'

'Did it work?' asks Nat.

'Nah,' replies Cordelia. 'She said the soup tasted funny and didn't finish the bowl. Made her vomit, that's all.'

'You should have used wolfsbane,' says Nat.

'What's that?'

'It's a plant. I heard about this gardener who died when he touched the leaves.'

'My mum doesn't like gardening,' says Cordelia, missing the point.

Guthrie passes the teddy bear to Evie. 'Your turn.'

'Nope.'

'Why not?'

'The details of my life are inconsequential.'

'That's not true.'

Evie sighs and leans forward, resting her forearms on her knees, squeezing the bear with both hands. Her accent changes.

'My father was a relentlessly self-improving boulangerie owner from Belgium with low-grade narcolepsy and a penchant for buggery. My mother was a fifteen-year-old French prostitute named Chloe with webbed feet . . .'

I laugh. Everybody looks at me.

'It's from *Austin Powers*,' I explain.

More blank stares.

'The movie . . . Mike Myers . . . Dr Evil.'

Still nothing.

Evie puts on a gruff Scottish accent. 'First things first. Where's your shitter? I've got a turtle-head poking out.'

'Fat Bastard,' I say.

Evie smiles. Guthrie is annoyed with me, as though I'm fomenting unrest.

He calls on another teenager, who has a blue streak in her hair and piercings in her ears, eyebrows and nose.

'What brings you here, Serena?'

'Well, it's a long story.'

Groans all round.

Serena recounts an episode from her life when she went to America as an exchange student at sixteen and lived with a family in Ohio, whose son was in prison for murder. Every fortnight they insisted Serena visit him, making her wear her sexiest clothes. Short dresses. Low-cut tops.

'He was on the other side of the glass and his father kept telling me to lean closer and show him my tits.'

6

Evie sneezes into the crook of her arm in a short, sharp exhalation, that sounds a lot like, 'Bullshit!'

Serena glares at her but goes on with her story. 'One night, when I was sleeping, the father came into my room and raped me. I was too frightened to tell my parents or call the police. I was alone in a foreign country, thousands of miles from home.' She looks around the group, hoping for sympathy.

Evie sneezes again – making the same sound.

Serena tries to ignore her.

'Back home, I started having problems – drinking and cutting myself. My parents sent me see to a therapist, who seemed really nice at the beginning until he tried to rape me.'

'For fuck's sake!' says Evie, sighing in disgust.

'We're not here to pass judgement,' Guthrie warns her.

'But she's making shit up. What's the point of sharing if people are gonna tell lies.'

'Fuck you!' shouts Serena, flipping Evie the finger.

'Bite me!' says Evie.

Serena leaps to her feet. 'You're a freak! Everybody knows it.'

'Please sit down,' says Guthrie, trying to keep the girls apart.

'She called me a fucking liar.'

'No, I didn't,' says Evie. 'I called you a *psycho* fucking liar.'

Serena ducks under Guthrie's arm and launches herself across the space, knocking Evie off her chair. The two of them are wrestling on the floor, but Evie seems to be laughing as she wards off the blows.

An alarm has been raised and a security team bursts into the group therapy room, dragging Serena away. The rest of the teenagers are ordered back to their bedrooms, all except for Evie. Dusting herself off, she touches the corner of her lip, rubbing a smudge of blood between her thumb and forefinger.

I give her a tissue. 'Are you all right?'

'I'm fine. She punches like a girl.'

'What happened to your neck?'

'Someone tried to strangle me.'

'Why?'

'I have that sort of face.'

I pull up a chair and motion for Evie to sit down. She complies, crossing her legs, revealing an electronic tag on her ankle.

'Why are you wearing that?'

'They think I'm trying to escape.'

'Are you?'

Evie raises her forefinger to her lips and makes a shushing sound.

'First chance I get.'

2

Guthrie meets me in a pub called the Man of Iron, named after the nearby Stanton Ironworks, which closed down years ago. He's perched on a stool with an empty pint glass resting between his elbows, watching a fresh beer being pulled.

'Your regular boozer?' I ask, sitting next to him.

'My escape,' he replies. His fingers are pudgy and pale, decorated with a tri-band wedding ring.

The barman asks if I want something. I shake my head and Guthrie looks disappointed to be drinking alone. Over his shoulder I see a lounge area with a pool table and fruit machines that ping and blink like a fairground ride.

'You're looking good,' I say. Lying. 'How's married life?'

'Terrific. Great. Making me fat.' He pats his stomach. 'You should try it.'

'Getting fat?'

'Marriage.'

'How are the kids?'

'Growing like weeds. We have two now, a boy and a girl, eight and five.'

I can't remember his wife's name but recall her being eastern

9

European, with a thick accent and a wedding dress that looked like a craft project that had gone horribly wrong. Guthrie had met her when he was teaching part-time at an English language school in London.

'What did you think of Evie?' he asks.

'She's a real charmer.'

'She's one of them.'

'One of who?'

'The lie detectors.'

I suppress a laugh. He looks aggrieved.

'You saw her. She knew when they were lying. She's a truth wizard – just like you wrote about.'

'You *read* my thesis?'

'Every word.'

I make a face. 'That was eight years ago.'

'It was published.'

'And I concluded that truth wizards didn't exist.'

'No, you said they represented a tiny percentage of the population – maybe one in five hundred – and the best of them were accurate eighty per cent of the time. You also wrote that someone could develop even greater skills, a person who wasn't disrupted by emotions or lack of familiarity with the subject; someone who functioned at a higher level.'

Christ, he did read it!

I want to stop the conversation and tell Guthrie he's wrong. I spent two years researching truth wizards, reading the literature, exploring the research, and testing more than three thousand volunteers. Evie Cormac is too young to be a truth wizard. Usually, they're middle-aged or older, able to draw upon their experiences in certain professions, such as detectives, judges, lawyers, psychologists and secret service agents. Teenagers are too busy looking in the mirror or studying their phones to be reading the subtle, almost imperceptible changes in people's facial expressions, or the nuances of their body language or their tones of voice.

Guthrie is waiting for me to respond.

'I think you're mistaken,' I say.

'But you *saw* her do it.'

'She's a very clever, manipulative teenager.'

The social worker sighs and peers into his half-empty glass. 'She's driven me to this.'

'What?'

'Drinking. According to my doctor I have the body of a sixty-year-old; I have high blood pressure, fatty tissue around my heart and borderline cirrhosis.'

'How is that Evie's fault?'

'Every time I talk to her I want to curl up in a ball and sob. I took two months off earlier in the year – stress leave, but it didn't help. Now my wife is threatening to leave me unless I agree to see a marriage counsellor. I haven't told a soul that information, but somehow Evie knew.'

'How?'

'How do you think?' Guthrie doesn't wait for me to respond. 'Believe me, Cyrus. She can tell when people are lying.'

'Even if that were true, I don't see why I'm here.'

'You could help her.'

'How?'

'Evie has made an application to the court to be released, but she's not ready to leave Langford Hall. She's dyslexic. Anti-social. Aggressive. She has no friends. Nobody ever visits her. She's a danger to herself and others.'

'If she's eighteen, she *has* the right to move on.'

Guthrie hesitates and tugs at his collar, pulling it away from his neck.

'Nobody knows her true age.'

'What do you mean?'

'There's no record of her birth.'

I blink at him. 'There must be something – a hospital file, a midwife's report, school enrolments . . .'

'There are no records.'

'That's impossible.'

Guthrie takes a moment to finish his beer and signal the barman for another. He drops his voice to a whisper. 'What I'm about to tell you is highly confidential. I'm talking classified. You can't breathe a word of this to anyone.'

I want to laugh. Guthrie is the least likely spy in history.

'I'm serious, Cyrus.'

'OK. OK.'

His beer arrives. He centres it on a cardboard coaster and waits for the barman to wander out of earshot. A shaft of sunlight is slanting through a window. Full of floating specks, it gives the pub the ambience of a church and that we're in a confessional.

'Evie is the girl in the box.'

'Who?'

'Angel Face.'

Immediately, I understand the reference, but want to argue. 'That can't be right.'

'It's her.'

'But that was . . .'

'Six years ago.'

I remember the story. A girl found living in a secret room in a house in north London. Thought to be eleven or twelve, she weighed less than a child of half that age. A mop-headed, wild-eyed, feral-looking creature, more animal than human, she could have been raised by wolves.

Her hiding spot was only feet away from where the police had discovered the decomposing body of a man who had been tortured to death, sitting upright in a chair. The girl had lived with the corpse for months, sneaking out to steal food and sharing it with the two dogs that were kennelled in the garden.

Those first images were flashed around the world. They showed an off-duty special constable carrying a small child through the doors of a hospital. The girl wouldn't let anyone else touch her and her only words were to ask for food and whether the dogs were all right.

The nurses dubbed her Angel Face because they had to call her something. The details of her captivity dominated the news for weeks. Everybody had a question. Who was she? Where had she come from? How had she survived?

Guthrie has been waiting for me to catch up.

'She was never identified,' he explains. 'The police tried everything – missing person's files, DNA, bone x-rays, stable isotopes . . . Her photograph went around the world, but nothing came back.'

How could a child appear out of nowhere – with no record of her birth or her passage through life?

Guthrie continues. 'She became a ward of the court and was given her a new name – Evie Cormac. The home secretary added a Section 39 Order, which forbids anybody from revealing her identity, or location, or taking any pictures or footage of her.'

'Who knows?' I ask.

'At Langford Hall – only me.'

'Why is she here?'

'There's nowhere else.'

'I don't understand.'

'She was placed in a dozen different foster homes, but each time she either ran away or they sent her back. She's also had four caseworkers, three psychologists and God-knows-how-many social workers. I'm the last one standing.'

'What's her mental health status?'

'She passed every psych test from Balthazar to Winslow.'

'I still don't understand why I'm here.'

Guthrie sucks an inch off his pint and looks along the bar.

'Like I said, Evie is a ward of the court, meaning the High Court makes all the important decisions about her welfare while the local authority controls her day-to-day care. Two months ago, she petitioned to be classed as an adult.'

'If she's deemed to be eighteen, she has every right.'

Guthrie looks at me plaintively. 'She's a danger to herself and others. If she succeeds . . .' He shudders, unable to finish. 'Imagine having her ability.'

'You make it sound like a superpower.'

'It is,' he says, earnestly.

'I think you're exaggerating.'

'She clocked you straight away.'

'Being perceptive doesn't make someone a truth wizard.'

He lifts his eyebrows, as though he expected more of me.

'I think you're trying to fob her off,' I say.

'Gladly,' he says, 'but that's not the reason. I honestly thought you could help her. Everybody else has failed.'

'Has she ever talked about what happened to her – in the house, I mean?'

'No. According to Evie, she has no past, no family and no memories.'

'She's blocked them out.'

'Maybe. At the same time, she lies, she obfuscates, she casts shade and misdirects. She's a nightmare.'

'I don't think she's a truth wizard,' I say.

'OK.'

'What files can you show me?'

'I'll get them to you. Some of the early details have been redacted to protect her new identity.'

'You said Evie broke someone's jaw. Who was it?' I ask.

'A male member of staff found two thousand pounds in her room. He figured Evie must have stolen the money and took it from her, saying he was going to hand it over to the police.'

'What happened?'

'Evie knew he was lying.'

'Where did she get the money?' I ask.

'She said she won it playing poker.'

'Is that possible?'

'I wouldn't bet against her.'

3

Angel Face

I enjoy the mathematics of smoking. Every cigarette takes fourteen minutes off my life, according to a poster I read in a doctor's surgery. When I add the six minutes it takes to smoke each one, it makes a total of twenty minutes. An hour for every three. I like those numbers.

I'm only allowed four a day, which I have to smoke outside in the courtyard while a member of staff watches over me, ready to confiscate the lighter afterwards in case I try to burn the place down.

Sucking hard on the filter, I hold the smoke inside my chest, picturing the toxic chemicals and black tar clogging my lungs, causing cancer or emphysema or rotting my teeth. A slow death, I know, but that's life, isn't it — a long, drawn-out suicide.

I'm sitting on a bench where I can feel the coldness of the concrete through my torn indigo-coloured Levis (which I stole from Primark). I slip a forefinger through one of the frayed holes and widen the tear as far as the seam. I press my thumb into the skin on my thigh, watching how the blood rushes back into the pale blotch. Although barefoot, I don't feel the cold. I've been in colder places. I've had fewer clothes.

Pulling my foot into my lap, I begin picking off my toenail polish, not liking the colour any more. It's too girly. Dumb. I should never wear pastel colours — pinks and mauves. I once experimented with black, but it made my toenails look diseased.

I think about the group session. Guthrie brought a guest — a shrink with a strange name: Cyrus. He was handsome for an old guy — at least thirty — with thick dark hair and green eyes that looked sad, as though he might be homesick or missing someone. He didn't say much. Instead he watched and listened. Most men talk too much and rarely listen. They talk about themselves, or give orders, or make decisions. They have cruel or hungry eyes, but rarely sad eyes.

Davina knocks on the window and shakes her dreadlocks. 'Who are you talking to, Evie?'

'Nobody.'

'Come inside now.'

'I'm not finished.'

Davina is one of the 'house mothers', a title that makes Langford Hall sound like a boarding school rather than a 'secure children's home', by which they mean prison. There are locks on the doors and CCTV watching the corridors and if I kicked off right now, a three-person 'control and restraint' team would wrestle me to the ground and truss me up like a Christmas turkey.

Davina knocks on the glass again, making an eating motion. Lunch is ready.

'I'm not hungry.'

'You have to eat.'

'I'm not feeling well.'

'Do you want another red card?'

Red cards are given for misbehaviour and swearing at staff. I can't afford another one, or I'll miss our Sunday excursion. This week we're going to see a movie at Cineworld. My life always seems better when I'm sitting in the dark with a warm tub of popcorn between my thighs, watching someone else's shitty life flash before my eyes.

Nobody ever gets a green card. You'd have to cure cancer or bring peace to the world or let Mrs Porter look at you naked in the shower — girls only, of course — she doesn't look at boys the same way.

Crushing the cigarette against the brickwork, I watch the sparks flare and fade, before tossing the butt into the muddy garden. Davina raps on the window. I roll my eyes. She jabs her finger. I retrieve the butt and hold it up, mouthing the word 'satisfied?' before popping it into my mouth, chewing and swallowing. I open wide. All gone.

Davina looks disgusted and shakes her head.

Back in my room, I brush my teeth and reapply my mascara and foundation, hiding my freckles. I won't earn another strike unless I'm fifteen minutes late for a meal. When I arrive in the dining room, most of the other kids are finishing because boredom makes them hungry. The room smells of baked cheese and overcooked Brussels sprouts. I take a tray and move past the hot food, collecting two pots of yoghurt, a banana and a box of muesli.

'They're for breakfast,' says a server.

'I didn't have breakfast.'

'Whose fault is that?' She takes back the muesli.

I look for a place to sit down. Whenever I spy an empty seat, someone moves quickly to deny me the place. They're all in on the game. Eventually, one of the girls doesn't react swiftly enough and I get to a chair first.

'Freak!' she mutters.

'Thank you.'

'Dyke!'

'You're too kind.'

'Retard.'

'You're welcome.'

I peel the top from a tub of yoghurt and spoon it into my mouth, turning the spoon upside down and pushing my tongue into the hollow. I'm aware of people moving behind me, so I keep one arm braced across my tray, preventing anyone from flipping it over.

I can't stop them spitting or putting bogeys in my food, but it doesn't happen so much these days, because most of them are frightened of me. The same is true of the staff, especially Mrs Porter who calls me 'that devil child'.

I don't mind the name-calling because I'm harder on myself than any member of staff. Nobody can hate like I can. I hate my body. I hate my thoughts. I am ugly, stupid and dirty. Damaged goods. Nobody will ever want me.

The bully barks. The bully laughs. The bully wins.

4

Sun sinking. Autumn cold. I run along Parkside, zigzagging through the gate into Wollaton Park, where a sign warns me that I'm entering a deer calving area and that no unleashed dogs are allowed. The sky is streaked from edge to edge with pale trails of jets that have passed in the stratosphere.

Jogging beneath a tunnel of bare trees, the asphalt path moves like a conveyer belt beneath my feet. Things come and go – park benches, garden beds, walkers and cyclists. I run twice around the lake before climbing a rise towards the Elizabethan country house that gives the park its name. Wollaton Hall once took my breath away, but I've grown tired of its grandeur because it seems to be showing off.

Deer raise their heads, pausing from their grazing, as I ghost past them along an avenue of lime trees towards the eastern entrance to the park. My right hip twinges, but I like the pain because it helps me focus. Wearing jogging shorts, a quilted red windbreaker, woollen hat and light-weight runners, I move in an easy rhythm, turning back at Middleton Boulevard and retracing my route through the park.

Running is many things to me. Calmness. Solitude.

Punishment. Survival. In a world beset by problems that I cannot control, I can tell my body what to do and it will obey for as long as it can. When I run my thoughts become clearer. When I run I imagine that I'm keeping pace with a planet that turns too quickly for me.

I think about Evie Cormac. More of the details have come back to me. She was discovered behind a false wall at the back of a walk-in wardrobe in an upstairs bedroom. The house, in north London, had been rented by a low-level crim called Terry Boland. It was his body police had found in the same bedroom six weeks earlier. He was strapped to a chair with belts around his neck and forehead. The killer or killers had used an eyedropper to put acid into Boland's ears, slowly burning through his eardrums, destroying his cochlea and auditory nerves. Once he was deaf, they heated a metal poker with a blowtorch and used it to burn through his eyelids and his corneas, until his pupils boiled in their sockets. I remember this because the tabloids seemed to revel in every prurient detail.

The murder was still under investigation when Angel Face emerged from her hiding place. Nurses cleaned off the muck and washed her hair, discovering a pale, pixie-faced thing with freckles and dirty-brown eyes, a child too small to hold her own history.

In the days that followed, she dominated the news cycle. The entire nation seemed to adopt her, discussing her fate over dinner tables, in hotel bars, across backyard fences and in supermarket queues. There were public appeals, newspaper rewards and offers to adopt her.

I know what it's like to be at the centre of a media storm. I was once the survivor – the lost little boy, whose parents and sisters were murdered. I have been there, done that, seen the movie, and stayed for the closing credits. Is that another reason Guthrie turned to me?

Speeding up over the last mile, I check my watch as I reach the front gate, holding my wrist steady because I'm breathing so hard. I'm forty seconds outside my best time. I'm happy with that.

Lifting the latch on the gate, I walk up the front path to a tall narrow house. My ancestral home. It once belonged to my grandparents who retired some years ago to the south coast, preferring a modest bungalow in Weymouth to a six-bedroom, Grade II listed house that looks like it should be haunted, or at least have a mad woman in the attic. It was crumbling then, it's falling down now – a masterpiece of urban decay.

The ground floor has two large bay windows and a hand-some carved doorway with fluted half columns and leadlight glass panels that throw red and green patterns onto the hallway rug when the sun is angled in the right direction. To one side, a garage is almost completely overwhelmed by ivy; and to the rear, beyond a stone wall, an uncut meadow, guarded by ancient trees, makes up a quiet corner of Wollaton Park.

As a child I knew every cubbyhole, nook and odd corner of this house. I explored them with my brother and sisters. We played hide-and-seek or other games that involved make-believe guns, or swords, or dungeons, or dragons. We practised jumping from one piece of furniture to the next, never touching the ground, which was molten lava, or covered in spiders. Now the house is mine. My inheritance. My folly. My last link to the past.

Periodically property developers or estate agents knock on the door or push their business cards through the mail-flap, trying to convince me to sell. I once made the mistake of letting one inside. He began talking about morning rooms and secondary kitchens and conservatories, offering quotes and discounted terms.

'You're sitting on a goldmine,' he said. 'But we have to act quickly, while the market is hot.'

'Before this place falls down,' he should have said.

I reach under a pot for the spare key. As I straighten, I notice an unmarked police car is parked opposite the house.

I know it's a police car because two-way radio antennas are sticking from the roof and a square-headed figure is behind the wheel.

Unlocking the door, I walk to the kitchen, a big, high-ceilinged room with a scrubbed wooden table and mismatched wooden chairs. I get a glass of water from a spitting tap.

The doorbell rings. Water spills down my chin. I want to ignore both things, but that's not going to happen.

The shadow behind the stained glass is a detective in a misshapen suit, or maybe it's his body. Medium height, with short arms and spiked hair.

'I'm sorry to bother you. I tried to call ahead, but nobody had your phone number.'

'I don't have one.'

'What sort of person doesn't have a phone?'

'One with a pager.'

He sneaks a glance at me as though I'm mentally challenged.

I turn and walk down the hallway. He follows, introducing himself.

'I'm Detective Sergeant Alan Edgar. Lenny sent me to collect you.'

'You call her Lenny?'

He looks at me sheepishly. 'Chief Inspector Parvel.'

I drink another glass of water. The silence plays on his nerves.

'We've found the body of a teenage girl who went missing last night.'

'Where?'

'In Clifton . . . beside a footpath.'

I rinse the glass and put it in the drainer.

'I need a shower.'

'I'll be in the car,' he says, glancing at the ceiling, as though the house might collapse at any moment.

In the upstairs bathroom, I strip down and turn on the tap. The pipes clank and shudder as I wait for the water to arrive, spitting and hawking from the showerhead. Some days it remains cold as though testing me, or scalding hot as though punishing me, but whenever I call a plumber he recommends ripping out the entire heating system and installing a new one, something I can't afford.

Hot water arrives. I'm clean for another day.

Dressed in old jeans, a flannelette shirt and an olive-green army coat, I fill the pockets with a chapstick, keys, chewing gum and my money-clip. I have no pets to worry about, no plants to water, no other appointments to keep.

DS Edgar opens the car door for me. I wonder if his mates call him 'Poe'. There are worse nicknames. I've had some of them. At school I was called 'Virus' because of the rhyme.

'You're a psychologist,' Edgar says. Not a question. 'You treated a mate of mine in the SWAT team. You said he had PTSD and recommended he be medically retired. Pissed him right off.'

'I can't talk about my clinical cases.'

'Right. Sure. You were probably right.'

'Probably' means he thinks I got it wrong.

I often get this reaction from police officers when they discover the work I do. I'm the specialist they see after they've been attacked, or shot at, or have discharged a firearm, or witnessed a tragedy. I judge their mental state. I look for signs of trauma. I prevent suicides. The thin blue line can be a mentally fragile one.

Edgar has grown uncomfortable with the silence.

'How do you know the guv?' he asks.

'We go way back.'

'Did you meet her on the job?'

'When I was a child.'

He doesn't react, but I recognise what he's doing. He's digging for details. He knows what happened to my family. I'm the boy who came home from football practice and found my father dead in the sitting room and my mother on the kitchen floor and my twin sisters hacked to death in the bedroom they

23

shared upstairs. Did I really discover my older brother sitting on the sofa, watching TV, resting his feet on my father's body?

I don't give him the opportunity. 'What do you know about the victim?'

'Jodie Sheehan. Aged fifteen. She was last seen at a fireworks display at the Clifton Playing Fields. Her parents reported her missing this morning. Her body was found just after midday in a wooded area next to Silverdale Walk.'

'Who found her?'

'A woman walking her dog.'

Why is it always someone walking a dog?

We partially circle two roundabouts and enter a small triangle of streets squeezed between Clifton Lane and Fairham Brook. The cottages and semi-detached bungalows are post-war, with low-pitched roofs, flat-fronted facades and postage stamp-sized front gardens.

I know areas like this one, full of hardworking, respectable people, who have pushed back against low pay, insecure employment and government austerity by working multiple jobs, driving second-hand cars, and setting achievable goals rather than aspirational ones.

Turning a corner, I see a crowd spilling onto the road. People jostle and press forward, hoping for a glimpse of the fallen girl, or to see a real-life tragedy unfold that isn't on their TV screens. Two police cars are parked across the entrance to the community centre. Forensic technicians clad in light blue overalls are unloading silver cases from the sliding doors of a van.

A handful of uniformed officers are keeping the crowd behind bollards and crime-scene tape. DS Edgar flashes his badge and raises the tape above my head. A big man steps from the crowd, yelling, 'Is it her? Is it our Jodie?'

He's wearing a fawn-coloured raincoat tight across his chest and his head seems to perch like a stone ball on top of his shoulders.

'Please go home, Mr Sheehan,' says Edgar. 'We'll tell you as soon as we know something.'

He tries to force his way past the police but is pushed back. A younger man grabs his arm. 'Come on, Dad,' he says. 'Let it go.' He's a smaller, deflated version of his father, with short hair and long sideburns that reach down his cheeks.

'Poor bastards,' mutters Edgar as we walk in single file along an asphalt path, entering a large copse of trees surrounded by a wild meadow. It's four-thirty and already growing dark. Ahead of us three lampposts cast pools of light that lengthen and shorten our shadows. Further on, we reach the footbridge with welded metal handrails and the sound of running water underneath. As we cross Fairham Brook, I glance over the side and see where the channel widens into a pond fringed by reeds. Eighty yards away, in a small clearing, tree trunks have been turned to silver by bright lights, and portable generators are throbbing like a drum track playing on a loop. A white canvas tent has been erected at the base of a steep embankment. Lit from within, it glows like a Chinese paper lantern with moths trapped inside.

Two Land Rovers are parked at the western side of the footbridge. Lenny Parvel is seated in one of them, talking on a two-way radio. I wait until she's finished.

She shakes my hand, wanting to pull me closer into a hug, but this is work. Her hazel eyes soften. 'I wouldn't normally.'

'Yes, you would.'

Dressed in a Barbour jacket and wellingtons that reach as high as her knees, she has pale, fine features and bottle-black hair cut short enough to brush against her shoulders. Lenny isn't her real name. She was christened Lenore Eustace Mary Parvel by parents who thought a long name would give their daughter added status, although Lenny would dispute this. She once told me she'd have earned an extra A level if she hadn't spent so much time filling out her name.

Lenny was the first police officer on the scene when my parents and sisters were murdered. She found me hiding in the garden shed where I'd armed myself with a mattock, convinced

25

I was the next to die. It was Lenny who coaxed me out and wrapped me in her coat and sat with me until the cavalry arrived. I remember her crouching beside the open door of the patrol car, asking me my name. She offered me a Tic Tac, holding my trembling hand as she shook them onto my palm. That moment, her touch, made me realise that there was still warmth in the world.

In the days that followed, Lenny sat with me during the police interviews and watched over me when I slept in a foldout bed at the station. During the committal hearings and the trial, she shielded me from the media and chaperoned me to court, keeping me company as I waited to give evidence. She was sitting at the back of the courtroom when I swore to tell the truth and tried not to look at my brother in the dock.

Back then she was a constable, barely a year into the job. Now she's head of the serious operations unit in Nottinghamshire Police; married, divorced, remarried, with two grown-up stepchildren. I'm like a third.

'How much did Edgar tell you?' she asks.

'Jodie Sheehan, aged fifteen, went missing last night.'

Lenny shows me a photograph of two girls, pointing to Jodie, a sloe-eyed teen with thick brown hair and a gap in her front teeth that braces didn't fix.

'She was last seen by her cousin, Tasmin Whitaker, at five past eight at a fireworks display less than a mile from here.' Lenny points to the second girl in the picture, who is taller and heavier, with a round face and a lopsided smile.

'Jodie told Tasmin she was going to a chippie on Southchurch Drive. They planned to meet up later at Tasmin's house. Jodie didn't arrive.'

Lenny leads me down the muddy path that switches back and forth and grows steeper in places. As we near the tent, duckboards are set out like stepping stones and arc lights create pools of bright light that turn dew-beaded cobwebs into jewelled threads.

A canvas flap is pulled back and I catch a glimpse of the body. Jodie Sheehan is lying on her right side with her knees pulled up towards her chest. Her jeans and knickers are bunched at her ankles above her suede boots, and her sweater has been pulled up beneath her chin. Her bra is unclasped and twisted to the side, exposing small, pale breasts that are stained with mud or blood. Her eyes are open, popping slightly, with a dull white sheen as though cataracts have grown across her pupils.

I feel embarrassed by her nakedness. I want to pull up her jeans and pull down her sweater and say how sorry I am that we're meeting like this. I want to apologise that people are taking photographs and scraping beneath her fingernails and swabbing her orifices. I'm sorry that she can't tell me who did this to her; or point him out from a line-up or scrawl his name on a piece of paper.

I crouch and notice the leaves and grass clinging to her hair. There are scratches on her hands and forearms, and bruising to her right eye, and a bump on her forehead. She's wearing a single earring – a delicate silver stud that catches the light. Where is the other one? Was it lost in a struggle, or taken as a souvenir?

A ghost-like figure steps into the tent. Clad from head to toe in shapeless hooded coveralls, Robert Ness is barely recognisable, but he makes the tent feel smaller because of his bulk.

The senior Home Office pathologist, sometimes called Nessie, is in his late forties with skin so dark it makes the whites of his eyes seem brighter. He's wearing rimless glasses that momentarily catch the light when he tilts his head.

'Do you two know each other?' asks Lenny.

We nod but don't shake hands.

'Let's make this quick,' says Ness. 'I don't want to leave her out here.'

'When did she die?' asks Lenny.

'Early hours. It was cold last night, which lowered her body temperature and kept the insects away.'

'Cause of death?'

'Unclear. She suffered a blow to the back of her head that didn't fracture her skull but might have rendered her unconscious. I'll know more after the post mortem.'

'Was she sexually assaulted?' I ask.

'There are traces of semen in her hair.'

A bubble of air gets trapped in my throat.

The pathologist drops to his haunches, pointing to Jodie's boots. 'They're full of water and I found pondweed in her hair. Fairham Brook is beyond those trees.' He indicates the bruising on her forehead. 'That's an impact injury, likely caused by a fall.'

'What about the scratches on her arms?'

'From branches and brambles.'

She tried to run.

Lenny turns away and summons DS Edgar. 'I want police divers here at first light. We're looking for her mobile phone and a polka-dot print tote bag.'

Leaving the SOCO tent, I keep to the duckboards until I reach the perimeter of the crime scene. A carpet of papery leaves squelches beneath my boots, hiding roots that bump up from the ground ready to catch my ankles. In daylight the clearing would be visible from the footpath, or the top of the embankment. At night it disappears and becomes darker than the meadow because overhanging branches block out the ambient light.

Lenny has joined me. We scramble up the embankment using the trees as handholds.

'Where does the footpath lead?' I ask.

'Once it crosses the footbridge it hits a T-junction. To the right is Farnborough Road. Turn left and it crosses the tramlines and eventually reaches Forsyth Academy, Jodie's school. Her family lives beyond, in Clifton. This would have been a shortcut home.'

'From where?'

28

'Her cousin's house. Tasmin Whitaker lives five minutes from here.'

Below us, a group of forensic technicians have lifted Jodie's body onto a white plastic sheet that is folded over her and sealed. A second layer of plastic is zipped up, cocooning her in a bag with handles that is carried by four men to a waiting ambulance.

Lenny watches in silence, her dark hair boxed on her neck.

'The tabloids will have wet dreams over this one. A pretty church-going schoolgirl; a champion figure skater.'

'Figure skater?'

'*The Times* profiled her during the summer. They called her the golden girl of British skating.'

Crossing the footbridge, we follow the asphalt path to the community centre. Most of the locals have gone home, escaping the cold, but TV crews and reporters have taken their places. Cameras are shouldered. Spotlights blaze.

'Is it Jodie?' someone yells.

'How did she die?'

'Was she raped?'

'Any suspects?'

The questions seem brutal in the circumstances, but Lenny keeps her head down, hands in her pockets.

We pause at the police car. 'What do you need?' she asks.

'Can I talk to her family?'

'They haven't been formally notified.'

'I think they know.'

5

The semi-detached house has a single bay window on the lower floor and a small square of soggy front garden surrounded on three sides by a heavily pruned knee-high hedge. Two vehicles are parked nose to tail in the driveway – one a black cab and the other a new-model Lexus with a darker-than-legal tint on the windows.

A police constable is waiting outside, stamping her feet against the cold. Lenny presses a doorbell. Dougal Sheehan answers and looks past us, as though hoping we might have brought his daughter home.

'I'm Detective Chief Inspector Lenore Parvel,' says Lenny. 'I wanted to speak to you and your wife.'

Wordlessly, he turns and leads us into an over-furnished sitting room with a lumpy sofa and two worn armchairs. A TV is showing football with the sound turned down.

Maggie Sheehan is standing in the arched doorway to the kitchen. Everything about her is crumpled and diminished. The forward cant of her shoulders. The dark rings beneath her eyes. A string of polished wooden rosary beads are clenched in her fist.

'Mrs Sheehan,' begins Lenny.

'Please call me Maggie,' she replies mechanically, before introducing her brother, Bryan, and his wife, Felicity, who are sitting at the kitchen table. The Whitakers are Tasmin's parents, come to offer support.

Lenny is standing in the centre of the living room with her legs braced apart and hands clasped like she's on a parade ground. Some people *own* every space they inhabit, but Lenny seems to conquer the room quietly, taking it inch by inch with the force of her personality.

Maggie takes a seat on the sofa. The skin above her collarbone is mottled and there are cracks in the make-up around her eyes. Dougal is next to her. She reaches for his hand. He takes it reluctantly, as though unwilling to show any frailty.

The Whitakers are side by side in the arched doorway, their faces filled with dreadful knowing.

Lenny begins. 'It is my sad duty to inform you that the body of a teenage girl has been found beside Silverdale Walk. She matches the description of your daughter Jodie.'

Maggie blinks and glances at Dougal, as though waiting for a translation. His eyes are closed, but a tear squeezes from one corner and he wipes it away with the back of his hand.

'How did she die?' he whispers.

'We believe her death to be suspicious.'

Dougal gets to his feet and sways unsteadily, gripping the back of the sofa for support. He's a big man, who looks like a builder or a butcher. Big arms. Big hands.

'We will need one of you to formally identify Jodie,' says Lenny. 'It doesn't have to be today. I can send a car in the morning.'

'Where is she now?' asks Maggie.

'She's been taken to the Queen's Medical Centre. There will need to be a post mortem.'

'You're going to cut her up,' says Dougal.

'We're investigating a homicide.'

Maggie Sheehan's fingers have found her rosary beads. She clutches the tiny crucifix in her fist, squeezing it so tightly it leaves an imprint when she opens her palm. She must have prayed all day, daring to hope, but nobody has answered.

Bryan and Felicity hug each other in the doorway. They're physically the same size but she seems to be holding him up.

'We need to establish Jodie's movements,' says Lenny. 'When did you last see her?'

'At the fireworks,' replies Maggie.

'We go to Bonfire Night every year,' echoes Felicity. 'Nobody calls it Guy Fawkes Night any more. Maybe it's not politically correct. The Gunpowder Plot and all that.'

She's a tall, striking woman, with a plume of silver flowing through her thick dark hair from the left side of her temple to the collar of her blouse.

'Who was Jodie with at the fireworks?' interrupts Lenny.

'Tasmin. Our daughter.'

'Anyone else?'

'Schoolmates. Friends. Neighbours. It was like a big street party. I took a bottle of champagne and glasses.'

Maggie retrieves a cotton handkerchief from the sleeve of her cardigan and blows her nose. It makes everybody turn.

'I should have made her come home after the fireworks,' she whispers, her voice breaking. 'I shouldn't have let her stay out.'

'This is *not* your fault,' scolds Felicity.

'She should have been home. She would have been safe.'

Dougal doesn't react, but I can already sense the tension between husband and wife. The recriminations are just beginning. Guilt has to fall somewhere when logic fails.

'What time did you last see Jodie?' I ask.

'She found me at eight o'clock,' says Maggie. 'She asked if she could sleep over at Tasmin's house. I told her she had to be up early for training.'

'Training?'

'The nationals are coming up,' explains Bryan Whitaker. 'We're on the ice by six-thirty, six mornings a week.'

'You're Jodie's coach,' I say.

'I taught her to skate.'

'Almost before she could walk,' echoes Maggie.

Brother and sister have similar eyes and the same shaped noses. Maggie is rounder and softer while Bryan has slim hips and slender hands. He looks like a dancer in the way he stands with a straight back, square shoulders and raised chin.

Attention shifts to the TV where the football has been replaced by a news bulletin. Drone footage shows the pale outline of a forensic tent, almost hidden from view by over-hanging branches. The next pictures are of police searching the uncut meadow, walking in a long straight line through knee-high grass. One of them pauses, crouches and picks up a discarded soft-drink can, which he places in a plastic evidence bag. The picture changes again. This time Jodie's body is being carried up the embankment.

'Turn it off!' begs Maggie. Dougal reaches for the TV remote. Fumbles. Curses. The screen goes black.

'Why would anyone hurt our baby?' whispers Maggie. Her shoulders heave, as though shifting weight from one to the other.

Lenny glances at me, but I have no words to make this right. I know what awaits them. In the days to come, Jodie's life will be picked apart by the media, who will feast on this story: the young 'golden girl' of skating, who dreamed of Olympic glory but died in a cold, muddy clearing less than a mile from her home.

As a forensic psychologist, I have met killers and psychopaths and sociopaths, but I refuse to define people as being good or evil. Wrongdoing is an absence of something good rather than something fated, or written in our DNA, or forced upon us by shitty parents, or careless teachers, or cruel friendships. Evil is not a state, it is a 'property', and when a person is in posses-sion of enough 'property', it sometimes begins to define them.

Would it benefit the Sheehans if I told them this? No. It won't bring them comfort when they lie beside each other tonight, staring at the ceiling, wondering what they might have done differently. People who lose children have their hearts warped into weird shapes. Losing a child is beyond comprehension. It defies biology. It contradicts the natural order of history and genealogy. It derails common sense. It violates time. It creates a huge, black, bottomless hole that swallows hope.

Dougal is pouring himself a drink at a bar cabinet. Most of the bottles have duty-free stickers still attached. Maggie seems more relaxed when he's not focused on her. She talks more freely. Remembers.

'When Jodie learned to ride a bike, I wouldn't let her leave the cul-de-sac because I didn't want her riding out of sight. People said I was over-protective, but I know how these things happen. Later, when she started school, I let her walk to Tasmin's house, but never in the dark – not on that footpath. We used to call it the Black Path because it had no lights. Even when the council finally put them in, we still called it the Black Path.'

'Why did Jodie and Tasmin split up last night?' I ask.

'Jodie went to get fish and chips,' says Felicity.

'By herself?'

Nobody answers.

'Does she have a boyfriend?' I ask.

'Not a proper one,' says Felicity. 'Sometimes she hangs out with Toby Leith.'

'The rich kid?' Dougal says, in a mocking tone.

'He's not *that* rich,' says Bryan. 'His father has a car dealership.'

'How old is Toby?' I ask.

'Too old,' says Dougal.

'He's eighteen,' explains Felicity, who doesn't like correcting her brother-in-law. 'They only hang out.'

Dougal reacts angrily. 'What does that even mean? Jodie was

supposed to be in training, not running around with some horny chav with a flash motor.'

Maggie flinches and looks even more miserable.

'When did you realise that Jodie was missing?' I ask, wanting to change the subject.

'She was supposed to come back to ours,' explains Felicity. 'Tasmin waited up until eleven and then fell asleep.'

'Did Jodie have a key?'

'Tasmin left the patio door unlocked.'

'She was out there all night,' says Dougal, his voice breaking.

Felicity sits on the edge of his armchair and brushes his cheek with her hand. It's an intimate gesture, like watching Androcles pulling a thorn from the lion's paw. These people are close, I think. They have raised their children together, celebrating birthdays, christenings, anniversaries and milestones. The highs and the lows.

'I went to wake Jodie for training, but she wasn't in Tasmin's room,' says Bryan. 'I figured she must have gone home last night, so I drove by here to pick her up. That's when we realised that she'd been missing all night.'

'And you phoned the police,' says Lenny.

The couples look at each other, waiting for someone else to answer.

'We looked for her first,' says Bryan defensively. 'I went to the ice rink. Tasmin began phoning her friends.'

Lenny studies Dougal. 'What about you?'

He motions to the window and the black cab outside. 'I was working last night. I got home around seven and went straight out again, looking for Jodie.'

'Where?'

'I walked along the footpath.'

'What made you immediately think of Silverdale Walk?'

'It's the way home,' he replies, as though it should be obvious. His voice catches. 'I must have walked right past her.'

Maggie is staring at the wall, as though looking into the past.

'What did you do?' I ask.

'I prayed.'

'Someone had to stay here in case Jodie called or came home,' explains Felicity.

Lenny seems to be quietly plotting the timeline of events. It made no difference when the police were called. Jodie had been dead for hours.

'Is there anyone who might have wanted to harm your daughter?' asks Lenny.

Maggie answers. 'What do you mean?'

'Did she talk about anyone following her? Someone who might have looked out of place or made her feel uncomfortable, or unsafe?'

Nobody responds.

'Is there anyone who might want to hurt your family?'

Dougal makes a scoffing sound. 'I drive a cab. Maggie works in the school canteen. We're not low-life crims or scumbags.'

Lenny doesn't react. Perhaps she should be talking to the parents separately to gauge their different responses. Dougal has the stronger personality and Maggie defers to him, never questioning his answers, or interrupting. She's not subservient, but neither is she an equal in the relationship.

I walk to the sliding doors and peer into the darkness of the garden. An outside light reveals a deck with a hot tub, covered for the winter. I try to picture Jodie here, but have too little information to breathe life into her pale corpse. I need to discover who she was *before* if I'm to understand what happened to her. Was she friendly and approachable? Would she say hello to a stranger who passed her on the footpath late at night? Would she nod and smile, or drop her head, avoiding eye contact? Would she run if attacked? Would she fight back? Would she submit?

'Can I see Jodie's room?' I ask, directing the question at Dougal.

He hesitates for a moment, before showing me up the stairs. Jodie's room is nearest the shared bathroom. Dougal won't come inside. He hovers in the doorway, as though waiting for permission to enter from a daughter who will never be able to grant it.

The pillow on Jodie's bed has a small indentation, where her head last rested. Next to it is a floppy rag doll with yellow yarn curls and button eyes. It is a typical teenager's room. Messy. Cluttered. Characterful. Dirty clothes are strewn near a wicker basket and a lone shoe has been thrown towards the wardrobe. I have to stop myself wanting to bend down and put it in place. A damp towel from yesterday is lying on the floor.

Studying the room, I imagine Jodie sitting cross-legged on the bed, a little girl playing with dolls and cutting and pasting pictures. She grew up and graduated from crayons to eyeliner, from Barbies to boy bands. Every detail resonates; the book on her bedside table, doodles on a piece of paper, a collection of lanyards hanging from the doorknob.

Her shelves are lined with ice-skating trophies and medals. The wall above her bed is covered in photographs and posters of skaters, some of whom I recognise. Katarina Witt is among them, as well as Tessa Virtue and Scott Moir. The camera has captured many in mid-air, seemingly defying gravity, while others glide across the ice with the grace of ballet dancers.

Polaroids are pinned to a corkboard above Jodie's desk. Most of them show Jodie and Tasmin together. They are sitting on each other's laps in a photo booth, pulling faces at the camera. Jodie is the prettier of the two. Tasmin is more self-conscious about her looks, tilting her face to hide the weight she carries around her neck. Jodie is smaller, with a skater's body, slim and muscled. She's more at ease with her body, showing it off in miniskirts and tight tops.

I notice a barrel bolt lock on the door, which has been affixed in a wonky fashion.

'That was Jodie's doing,' explains Dougal. 'She wanted her privacy.'

'Who was she trying to keep out?'

'Her brother, mainly. Felix can push her buttons.'

'He's older?'

'Twenty-one.'

I remember the youth I saw at the community centre, urging Dougal to go home.

'Does Felix live here?' I ask.

'He comes and goes.'

There are more trophies on a shelf above Jodie's bed. Some have come from junior competitions in Moscow, Berlin and Hungary.

'You must have been very proud,' I say.

'Every time I watched her skate.'

Dougal inhales, holds his breath and exhales.

'Most people take figure skating for granted. They don't realise what goes into it – the courage and skill it takes to glide across the ice and spring into the air and spin three or four times before landing on a single blade as sharp as a knife. I'm a boneheaded man. I don't read books or recite poetry or understand paintings, but Jodie was beautiful on the ice . . . truly breath-taking.'

Lenny calls up the stairs. She's ready to go.

We offer our condolences and leave two devastated families to their grief. Outside, as I reach the police car, I pause and turn back towards the house. A figure is standing motionless in an upstairs window, gazing steadily in our direction. Felix Sheehan is shirtless, or perhaps naked, his lower half shielded. He flicks at a cigarette lighter, triggering a flame and dousing it, while looking directly at us with a hatred that sustains rather than corrodes him.

What does he want to burn, I wonder, and why does he want to burn it?

6

Angel Face

'Do you remember your mother?' asks Guthrie.

'With her long blonde hair and eyes of blue, the only thing I ever got from her was sorrow, sorrow.'

'You're quoting David Bowie.'

'I like David Bowie.'

Guthrie is wearing a funky patterned jumper that was probably knitted by his mother. It's too heavy for the central heating, but he won't take it off because he doesn't want to show his paunch.

'What about your father?' he asks.

'Papa was a rolling stone. Wherever he laid his hat was his home. And when he died, all he left us was alone.'

'The Temptations.'

'It's a good song.'

'You're not taking me seriously.'

'You've asked me this stuff before.'

'And you haven't answered.'

'Recognise the pattern?'

Leaning back in my chair, I rub the instep of one foot with the arch of the other. I'm not wearing shoes or socks – preferring bare feet because I like to feel the ground beneath me. My electronic tracker looks like a manacle minus the ball and chain. I tested it once. I made it as far as the parking area before the alarms starting sounding.

'I want what's best for you,' says Guthrie, giving me his hangdog look.

'Then let me go.'

'Answer my questions.'

Isn't my silence loud enough, I think. Don't tell me that my silence doesn't have a sound. I can hear it, loud and clear, screaming between my words.

Guthrie sighs and scratches at a razor burn on his neck, lowering his eyes to look at my file. He's going bald in a neat round dome on top of his skull. Does it happen to all men? I quickly draw up a mental list. Alfie and Dylan from the kitchens have full heads of hair. Paddy the gardener is a little bald and Reno, one of the counsellors, shaves and oils his head, so it's hard to tell. Terry Boland had hair, which fell out after he'd been dead a few weeks, which isn't the same. Some do, some don't, is my guess.

Guthrie has been talking to me. He lectures more than talks. His voice is so boring he should make meditation tapes. 'Soporific' is my word for the day. Every morning I choose a new one from the dictionary and try to put it into a sentence. Certain words stick in my mind like 'peripatetic' and 'serendipitous' because they sound so musical. Others I've forgotten already.

When my mind wanders the walls seem to drop away, and the streets and houses and cities disappear, until I find myself lying in the shade of a tree, smelling the grass and turned earth and wood smoke. Nearby, my mother is moving between the rows, filling a wicker basket with raspberries and redcurrants. I don't know if this is a real memory, or if someone has planted it in my mind to make me believe that I had a childhood, but I can remember the soft golden light and the buzz of bumblebees in the hedgerows and the coarseness of the grass. I remember my mother's dark hair, which curled over her shoulder as she worked.

Guthrie's voice intrudes. 'What would you do if you could leave?'

'Get a job. Find somewhere to live.'

'I could help make that happen.'

'Good.'

'We could process the paperwork today – all I need is a few details.' He clicks the top of a pen. 'Firstly, your date of birth, and your real name, and where you were born.'

I sigh as though I'm dealing with a moron.

Guthrie continues. 'How do we know you're eighteen?'

'You've checked my teeth and my wrist bones. You've taken x-rays and measurements.'

'Those tests have a margin for error.'

'I'm in the margin.'

'How did you meet Terry Boland?'

I don't answer.

'Did he kidnap you?'

More silence. I toy with the cord of my track pants, twirling it between my fingertips. There's no point getting annoyed or acting the way I feel, which is bored shitless, because I'll get another red card.

'Can I have a drink of water?' I ask.

'No.'

'I'm thirsty.'

'Not until you answer the question. I'm trying to help you, Evie, but we have to meet each other halfway.'

Halfway to where, I think. People always say that when they have no idea of the distances involved. I could come from another planet. I could come from another time in history. But they want to meet me halfway.

I'm happy with who I am. I have pieced myself together from the half-broken things. I have learned how to hide, how to run, how to keep safe, despite never knowing a time when my blood didn't run cold at the sound of footsteps stopping outside my door, or the sound of someone breathing on the opposite side of a wall.

I know the jittery, crawling sensation that ripples down my spine whenever I feel the weight of eyes upon me. Searching my face. Trying to recognise me. And no matter how many times I step into doorways, or look over my shoulder, or yell, 'I know you're there,' the street is always empty. No footsteps. No shadows. No eyes.

41

'I understand your pain,' says Guthrie. 'I know how it separates you from a normal life, from what's true and real.'

How does anyone know what's true or real? Things we once accepted as facts are now accepted as being wrong. The Earth is not flat, smoking isn't good for us, Pluto isn't a planet, witches weren't burnt at the stake in Salem, and humans have more than five senses. Everything has a half-life – even facts.

Guthrie rocks back in his chair and looks at me impatiently. He begins quoting from my file – which he seems to know by heart – the foster homes, my escapes and arrests, the alcohol and drug abuse.

I interrupt him. 'Why are you so determined to keep me here? You don't even like me.'

'Yes, I do.'

'You're frightened of me.'

'No.'

'Really? How is your wife? Has she asked you for a divorce yet?'

'That's none of your business.'

'Are you seeing a counsellor?'

'No.'

'Liar! Are you having an affair?'

'No!'

'Is she?'

'Of course not.'

'She is!'

'Shut up, Evie.'

'Is he an old boyfriend or someone new? Someone she met at work. A colleague.'

'That's a red card.'

'I overheard you talking to Davina. You told her that you didn't want your wife going back to work, but you couldn't afford the mortgage on a single wage. You said her boss was a sleazebag. Is he the one?'

'Please stop,' groans Guthrie.

'Let me go.'

'You're not ready.'

'Who was that man who came to see me today?'

42

'A psychologist.'

'What did he want?'

'He came to look at you.'

'Why?'

'I think he can help you.'

'Can he get me out of here?'

'Maybe.'

I know he's telling the truth, but not the whole truth. The idea makes me shake with dread and excitement.

'Is he coming back?'

'I hope so.'

I do too, but I say nothing.

7

Two photographs of Jodie Sheehan dominate the front page of the *Nottingham Post*. One shows her dressed in her school uniform with her hair neatly brushed and the barest hint of make-up. Jodie is smiling cheekily at the camera, as though someone behind the photographer has made her laugh. The second image captures her in motion on the ice in a costume that sparkles with sequins.

ICE PRINCESS is the banner headline, above a subheading: *Missing Jodie, 15, found dead*. Further below is a breathless commentary, describing the discovery of Jodie's body and the search for clues. As expected, she is portrayed as a fairy-tale victim – Little Red Riding Hood snatched from a lonely footpath by a crazed beast who had been lying in wait for her.

There are quotes from neighbours, schoolfriends and fellow skaters, all of whom are shocked and saddened.

'I can't believe it could happen here.'

'This is such a nice area.'

'We look out for each other.'

'Who would do such a terrible thing?'

I often wonder how people can live in such a state of

innocence. Then again, what is the alternative? Fear. Suspicion. A siege mentality.

Inside there are two more pages of photographs, some showing lines of police searching the meadow, or the crowds of onlookers and the glowing white tent amid the trees. This is just the beginning. Certain crimes generate their own energy, like bush-fires racing across treetops, moving faster than the wind, sucking oxygen from every other story. They consume the news cycle until they burn out or some other tragedy takes their place. Angel Face had been like that.

Overnight Guthrie has sent me the files on Evie Cormac. There are thousands of pages: admission records, ward notes, psychiatric assessments, escapes and offences.

I begin by familiarising myself with the original case, pulling up the earliest newspaper stories about the discovery of Terry Boland's body. He was murdered in a house in Hotham Road, in East Barnet, where his body lay undiscovered for two months, until neighbours complained about the smell and the landlord was summoned. Police broke down the door and found a mound of rotting flesh tied to a chair. Fingerprints were impossible, given the state of decomposition, and whoever killed Boland had cleaned the house so thoroughly – bleaching floors, vacuuming rugs and wiping down every surface – that only one set of prints remained, which didn't show up on any police database until Angel Face was printed six weeks later.

It took facial recognition technology to reveal the victim's identity. A computer-generated photograph was released to the media and triggered a call from a woman in Ipswich who identified Terry Boland as her ex-husband – an unemployed truck driver, aged thirty-eight, born in Watford, twice married, twice divorced, with a history of petty crime and low-level violence.

Two Alsatians were found in a kennel in the rear garden of the house. The animals were in surprisingly good condition given how long Boland had been dead. Clearly someone had been feeding them, which generated the theory that the killer, or killers, might have returned to the house, showing more compassion for the dogs than for the man they killed.

When details of the torture were leaked, the murder took on a greater sense of urgency. Various theories emerged, including foreign crime syndicates, or money-laundering, or a drug deal gone wrong.

Without any new leads to feed the story, the media became more interested in the fate of the dogs, which were given names, William and Harry. The *Sun* and *Daily Mirror* ran competing campaigns to find them new homes. Hundreds of readers offered to adopt the animals, while others donated money, until the Alsatians risked becoming the richest dogs in England before the deputy mayor of Barnet Council stepped forward and adopted them, promising to use the donated funds to build an animal shelter.

In the weeks that followed, the story slipped from the headlines until Angel Face was discovered and it became an international news event. A mysterious child in a secret room – it sounded more like a Grimm's fairy tale than reality.

Among the files that Guthrie has sent to me is the original admission form from Great Ormond Street Children's Hospital.

Gender: Female
Name: Unknown
DOB: Unknown
Height: 50 inches
Weight: 57lbs
Condition: Underweight. Filthy. Evidence of scabies, headlice and rickets. Physical signs of long-term sexual abuse, including deep perineal and vaginal lacerations and scar tissue.
Markings: Birthmark on her left inner forearm the size of a penny. Scar on her right thigh, four inches above the knee.

Multiple lesions on her back and chest most likely caused by cigarette burns.
Property: Eight pieces of coloured glass. A large tortoiseshell button.
Clothing: Soiled jeans. A woollen jumper with a polar bear on the chest. Cotton knickers.

The admitting officer is listed as Special Constable Sacha Hopewell. She was photographed carrying Angel Face into the hospital – an image that flashed around the world and became synonymous with the case. I call it up on my computer. Constable Hopewell is dressed in dark gym gear – leggings and a jacket and trainers. Her knees and elbows are smudged with some sort of white powder. The girl in her arms looks filthy and emaciated, her hair a tangle of snakes, her face gaunt. She's dressed in the clothes described in the hospital admission form.

Sacha Hopewell was twenty-two when she found Evie. She'd be twenty-eight now. A lot of people become special constables as a stepping stone towards a full-time career in policing. Sacha could still work for the Met. I want to ask her how she found Evie. What made her go back to the house so long after the murder?

I call Barnet Police Station in north London and negotiate a maze of automated choices before reaching a desk sergeant.

'Never heard of her,' he says, wanting to get rid of me.

'She was the officer who found Angel Face.'

'Oh, her! She doesn't work here any more.'

'Where can I find her?'

'No idea. She was only a volunteer.'

'She was a special constable.'

'Yeah, same thing.'

I hang up and type Sacha's name into Google, hoping she might have a Facebook page or Twitter account, but come up with nothing. Instead I stumble across several newspaper photographs of her leaving a house identified as being in Wembley

Park – possibly her parents' place. She is surrounded by photographers and reporters, forcing her way grimly through the pack.

Further down the screen, I find a story from the *Harrow Times*. Sacha's father, Rodney, is quoted, asking the media to leave his daughter alone. 'She's not allowed to speak to you. She doesn't have anything to say. Please, let Sacha have her life back.'

A street name is mentioned. I try the reverse phone directories, but the family's number is unlisted. Eventually, I call an old friend who works for the DVLA. Donna Forbes was a year ahead of me at school and is one of the good ones.

'How do I know you're not trying to trace an old girlfriend?' she asks.

'I'm not.'

'Yes, but I how do I know?'

'I'm trying to find the special constable who found Angel Face. Do you remember the case?'

'Of course. Why her? I'm going to assume it's police business,' says Donna, sucking air through her teeth. 'But if I get caught, I could lose my job.' I can hear her typing in the background. 'Every search creates a data trail.' More typing. 'There's a Rodney Hopewell in Wembley Park.' She gives me an address and phone number.

'I owe you a drink,' I say.

'I expect dinner.'

'You're married.'

'A girl still has to eat.'

Rodney Hopewell answers on the fourth ring. A gruff-sounding man, he recites the phone number before saying, 'Can I help you?'

'Is Sacha there?'

There is a pause.

'Who are you?'

'A friend.'

The phone goes dead. I don't know if he hung up, or the line dropped out. I call again. The number rings off. I try one more time. Someone picks up the receiver and drops it into the cradle.

I'm listening to dead air.

8

The major incident room at West Bridgford Police Station has a makeshift feel, as if put together in a hurry. Computer cables snake haphazardly across the floor and desks are pulled into clusters. A series of whiteboards dominate the space, covered with data collected over the past twenty-four hours – crime scene photographs, timelines and phone wheels. Some of the information is highlighted or circled with fluorescent markers or linked by hand-drawn lines, creating a storyboard of Jodie Sheehan's final hours.

Forty detectives are working on the case, collecting CCTV footage, knocking on doors and taking statements. Many of them have been up all night and their eyes sting with tiredness and too much caffeine. Most are men. Lenny has done her best to get more women into the CID, but politics and sexism trickle down from the top. Regardless of the difficulties, she rarely complains, although she has become more outspoken with age. Professionally and publicly, she enforces laws that she sometimes regards as being antiquated and unfair – protecting property rather than people – while privately she rails against the *real* causes of crime: poverty, boredom, stupidity and greed.

None of these are excuses. In Lenny's view, deprivation doesn't force someone to put a needle into his or her vein, or gamble away a welfare cheque, or put a rubbish bin through a shop window, or set fire to a homeless man.

'Every society gets the criminals it deserves,' is her philosophy. 'And the police force it's willing to pay for, rather than the one it insists upon.'

The ten o'clock briefing is under way. Lenny is perched on a desk with her feet on a chair, listening as various detectives bring her up to speed. Some I've met before. Many have nick-names. Monroe gets called 'Marilyn' for obvious reasons, although she does have blonde hair. Her partner is known as 'Prime Time' because he manages to get himself on camera so often. My personal favourite is David Curran, a sharply dressed younger detective they call 'Nobody' because 'nobody's perfect'.

An estimated two thousand people were at the fireworks display on Monday, with as many as three hundred vehicles. Parking was ticketed, but anyone could walk from the surrounding streets and set up a picnic blanket for the show. There were no CCTV cameras focused on the crowd, but the rugby club had one in the parking area and another covered the traffic lights on Clifton Lane.

A detective sergeant with a crew cut consults a laptop. 'Twenty-two names have come up on the Sex Offenders Register, living within three miles of the murder scene. We've spoken to eight of them and will get to the others today.'

'Any of them known to Jodie?' asks Lenny.

'Kevin Stokes lives three doors away. He served seven years for molesting two boys at a swimming centre in Coventry. The victims were five and seven.'

'When was that?'

'He was released eight years ago.'

'Anything since?'

'Nah. He's on a disability pension. Needs a mobility scooter to get around.'

'Check with his doctor,' says Lenny, turning to another detective. 'Where are we with the family?'

Prime Time licks his finger and flips a page of his notebook. 'Dougal Sheehan is a cabbie. He says he left home at seven and did a twelve-hour shift, but it's proving difficult to track down his movements. We're going to look at his logbooks and credit card machine. The uncle, Bryan Whitaker, teaches at the National Ice Centre. He's a recovering alcoholic, who briefly lost his coaching licence eight years ago, following a complaint about inappropriate behaviour from one of his students. The allegations were withdrawn.'

'What sort of complaint?'

'She accused him of taking pictures of her in the showers. He denied it.'

'Were there photographs?'

'None were found.'

'Talk to the girl.' Lenny turns to Monroe. 'What about Jodie's brother – Felix?'

'He was at the fireworks early in the evening but left with friends before eight. He says they went to a nightclub where he picked up a girl around midnight and went back to her place. He can't remember the address or her name.'

'Convenient,' mutters Nobody.

'He seemed pretty cut up about what happened to Jodie,' says the constable I saw outside the Sheehans' house last night.

'You talked to him?' asks Lenny.

'Yes, Guv, but he didn't say much. I'd call him strong and silent, but it's more like brooding and sulky.'

'Did you clock his car?' says Edgar. 'A top of the range Lexus. Business must be good.'

'Find out *what* business,' says Lenny, before turning to Nobody. 'Where are we with Jodie's phone?'

'Her mobile puts her at the fireworks until about eight o'clock but it stopped transmitting at eight-twelve. I figure she must have turned it off.'

Lenny looks at him askance. 'Do you have kids, Nobody?'

'No, Guv.'

'For future reference, should you ever find a woman who wants to give birth to a little Nobody, you'll discover that teenagers can't go five minutes without their phones. Jodie wouldn't have turned it off without a very good reason.'

'Maybe it ran out of juice,' suggests Monroe.

'Perhaps,' says Lenny, clearly not convinced. 'Find out what sort of phone she was using. She might have had tracking software, or some app that allows us to turn it on remotely.'

'Yes, Guv.'

'When and where did we lose the signal?'

'A fish and chip shop called the In Plaice on Southchurch Drive.'

'Talk to the staff. See if anyone remembers her. Where are we with her call log and text messages?'

'We're waiting on her service provider to release them,' says Edgar.

'And her laptop?'

'Nothing out of the ordinary in her search history – apart from the fact that she wiped it regularly. Mostly it was homework assignments, music videos, clothes, make-up, et cetera. We're still trying to access her iCloud account, but these tech companies treat every request like it's an attack on civil liberties.'

'That's because we're fascists,' grunts Prime Time.

'The Deep State,' says Monroe.

Lenny gets to her feet, hitching her houndstooth trousers and running her hands through her hair. 'OK, I want interviews with everybody who had contact with Jodie on Monday evening and that includes friends, neighbours, secret admirers. Also look at anyone who follows her on social media and who comments on her posts.'

She divides the task force into four teams, each with a senior officer in charge. One group will concentrate on the door-to-door interviews, another will trace Jodie's movements, a third will track down known sex offenders in the area, and the fourth will search for anyone seen talking to Jodie at the fireworks.

The briefing ends and detectives disperse, some pulling coats from backs of the chairs and heading out. I get a nod from Lenny. She wants to talk to me privately. Closing her office door, she sits in her high-backed chair and opens a desk drawer, pulling out a scented candle, which she lights with a match, filling the room with the chemical reek of lemons.

'My personal trainer suggested them,' she says. 'Apparently they relieve stress. I think they mask the smell.'

'Of what?'

'Forty detectives, fast food and too much caffeine.'

I notice a wedding gift register open on her laptop.

'My sister is getting married again,' she explains. 'You'd think after two husbands she'd be gun-shy but she's having all the bells and whistles – a horse-drawn carriage, white wedding gown and a reception in a manor house. The whole family has to show up and watch her pledge her undying love for some guy she met on a Caribbean cruise in August.'

'Third time's a charm.'

'He's a sodding dentist!'

Lenny closes her laptop and moves away from her desk, pressing her back against the window frame. 'You got anything for me?'

'Not yet.'

'What does your gut tell you?'

'Strangely, my colon hasn't said a word since this morning.'

Lenny nods, as if to say, 'Point taken.'

Despite our closeness, Lenny has never fully embraced psychology as being a science and criminal profiling as an important tool. She's not a complete philistine, but regards it more like a dark art akin to psychic readings or ESP. Lenny doesn't try to understand the moral insanity of a perpetrator or put herself in his or her shoes. She doesn't want to look at the world through a criminal's eyes, or imagine their torment, or sympathise with their motives, because it might interfere with catching them and locking them away.

Psychologists care about motive, as do juries and actors and people who've lost someone to suicide. For a homicide detective 'that which moves' and 'that which impels' is never as important as the action itself. 'Fuck the why,' Lenny would say. 'Tell me the what, where, how and who.'

Her arms are folded. She waits.

'Jodie was a low-risk victim for her attacker,' I say. 'She was young and small for her age, which made her easier to subdue. The attack site was also low risk – a quiet footpath, deserted at that time of night. Jodie wasn't expected to be there, so most likely he's an opportunist, unless they arranged to meet earlier. More likely, it was unplanned. She was hit from behind and subdued quickly. He didn't bring anything to bind her and made little attempt to clean up afterwards.'

'He tried to hide her body.'

'With a few branches – a token gesture. He may have panicked, or something spooked him. I think he's inexperienced. Disorganised. He didn't plan the rape. He didn't plan the murder.'

There's a knock on the door.

'Got something, boss,' says Edgar.

He leads us back to the incident room where two detectives are going through CCTV footage collected from cameras in Clifton on Monday evening. Chairs are pushed back to give Lenny room. I watch over her shoulder.

Edgar presses the 'play' button. The footage shows a deserted footpath outside a row of shops that includes a nail salon, convenience store, hairdressing salon, carpet cleaning company and the fish and chip shop. A group of four teenagers comes into view – a girl and three boys. Two of them are drinking from cans of beer. The girl is wearing tight jeans, boots and a puffa jacket. Jodie Sheehan. The tallest of the boys puts his arm around Jodie's shoulders and she shrugs it away, knocking the lager from his grasp. He glares at her angrily and picks up the foaming can, shaking spilled beer from his hand. He runs to catch up with the others, disappearing from view.

'This is fourteen minutes later,' says Edgar, as he fast forwards through the street cam footage. Jodie walks back into the frame, seemingly alone. She stands beneath the street light and reapplies her lipstick, using her mobile phone as a mirror.

'Is she waiting for someone?' asks Lenny, leaning closer to the screen.

At that moment, Jodie looks up and waves to someone out of shot. A few seconds later, she steps off the kerb and disappears from view.

'That's all of it,' says Edgar, pressing pause. I look at the time code at the bottom of the screen: 20:48.

'What time did Jodie's phone stop transmitting?' I ask.

'Twenty-twelve,' says Edgar.

'If her mobile was turned off at twenty-twelve, how was she still using a phone under the street light fifteen minutes later?'

'She had a second phone!' exclaims Lenny.

I tap Edgar on the shoulder and ask him to play the footage again.

'Slow it down.'

Jodie is under the street light. She waves. She steps off the kerb.

'There!' I point to the screen. None of them reacts. 'Her shadow changes. It doesn't just lengthen, it moves from left to right. I think a car was doing a U-turn.'

'He's right,' says Lenny. 'Someone picked her up.'

9

A buzzer sounds. The door unlocks. Each new section of Langford Hall has added cameras and extra staff, but most of the security is understated or invisible. There are louvred observation panels and tamperproof locks on the doors. The windows are made of Plexiglas and the bathroom mirrors are plastic. Nothing can be unscrewed, unhooked, unhinged or rendered into a weapon, or a noose.

Evie's room has a single bed, a desk and a wardrobe that is divided between hanging space and drawers. There are pictures of dogs on every smooth surface. Cut from magazines and glued closely together, they form a collage of mismatched sizes, shapes and breeds. A poodle looks bigger than a Great Dane. A beagle seems to be balancing on a Jack Russell's nose.

A dictionary sits open on Evie's desk. Pages are marked. Words underlined. Nearby, a worn set of playing cards is fanned out, face down, as though waiting for someone to pick a card. Unlike Jodie Sheehan's bedroom, Evie has no posters of sporting heroes, or pop stars, or photographs of her friends.

'Can I sit down?' I ask.

Evie shrugs ambivalently. I turn the only chair towards the

bed where Evie has her back against the headboard and her legs stretched out. Her hair is gathered into a wet ponytail on one side of her neck and she's wearing so much make-up that her eyelashes look heavy to lift. She clicks a ballpoint pen open and closed with her thumb.

'You like dogs,' I say, glancing at the walls.

'Is that a question?'

'An observation.'

'Well done, Sherlock.'

'How long have you been here?' I ask.

'This admission: ten months, four days and eleven hours.'

'What was your index offence?'

'You know that already.'

'I wanted to hear it from you.'

'I broke someone's jaw with a half-brick.'

'Why?'

'He stole my money.'

'You think he deserved it?'

'Yep.'

Her eyes narrow and she looks at me dismissively. 'I know what you're trying to do. You want me to feel sorry for him. You think if I show remorse, I won't do it again, but if people steal from me, or hurt me, I won't take it lying down.'

Evie pulls up her legs and hugs them with her forearms.

'What do you most want, Evie?'

'I'll tell you what I want, what I really really want,' she says musically, singing a Spice Girls song, before riffing into Prince: 'I want to be your lover. I want to turn you on, turn you out, all night long, make you shout.'

I interrupt her before she goes on.

'What would you do if you were allowed to leave here?'

'Anything I damn well please. I wouldn't have to deal with social workers, or people like you. No offence.'

'None taken.'

Reaching across the bed, she picks up a bottle of nail polish

58

and unscrews the lid. Pulling her right foot into her lap, she begins painting her toenails with small, delicate strokes. Purple.

'Are you going to give me a psych test? I'm very good at them.' She licks an imaginary pencil and prepares to take notes. 'When you see a sick or a sad person, can you put yourself in that person's place?' Her accent is Swedish. 'A: Not at all. B: Just a little. C: Somewhat. D: Moderately. E: Quite a lot. F: All the time.'

I don't answer her. She carries on.

'Do you believe others control how you think and feel? A: Not at all. B: Just a little. C: Somewhat. D: Moderately. E: Quite a lot. F: All the *fucking* time.'

I interrupt her. 'Have you done many psych tests?'

'Dozens.'

'Why is that, do you think?'

'People think I'm crazy.'

'Why?'

'You tell me. You're the shrink. You're here to poke the bear with a stick. See if I bite.'

'Do you enjoy shocking people?'

'Yeah.'

'Why?'

'It's so easy.' Evie tucks her imaginary pencil behind her ear. 'Are you an ex-junkie?'

'What makes you ask?'

'A lot of the case workers here are former addicts. Why do you think that is?'

'Maybe they understand addiction.'

She points to my wrist, where my shirt cuff has ridden up, revealing the edges of a tattoo.

'Some people get tattoos to hide the needle tracks.'

'Not me.'

'Do you smoke dope?'

'Not any more.'

'Why did you stop?'

'It was a crutch.'

'That's very honest of you . . . and boring.'

'Do I bore you?'

'This place does.'

'Is that why you tell lies and take off your clothes and disrupt group therapy sessions?'

'Not really. Maybe. I have my wheel.'

'What's that?'

'My hamster wheel – everybody needs one in a place like this. It keeps you sane.'

'What's yours?'

'I stopped caring.'

'I don't believe that's true.'

'Suit yourself.'

Evie pulls up her foot and blows on her toes.

'Do you have any friends here?' I ask.

'No.'

'Why not?'

'Some of them are OK. Nathan and Cleary have been to prison and try to big themselves up, hoping the girls might sleep with them, but no bed-hopping is allowed.'

'Would you like to bed-hop?'

She raises one eyebrow. 'Are you suggesting I'm promiscuous?'

'I'm asking if you have a boyfriend.'

'Maybe I fancy girls. You shouldn't assume. I once kissed Charlotte Morris – with tongues – but that was for a dare.'

'Was Charlotte a friend?'

'Not really. She went home. They all go home eventually.'

'Except for you.'

Evie shrugs and I can see a timeless humanity in her.

'What about foster parents?' I ask.

'I've had loads.'

'What happened?'

'They sent me back.'

'All of them?'

'Sometimes I ran away.'

'Tell me about the last family who fostered you.'

'You mean Martha and Graeme. They were hippies. Vegan. They treated their herbalist like he was a brain surgeon and kept blaming my behaviour on my diet, wanting me to eat weird shit.'

'Is that why you ran away?'

She pauses and thinks. 'I don't know. Maybe.'

'Where did you go?'

'Edinburgh.'

'You were six weeks on your own.'

'And I would have been fine if they'd left me alone.'

'You were arrested for gambling.' I glance at the deck of cards on her table. 'Do you like playing cards?'

'I'm good at it.'

It doesn't come across as bragging.

'You were quite tough on Serena the other day.'

'She was lying.'

'You don't know that.'

'Yes, I do.'

Evie looks up from painting her nails, the brush poised above her big toe. Wet strands of hair have escaped from her ponytail.

'Can I call you Cyrus?'

'Sure.'

'If you'll permit me to say this, Cyrus, I don't think it's fair for someone like you to be studying me and not to tell me why.'

'You think I'm studying you?'

'Yes.'

Evie screws the lid onto the nail polish and points her toes towards me. 'What do you think?'

'Nice.'

'I have pretty feet, don't you agree, Cyrus?'

She stretches out her legs, resting her feet in my lap. This time when she points her toes, they press against my groin.

'Are you one of those guys who get off on women's feet?'

'No.'

I lift her legs and put them back on the bed.

Evie smiles. 'Definitely not gay. Are you married?'

'No.'

'Do you have a girlfriend?'

I hesitate before answering. 'Yes.'

'Mmmm,' says Evie, as though not convinced. 'What's her name?'

'Claire.'

'Do you live together?'

'She's working overseas.'

'When is she coming back?'

'I'm not sure.'

'Mmmmm,' Evie says again.

I'm annoyed at myself. Guthrie has me spooked. Is that why I'm being so truthful?

Technically, Claire and I are still together, by which I mean we haven't broken up, although our Skype calls have gone from daily to weekly and lately once a month. She's in Austin at the moment, working on appeals for death-row inmates on behalf of the Texas Defender's Service. It was supposed to be a six-month assignment, which has stretched to ten months. Initially we had planned to spend this Christmas together in New York, but Claire told me two weeks ago that she has to work through the holidays. I offered to come to Austin. She told me I'd have more fun at home.

'What were the dogs called?' I ask.

Evie hesitates. 'What dogs?'

'The Alsatians that you kept alive in the garden. The newspapers called them William and Harry, but you must have had names for them.'

Fear ignites in Evie's eyes. She's not used to people knowing about her background.

'You can't tell anyone who I am,' she says, glancing anxiously at the door. 'It's against the law.'

'I know.'

I give her a moment to relax.

'Sid and Nancy,' she says, referring to the dogs.

'Did you name them?'

'No.'

'Terry must have liked The Sex Pistols.'

'I guess.'

'Why didn't you let the dogs loose? You were sneaking out at night to steal food for them – you could have set them free.'

Evie has gone quiet. Someone shouts along the corridor. A voice answers. A third person tells them to shut up.

'I think you wanted their company,' I say. 'Sid and Nancy were your friends.'

I can almost see the wheels turning in Evie's mind. She's steeling herself for the next question. The obvious one. The most offensive one. Why didn't she run when she had the chance? I won't ask it because it would imply that she was somehow complicit – that she was responsible for what happened, when nothing could be further from the truth.

I know the answer already. Elizabeth Smart, Jaycee Dugard, Shawn Hornbeck, Natascha Kampusch – all victims of celebrated kidnappings, all of whom had opportunities to escape but chose to stay with their abductors out of misplaced loyalty and love; or a 'learned helplessness'.

The same was true for Evie. She was drawn into a binding, dysfunctional, yet compassionate relationship with her abuser. She was brainwashed using the classic methods of sensory deprivation, threats, violence and kindness. He created a new normal for Evie, convincing her that her parents were dead, or had abandoned her; or that others wanted to kill her and only he, Terry Boland, could keep her safe.

'Did you stay in touch with Sacha Hopewell?' I ask.

'Who?'

'The officer who found you.'

Evie shrugs, pretending not to remember her name.

'How did she find you?' I ask.

'She got lucky.'

'I think she was very clever.'

Evie pulls a face.

'That famous photograph – the one where she's carrying you into the hospital – she had white powder on her knees and elbows. You had white powder on your bare feet. It bugged me for a while. Then I realised it was talc. I think she suspected you were hiding somewhere in the house, so she waited until dark and she sprinkled baby powder over the floors. The next morning, she saw your footprints, up the stairs, across the landing, into the wardrobe. That's pretty clever, don't you think?'

Nothing from Evie.

'Tradesmen were renovating the house. It was up for sale. What did you think was going to happen?'

'I would have found somewhere else to hide,' she replies, making it sound obvious.

'What about Sid and Nancy?'

She can't answer me. It annoys her. 'I want you to leave.'

'Why?'

'You ask too many stupid questions.'

'Does that make you angry?'

'Yes.'

'What else makes you angry?'

'Sweeping generalisations. Hypocrites. Being blamed for something I didn't do. People who hurt children.'

'Were you hurt?'

'Why do you jump to that?'

'I'm interested.'

'It's all in the files.'

'No, it's not,' I say. 'You keep telling different stories to different people.'

'Maybe the truth changes.'

Evie reaches for my arm and pushes up the sleeve, rolling it over my forearm to reveal a hummingbird hovering above a flower.

'I'm going to get a tattoo,' she says.

'Anything in particular?'

'Something bold and unexpected. No butterflies or flowers or birds.'

'I like birds.'

'Mine is going to make a statement.' She traces the outline of the hummingbird. 'Does it hurt?'

'Yes.'

'You're being honest.'

'Always.'

'That's a lie.'

'Do you ever hear voices, Evie?'

'No.'

'Are you anxious?'

'Not especially.'

'What are you most frightened of?'

'The people who want me dead.'

'Who are they?'

'Nameless men.'

'Do you have a gift?'

'No.'

'What about a curse?'

Evie lifts her head to look at me, her eyes like a mirror, reflecting my image back to me.

'Yes.'

10

The mortuary manager is a thin man, with a hook nose and nostrils like sinkholes that draw attention away from everything else on his face. I try not to stare at them as I show him my business card, asking to see Dr Robert Ness.

'You're not police,' he says, stating the obvious.

'I'm assisting in a murder investigation.'

The manager eyes me suspiciously, as though my true mission is to steal body parts. A call is made. Permission granted. I sign the visitors' book and look into the camera, letting my picture be captured, laminated and hung around my neck.

The mortuary is on the fourth floor of the Queen's Medical Centre, which has always seemed odd to me because I feel like it belongs in the basement, closer to where we all finish. Dust to dust and all that.

A trainee pathologist in green scrubs collects me from the reception area and leads me down a long corridor past post mortem suites with stainless steel operating slabs and banks of halogen lights angled from above.

'You're late,' says Ness, peeling off his gloves and tossing them into a hazard waste bin. His dark hands are preternaturally pale from the talc that lingers on his fingers. He raises his arms and an assistant unties his stained scrubs and takes the protective glasses from his forehead.

Jodie's body is lying on the slab with cross-stitches running from her torso to her pubic bone, showing where her organs were removed, weighed and examined. The stitches are haphazard because Jodie has no need of a pretty scar. Under the bright lights, the whiteness of her flesh makes her look like a marble statue with a tangle of blue veins lying just beneath the surface of her skin. Small for her age with narrow hips and muscled legs from skating, her arms are scored by scratches and her eye sockets look like pools of purple dye.

Ness reaches up and switches off the microphone above his head and turns away, grimacing in pain when he puts weight on his right leg.

'Everything OK?'

'Gout,' he mutters, as if no other explanation were needed. 'My doctor wants me to give up smoking, drinking and eating rich foods. I think he's in cahoots with my wife. Maybe they're sleeping together.'

'If she wanted you dead she wouldn't care so much.'

'True.'

Another assistant approaches with a clipboard, needing a signature. Ness signs with a flourish. 'Tell the lab I want those bloods done by the morning.'

'What did you find?' I ask.

'More questions than answers.'

Stepping towards the bench, he picks up a white sheet, which he draws over Jodie's body, leaving only her face exposed. Tucking the sheet beneath her chin, he strokes her cheek like a father saying goodbye to his daughter. Finally, he moves away, as though not wanting to speak in front of her.

'The semen in her hair will give us a DNA signature. She had nothing internally, but a small trace on her right thigh, along with evidence of a lubricant, which suggests a condom was used. I found no evidence of vaginal tearing or bruising, so the intercourse may have been consensual – at least at first.'

'Why have sex with her and then ejaculate in her hair?'

'That's your area, not mine,' says Ness, drinking from a bottle of water, not letting the plastic touch his lips. He wipes his mouth. 'Jodie had dirt under her fingernails, but no skin cells or obvious defence injuries. The scratches came from brambles and branches.'

'You mentioned a blow to the head.'

'Some sort of blunt force trauma, which caused a hairline fracture of the parietal bone, but no internal bleeding.' Ness indicates the back of his skull. 'She might not have seen it coming. Most likely it knocked her unconscious or disorientated her. She had pondwater in her lungs, which suggests she either fell or was pushed from the footbridge.'

He tosses the empty water bottle in a bin. It rattles around the edge before it drops.

'Jodie didn't remove her own clothing. Her jeans were pulled down while she was lying on her back. She didn't get up again.'

'How did she die?'

'That's a good question,' says Ness, in no hurry to answer it. He walks to a nearby bench and begins swapping his shoes. 'Have you ever heard of dry-drowning?'

'No.'

'When we inhale water into our lungs, we cut off oxygen to the body, which begins to shut down. Once we take a lungful of air, we cough up the water and usually begin breathing normally again. Everything is fine . . . except for when it's not.'

Ness can see my confusion.

'There is a condition called secondary or delayed drowning. With young children it can happen in a matter of seconds, but the process typically takes longer in adults – hours or days. It tends to affect people who have damaged lungs, or pulmonary illnesses. Jodie Sheehan suffered a bout of pneumonia eight months ago and was hospitalised.'

'You're saying she drowned on dry land.'

'Possibly. Theoretically. I think she fell or was thrown from the footbridge. Maybe the cold water brought her round. She crawled out but was struggling to breathe because her diaphragm couldn't create the necessary respiratory movements. This made her sluggish. Slow.'

'An easy target.'

'Just so.'

Ness slides his arms through the sleeves of his coat. 'I can't tell you the exact cause of death, but the temperature on Monday night fell to below freezing. Jodie was cold and wet and barely conscious. She was always going to die unless someone found her.'

As I'm leaving, I pass the viewing suites and the waiting room. A lone figure is sitting on a plastic chair, bent forwards with his elbows on his knees and his eyes fixed on the floor. Even without seeing his face, I recognise Felix Sheehan.

'We haven't met,' I say. 'I'm Cyrus—'

'I know who you are.'

'I'm sorry about your sister.'

'You didn't even know her.'

'That's true – but I'm still sorry for your loss.'

I notice a cigarette tucked behind his ear. He touches it occasionally, before lacing his fingers in his hair. He's dressed in baggy jeans and a hooded sweatshirt, that hang so loosely on his lanky frame they could be draped on a wire coat hanger.

'Have you been waiting long?' I ask.

'I want to see Jodie.' The words catch in his throat.

'Can I ask why?'

'She's my sister. Isn't that enough?'

'The post mortem has just finished. They'll be getting her ready.'

I can picture them dressing Jodie in clean nightwear and brushing her hair. Afterwards, her body will be arranged in a supine position and covered in a white sheet with only her face and hands visible.

'When did you last see her – Jodie?'

'At the fireworks.'

'What time did you leave?'

'More fucking questions,' he snarls, rattling off the same answers he gave to the police about visiting a nightclub and picking up a girl. 'First I knew about Jodie was when Mum phoned me.'

'Did you get on well with your sister?'

'What sort of question is that?'

'I'm trying to learn more about her.'

His eyes narrow, fixed on mine. Black. Hard. 'You think I killed her.'

'No.'

He can't hold my gaze. Relaxes. Shrugs. 'We got on OK. I saw less of her when I moved out of home. She had her skating. I had my shit to do.'

'What do you do, Felix?'

'I buy and sell stuff, on eBay mostly. Somebody's trash is somebody's treasure, right?'

'Is there much money in that?'

'You'd be surprised. People throw all sorts of stuff away. I picked up a box of vinyl the other day and came across a mint copy of *Sticky Fingers.* Classic Rolling Stones. Sealed. Unopened. Worth three grand, at least.'

He's watching me closely as he relates the story, as if gauging my reaction. Suddenly, he changes direction. 'Was she raped?'

'She was sexually assaulted.'

He swallows. 'Did she suffer?'

'I don't know.'

His fingers are opening and closing into fists, while his knee jiggles rhythmically. A nurse interrupts. Jodie's body is ready for viewing. Felix hesitates. His lower lip disappears as he bites down.

'I've changed my mind. I don't want to see her.'

He brushes past me, striding along the corridor, jabbing impatiently at the button on the lift, desperate to be outside, away from this place. It's like he's holding the sick in his mouth, looking for somewhere to vomit. As the lifts doors close, his arms form a tent over his head and his eyes shine like gemstones in a dark cave.

11

Silverdale Walk is a different place with the sun shining. Trees blaze orange and red, while others stand naked and grey; as if the artist ran out of paint on his palette before he could finish the landscape. Daylight has given context to the location, revealing landmarks and lines of sight. A thickly wooded ridge. A grass-covered coppice. The reed-fringed pond.

It has taken me twelve minutes to walk from Jodie's house to the clearing where her body was found. A young police constable is standing guard at the scene, stopping bystanders from getting too close. A makeshift memorial has sprung up, a mound of flowers, cards and soft toys. Someone has made a sign saying, 'Justice for Jodie'. Remnants of crime-scene tape flutter in the breeze.

A team of police divers are packing up their gear, loading air tanks into wooden racks and hanging damp wetsuits over railings. The last of their number emerges from the water. Dripping in wrack and weeds, he looks like prehistoric sea monster, crawling before he can walk.

He stands and pulls off his mask, letting his respirator dangle against his chest. Clad in a wetsuit, his short, barrel-shaped body appears to be carved from granite or ebony. He swings his air tank to the ground and unhooks the harness.

Ducking under the tape, I clamber down the embankment and join him beside the pond. The diver gives me a momentary glance and peels back the hood of his wetsuit, revealing a nest of shaggy hair.

'Dr Haven,' he says.

'Sergeant Thorndale.'

We shake hands damply and I fight the urge to wipe mine on my thighs.

Jack Thorndale is a former patient, a hostage negotiator, who came to see me after a sixteen-hour police siege went south. A disgruntled employee gunned down four of his workmates before turning the weapon on himself. Jack took the failure personally and it almost cost him his marriage and his career. Eventually, he retrained as a police diver, saying he'd 'rather wade through filth' than negotiate with madmen.

'Any news?' I ask.

'The more we dive, the more shit we stir up. If she dropped her phone it could have drifted downstream or be deep in the mud by now.'

He points to a tarpaulin that is covered in a pile of rubbish retrieved from the pond. There are bicycles, a shopping trolley, broken concrete, metal pipes, half-bricks and nondescript machinery parts, all caked in mud.

'Forensics are coming to take a look. Maybe we've stumbled upon a murder weapon, although I doubt it.'

Someone yells from the van. His colleagues are cold and want to go home.

Jack holds up a thumb. 'You working this one?'

'Yeah.'

'I'd wish you luck, but you don't believe in it.' He grins.

During our sessions I talked to Jack about the difference between chance and luck. Chance is a random outcome in the real world whereas luck is the value we place upon it when we label it good or bad. Whether the police find Jodie's phone isn't lucky or unlucky, it's the same chance event.

Slinging the tank over his shoulder, Jack makes the embankment look easy as he joins his team. I walk to the footbridge and lean over the side. The brook, swollen by recent rain, is running freely and foaming as it enters the pond.

In this quiet, lonely place, two people came together and one of them died. There must have been an interaction, however brief or violent. What did they say to each other? How did they spend their last moments together? What relationships and experiences shaped their personalities?

No two people respond to the same situation in the same way. If Jodie met a stranger on the path on Monday night, would she automatically see him as being dangerous, or would she smile and say hello? Would she start up a conversation, or respond to a question? Would she turn her back? Would she run? Fight? Plead?

Perhaps it was someone she knew. She could have been brought here, or lured by somebody she trusted. She was picked up in a car earlier in the evening. She had a second mobile phone. This suggests a secret liaison. A boyfriend or a casual hook-up.

At some point Jodie was struck from behind, most likely without warning. She had turned her back. She either trusted this person, or she was trying to flee. Barely conscious, she fell or was pushed off the bridge. The cold water shocked her awake. She swallowed some of it. Almost drowned. Her attacker dragged her from the pond or followed Jodie after she saved herself. She ran, disorientated by the darkness. Branches and brambles tore at her face and skin. She collapsed, close to death. Dying.

He undressed her hurriedly, clumsily. He unwrapped a condom . . .

No! It doesn't make sense. Use of a prophylactic suggests forensic awareness. He wanted to conceal his identity. But why use a condom and then ejaculate into her hair? That's an act designed to humiliate or mark his territory or signify unconditional acceptance.

Maybe they had sex and she denied him a second round. More likely he couldn't maintain an erection and grew frustrated? Which means he's not experienced around women. He's a loner. Socially inept. He wants a girlfriend, but nobody wants him. He knows this area. This place.

Some rapists panic and kill victims to protect their identity. Others take pleasure from abusing a victim at the moment of his or her death or afterwards. The timing of the penetration reveals clues about them. I don't know the exact sequence of events, but this man and his corrupt lust sacrificed a human life for an orgasm. Afterwards he left her to die, or he watched her take her last breath. He covered her body with branches, trying to hide what he'd done.

He went home. Showered. Changed his clothes. Tried to forget. But he won't stop thinking about this. Part of him will be horrified, but another voice will tell him that she deserved it, that she led him on, that she was like all the other women who ignored him, belittled him, laughed at him . . .

My knees are hurting. I've been squatting on my haunches for too long. I straighten, drinking in the cold air and begin to move away from the footbridge, walking in a widening circle, feeling the softness of the ground beneath my feet.

Everywhere I see signs of the police search – evidence markers, broken twigs, boot prints – but I'm not looking for the same things they were. A psychologist views a crime scene differently from a detective. Police search for physical clues and witnesses. I look at the overall picture and the salience of certain landmarks and features. Where are the obstacles and boundaries that alter behaviour? How quickly does someone disappear from sight? How far can I see in each direction? What are the vantage points and the shortcuts?

Ahead of me, I glimpse something straight edged through

the trees, embowered by ferns. It's an old groundkeeper's cottage or hunting lodge, which has fallen into disrepair. Grey with age, the walls are streaked with rust from the downpipes and creepers have twisted around the spindle wood railings that fence in a small front veranda.

The path is overgrown, but not unused. There are muddy boot prints and torn cobwebs. The police must have searched here yesterday. Stepping inside the derelict cottage, I take a moment to let my eyes adjust to the darkness. The wooden floorboards are splintery with age and stained by innumerable spills and leakages. Rubbish is strewn across the floor and the walls are covered in graffiti, none artistic, some of it obscene or as harmless as initials inside a heart. An old mattress yellowing with age has been positioned in front of a hearth, which is full of crushed beer cans, blackened by a recent fire. A half-drunk bottle of apple cider is within reach. Two more empties are nearby.

I move to the next room – a kitchen that reeks of damp and decay. Rubbish floats in an ankle-deep puddle. Crisp packets and condom wrappers. Someone has ripped out the copper pipes, no doubt for scrap metal. The final room, most likely a bedroom, has a roof that has partially collapsed, giving me a glimpse of blue sky and the tops of trees.

I understand instinctively where I am – not the original purpose of the building, but what it has become: a place where youngsters can avoid the gaze of adults. Where they break up, make up, hang out and make out; where they experiment with alcohol, drugs and sex. Did Jodie ever come here? Did this place mean something to her, or her killer?

The police have searched the cottage, but I doubt if any of them recognised the likely salience. Detectives don't understand the ley lines that teenagers use to navigate their world. The shortcuts. The meeting places. The secret language.

Later I call Lenny from a phone box opposite the school. It goes to her voicemail.

'The killer is in his late teens or twenties. Physically strong, but not overly intelligent. He's local. This is *his* territory. He knows the area. He knows the footpath and maybe the cottage. Look for someone who's been arrested or questioned for lesser offences like exposing himself to women or stealing their underwear.

'I don't think he planned the rape, or the murder – it was too disorganised – but he possibly knew Jodie or was aware of her and she may have played a part in his sexual fantasies.

'He's going to feel bad about what he's done. Ashamed. This is the first time for him. His first murder. He'll be following the police investigation closely, frightened and appalled, but also fascinated, which means he could return to the scene as an onlooker, or bystander. Look for his face in the crowd. He's somewhere close by. Watching.'

12

Angel Face

I hear a knock.

'Are you decent?' asks Davina.

She's a big woman with coloured beads woven into her dreadlocks that tumble to her shoulders, curling at the ends like pigs' tails. She leans on the frame; thrusting out one hip.

'You have a visitor.'

'Who?'

'Dr Haven.'

I feel a surge of excitement. Tossing aside my magazine, I swing my legs off the bed and go to the mirror, touching my hair and brushing my fingertips along my eyebrows. I reach for my make-up bag.

'He's not your boyfriend,' Davina chuckles. She's still standing in the doorway.

I want to slap her for being a bitch.

'Shall I tell him you're coming? I could throw rose petals in your path.'

'Fuck off!'

'That's a red card.'

I pull the hood of my sweatshirt over my hair and follow Davina down the hallway, less certain than before. Normally, I don't care about shrinks and social workers. I've dealt with so many. But this one unsettled me the last time. It was nothing he did or said. He didn't ask about my family, or my real name, or where I came from, or what happened to me as a child. Instead he seemed to hold up a mirror to me, wanting me to look.

Entering the dining room, I find him sitting at a table nursing a cup of tea. He stands and bows in an old-fashioned way like he's Prince Charles, which makes me smirk.

I take a moment to decide where I should sit. Opposite is best, so I can see his face.

Cyrus is smiling. He looks tired, like someone is blowing air into his eyes, making him blink.

'Why are you smiling?' I ask, guardedly.

'I'm pleased to see you.'

I make a scoffing sound and study his face but cannot find a lie.

'I told you I'd come back. How have you been?'

I shrug.

Cyrus picks a chocolate finger biscuit and nibbles one end.

'That's not how you should eat them,' I say.

He looks at the biscuit.

'You have to bite off both ends. Then you can use it like a straw.'

'In my tea?'

'Exactly.'

Cyrus bends his head and sucks tea through the biscuit.

'Eat it before it gets too soggy,' I say.

He stuffs the biscuit into his mouth and chews, showing his chocolate-stained teeth. 'That's really good.'

'I don't think you should try it at the Ritz.'

'Have you ever been to the Ritz?'

'Oh, all the time,' I say, putting on my posh voice. 'I do so love their High Tea – the scones and clotted cream and strawberry jam. Although, one doesn't understand the point of cucumber sandwiches. They taste of nothing, don't you think?'

'Do you lie a lot, Evie?'

'What do you consider a lot?'

'Enough for people to think you're a liar.'

'I've been called worse.' I feel my jaw tighten. I don't want Cyrus to be like the others. 'So sometimes I lie. Is that so weird? You'd lie as well if you were stuck in here. You'd make up stories. Amuse yourself.'

'What do you lie about?'

'Random stuff. I don't even know why I do it half the time. It's automatic – like sneezing. Sometimes I hear myself say something and I think, that's not even remotely true – not even fucking close – but I still keep going. The other day, I told this new girl that my father is a treasure hunter looking for a Spanish galleon that sank in the Bermuda Triangle. I told Cordelia that I won a scholarship to a cheerleading school in California but had to turn it down because I'm on a no-fly list as a suspected terrorist. Stupid cow believed me.'

Cyrus laughs. He has a nice smile. It makes his eyes go crinkly at the sides.

'You want to play cards?' I ask, taking a deck from the pocket of my hoodie.

'OK.'

'Poker. Texas hold 'em. Is that all right?'

I divide, bridge and flip the deck, overlapping the edges and sliding the cards together. I do it twice more before racking the deck loudly against the table. With a flick of my fingers, I deal, sending cards spinning across the Formica.

I peel up the corners and check the hole cards. Cyrus takes longer. He doesn't play cards very often. I can tell from how he arranges them in his hand.

'What are we going to bet?' I ask.

'I don't think we should gamble.'

'It's poker. We have to bet.'

'Not money.'

'How about we gamble for questions?'

Cyrus agrees, but looks at me suspiciously.

'This is called the flop,' I explain, putting three cards face up on the table. 'You want to bet?'

'Yes. I'll bet one question.'

'I'll match you.'

I deal another card and we go through the process again. Eventually, there are four questions on the table. I have two pairs – aces and sevens, to his two kings.

I rub my hands together. 'Right, let's get started. Do you have any family?'

'A brother,' he replies.

'What about your parents?'

'They're dead.'

'How did they die?'

'They were murdered.'

I look for the telltale signs that he's lying but see nothing except sadness and regret.

'How old were you?'

'Thirteen.'

'Who killed them?'

'You've had your four questions.'

Annoyed, I deal another hand. Win again.

'Who killed them?'

'My brother.'

I take a moment to digest the news. I wonder if I'm missing the lie but can see only the truth. I want to know the details. At the same time, I wish I could take my questions back and give Cyrus some privacy.

'I don't want to play this game any more,' I say, pushing my chair away from the table.

'But I didn't get to ask a question.'

'You were never going to beat me.'

'Are you that good?'

'Yes.'

Inwardly, I curse my bravado. What have I got to boast about?

'You can ask me one thing,' I say softly. 'But not my name, or where I came from, or anything about Terry.'

'What will you do if you get out of here?'

It's always the same question, I think. 'What do you want to be *when you grow up, little girl?' It's as if jobs come on racks like clothes, hanging up before you: butcher, baker, tinker, tailor, waitress, receptionist. Pick one. Try it on for size.*

'I want to start my life,' I say. 'I've spent six years in places like this. It's my turn.'

'Your turn for what?'

'To be normal.'

13

Looking at Evie now, it is difficult to picture the filthy urchin they discovered in a secret room six years ago. The child who came out at night and hid during the day; who stole food from neighbouring houses, drank from garden hoses and kept two Alsatians alive; who quite possibly heard a man being tortured to death and later watched his body putrefying.

Clearly intelligent, despite her lack of formal education, every escape and failed fostering attempt set Evie back academically, but she hasn't fallen too far behind her peers. Dyslexia makes reading difficult, but she has good language and numeracy skills.

I spent last night going over her earliest interviews with counsellors and social workers. They were searching for clues about her background, but Evie revealed almost nothing. She asked for food when she was hungry and water when she was thirsty. She didn't start conversations, or answer questions with more than a yes or no. Linguists and dialect experts were brought in to study her speech patterns and accent. One said that Evie had spent time in Scotland. Another detected possible East European traces in her voice, in particular how she made 'rainbow' sound like 'ranbow' and mixed up her tenses.

I don't recognise any trace of an accent. Instead, I see a teenager with heightened defences, who trusts nobody. Right now she's slouching in a chair, rolling her tongue, acting bored.

'Why do you wear so much make-up?' I ask.

'I hate my freckles. They make my face look dirty.'

'Your freckles are the best part.'

Evie looks at me with a mixture of pity and disgust. She doesn't like being complimented. Praise is for other people.

'You didn't answer my question – what will you do?'

'I'll get a job.'

'Doing what? Don't say you'll play poker.'

'There are professional poker players.'

'They have funds. A stake. Where will you live?'

'I'll rent somewhere.'

'Do you know how much it costs to rent a flat? What about electricity, gas, phone bills, the TV licence fee?'

'I'll get a room in a shared house.'

'You don't like people, Evie. You don't trust them.'

She gives me a pitying stare. 'Guthrie said you wanted to help me. Another fucking lie. You're like all the others.'

'No, Evie, but even if you had savings and a job and a place to stay, a judge might still not let you go. He's going to ask for a mental health assessment, which means getting evidence from social workers, doctors, therapists . . .'

'Fuck them,' spits Evie. 'I'm not a freak.'

'Nobody thinks that.'

'Yes, they do.'

Before I can respond, a clanging bell rattles the air, reverberating from speakers in different parts of the building.

'Lock down,' says Evie. She's on her feet. 'I have to go back to my—'

Her words are cut short by a scream from the corridor. A woman stumbles through the door, holding her stomach. The front of her dress is changing colour, growing darker towards her thighs and knees.

84

'He stabbed me,' she says, disbelievingly. 'Where did he get a knife?'

I pull her further into the room. People are running. Two male orderlies flash past the open doorway and then retreat, just as quickly. 'Knife!' yells one of them. 'Stay back!'

A moment later a teenage boy appears, wild eyed and wired, edging backwards into the room. He looks over his shoulder and spins around, pointing a knife at me. I raise my hands and retreat. He pushes the table across the doorway, barricading the entrance. Our escape.

I make the wounded woman sit down, telling her to stay calm.

'What's your name?'

'Roberta.'

'You must keep still and keep pressure on the wound.' I show her how to make a fist and push it hard into her stomach.

'How are things, Brodie?' asks Evie, making it sound like they're discussing the weather. The boy blinks at her, his thin face bubbling with acne and switching between rage and misery.

'The bitch! The fucking bitch!'

'What did she do?' asks Evie.

'Took my magazines.'

'Your porn?'

'It weren't all p-p-porn,' stammers Brodie, wiping the back of his mouth. 'This is f-f-fucked. This whole p-p-place.' His face folds like an accordion, grimacing and twitching.

'She needs a doctor,' I say, still crouched next to Roberta.

'I hope she d-d-dies,' says Brodie, carving at the air with the knife. The alarm is still clanging, almost drowning out his words.

Evie has moved closer. I tell her to stop.

'You want some of this?' says Brodie, swishing the blade at her face.

'You're not going to stab me,' she responds, opening her arms as if saying, 'Here I am.'

'Maybe I'll f-f-fuck you first.'

'Why?'

'Because you're an uppity b-b-bitch who thinks your shit don't stink.'

'You barely know me.'

Davina and two male orderlies are standing in the doorway, watching in horrified silence. Evie has stepped closer. Her voice is calm and nothing about her seems tense or uncertain.

'Please, stay back,' I tell her.

She ignores me and moves into range.

'Do you really hate me, Brodie? I don't hate you. We're all victims in here. Prisoners. Pawns. You say I never talk to you – I'm talking now. What do you want to say?'

'It d-d-doesn't work like that.'

'What doesn't?'

Brodie tries to speak, but the statement gets lost in his stuttering. He swallows and curses himself.

'How does it work?' asks Evie, who is standing next to him now. She takes Brodie's wrist and pulls the knife towards her chest, pointing it at her heart. 'This is the best place. One push and I'll be dead.'

Brodie tries to pull the blade away. Evie holds it steady. She leans her head forward until her forehead touches his and they're staring into each other's eyes.

'If you do it quickly, I won't feel a thing,' she whispers. 'You'll be doing me a favour.'

'I don't hate you that much.'

'You called me an uppity bitch.'

'You d-d-don't talk to people.'

'I've got nothing to say.'

Davina is pleading with Evie to step back, but nobody dares to move because the knife is so close to her heart. Brodie looks confused. Lost. He tries to pull away again. Evie groans and I can't tell if the knife has entered her chest.

'D-d-d-don't,' Brodie stammers, but doesn't get to finish the statement before Evie rams her forehead into his face. The crack of bone and spray of blood tell me she's broken his nose. Brodie teeters back, uttering a curse, holding his face. The knife clatters to the floor.

Two male orderlies vault over the table and wrestle Brodie to the ground. Evie touches her forehead, as though concerned she might have a bruise. Then she bends and picks up the knife.

'Give it to me,' says Davina.

Evie caresses the blade almost lovingly, before spinning it across her palm, so the handle is facing Davina.

Moments later the paramedics arrive, calling out numbers and driving needles into Roberta's veins, giving her fluids before strapping her to a stretcher and wheeling her through the reception area to a waiting ambulance.

I escort Evie back to her room where she checks herself in the mirror, making sure that her make-up hasn't smudged.

'Do you have a death wish?' I ask, after a silence.

'He was never going to stab me.'

'How do you know?'

She sighs and shrugs wearily. 'I could tell.'

14

Lenny Parvel's secretary Antonia is a plump, playful woman with cat-eye spectacles and wrists that jangle with multiple metal bracelets. Her desk is wedged between three filing cabinets that look like grey standing stones.

'Milk no sugar,' she says, bringing me a cup of tea. 'Digestive or Hobnob?'

'Not for me.'

'Don't tell me you're on a diet. There's nothing of you. Women like a little meat on the bone.' She winks at me wickedly and takes a biscuit.

I notice flat-packed boxes leaning against a wall.

'Are you moving?' I ask.

'Haven't you heard? DCI Parvel is being transferred.'

'To where?'

'Uniformed operations.'

'She's an investigator.'

'I don't think she was given a choice.'

My surprise borders on shock. 'Why?'

Antonia gives me an exaggerated shrug. 'Nobody tells me anything.' Then she leans closer and whispers the name Heller-Smith.

Timothy Heller-Smith is the rising star of the Nottinghamshire Police; a future chief constable if the pundits are to be believed, as well as the conga line of hangers-on. Heller-Smith has overseen intelligence and operations for the past five years, claiming credit for a string of major drug busts and the arrest of a gang of British-born Islamists, who had returned after fighting with ISIS in Syria.

There's no way Lenny would have asked for a transfer. Ever since I've known her, she's worked towards becoming a detective.

'If you ask me, Heller-Smith wants her out of the way,' whispers Antonia, brushing biscuit crumbs from the shelf of her bust.

'Lenny isn't a threat.'

'A lot of people are suggesting that the next chief constable should be a woman.' She taps her nose as if she's giving me the name of a sure thing running in the three-thirty at Doncaster.

The office door swings open and Lenny emerges, shrugging on her overcoat. 'There's a car downstairs.'

'Where are we going?'

'Jodie Sheehan had a school locker.'

Lenny picks up keys at the front desk and we take a side door into the parking area. She presses the fob and waits for the telltale blink of lights to show her to the car.

'Why didn't you tell me?' I ask.

'About what?'

'Uniformed operations.'

'We're not married, Cyrus.'

'You love this job,' I say.

'We're not talking about it.'

'Isn't there something you can do?'

'Yeah. I can tell people to mind their own business.'

Lenny eases out of the car park and we head south-west along Rectory Road until we reach the West Bridgford Baptist Church and turn right towards the River Trent. It's ten minutes before she speaks again.

'I'm thinking of retiring. I can take it next year and get a full pension.'

'And do what?'

'What do other people do? They travel, read books, binge watch TV . . .'

'They die young.'

'Not all of them.'

There is another long pause before her shoulders rise and fall in a sigh. 'There are some right bastards loose on this earth, Cyrus. And some of them are supposed to be on the side of the angels.'

Forsyth Academy takes up a corner of the Clifton Playing Fields less than five hundred yards from where Jodie's body was found. Knocked down, rebuilt and renamed eight years ago, it looks more like a germ warfare laboratory than a secondary school.

Lenny pulls up in front of a green electric barrier and presses the intercom, announcing herself to the office. The gate slides open and we drive past all-weather pitches where boys in black trousers and untucked white shirts are playing football. Meanwhile, the girls are sitting on benches in the weak sunshine, or clustered around tables in the quadrangle.

A young student comes to escort us, her blonde ponytail swinging as she walks. A piece of colourful braided rope is tied around her wrist.

'Some of the girls are making them,' she explains. 'They're in memory of Jodie. Would you like one? They're free.'

She reaches into her pocket and produces four similar-looking bracelets of different colours. I choose one as Mr Graham appears, the executive head teacher.

'Thank you, Cassie,' he says, nodding to the girl. 'That bracelet isn't part of the official uniform.'

He notices me tying one around my wrist and lets the subject drop.

Mr Graham is in his late fifties with a long, thin face that falls like a landslip towards his chins. He whispers his greetings.

'Dreadful business. Such a shock. We're all feeling it – the staff, the students . . .' The office door closes. 'Some girls have been crying for days. I've called a school assembly for midday. What do I say to them?'

He seems to be addressing me. Instinctively, I understand why. He knows who I am – about my family – and this somehow gives me some special insight or monopoly on words that might help children cope with loss. I'm transported back to my first day at school following the funerals of my parents and sisters. My grandparents wanted to keep my life as normal as possible, so I went back to the same school. Miss Payne escorted me to my first class. Biology. As I walked into the room, I was greeted with absolute silence. A pin dropping would have sounded like a crashing cymbal. My eyes didn't leave the floor. I don't blame my classmates for staring at me. I blame Elias. It was *always* my brother's fault.

'Should I tell them Jodie was murdered?' asks Mr Graham.

'I think that ship has sailed,' I reply, regretting my sarcasm. I start again. 'Be honest. Don't manufacture emotions. Don't say, "I know what you're going through," or tell them you've lost someone too. Don't offer your thoughts and prayers. Don't look for a bright side. There isn't any.'

'What do I say?'

'Listen.'

'I can't listen to them all.'

You can't even listen to me.

'Children are especially vulnerable to grief. Some will struggle with how to communicate their sadness, or fear, or confusion. Accept their feelings. Not all of them will have known Jodie, so don't say that everyone will miss her. Say that you're sad for her friends and her family.'

I want to warn him about inviting bereavement counsellors into the school, because they can reinforce the idea that people *should* be traumatised. I know this because I've been there, passed between psychiatrists, therapists and counsellors, who squawked at me like seagulls fighting over spilled chips; spending hours telling me *how* I should be feeling or asking me to vent, when I simply wanted to be left alone.

Lenny interrupts: 'We're here to look inside Jodie Sheehan's locker.'

'Yes, of course,' says Mr Graham, picking up his phone and asking his secretary to get 'Mr Hendricks'.

'Ian is Jodie's form tutor,' he explains. 'Every child at Forsyth Academy is assigned a tutor who becomes their main adult contact at the school; someone they see every day, who calls the roll and checks their uniforms. Students are encouraged to talk to their tutor about any problems at home or at school. Issues around bullying, or homework, or participation.'

'Did Jodie have any problems?' I ask.

'Ian will certainly know.'

'How long was Jodie a student here?'

'Since Year Seven. She was quite special because of her skating. Her parents approached me and asked if we could offer her extra tutoring and waive some of the normal rules regarding attendance. We accommodated Jodie's absences as best we could.'

Someone knocks. The door opens. Ian Hendricks is wearing casual trousers and an open-necked shirt. He's in his mid-thirties, slim and athletic, with flecks of grey in a ponytail that he has twirled into a Samurai knot at the back of his head. Straight away, I clock him as the 'cool teacher'; a John Keating figure, who wins over his students by reading poetry, or standing on his desk, or listening to the popular music. I bet he has an Instagram account and uses Snapchat.

'DCI Parvel and Dr Haven wish to look inside Jodie Sheehan's locker,' explains Mr Graham. 'They also have some questions about Jodie. I thought you were the best person to ask.'

Hendricks looks less than keen. 'I don't have a key to her locker.'

'Well, call maintenance and get bolt cutters.'

Moments later we're escorted along a covered walkway to a two-storey brick building with stairs at either end. Children call out to Hendricks who waves back, using their first names.

'Do you know them all?' I ask.

'Eight hundred students – I don't think so.' He forces a laugh.

'What about Jodie?'

'I've been her form tutor since last year. She missed a lot of school with her skating. I helped her to catch up.'

'How did you do that?'

'I collected the relevant notes from her teachers and emailed her homework and assignments.'

'Was she popular?' I ask.

'I think so. Everybody knew her.'

'Outgoing?'

'Yes.'

'Academic?'

'Not really.'

He gazes past me at a window, high up on the stairwell. 'Some students are naturally gifted, but Jodie had to work hard to keep up. Some of her teachers complained that she fell asleep in class, but most understood the hours she trained.'

'Did you ever see her compete?' I ask.

'No, but I used to wonder if it was cruel.'

'In what way?'

'Making a child work that hard – up every morning at six; a special diet, gym sessions, weight work, dance classes, acrobatics. She didn't have time for a childhood.'

'You make it sound like child abuse.'

'More like white slavery.' He smiles wryly. 'Some parents expect too much of their children and others expect too little. Both can be equally damaging.'

The metal lockers are lined along the walls around the base of the stairwells. A maintenance man in a grey uniform arrives with a set of bolt cutters that slice easily through the soft metal of a cheap padlock.

Lenny tosses me a pair of disposable gloves and puts on a similar pair, smoothing them over her fingers. The locker door squeaks on stiff hinges. The inner surface is plastered with photographs cut from magazines. There are no skaters this time. Instead Jodie has chosen boy bands, pop singers and film stars. I recognise Justin Bieber and Ed Sheeran.

Lenny takes photographs of the undisturbed locker, which is divided by two metal shelves. School textbooks are stacked upright at the bottom, along with several ring-bound folders, which Jodie has decorated with stickers. The top shelf has brightly coloured storage containers, full of pens, highlighters, flash cards, hand cream, hair bands, cough drops, chapsticks, chewing gum, a small zippered make-up bag, a bundle of greetings cards . . .

Lenny is flicking through the ring-bound folders. I look at the cards. Some of them celebrate Jodie's birthday, while others are valentines from secret and not-so-secret admirers. I look for names. Clues. One has a flower pressed between the pages, a blue forget-me-not. The inscription reads: 'I am not too young. You are not too old. I am your Ruth and you are my Tommy. Never Let Me Go.'

'What is it?' asks Lenny, looking over my shoulder.

'A valentine.'

'Is that Jodie's handwriting?'

I compare it to the notes in her subject folders. 'She must have written it and run out of courage.' I look at the quote again. 'It's from a novel by Kazuo Ishiguro, *Never Let Me Go*.'

'What's it about?'

'A doomed love affair.'

Ian Hendricks is sitting on the stairs, looking at his mobile. I ask him what texts Jodie was studying for her English classes.

'We were reading dystopian stories.'

'You're her English teacher?'

'Yes.'

Lenny continues searching. She unzips the make-up bag and quietly nudges me. I glance down and see a box of condoms. Open. She pulls back the flip-top and counts. Four of the twelve are missing.

'Parents are the last to know,' she whispers.

The condoms are put into a sealed evidence bag that she marks with a time, date and location.

A black rubberised torch is standing upright at the back of the locker, looking out of place. Weighing it in my hands, I unscrew the battery cap and shake out a single D-sized battery into my palm. There should be more. Holding up the torch, I peer inside and see a roll of paper. Not paper. Bank notes: hundreds, fifties and twenties.

Lenny takes the bundle from me. 'It has to be five, maybe six thousand.'

'Where would Jodie get that sort of money?'

The question echoes in the stairwell, unanswered, and we both realise that Jodie is not the girl that we imagined.

15

I've been standing outside the house in Hotham Road for twenty minutes, studying the way the sun throws shadows beneath the eaves and highlights the coloured glass in the lead-light panels above the windows. A wind-vane of Father Time on the pitched slate roof is pointed fixedly towards the west, regardless of the breeze.

No. 79 is an ordinary house in an ordinary street in north London, lined with plane trees and dotted with estate agents' signs and posters for the local primary school's autumn fete.

This is where Evie Cormac emerged from hiding six years ago. Back then, the house was being renovated and the garden was overgrown, the downpipes were streaked with rust and the window frames needed painting. Wisteria had grown wild during the summer, twisting and coiling up the exterior wall, creating a floral curtain that half covered the front door. The house is in order now, but the wisteria remains, littering the steps like mauve confetti left behind by a weekend wedding.

A woman emerges from the house. She has red hair and a pinched face and she's holding a mobile phone to her ear.

'Can I help you?' she shouts, not leaving the front steps.

'No. Thank you.'

'Well, piss off!'

'Pardon?'

'We don't like your sort around here.'

'What sort is that?'

'Whatever you are – a ghost-hunter, psychic, true-crime writer, or general sicko.'

'I work with the police,' I say, taking out my business card. She edges closer, squinting as she reads.

'A psychologist! You're not the first.' She's still holding her mobile to her ear. She speaks to someone, 'Yeah, he's one them . . . I will . . . Bye, love.'

She lowers the phone and rattles off a list of answers to questions I haven't asked. 'You can't come inside. The secret room doesn't exist any more. There are no ghosts, no hauntings, no strange sounds, no dog kennels in the garden. And we don't know what happened to Angel Face.' Defiantly, without prompting, she says: 'We bought this place *after* the murder, OK? I know we got a bargain, but we didn't expect to be in the bloody guidebooks.'

'I didn't mean to trouble you,' I say.

'Well, don't.' She turns in her slippers and disappears inside the house, slamming the door so violently it shakes the windows.

'Don't mind Francine,' says a voice from across the fence. 'She's never been very friendly.' The jug-eared old man has a Scottish accent and is leaning on a rake in his garden. His baggy trousers make him look bow-legged. 'I don't know what she's complaining about – she didn't live here when it happened. That was a real circus.'

'Circus?'

'The police and the reporters and the TV vans. We could barely get into the place. And the smell.'

He holds out his hand and introduces himself as Murray Reid. 'It was me who called the landlord because the dogs were howling at night and the lawn hadn't been mown for weeks. I figured the tenant had done a runner – skipping on the rent, you know – so I knocked on the door. When nobody answered, I pushed open the mail-flap. That's when I got a whiff. That smell could have routed an army.'

'How well did you know Terry Boland?'

'I didn't know anyone by that name. Called himself Bill. We said hello a few times. Waved over the fence. I'd see him outside, working on his car, or carrying stuff back and forth.'

'Did you ever see him with the girl?'

'Never. I mean, people came and went – the killers obviously, although nobody took much notice – but I never saw that wee girl. Still makes me shudder – the thought of her alone in that house with a dead body. Then again, maybe she was better off.'

'What do you mean?'

'He couldn't hurt her any more.'

The temperature seems to drop, as though a cloud has suddenly passed across the sun.

'Why do you think they tortured him?' I ask.

Murray shrugs. 'At first, I figured he must have been a gangster or a drug dealer, you know. He pissed off the wrong people. But when they found Angel Face that all changed. Paedophile like that – kidnapping a wee girl – he deserved everything he got.'

A group of school-age children are pushing bikes along the footpath. As they get nearer, their chatter ceases.

Murray yells out to one of them. 'Hey, George.'

A teenage boy looks up, embarrassed to be singled out. Leaving the group, he wheels his bike towards us.

'This is Dr Haven – he works with the police,' explains Murray. 'George lives over the road. He saw Angel Face.'

'Only one time,' says George, who is tall and gangly, with a foppish fringe that falls over his eyes, while the rest of his hair is cut short in a wide band.

'When did you see her?' I ask.

'My dad says I'm not supposed to talk about it.'

'Why not?'

'Property prices.'

Murray finds this funny. George doesn't like being laughed at. 'Dad says we get too many rubberneckers driving up and down the street, looking for the house. He says the police are useless. No offence.'

'None taken. Did you ever talk to the man who was murdered?'

'No.'

'But you saw him.'

'Sure.'

'You must have been young when it happened.'

'Ten.'

'And you saw the girl.'

George shrugs. 'I didn't know she was a girl. I thought she was a boy because she had short hair.'

'Where did you see her?'

'In the window, upstairs.' He points towards the house. 'I waved to her, but she didn't wave back.'

'Did you tell anyone?'

'Only the policewoman.'

'Sacha Hopewell.'

He nods.

'She came to talk to us about the robberies,' says Murray.

'What robberies?'

'A lot of us had stuff going missing. Little things, you know. I lost a cashmere blanket and a bag of Liquorice Allsorts. Mrs Vermeer had dog food stolen.'

'Someone took my Harry Potter books,' adds George, 'and my snow dome of the Eiffel Tower.'

'We thought it was local kids until Constable Hopewell found Angel Face,' says Murray. 'It's amazing how that wee lass survived all those weeks. I often wonder what happened to her. If she made it back to her family. I hope she's OK.'

* * *

A different house in a different street. A shadow passes behind the frosted glass.

'Who is it?' asks a woman from behind the door.

'Dr Cyrus Haven. I'm looking for Sacha Hopewell.'

'She's not here.'

'I work with the police. Can you tell me where she is?'

'No.'

'I'm going to slide my business card under the door.'

I push the card halfway and it disappears onto the far side. After two beats of silence, the deadlock releases. A woman with burnt orange hair and thick spectacles peers at me over the security chain.

'Why do you want Sacha?'

'I'm looking for information about a cold case.'

'Angel Face?'

'Yes.'

'Go away!'

She shuts the door. I put my finger on the bell, letting it ring constantly. This time a man answers, her husband, telling me to leave or he'll call the police.

'I *am* the police,' I say.

'They all say that.'

'Who do?'

'Leave us alone.'

'It's Rodney, isn't it? I talked to you on the phone. Give me five minutes. Please. It's important.'

The door closes and I can hear them arguing, whispering urgently.

'Sacha told us not to . . .'

'He doesn't look dangerous.'

'What if it's a trick.'

'But he's a psychologist.'

'The card could be fake.'

After a few more moments, the chain is unlatched and the door opens. They're standing side-by-side in the hallway like parents ready to scold a child for coming home late.

'We're not going to tell you where she is,' says Mr Hopewell.

'I understand. Can I come in?'

They look at each other as though trapped by their natural politeness. Mrs Hopewell is a heavy-set woman in a floral dress and cardigan. Her husband is tall and lean and hunched over, as if bent by some invisible weight.

He whispers to me as I pass him. 'Please, don't upset Dominique. She's not well.'

Their kitchen is cold. Used teabags have solidified in the sink and a dripping tap rings the same note over and over. Mrs Hopewell offers to turn on the heating. She's in her mid-sixties with a fine head of chemically coloured hair, swept back and held in place by a hairband. They sit close. Shoulders touching. Arms crossed.

'I've been asked to look into a police cold case. I was hoping your daughter, Sacha, might be able to help me.'

'She can't,' says Mr Hopewell.

'She won't,' echoes his wife. 'Haven't you done enough to hurt her?'

'I don't understand what you're talking about.'

'I wish Sacha had never found Angel Face.'

'Why?'

'Because we lost a daughter,' says Mrs Hopewell, her chest expanding and collapsing in a sigh.

I don't know what these people are talking about, but their pain is real.

'Please, can you start at the beginning?'

A look passes between them. They don't trust me, but whatever has happened has gone on too long.

'When Sacha finished school, she applied to join the police force. I didn't think it was a proper career for a woman – not like nursing or teaching – but she had her heart set on it. She tried twice to join the Metropolitan Police but missed out. She was too young the first time. Then they said she had to live in London to be eligible.'

101

'That's why she became a special constable,' adds Mr Hopewell. 'She said it was a stepping stone. The next best thing.'

They both fall silent. I wait.

He begins again. 'That all changed when she found Angel Face. It made her famous for a while. Everybody wanted to talk to her – the newspapers, TV shows, magazines. She thought it might help her career, but it caused her nothing but grief.'

'Why?'

'It never stopped – the late-night phone calls and the people following her.'

'Are you talking about reporters?'

'At first, yes, but then other people came calling. Some wouldn't take no for an answer. We had two burglaries and her car was vandalised.'

'When you say "they" – who did these things?'

Mrs Hopewell erupts. 'You tell us!'

I can't answer her.

'Where is Sacha now?'

'Travelling.'

'Can you be more specific?'

'Last week she was in France. A month ago it was Germany. Before that we got postcards from Scotland, Italy and Ireland.'

Mr Hopewell motions to the fridge, which is entirely covered in cards. 'She never stays in the same place more than a few days. That's why they can't find her.'

'Who?' I ask.

'The people who are looking for her.' He makes it sound so obvious.

'Have you ever met these people?'

'No.'

'Does Sacha know their names?'

'No.'

'Was she ever threatened?' I ask.

'Everything was a threat,' says her father.

102

We're going around in circles.

'They weren't reporters,' says Mr Hopewell. 'They didn't leave their names. Sometimes they watched the house or they followed Sacha to work, or when she went to the shops. They thought she could lead them to Angel Face.'

'Did Sacha tell the police?'

'Nobody believed her. They thought she was being paranoid. That's why they wouldn't let her join the Met, they labelled her as too unstable.'

'Can I phone her?' I ask.

'She doesn't have a phone.'

The irony isn't lost on me.

'She rings us,' says Mr Hopewell. 'We never know when she'll call. Sometimes she contacts her brother, or her aunt.'

She's covering her tracks.

'Can you bring Sacha back?' asks his wife. She's holding his hand beneath the table.

What do I say? I don't understand why she's gone.

Mr Hopewell turns to me and struggles to speak.

'You want to know the worst thing . . . I'm angry with Sacha. I wish she had never grown up. I wish we could have locked her in a room and stopped her leaving home.

'We sit here, waiting for the phone to ring or hoping for a postcard. That's our future. That's what we look forward to when we wake up every morning. Each day begins and ends with her.'

On the drive back to Nottingham, the rain arrives, sweeping in from the west in sheets that blur the landscape of fields and forests. My wipers struggle, slapping against the side of the windscreen like a soggy metronome.

I go over my visit to the Hopewells. A part of me wants to dismiss their suspicions as paranoia, but neither of them had been looking for confirmation or justification. Paranoid people believe the world is conspiring against them and that mistakes are never their fault. Paranoid people focus on what they *want* to see.

At the same time, I don't buy into conspiracies. I'm not saying they don't exist, but too many people are drawn to complicated answers, rather than obvious ones. They want to believe that arch-villains, or shady organisations or the 'deep state' are manipulating society, pulling the strings.

In reality, there isn't some shooter in the grassy knoll or child sex ring in the pizza shop or secret group controlling the world. To misquote Mark Twain: 'It isn't what we don't know that gets us into trouble. It's what we know for sure that just isn't so.'

16

Angel Face

The minibus is supposed to leave at noon. I stand back while the others jostle to get on board, calling 'shotgun' on certain seats or demanding to sit next to the window.

'Will you get on the sodding bus,' says Miss McCredie, pinching Nat on the forearm.

'Ow! What did I do?'

'You're being a twat,' she says under her breath, but loud enough for me to hear.

Miss McCredie's partner, Judy, is driving the bus. She looks like a nightclub bouncer, or a rugby manager, with her square head, boxy clothes and tightly cropped hair.

'I know who wears the pants in that relationship,' whispers Chloe.

'What does that mean?' I ask.

'She's the butch one. She goes on top.'

Do lesbians worry about tops and bottoms, I wonder.

Chloe considers herself an expert on sex, having boasted about giving blowjobs to her older brother's friends and her biology teacher, who got sacked when he texted her a picture of his dick. He thought it was anonymous, but he forgot to crop the image, which included a coffee cup that said: 'Old teachers never die, they just lose their class.' Irony 101.

I take a seat near the front where I'm less likely to be hassled. I plug in my music but can still hear Chloe commandeering the back seat and choosing who gets to sit next to her.

Miss McCredie does a head count and tells everybody of the penalties that await anyone who misbehaves. She's almost finished when Reno steps on the bus. A cheer goes up because Reno is one of the most popular members of staff. He's young and into music and he likes discussing last night's episode of Love Island. He also plays keyboards in a pub band called Roadkill. They once came to Langford Hall and did a gig, which was the most fun anyone could remember – unless you ask the neighbours.

Reno sits next to me and holds out his fist for a bump. I do it reluctantly, glancing at him quickly before looking away again, seeing the stubble on his cheeks and the stud in his earlobe. Some of the boys' wolf-whistle and chorus, 'Oooooh.' I don't react, but I'll get them later.

Reno is just back from his honeymoon in Sri Lanka. He showed me where that was on a map, but I couldn't tell if it was a long way away because I have no sense of distance.

The bus pulls out of the driveway and heads through the streets until the houses give way to pound stores and pawnshops. We pass an Islamic bookshop, a kosher butcher, an Arab grocer and an Asian supermarket. People call it the great melting pot, but nothing is melting, or blending. I like it that way – with everybody being different.

What I don't like are the old people, who keep complaining about stuff – the noise and the traffic and the cost of living. Grey and puffy as dumplings, they hobble along footpaths and wait at bus stops and count out their change at supermarket checkouts, humming with disapproval every time a young person speaks too loudly, or moves too quickly, or simply breathes. Don't ride your skateboard. Don't play your music. Don't wear those clothes.

The minibus stops at a red light. Reno is reading a story on his phone. It's about a schoolgirl who was raped and murdered in Nottingham.

'Who did it?' I ask.

'Some sicko.'

'How can you tell?'

'What?'

'How do you know when someone is sick in the head, or when they're just plain bad?'

Reno shrugs.

'Is that why we're in Langford Hall?' I ask.

'Nobody thinks you're sick or bad.'

I turn away, resting my forehead against the glass, watching the window grow foggy with each breath.

At the cinema we wait while Miss McCredie buys our tickets. Arcade machines beep and blink with bright lights. A group of teenage boys are playing table football, knowing the girls are checking them out. Chloe grabs Reebah and pulls her over to the boys. Chloe has all the moves – pointing her front toe, pushing out her boobs and smiling coyly. Straight away, she's targeted the best-looking one, who has blond hair, cut short and gelled into spikes like he's channelling his inner hedgehog. I notice his smoky-grey eyes and his clear skin, but most of all his confidence. Where does it come from? Does it come with age, or testicles, or can it be ordered online from Amazon – next-day delivery?

The boy has his arm around Chloe, running it down her back, letting it drift lower.

'Chloe Pringle!' barks Miss McCredie, giving the boy the evil eye. She marches Chloe back to the group. Chloe looks over her shoulder and mouths the word 'Later', tossing her hair again for the sake of tossing it.

We queue for popcorn. I let the others push past me. Reebah takes an age to choose what she wants because she's careful with her money. The guy behind the counter acts like he's got a plane to catch. He hands Reebah her change. She looks at her hand, saying, 'This isn't enough.'

'What?'

'I gave you twenty quid.'

'You gave me a tenner.'

'No.'

He opens the till and holds up a ten-pound note. 'See!'

'I gave you a twenty,' says Reebah, growing anxious and looking around for support.

'Next,' says the man, looking past her.

'I brought twenty quid. I know I did.' Reebah looks at Miss McCredie, then at Chloe and Nat and the rest of the group. 'I gave him a twenty, I swear.'

'You must be mistaken,' says Miss McCredie.

'It's my birthday money. Mum sent it to me.'

The man behind the counter interrupts. 'She gave me a tenner, OK? I get kids coming in here all the time trying to pull this scam.'

'It's not a scam,' says Reebah, her voice changing pitch.

Miss McCredie tells her to calm down and step away from the counter.

'But he stole my money.'

'Be quiet, Reebah!' she scolds, and apologises to the man, saying she's sorry for causing trouble.

I've been watching from the back of the queue. Reluctantly, I step forward. 'She's telling the truth.'

Miss McCredie frowns. 'Did you see her hand over the money?'

'She's not lying.'

Miss McCredie pulls me closer to the counter. 'You were standing way back there, Evie. How could you see what money she handed over?'

'She gave him a twenty.'

'They're both in on it,' says the man. 'It's a scam.'

'You're trying to rip her off,' I reply, shifting my slouch from one hip to the other.

The man behind the counter grows flustered. 'I'll call the manager. You'll all have to leave.'

'You won't call the manager,' I say.

'Maybe I'll call the police.'

108

'Go on then.'

The conviction in my voice seems to surprise him. He's not used to being contradicted – not by a girl. He leans towards me and I brace myself, expecting to be slapped. Reno intervenes, protecting me, giving me confidence.

'I think you've done this before,' I say. 'I bet you put that twenty straight into your pocket.'

The man reacts with fake outrage.

'Empty your pockets,' says Reno.

The man mutters something under his breath and opens the till. He takes out an extra ten-pound note and tosses it towards Reebah. She picks it off the floor and puts the money deep into the back pocket of her jeans.

'I hope you weren't lying,' mutters Miss McCredie, as she walks behind me into the cinema.

Reebah is ahead of us. She looks over her shoulder, as though wanting to say thank you, but not remembering the words.

17

Sunday afternoon in the shadows of Nottingham Castle, two boys and a girl, roughly the same age, are pushing a wheelbarrow across the square. Slumped inside is crude effigy of Guy Fawkes, stuffed with straw or rags, with red woollen hair, a flat cap, and mismatched buttons for eyes.

'They're a bit late,' I say. 'Bonfire night was a week ago.'

'Maybe they're getting a head start on next year,' says Caroline Fairfax. Evie Cormac's lawyer is in her early thirties with dark wavy hair held back from her face by an Alice band. She's dressed in a cream-coloured blouse and blue denim jeans that look brand new. She reaches for the sugar and fills a spoon twice, stirring as though it might solidify if she didn't.

'You don't see Guy Fawkes effigies very often any more,' I say.

'That's not a bad thing,' she replies. 'Anti-Catholic rituals are rather outdated.'

'Are you Catholic?'

'Heavens, no! I'm an equal opportunity atheist.' She licks foam from her spoon.

Across the road, Japanese tourists are posing for photographs in front of a Robin Hood statue. Cast in thick bronze, Robin has a green tinge and is about to unleash an arrow at a tourist stand selling felt hats, medieval tunics, Maid Marian wimples and Friar Tuck teddy bears.

'Where do you stand on Robin Hood?' I ask, enjoying the banter.

'He was a dangerous progressive who gave money to spongers and welfare cheats. Nowadays they'd lock him up, or make him leader of the Labour Party.'

She smiles, and I feel a jolt of attraction as her eyes meet mine. In that moment it feels like she has mentally grabbed hold of my testicles and given them a tug. I look away and try not to blush. I expect her to look away as well, but Caroline's eyes are still searching my face. She licks the spoon again.

'Evie's case is on Wednesday,' I say.

'Are we allowed to be talking?'

'What do you mean?'

'Maybe you're going to be a witness for the other side.'

'Are there sides?' I ask. 'We all want what's best for Evie.'

She looks at me doubtfully. 'Why do people always say that when they're taking the choice away from someone?'

'Do you think Evie is ready?'

'My job is to ask questions of people like you, who seem to think she's too damaged to be allowed out into the big bad world.'

'You must have an opinion.'

'I'm a legal aid lawyer, not a psychologist.'

'How old were you when you left home?' I ask.

The question annoys her. 'I don't see what difference that makes.'

'Was it university?'

'Yes.'

'You went home for the holidays. You had a student loan, a car, regular money from your parents.'

'What are you trying to say?'

'Evie doesn't have any support. No family to fall back on.'

'We can't keep people locked up because they don't have parents, or family money.'

I hesitate, about to ask another question, but Caroline gets in before me. 'I know who she is.'

'Pardon?'

'Evie. I know the truth.'

I play dumb.

'She's Angel Face.' There is a beat of silence. Caroline lowers her voice. 'I guessed. How many people her age can't prove how old they are?'

'You can't tell anyone.'

'I know the law, Dr Haven.'

'Please call me Cyrus.'

Outside, another group of tourists are carrying matching red shoulder bags and following a guide who is twirling a yellow umbrella like a baton.

Caroline speaks next. 'Do you want to keep Evie locked away?'

'No.'

'Then why are you here?'

I don't know how to answer her, or if it's appropriate to tell her the truth. How do I explain that Evie Cormac has lodged under my skin like a splinter that irritates me at unexpected moments? She fascinates and alarms me and makes me realise why I became a psychologist.

Normally, when someone is balanced and copes well with day-to-day life, there's no point in trying to unlock their psyche. More importantly, it can be dangerous to tinker with a 'machine' that isn't broken. Most people learn to live with trauma and deprivation, by developing coping mechanisms. They get on with life rather than dwelling on failure or loss.

I don't know if Evie remembers what happened to her or has chosen to forget. The idea of traumatic memories being suppressed and coming to the surface later has divided psychologists and neurologists for thirty years, but the memory wars of the 1990s were never resolved. I don't think Evie has suppressed memories. We know some of what she endured. She listened to a man being tortured to death. She spent weeks in a house with his decomposing body. She was sexually abused from a young age and doctors doubt if she'll ever be able to have children.

Yet, despite being treated by a legion of therapists, counsellors and psychologists, she has never spoken about what she witnessed or how she came to be in the secret room. I don't care how untouched or untroubled she may appear to be, she *will* have scars. She *does* remember.

Caroline runs her finger around the rim of her coffee cup, collecting the remaining froth.

'Would you like another?' I ask.

'I don't have time,' she replies, glancing at her phone. 'About Evie. Can I call you as a witness?'

'No.'

'But you've talked to her.'

'She's told me nothing.'

'You've read her files.'

'Same answer.'

'Was it really so bad – what happened to her?'

I lean closer. 'So far I haven't found anyone who doesn't consider Evie to be a danger to herself and to others.'

'And you agree?'

'Not completely. I think Evie is self-destructive, self-hating, anti-social and impervious to criticism, yet she's also the most self-aware, undaunted, sanguine person I've ever met. She doesn't appear to need friends, or approval or human interaction. That doesn't make her dangerous to anyone other than herself, although she has a history of attacking people whom she perceives as having wronged her in some way.'

'You think she should be locked up indefinitely,' says Caroline.

'I didn't say that. I want to help Evie but I haven't worked out exactly how to do it.'

'That's still not a reason to keep her at Langford Hall.'

'No.'

Caroline's face seems to transform, growing softer.

'Nobody else in my office wanted this case. They gave it to me because I'm the newbie. I've litigated two cases in my short career and now I'm appearing before the High Court.'

'You'll be fine,' I say, hoping I sound convincing.

'But you're right. They're going to ask Evie how she can support herself, where she'll live . . . I don't have anything to tell them.'

'I wish I could help you.'

Caroline collects her briefcase from beside the table.

'Are you going to put her on the stand?' I ask.

'I don't think I have a choice.'

'Don't do it. She's not . . . she'll . . .' I can't finish.

'What else can I do?'

'Anything but that.'

18

Chief Superintendent Timothy Heller-Smith strides into the incident room, yelling, 'We got him!' and pausing to punch at the ground like he's pull-starting a lawn mower.

Cheers echo across the open-plan office, accompanied by fist bumps and high fives. Three words have changed the entire mood of the task force, sweeping away the exhaustion and fatigue. Lenny Parvel is with him, along with a uniformed constable, nervous at being thrust into the spotlight.

Lenny doesn't seem to share Heller-Smith's enthusiasm, but says nothing as she lets her superior take charge of the briefing. Detectives gather to hear the details. I join them, standing at the back, leaning against the wall.

Heller-Smith looks more like a politician than a senior police officer, dressed in an expensively cut suit and red silk tie. His thin sparse hair is dyed black and heavily oiled and his mouth is permanently open, like a thick-lipped fish.

'This is Constable Harry Plover,' he announces, getting the name wrong and having to be corrected. 'PC Glover has provided us with a breakthrough in the Jodie Sheehan case. But let's hear the story from him.'

I can see Lenny seething, but she's not going to create a scene.

The young PC looks nervously around the room, holding his hat in his hands.

'It was last Wednesday afternoon . . . the day after we found Jodie. I was at Silverdale Walk, protecting the crime scene, when this guy came along walking his dog. He got all chatty with me, saying he used the footpath most days and knew the area well. I asked him if he'd noticed anyone odd hanging around the footpath, maybe someone who was following women and such. He said I should show him a photograph if we find a suspect. I took down his name and address.'

Lenny motions for him to go on.

'Later that afternoon I had a couple of girls come up to me. They were putting flowers on Jodie's memorial – the makeshift one – near the Community Centre. One of them said she went to school with Jodie. I asked her when she heard the news and she said she'd been waiting at a bus stop on Southchurch Drive on Tuesday afternoon when a guy came up to her. He had a dog – a kelpie. He told them not to use Silverdale Walk because the police had found a girl's body beneath the footbridge. I asked Jodie's friend what time this was, and she said about half-three. People knew Jodie was missing by then, but this guy had knowledge that a girl's body had been found. He pinpointed the location.'

'Exactly,' says Heller-Smith. 'That information wasn't released until the six o'clock media conference and we made no mention of the footbridge.' He holds aloft Glover's police-issue notebook. 'Not only did the constable recognise the discrepancy, but he asked the girl for a description and realised that she was talking about the same person he'd spoken to earlier in the day. Outstanding work. Simply outstanding.'

He claps PC Glover on the shoulder, mispronouncing his name again.

Lenny smiles wryly and thanks Heller-Smith for his 'insightful summary'. The words seem innocuous enough but land like a punch. Looks are exchanged. Mutual antipathy.

The chief superintendent leaves and Lenny relaxes, propping herself on a desk.

'Our prime suspect is Craig Farley, twenty-six. He lives alone in Bainton Grove, which is less than a mile from where Jodie was found. He was taken into custody an hour ago and SOCO are examining his bungalow. We know that Farley works as a porter at the Queen's Medical Centre – which is where Jodie was hospitalised with pneumonia eight months ago. He may have seen her there and developed an infatuation.

'More importantly, he has form – two arrests for exposing himself to women in Central Park, near Nethergate Stream. Both times he claimed to be nude sunbathing. The second time he was given a suspended sentence and a good behaviour bond. At aged eighteen he was picked up for having sex with a minor. The girl was fourteen. Her parents chose not to press charges, which means Farley escaped with a caution and wasn't put on the Sex Offenders Register.'

Lenny looks from face to face, making sure that everyone is on the same page.

'One of Farley's neighbours saw him on Tuesday morning carrying a bundle of clothes in a bin bag. He said he was giving them to charity, which is why we're going to check every second-hand shop and clothing bin in Nottingham.'

There are groans from the detectives. Lenny ignores them, glancing instead at the clock.

'We can hold Farley for another twenty-three hours, unless we apply for an extension. The clock is ticking. I want to know everything about him. Talk to workmates, friends, family, ex-girlfriends, neighbours. Trace his movements. This is our guy – I can feel it in my water.'

'What about DNA?' asks Monroe.

'The results will take three or four days. I want a confession before then. I'm going first team with Edgar. Monroe and Prime Time, you're second team.'

'Has he lawyered up?' asks Nobody.

'Not yet, but we do everything by the book. We give him a break every two hours. Plenty of liquids and regular meals. Go in hard, but don't bully him. Next briefing is at four o'clock.'

As she turns away, she is handed a phone. The chief constable is on the line. I hear Lenny responding: 'Yes, sir . . . about an hour ago . . . reasonably certain . . . we're about to start now . . . yes, sir. I will, sir. You'll be the first to know.'

Lenny hangs up and motions for me to follow. We head downstairs to the interview suites, located at the rear of the building. The white-painted room is furnished with a table, three chairs and a one-way mirror that allows the interrogations to be observed and filmed.

Craig Farley is alone, slouching in a chair, biting at a hangnail as though it's a splinter. He stands suddenly and walks to the door. He raises his fist, as though ready to knock but changes his mind. Now he's in front of the mirror, glancing past his reflection with a studied casualness, as if he's aware there might be someone watching him.

There is nothing unusual about his looks. He's five-ten, brown-haired and thirty pounds overweight. Although anxious, his face is strangely blank, as though he's not completely sure how he managed to get here.

Lenny and DS Edgar enter the room and introduce themselves. They ask Farley if he'd like something to eat or drink. He says he wants to go home.

'You're under arrest,' Lenny explains.

'There's been a mistake. You got the wrong person.'

'For what?'

Farley hesitates. 'For whatever you think I did.'

'I'm glad to hear it,' says Lenny. 'Because things were looking pretty serious for you, Craig. But if it's all a misunderstanding, we should be able to sort this out tout suite.' She pulls her chair closer. I watch how Farley examines her, checking out her breasts and her hips. He can't help himself.

'Exactly what mistake have we made?' asks Lenny.

'I had nothing to do with that girl.'

'What girl?'

'The one in the papers.'

'Do you know her name?'

'Jodie something.'

'You mean this one,' says DS Edgar, opening a file and taking out a photograph. 'For the record, this is a recent picture of Jodie Sheehan. It was taken by a school photographer in March 2018.'

Farley looks at the image and away again.

'Pretty, isn't she?' asks Lenny.

'Not my type.'

'What's your type, Craig? We know you like them young.'

He doesn't answer.

'You had sex with a minor.'

'I was never charged.'

Lenny corrects him. 'You were never convicted. According to the medical report, you really tore her up.'

Farley nods. 'She wanted it.'

'And she was your girlfriend.'

'Yeah.'

'So why be so rough on her?'

'Her dad was the problem, not me.'

He looks from face to face, wanting to be understood.

Lenny switches focus. 'So where did you meet Jodie?'

There is a momentary glimmer of recognition in Farley's eyes, but he's taken too long to answer.

'I never met her.'

'What about at the hospital?'

He frowns.

Lenny produces a small plastic test tube from her pocket. 'Do you know what this is, Craig? It collects skin cells from inside your cheek. Open wide and I'll have a quick brush around.'

Farley shakes his head. 'I don't trust you. You're going to plant my DNA at the scene.'

'What scene?' asks Edgar.

'On that girl. You'll take my spit and you'll spill it around.'

'We're trying to remove you from our list of suspects.'

Farley presses his lips together and shakes his head.

'It won't matter, Craig,' says Lenny. 'We can hold you down if necessary. I can get four officers in here right now and we'll do this the hard way.'

Farley shrinks from her and glances at his reflection in the mirror, raising his hand as though he's unsure if he's watching someone else being interrogated.

'What's your dog's name?' asks Edgar.

Farley reacts as though every question is loaded.

'Clancy.'

'What breed?'

'A kelpie.'

'Do you walk him every day?'

'She's a bitch.'

'Where do you normally take her?'

'Lots of different places – along the river mainly. Sometimes I go to Rushcliffe Country Park.'

'How about Central Park?' asks Lenny.

'No.'

'That's right – you prefer to nude sunbathe,' says Edgar.

Farley bristles. 'That was a misunderstanding.'

'What about Silverdale Walk?' asks Lenny. 'You told Constable Glover you used that footpath every day.'

'Not every day.'

'What about on Monday night?'

There is another pause. Silence. I can see Farley's mind working overtime because he doesn't have the intellect or the speed of thought to maintain his lies or second-guess what the detectives know or don't know. He has a below-average IQ and limited social skills, which fits with the clumsy attempt to hide Jodie's body and his lack of forensic awareness and his history of underage sex and lower-grade sexual offences.

Lenny and Edgar slowly ratchet up the pressure, unpacking Farley's movements on Monday evening. There is nothing subtle about their approach. Everybody in the room knows what role they have to play – even Farley.

If he were a patient of mine, I would interview him differently. I'd begin by exploring his childhood, his schooling and his family relationships. After taking his history, I would slowly explore his sexuality and fantasies. What does he look for in a woman? What turns him on? What does he picture when he masturbates? Is it their smell, or the clothes they wear, or the way they walk? Over numerous sessions, I would identify the progression that led his normal, consensual romantic fantasies to become corrupted by thoughts of violence, exploitation and coercion. Perhaps he was abused as a child, or maybe his first attempts at having ordinary relationships were rebuffed. Girls ignored him, or laughed at him, or belittled his failings.

That's when his fantasies were formed – richly detailed scenarios in which he won the girl and landed the job and got a nice car and cool friends. But the more his real-world attempts at intimacy failed, the more his fantasies changed. Instead of romantic love and sexual compatibility, he imagined punishing the women who shunned him, the bosses who sacked him, and the bullies who bullied him. In his imagination, he didn't just *get* the girl, he made her pay. He made them *all* pay.

Fantasies of sexual revenge have to be fed. Pornography and violent films provided some of what he needed, but soon it wasn't enough. He sought out real-world details – locations, victims, souvenirs . . . He began following women home, or stealing underwear from their clothes lines, or peeping through their windows. When he *did* approach women, they tended to be young and impressionable and easier to talk into having sex.

All of this behaviour is part of a progression, yet raping and killing Jodie was way ahead of anything he'd done previously. Something must have triggered the escalation – a family tragedy, getting fired from a job, some unexpected setback or humiliation.

If I were asking the questions, I would take my time, but the police don't have that luxury. Unless they seek an extension from a judge, they have twenty-four hours to either charge Farley or let him go.

After two hours, the team takes a break. Lenny arrives in the observation room. She looks pleased with how it's gone. Farley is still in the interview room, pacing the floor, muttering to himself.

'What do you think?' she asks.

'I think you'll get a confession.'

She waits, expecting more.

'I think he's highly suggestible.'

'We're not putting words in his mouth.'

'Pushed hard enough he'll say almost anything.'

Lenny frowns so deeply that her eyes disappear. She's angry in a hip-jutting, pissed-off way.

'He's not going to make up a murder.'

'I know, but you'll get his DNA and fibres from his clothes. You don't have to break him. Farley is isolated and confused. The adrenalin rush that led him to raping Jodie has disappeared and he's realising the magnitude of what he's done . . . of what he is.'

'You think he's a suicide risk?'

'Yes.'

'Saving us a lot of time and expense.'

'I'll pretend I didn't hear that.'

19

'Christ! That's all I need,' mutters Lenny, looking through the glass doors of the station.

A crowd has gathered on the pavement, spilling onto the road.

'They've been arriving for the past hour,' says a uniformed sergeant.

'That's because this place leaks like a church roof,' grunts Lenny.

I recognise Felix Sheehan among the crowd. He's with another young man and two teenage girls who look school age but are dressed to look older or colder, depending what you consider functional or fashionable.

Two uniformed officers are guarding the main doors.

One of the protesters yells, 'What's his name? Has he confessed?'

Others react and begin chanting, 'Bring him out! Bring him out!'

I notice a TV crew arriving, hoisting cameras onto shoulders and bathing the crowd in a spotlight. The escalation is immediate and the noise level increases. I've always been fascinated by the psychology of the mob, how it provides anonymity and abrogates responsibility and diminishes any sense of 'self'. People don't *lose* their identity when they join together – they gain a new one as part of a tribe.

'Get some more bodies down here,' mutters Lenny, pushing through the glass doors. Cameras fire and reporters jostle to get to the front.

'I'll make a short statement, then I want you all to leave,' she says. 'A local man has been taken into custody and is helping us with our enquiries into the murder of Jodie Sheehan. That is all I can say.'

'Who his he?' yells one of them.

'We won't be releasing his name.'

'Let us talk to him.'

The statement triggers laughter.

Lenny continues. 'Please, go home. Let us do our job.'

'We have every right to be here,' yells the ringleader, who has tattoos on his shaven head and a T-shirt that says FREEDOM ISN'T FREE, with a picture of Tommy Robinson, the far-right activist, emblazoned on a Union Jack flag.

Lenny ignores him. The crowd starts chanting, 'Scum! Scum! Scum!'

I notice Felix slipping back through the bodies, trying to fade into the background. Stepping out of the main doors, I walk along the pavement, skirting the crowd keeping him in sight among the heads. I spy him crossing the road, ducking between stopped cars. He's with the same group, the young man and teenage girls. I follow from a distance, watching them saunter along Rectory Road, slouching and smoking. Felix has his arms around the two girls, sliding his hands down their spines until his fingers tuck into the pockets of their denim shorts.

I want to talk to him. I want to ask about the money we found in Jodie's locker, but now isn't the time. Instead I follow him from a distance. This is how I learn things about people.

I watch them. I study the way they walk and talk and interact with the world. When a structural engineer looks at a bridge or a building, he automatically thinks about axial forces, load-bearing points and tensile strength. I look at how people use their bodies, faces and voices; what they wear, how they drive their cars and relate to each other. Without trying or wanting to, I learn things about them – not the detail of their lives but the shape of their personality and what influences their behaviour.

I'm not far behind Felix. I half expect him to notice me and turn, but he's too busy flirting with the girls. He's reached his Lexus. My ageing red Fiat is parked opposite. That's when I make the decision. I cross the road and open the car door, while Felix says goodbye, bumping fists and shoulders. One of the girls whispers something in his ear. He brushes her off.

I've never tailed a car before. It's not like following someone home from the pub or to a picnic spot in the countryside. Felix drives impatiently, accelerating hard between lights. Twice I think I've lost him, but the traffic is so heavy that he can't get too far ahead of me. We cross Trent Bridge and follow London Road past Meadow Lane Stadium before turning left into Queen's Road. He pulls into a multi-storey car park near Nottingham Railway Station and drives to the rooftop level. He parks and locks the Lexus, twirling the keyless fob around his forefinger, as he walks quickly down the stairs. I can hear his footsteps echoing below me, masking the sound of my own progress.

I emerge thirty yards behind him, watching him enter the station concourse, past the taxi rank and through the automatic doors. He stands beneath the arrivals and departures board but isn't studying the timetable. Instead he seems to be looking for someone. Maybe he arranged to pick them up.

He walks slowly along the concourse, checking out the cafés, the booking hall and the men's toilets. Beside a row of vending machines, he stops and studies two backpackers, who are lying on the floor with their heads resting on their rucksacks. Felix says something. A baseball hat is lifted. A shake of the head.

Leaving the main entrance, he crosses Station Street to a Jobcentre Plus on the opposite side of the road. The automatic doors open to reveal a queue of job seekers waiting for interviews. Felix loiters near the access ramp, watching people arrive and leave. Occasionally he approaches one of them, but the conversations are brief.

Another youth emerges, hands in pockets, a hooded sweatshirt covering his head. Felix greets him, his face full of boyish good cheer. A cigarette is offered. Accepted. Lit. Exhaled smoke mingles and dissipates in the cool air. They don't know each other. This is a first meeting.

They chat for a few minutes before Felix reaches into his pocket and takes out a pen. He motions for the teenager to pull up his sleeve and then writes something on his forearm. A phone number? An address? I'm too far away to see.

They separate. The youth doesn't look back. Felix checks his phone. Types. Two-handed. Seemingly satisfied, he turns away from the Jobcentre and heads back to the railway station. I'm not exactly sure what I've just witnessed. Some sort of recruitment, or business arrangement.

I still want to ask Felix about the money in Jodie's locker but not now, not yet. I don't want him to know that I've followed him. He's passing a homeless man, dozing beside a dog. Felix pauses and takes a ten-pound note from a money-clip and tucks it into the man's pocket, before walking away with a lightness to his step, as though all is now right with the world.

20

Wednesday morning and the wind hints of winter. Mottled clouds are being driven across the sky, heading towards the Peak District and beyond to Ireland. I had planned on going for a run but quickly went off the idea when I saw the temperature outside. The central heating didn't trigger again. The pilot light had gone out. It takes twenty minutes and a sore thumb before the spark becomes a solid blue flame.

I order a cab for nine o'clock and slide into the back seat. The driver is listening to the radio. I can only see the back of his head, which is shaved and oiled and the colour of an old leather football.

'*A hospital porter has been charged with the rape and murder of Nottingham schoolgirl Jodie Sheehan, whose body was found a week ago beside a local footpath. Craig Farley, aged twenty-six, was arrested on Sunday at his Bainton Grove bungalow, which is less than a mile from where Jodie's body was discovered.*

'*At a press conference held late yesterday, Detective Chief Inspector Lenore Parvel said that Farley had made a full confession and would appear in Nottingham Crown Court this morning.*'

I hear Lenny's voice take over the commentary.

'*By choosing to co-operate with the police, the suspect has spared Jodie's family added heartache. I would like to thank my team, who have had very little sleep over the past week. This quick arrest is down to their professionalism and hard work. They did it for Jodie and for everyone whose life she touched. We cannot bring her back, but we can make sure she's not forgotten.*'

The driver is talking to me.

'Sorry, did you say something?' I ask.

He nods towards the radio. 'Me and my mates got it wrong.'

'About what?'

'Jodie Sheehan. We figured it was going to be family, you know. Someone close to her.'

'Any particular reason?'

'Normally is, eh? Eighty per cent of the time.'

Where do people get figures like this?

He's waiting for me to agree with him.

'Do you know the family?' I ask.

'The old man. He's a cranky prick.'

I want to say the name Dougal Sheehan, but leave it unsaid.

'He's one of us – a cabbie,' says the driver. 'Had some trouble a while back. This woman complained that he assaulted her. He'd driven her all the way out to Calverton before she told him she couldn't pay. Said her purse had been stolen. Dougal threatened to call the cops, but she got in first and accused him of holding her hostage. She had bruises on her arm. Could have been Dougal did it. Could have been her boyfriend.'

'What happened?'

'Never went to court.' He glances into the rear-view mirror. 'That's why I got myself one of these.' He points to a small box on the dashboard. 'You're on candid camera. Say cheese!'

We're heading along Derby Road past Lenton Abbey and the university. Taking the first exit on a roundabout, we cross the River Leen, little more than a concrete culvert, and follow Abbey Street. The plane trees form a golden tunnel that is crumbling in the wind, and between the branches I get a glimpse of Nottingham Castle perched on the aptly named Castle Rock. Having been conquered, razed, rebuilt and conquered again, it now looks more like a grand house than a fortress with turrets and battlements.

The cab drops me outside the Crown Court, a modern building with an arched glass entrance. TV crews are sheltering inside the main foyer, away from the wind. They have set up their cameras in front of the large coat of arms, ready for reporters to cross live to the studio with news of Craig Farley's first court appearance.

High Court hearings are in a different part of the building. Evie Cormac's case has been listed for ten-thirty. I try to imagine her being anxious, but it's not an emotion I associate with Evie.

The corridors are bustling with lawyers and clients. This part of the precinct handles family law matters – divorces and child custody applications. I recognise the couples because they avoid eye contact, while their respective lawyers mingle with each other, chatting and smiling. Marriages that began with heartfelt promises 'to love and honour and respect' have been reduced to ring-bound folders that detail who gets what and when and where. The arguments have led to this, a hearing before a judge, who will undo what God put together and no man was meant to put asunder.

I spot Caroline Fairfax. She is wearing her 'court clothes', a matching skirt and jacket, both black, over a white collared blouse. As I draw nearer, I realise that she's not alone. Details slowly register – the freckles, bird-like skeleton and upturned nose. Evie has been transformed. Her hair is dyed to a more natural colour and she's wearing a dress and cardigan buttoned up to her neck. Ankle-length boots give her another few inches in height. She looks great, yet miserable, as though forced to wear sackcloth, or a hair shirt.

I smile.

'What are you looking at?' she snaps.

'Doesn't she look great,' says Caroline.

I nod. Evie tells me to fuck off.

'You have to stop doing that,' says Caroline.

'What?'

'Swearing. It can't happen in the courtroom.'

'I'm not a complete moron,' says Evie, who tugs at the collar of her cardigan and adjusts the elastic of her knickers in a less than ladylike manner.

Caroline must have helped her with her make-up, which is understated and subtle rather than plastered on with a trowel.

I hear someone call my name. Guthrie waves to me, wanting me to join him. He's standing with two men, lawyer-types in charcoal-grey suits. By comparison, the social worker is his usual slovenly self in baggy corduroy trousers and a tweed jacket with a canary-yellow fleck that makes his skin look jaundiced.

The taller of the lawyers introduces himself as Derek Hodge, QC, the silk representing Nottingham City Council. His colleague is the instructing solicitor, Stephen Carter. Hodge has a finger-mangling handshake and a way of leaning forward, as though trying to intimidate or establish the pecking order. Carter has his arms full of ring-bound folders and can only nod a greeting.

'It's good that you're here,' says Guthrie. 'Mr Hodge wants to call you as a witness.'

'Me?'

'Evie Cormac wouldn't agree to see a court-appointed psychologist, but I told him that you'd spoken to her.'

'I've met her twice – not in a clinical setting.'

'But you were there during the knifing incident,' says Hodge, looking at me straight and steady, as if to say, 'No pretending, no ducking out.'

'What difference does that make?'

Hodge answers. 'Evie Cormac asked a highly agitated adolescent to stab her?'

'That's not what happened.'

His right eyebrow arches up his forehead as though trying to join his hairline.

'I've seen the CCTV footage. She points the knife at her heart and pulls it towards her chest.'

'She disarmed him.'

'She asked the young man to stab her.'

'She knew he wouldn't do it.'

'And you know this because . . .?'

'She told me.'

Hodge chuckles without warmth, or humour, and I realise that I don't like him.

'I'm not comfortable giving evidence,' I say. 'I only came to observe.'

'On whose behalf?'

'Mine.'

Guthrie looks embarrassed for me. 'I thought you wanted to help Evie.'

'I do.'

'Don't worry about it,' says the barrister. 'The judge has Evie's history and the written submissions, which should be more than enough.' He glances towards Caroline. 'And we're not facing the big guns.'

I like him even less.

A loudspeaker interrupts us. The case is being called. Hodge nods at the solicitor. 'This shouldn't take long.'

The hearing is closed to the public to protect Evie's identity and the details of her past. I'm allowed to sit in the small public gallery because I'm a court-accredited expert witness, whether I give evidence or not.

Caroline and Evie take chairs at one end of the bar table, while Hodge and Carlton are at the other. Guthrie sits close behind them, ready to consult or pass notes. Judge Sayle enters through a side door. Middle aged, with tea-black hair and strangely grey eyebrows, he smiles and welcomes everyone, making a note of their names, before addressing Evie directly.

'It's nice to meet you, Miss Cormac. I know this place may seem intimidating, but we're not here to punish or repudiate anyone. This is a safe space, where you can speak freely and honestly.'

He then addresses the lawyers. 'I'm sure you all appreciate the strict secrecy provisions that apply in this case. I have read all the relevant submissions and will give each of you an opportunity to present closing arguments before I make my ruling. I would also like to hear from Evie – if that's all right with you.'

Evie doesn't react but seems to be holding herself in check.

'Perhaps you'd like to begin, Miss Fairfax,' says the Judge.

Caroline gets to her feet and gives Evie a fleeting look. She consults her notes and pulls back her shoulders.

'Evie Cormac became a ward of this court six years ago after all attempts to establish her identity and find her family proved fruitless. It was hoped that eventually somebody would come forward, or that Evie would be successfully fostered or adopted but none of these things have occurred.

'Normally care orders are put in place because a child is believed to be at risk of suffering significant harm. In Evie's case, that harm had already been done. She was discovered in a house in north London, hiding in a secret room. She was dirty, malnourished and suffering from rickets, among other ailments.'

Hodge gets to his feet. 'Your honour, I hope my learned friend isn't planning to give us a complete history lesson. None of these facts are in dispute.'

'But they are,' says Caroline. 'The most important fact. Evie's age.'

Judge Sayle motions her to continue.

'Your honour, the duty of care exists in common law, derived from the historic judgements made by the courts, that places an obligation upon an individual or organisation to take proper care of a child, or to avoid causing foreseeable harm. In the case of Evie Cormac, the local authority has done that job and she is now asking to be released because she is eighteen.'

'She could be sixteen,' interrupts Hodge, twirling a pen across his knuckles.

'Or nineteen,' counters Caroline. 'My client is an adult and wants to be treated like an adult.'

'She can't have it both ways,' says Hodge. 'She is trying to divorce the local authority like a child divorcing a parent.'

'What case law can she use to seek redress?' argues Caroline.

'Perhaps if she'd acted more like an adult,' says Hodge, who has stayed on his feet. Caroline tries to object, but Hodge ignores her. 'Setting aside the issue of Evie Cormac's age, we cannot ignore her mental fitness and her propensity for self-harm and violence. On twelve occasions, she has been fostered by safe, stable, loving families, but each time she has chosen to fight the system. She has run away from care at least twenty times, going missing for weeks at a time. Stealing, taking drugs, gambling, drinking, abusing police, resisting arrest . . .'

'Now who's giving a history lesson?' asks Caroline.

'A very pertinent one, Miss Fairfax,' chides Hodge. 'Evie Cormac has spent the past four years in a high-security children's home because of her refusal to obey the rules or, dare I say, to *act* her age. She has abused staff, her peers, mental health care workers, therapists, psychologists and psychiatrists – many of whom have provided submissions to Your Honour. Evie's case officer is in court today and he regards Evie as the most damaged child he has ever encountered. Only last week she was involved in a malicious wounding incident at Langford Hall where she grabbed a knife, pointed it at her heart and asked a highly disturbed young man to kill her.'

'Evie disarmed the man,' says Caroline.

'By offering herself as a victim.'

'It was a ploy.'

Hodge snorts and waves his hand dismissively, as though Caroline were resorting to semantics.

'Evie Cormac is not mature enough, or stable enough, to be released from care. She has no means of support, no job training, or anywhere to live. I should also point out that crime figures show that children in care go on to make up a disproportionate percentage of our prison population.'

'Hardly a glowing endorsement of local authority care,' says Caroline.

'The onus is not on the council to prove Evie Cormac's age,' says Hodge.

'Whose job is it?'

'Her own. It is Mr Guthrie's submission that Evie Cormac *knows* her real name and her age but refuses to co-operate. She is her own worst enemy. She is not ready to be released from care and even if she were deemed to be an adult in this court today, the local authority has instructed me to immediately seek to have her sectioned under the Mental Health Act and sent to a secure psychiatric hospital.'

'That's outrageous,' argues Caroline.

'You can't fucking do that!' yells Evie, leaping to her feet. Her chair topples over with a bang. She is on the bar table, crawling towards Hodge, as though ready to rip out his throat. Caroline has to pull her back, holding her around the waist. Evie is so small that Caroline lifts her easily but has to avoid her kicking feet.

Hodge has backed away. 'I think that proves my point.'

'You're a fuckwit!' screams Evie.

'Please be quiet,' Caroline pleads, glancing helplessly at me.

Judge Sayle waits until Evie is back in her chair before warning her, 'There can be no more outbursts.'

Evie's shoulders are shaking with rage, or maybe she's crying. I can't see her face.

The judge opens a folder and turns the pages. I glimpse notes scrawled in the margins and paragraphs that are underlined.

'I'd like you to approach the bench, Miss Cormac,' he says. 'Come up and take a seat.'

Evie stands awkwardly, slightly pigeon toed, and looks over her shoulder as she makes her way forward. The judge points to a wooden chair, which has been positioned to be on the same level as his own seat.

'I'm sorry you had to listen to that,' he says gently. 'It can't be easy hearing yourself described in such a way.'

Evie doesn't answer.

'I have read your application and I think I understand how you feel. Children are taken into care for many reasons, primarily due to parental abuse or neglect, but also because there is nobody else to look after them. Your case was considered to be so serious that you were made a ward of this court and we are your guardians.'

Sitting with her back straight and knees together, Evie listens with a disquieting intensity.

'Do you know how old you are?' he asks.

'Eighteen.'

'When were you born?'

'I can't tell you the exact date.'

'You look small for your age.'

'You look young to be a judge.'

He smiles at that.

'I have at least eight statements here from child care experts who say you're a danger to yourself and a risk to the community.'

'I'm not.'

'In fact, the only submission that supports your application was delivered to me yesterday.' Judge Sayle searches his folder and fumbles to put his glasses on his nose. 'The one person who thinks you are mature and stable enough to be released is a psychologist, a Dr Haven.'

Evie turns her head to look at me. Caroline does the same. For the briefest of moments, I'm the subject of everyone's attention, until Judge Sayle reclaims the focus.

'What will you do, Evie? Where will you live?'

'I want to go to London and get a job.'

'You have no qualifications or record of employment. You don't have a National Insurance number or a bank account, or any savings. Mr Hodge may be right – you could be sixteen.'

'People get married at sixteen.'

'With parental consent.'

'They join the army.'

'If their parents approve.'

Evie stops. She's not winning the argument.

Judge Sayle continues. 'I could order you emancipated, but only if you could prove that you are economically self-sufficient and emotionally capable of living alone, or going to a home environment that is entirely suitable for a minor.'

'I'm eighteen.'

'But you can't prove it.'

'Neither can anyone else.'

'Exactly. That's the rub, isn't it?'

Judge Sayle takes off his glasses and pulls a cloth from his pocket, breathing on each lens before polishing them.

'I don't want to see you remain in care, Evie, but I don't have any alternative unless you can find the means to support yourself or can prove your real age.'

Evie is shaking her head from side to side. I expect anger or an explosion. Instead I see tears prickle at the corners of her eyes, but she refuses to let them fall. Hodge grins triumphantly.

Judge Sayle hooks the glasses over his ears, jotting notes as he talks.

'I have decided to nominate a birth date for the appellant, Evie Cormac. According to the records, she was found on September 6, six years ago. For that reason, I'm going to nominate September 6 next year as the date that she turns eighteen. In the meantime, she will remain in council care.' He addresses Evie. 'Use that time well, young lady. Listen to your counsellors, study hard and sort through your issues.'

Evie is staring right through Judge Sayle, as if unable or unwilling to believe how quickly her fate has been decided. The speed of the decision. The complete reversal.

Instinctively, I realise this isn't over; that some unseen part of Evie's personality is stirring, uncoiling, waiting for the right moment to vent her fury upon the world.

21

Angel Face

The hate climbs inside me. It rises from my stomach into my throat, up my neck to my cheeks. In the near silence of the courtroom, I want to scream. I want to hurt someone. I want blood and carnage and destruction.

Willing myself to stand, I make my way back to the bar table. Caroline touches my arm. I pull away as if scalded. Instantly, I loathe this woman with her blemish-free skin and her expensive clothes and her lovely straight hair that smells of coconut; who has had everything handed to her by an accident of birth, born into the right family, sent to the best schools, taken on holidays abroad, given ballet and violin lessons. Everything has come easily to her – university, a career and a fiancé; I bet Mummy and Daddy helped her buy a flat. Even her name, Caroline Fairfax, sounds like it belongs to a film star or a fashion designer.

I hate her. I hate all of them – the judge and Guthrie and the braying lawyers. Fuckwits! Dickheads! Scumbags! I will not look at them. I will not show my disgust. Why did they raise my hopes and then tear me down? Why not just beat me up, break a few bones and dump my body in a ditch? Why not swing a fist into my stomach, or boot me in the groin?

That's what it feels like. I know because I've been here before.

I'm the problem. I'm worthless, detestable, a receptacle for refuse, a sewer, a punch bag, a piñata, a cunt, an ignorant, stinking slit.

I cannot escape my past. I'm a child again, sullen and whining, being passed from person to person, greeted like a special delivery. Dressed up. Painted. Pampered. Playing a role.

'Call me Daddy.'

'Call me Uncle Jimmy.'

'Call me Aunt Mary.'

'Yes, Daddy. Please, Daddy. Don't hurt me, Daddy. No more. We'll be good next time.'

In the background, I can hear voices. Cyrus is talking. The judge. Caroline. I'm not listening. Nothing is worth hearing, anyway. The cardigan is tight around my neck. The boots are hurting my feet.

Suddenly, I picture myself in the same courtroom, this time with a machine gun. I press the trigger and bullets rattle through the air, punching holes in stomachs and chests and eye sockets, painting the walls with blood and gore.

When they're dead, when their bodies are strewn around me, I walk out the door into the corridor, down the stairs, across the foyer, into the street, yelling to the armed guards. 'Come and get me. Shoot!'

Caroline shakes my shoulder. 'Evie, can you hear me?'

My heart creaks. Cyrus Haven is in the witness box. Why? When did he—?

'Dr Haven wants to know if you'd agree to live with him?'

'What?'

'As a foster child.'

'I don't understand.'

Judge Sayle speaks: 'Dr Haven would become your foster carer. Of course, he has to pass the necessary local authority and police checks, but he wants to know if such an arrangement might work for you.'

'We haven't talked about it,' says Cyrus, addressing me directly. 'I appreciate that this offer is quite spur of the moment and you don't know me well, but I'm serious. I have a big house in Nottingham. It's old and pretty run-down, but comfortable. You'd have your own room and bathroom.'

'And you'd have to continue your studies,' says the judge, 'or undertake training or get a job. You will remain a ward of the court until next September and your foster arrangements will be monitored regularly by the local authority.'

I still haven't responded. Where's the catch, I think. Why would he do this? I'm not going to sleep with him. If he lays one finger on me . . .

'You can't keep running away, Evie,' says Judge Sayle. 'You have to behave yourself until next September.'

I look from face to face and back down to the boots that are hurting my feet. I won't talk to him. I'll never tell.

22

'What in God's name were you thinking!' mutters Guthrie in a stage whisper. He has marched to the back of the courtroom, where he wrestles with the door, pushing instead of pulling. Evie and Caroline are still at the bar table. They look like they're arguing. Evie is probably saying the same things as Guthrie.

'I asked you to help her, not foster her. You have no idea how dangerous she is.'

Evie is glancing in our direction, her eyes full of suspicion or bloodlust.

'Look at her,' says Guthrie, following my gaze. 'She's already working out how to destroy you.'

'It won't be like that.'

'She broke someone's jaw with a brick. For all we know she killed Terry Boland.'

'Now you're being ridiculous.'

'Within a week you'll send her back.'

'No.'

'Either that or you'll throttle her.'

'Rubbish.'

'She'll find your weaknesses, Cyrus. She'll make you question yourself.'

Would that be such a bad thing?

Guthrie runs his fingers through his hair and makes soft noises by opening and closing his lips. 'You can still back out. Tell them you made a mistake.'

'It's done. Leave Evie alone.'

'Christ!' he mutters.

'I thought you'd be pleased. She's not your problem any more.'

Then it dawns on me that it was Guthrie who had his jaw broken. He stole the money from Evie and lied about taking it to the police, but she saw through him.

'You're going to publish, aren't you?' he says, with a new look in his eyes.

'What?'

'You're going to write about Evie Cormac like you're some sort of Oliver Sacks. She'll be your Solomon Shereshevsky.'

He's talking about the famous Russian mnemonist who could remember astonishing lists of random numbers or words in order, forwards or backwards, even in languages he didn't speak. He was discovered in the 1920s by a neuropsychologist called Alexander Luria, who published a famous book.

Guthrie is on a roll. 'I thought you were one of the good guys, Cyrus, but you're just another hypocrite. You're going to use Evie like everybody else.'

I feel the blood warming in my cheeks and want to throw a quick rabbit punch into Guthrie's soft belly, sending him down winded and sucking at air. I want to call him a self-deceiving, time-serving public servant, who looks for the worst in people unless someone forces him to see the good. Evie isn't a prize that people should be fighting over.

Caroline Fairfax is approaching us. Guthrie gives me a look of pity and pushes open the door with a grunt.

'What was that all about?' asks Caroline.

'Nothing,' I reply, glancing at Evie, who is sitting alone in the courtroom.

'She wants to talk to you,' says Caroline.

I nod and suggest we go somewhere for lunch. Caroline offers to pay, calling it a celebration, although Evie doesn't look convinced. We opt for a restaurant around the corner because it's too cold outside to walk far.

Evie sits opposite me. I'm waiting for her to say something, but she stares at her fingernails, which have been picked clean of nail polish. She's not hungry. Caroline orders for her anyway: a hamburger.

'I'm a vegetarian,' says Evie, as though it should be obvious.

'They have sweetcorn fritters.'

Evie shrugs. Caroline excuses herself and goes to the ladies – or perhaps she's giving us some privacy.

'I don't need a foster carer,' says Evie, sounding out each word like I'm dim-witted.

'The judge thought otherwise.'

'Are you a pervert?'

'No.'

'I'm not going to fuck you.'

'Good!'

'I wouldn't fuck you for a million pounds.'

'Wow! You *are* expensive.'

I'm coming across as being equally childish, which annoys me.

'I'm trying to help you,' I say, but my voice sounds like I'm an exasperated father talking to his daughter. I see her face go fixed and hard, like the bricks of a wall going up.

'At least come and have a look,' I say.

'I won't talk about what happened to me.'

'Understood.'

'And I won't play happy families.'

'I don't know that game.'

Evie seems to be evaluating me, chewing at her bottom lip. 'So how would this work?'

'You'll live with me. You'll have your own room and bathroom. It's nothing fancy, but I'm sure you'll cope. We'll share the chores.'

'I'm not your slave.'

I ignore her. 'I'll pay the bills. You'll study or get a job – in which case I'll charge you board.'

'Don't you get paid for being a foster carer?'

'I'm going to save that money for you. You'll get it when you turn eighteen – as long as you don't steal from me, lie to me or run away.'

Caroline returns, taking a seat between us.

'I don't think I've ever seen a case turn around like that,' she says, brightly. 'I don't have a lot to compare it with, of course. Was any of that planned?'

'No.'

'But your letter to the judge . . .?'

'I wrote it two nights ago.'

Evie has unzipped her boots and is rubbing her heels. I see the blue veins beneath her pale skin on her ankles. She interrupts.

'Do you have a dog?'

'No.'

'Why not?'

'I'm away a lot.'

'I could look after a dog.'

'You're not with me for long enough.'

'Two hundred and ninety-eight days,' she says, having done the maths. 'If you get a dog, I could take it with me.'

'We're *not* getting a dog.'

'And the bossing starts,' she mutters, but doesn't fixate on the rejection. I haven't seen Evie this animated before. Normally our conversations have been stilted and defensive, where each question is treated like a landmine to be avoided or disarmed. I could be winning her trust. I could be deluding myself.

'When can I see the house?' she asks.

'Why not today?' asks Caroline.

'I need to get it ready. Clean it up.'

'Prepare the dungeon in the basement,' says Evie.

'Very funny.'

'You said I could see it before I decided.'

'OK.'

We eat lunch. Caroline chats about the case, wanting to replay every highlight, wishing her immediate boss had been there to see it.

Evie watches us, as though trying to read something between the words. Occasionally, she wrinkles her nose, or makes a spitty sound in her throat, or blows air across the top of her soft drink bottle, making a tooting sound.

Caroline disappears to pay the bill.

'Is everything OK?' I ask.

Evie leans closer. 'You're flirting.'

'I'm not flirting.'

'Yes you are. And she's engaged.'

'How do you know?'

'I'm not blind.' Evie holds up her left hand and wiggles her wedding ring finger. 'You said you had a girlfriend.'

'I do.'

'But you're not sure.'

'Please don't do that.'

I look away, which Evie finds amusing.

Caroline returns. 'What are you two whispering about?'

'Nothing,' I say too sharply.

'Cyrus has a thing for lawyers,' says Evie with a glint in her eye.

Caroline pauses, clearly uncomfortable, and I feel myself shrink in her estimation. I want to shove a serviette in Evie's gob, but I know this is what she does. I can't say that I wasn't warned.

Moments later, we're outside on the footpath, buttoning coats, wrapping scarves and flagging down a cab. I try to remember what state I left the house in this morning. I hope the central heating has stayed on.

We retrace the route of my earlier cab ride, past the university and Wollaton Park. As we reach my road, I picture Parkside Avenue through Evie's eyes. It must look like I'm rich, almost posh, until the cab slows and stops. The house appears instantly shabbier than I remember, set amid a dense throng of rambling roses and clematis.

'It's huge,' says Caroline, being polite.

'It's falling down,' says Evie.

'It belonged to my grandparents.'

'Are they dead?' asks Evie.

'They've retired to Weymouth.'

'Can I live with them?'

Junk mail tumbles from the mesh-basket beneath the mail slot as I open the door.

'How long have you lived here?' asks Caroline, ever the optimist.

'A little while,' I say.

Seventeen years.

I give them a tour of the ground floor – the parlour, the study, the library, the drawing room, the kitchen. Evie opens the fridge.

'You have no food.'

'I buy when I'm hungry.'

'You order takeaway.'

'No. I can cook.'

Evie has moved on. 'Do you have a computer?'

'Yes.'

'Wi-Fi?'

'Of course.'

'Can I get a phone?'

'I don't have one.'

'What?'

'I don't like phones.'

Evie looks at Caroline as though they've stumbled upon the Missing Link. I try to explain but sound like a Luddite.

'I'll need a mobile phone,' she says adamantly.

I don't say yes or no, but a part of me is pleased that she's making plans. This might work.

Caroline has returned to the drawing room, where the rugs are worn and old furniture gleams with polish. She pulls open the curtains and dust motes dance in the shaft of light. The large fireplace has decorative tiles around the edges of the hearth and family photographs arranged on the mantelpiece. Most are casual snapshots, random moments captured when the subjects were unaware of the camera. I'm feeding ducks with my mother at Henley, or riding on my father's shoulders, or eating an ice-cream on Brighton Pier. My favourite is a black and white portrait of my parents on their wedding day in 1975. My father was twenty-nine and my mother twenty-six. They are doubled over laughing, my mother holds the train of her dress, trying not to drop her bridal bouquet. The only official family portrait was taken in a studio and looks so staged and unnaturally bright that I wonder if the colours were painted in afterwards.

Evie seems fascinated by the photograph. She picks it up and traces her fingers over the faces.

'What were their names?'

I point to each of them. 'April and Esme were the twins. They were seven when this was taken. I was nine. Elias was fifteen.'

'Where are they now?' asks Caroline.

'His parents are dead,' replies Evie. She points to my brother. 'He did it.'

Caroline looks shocked. 'What about your sisters?'

'They're dead, too,' I say, taking the photograph from Evie. I place it back on the mantelpiece, arranging it at exactly the same angle as before.

'You didn't tell me that,' says Evie, sounding aggrieved.

'You didn't ask.' I change the subject. 'I'll show you upstairs.'

They follow. Whispering. Evie is limping from her blisters.

'This can be your room,' I say, opening the door. The room has a single bed, a chest of drawers, a wardrobe, and a window that's so dirty we could be underwater. Evie looks unimpressed.

'I'll tidy it up, of course,' I say.

'And get me a new bed.'

'What's wrong with that one?'

'Your grandparents probably had sex in it.'

'This was *my* bedroom.'

'Ew! Even worse.'

Caroline admonishes her. Evie isn't fazed.

'Can I redecorate it?'

'If you wish.'

Evie turns in a slow circle, as if mentally measuring up the room and deciding on colour schemes.

I can see Caroline having second thoughts. 'Are you sure about this?' she whispers.

'Why?'

'Child and Family Services will have to approve everything . . . this place.'

'I'll clean it up, I promise.'

Evie steps outside the room and glances up the stairs. 'What's up there?'

'It's closed up.'

'Why?'

'Because I don't need any more rooms.'

'Can I see them?'

'No!'

My tone is harsher than I intended. I wish I could take it back. The moment registers with Evie, but she doesn't react. Instead, I imagine her storing it away, stockpiling weapons for later skirmishes.

'We should get Evie back to Langford Hall,' I say.

'I'll take her,' says Caroline.

Downstairs, Evie puts on her old duffel coat, which looks

incongruous with her new clothes. Caroline gives me a quick hug and Evie hesitates, wondering if she should do the same. Her arms go up and out, but never quite reach me.

'I'm sorry it's so messy and old,' I say.

'At least it's not haunted,' Evie replies.

'How can you tell?'

'I've been in haunted houses.'

23

That night I dream the dream.

My mother was the first to die, while cooking saffron chicken and prawn paella with peas. My mother with her wicked laugh, her soft spot for underdogs, her hatred of hypocrisy, her love for school teachers, dark chocolate and Bailey's Irish Cream. My mother with her posh phone voice and pink lipstick, potpourri-smelling lingerie drawer; her bubble baths behind a locked door, no children allowed. My mother, who could make rice pudding from leftover boiled rice and made us each take turns to get the wishbone when we ate roast chicken. My mother who grew up on a farm and had a pony called Twelve (because it was twelve hands high), yet who refused to let us have a dog because she still mourned the loss of her own beloved childhood pet, a boxer called Sinbad.

On that night she was standing in front of the freezer, with a bag of frozen peas in her hand, when the knife scythed through her carotid artery, spilling green and red onto the white tiled floor. She had always complained about choosing white tiles because they showed every spilled crumb, scuff mark and dropped pea.

The plume of blood sprayed in an arc across the kitchen bench and the sink and the cutlery drawer, which was open, and Tupperware boxes, which she always arranged neatly so she could find the lids when she needed them. The blood stretched all the way to the cat-food bowl in the corner where Tibbles would later lick it into a smear and track it across the floor with her paws.

Dad was next. My father who worked in property management – a fancy way of saying he collected rents and organised building leases. My father who taught Elias how to drive and would get him to practise his parking outside a succession of pubs, whereupon Dad slipped inside for a quick half. The White Lion, the Last Post, the Beekeeper and the Commercial Inn. Later Dad would fall asleep on the sofa, snoring through *Midsomer Murders*.

My father who brewed his own beer, collected vinyl LPs and once scored a golfing hole-in-one that ran all the way along the ground, but he still framed the scorecard. My father who didn't like using the word 'hate', but instead said he disliked racists, reality TV shows, Manchester United, pistachios that don't open and people who spend fifteen minutes in a queue and don't know what to order when they get to the counter.

Dad died on his hands and knees, crouching in front of the DVD player because one of the twins had managed to get a disc stuck in the machine. The knife severed his spine, paralysing him from the waist down. He managed to roll onto his back and hold up his arm, trying to ward off the blows, losing two fingers on his left hand and his right thumb. For a long while they couldn't find his thumb because it had rolled under the TV cabinet.

My twin sisters were doing their homework or playing in the bedroom they shared. They must have known something was wrong because they locked the door and barricaded it with beanbags and soft toys and a rocking horse that belonged to my grandmother and had no hair on its mane.

April was the eldest by twenty minutes and always acted like an older sister. Earnest and bossy, she was the hoarder, the show-off and the baker of cupcakes, partial to strawberry lip gloss and jelly snakes, and able to name every king and queen of England using a rhyme she'd learned off by heart.

Esme was different, but the same – part of a collective child, or two halves with the same face, each slightly different, but in symmetry. Esme the shy, the meek, the songbird, with a dancer's grace and tiny feet. Esme the peacemaker, the advocate, the knitter. Esme, who pressed flowers in the pages of her diary and gave names to every animal she ever met.

Elias used an axe to break a hole through the door before reaching inside and turning the key. He tossed aside the rocking horse and the beanbags. April fell first, which followed the natural order of how the twins handled everything. She ran towards Elias and the knife entered her ribs and came out near her spine. Blood splattered across the wallpaper and the bedspread, the bald rocking horse and the doll's house.

Esme tried to crawl beneath her bed but was dragged out by her ankles, scratching at the floor and bunching the rug under her body. I try not to imagine her fear or the sound of metal on air, or metal on flesh, or the silence that followed.

People always ask, where was I?

At football practice, or on my way home. It was the second training session of the season and my first year with the Sherwood Strikers. I had moved up to under-fifteens and felt a little over-awed.

We trained at Brelsford Park, about two miles from the house, or ten minutes if I rode my bike along the towpath. Mum had told me to be home by six. She also told me not to 'even think about' stopping for chips. Of course, I didn't listen. I hadn't eaten since lunch time at school and the Fat Friar did a cone of chips for a quid (although I had to forego the vinegar, or Mum would smell it on my breath).

I scoffed the chips and still had time to ride past Ailsa Piper's house in the hope I might glimpse her in the garden or coming home from netball practice. Ailsa was a year older than me. I once helped her find a bracelet that she lost on her way to school. We hadn't spoken since then, but she always smiled when we bumped into each other – happenstances that I tried to orchestrate as often as possible.

Running late, I had to stand up on the pedals and push hard to make it home by six. I wheeled my bike through the side gate and rested it up against the shed. Then I took off my muddy football boots and banged them against the back step. I could hear canned TV laughter coming from the front room as I opened the back door. I called out to Mum. She didn't answer.

In my dream this is where I wake – as I step into the kitchen – seeing the smear of blood near the litter box. I don't wake screaming, or bolt upright in my bed, but my cheeks are sometimes wet and my voice hoarse. That's when I get up. That's when I run.

On my second circuit of Wollaton Park, a car pulls alongside me, slowing to my speed. Tyres crunch over fallen leaves, acorns and seed pods. The window lowers.

'You're not allowed to drive on the footpath,' I say.

'I'm pursuing a suspect,' says Lenny.

'What's he done?'

'He refuses to have a phone.'

'That's hardly a crime.'

'No, but it's bloody annoying.'

Her wrist is draped over the steering wheel. Her collar is turned up.

I kick ahead and take a shortcut past the playground. Lenny accelerates and catches up as I reach the lake. She pulls alongside me again.

'We have a problem.'

'In my experience, whenever someone tells me they have a problem, they're trying to make *their* problem into mine.'

'I need your help.'

She looks tired. I wonder if, like me, she is kept awake by an unsettled mind or a past that will not stay buried. Slowing down, I walk to a nearby bench seat where I begin stretching, straightening each leg and bending my body over it until my forehead almost touches my shins.

Out of her car, Lenny takes a seat next to me, wrapping her coat around her chest and slipping her hands in the pockets where keys and spare change jangle.

'The DNA tests are back,' she says, taking out a chapstick and running it along her lips.

'And?'

'The semen found in Jodie's hair belonged to Craig Farley.'

'So that's it.'

'They also tested the second trace of semen found on her thigh, which was too degraded to get a complete profile, but enough to show that it didn't come from Farley.'

'Jodie had sex earlier in the evening.'

'Or Farley had an accomplice.'

'Nothing else indicates a second perpetrator.'

Lenny scratches at her cheek leaving a mark on her pale skin. 'Farley says he found Jodie in the woods. He says she was already unconscious.'

'Do you believe him?'

'Of course not! He's a lying sack of shit, but the second semen sample worries me because it creates doubt. A good defence lawyer is going to ask why we haven't identified an accomplice, or a boyfriend or another suspect. That's why we need to tighten up the case – make sure Farley doesn't weasel his way out.'

'What do you want me to do?'

'Review the evidence.'

'In what capacity?'

'You work for the police.'

'Part time.'

Lenny ignores the distinction. 'Just look at the interviews with Farley and tell me if we missed anything.'

'Can I talk to him face to face?'

'No. His lawyer claims we browbeat Farley into making a confession.' Lenny notices my look. 'Don't even go there. We followed procedure. Regular breaks. Kid gloves.' She sounds annoyed at herself for being defensive.

'Are you looking for anyone else?'

'Officially, no.'

'And unofficially?'

'I'm keeping an open mind.'

I've been standing still for too long and grown cold. Lenny offers to drive me home. In the car she turns up the heater full blast and negotiates her way out of the park and onto the street.

Silence hangs between us; not a solid divide but one that feels soft and familiar like an old pair of slippers or a favourite sweater. Lenny has known me since I was thirteen and she was in her early twenties. Since then she has been my greatest supporter and harshest critic, a stepmother, rebellious aunt, friend, sounding board and the person who knows me best.

'I had an interesting call from Child and Family Services the other day,' she says, as the car pulls up in front of the house. 'Seems that someone listed me as a referee on a foster care application.'

I stay silent.

'Apparently, this person wants to foster a young lass with behavioural problems. I took it as a prank call at first. I still think it might be.'

'It's not,' I say, opening the car door.

'I hear she's a nightmare.'

'She's fine.'

'Have you any idea what you're doing?'

'I hope so.'

'It's not easy to look after a teenager.'

'I used to be one.'

'You skipped those years,' says Lenny flippantly, but I know she's right.

'What did you tell them?' I ask.

'I told them you didn't torture kittens or shoot dolphins.'

'Thank you.'

Lenny leans forward and peers out of the windscreen at the overgrown garden and filthy windows. 'You should sell this place. It's too much for you.'

'Maybe I'll foster more kids.'

She knows I'm joking. Leaning behind her, she produces a padded envelope from the back seat. Inside are six DVDs.

'Twenty-two hours of interviews – finish that lot and you'll need a shower or a noose.'

24

'Can I help you?' asks the salesman at Dreamtime Warehouse.

His name is 'Brad' and he has shaved the sides of his head, but left hair on the top to grow untrammelled like weeds on a new allotment.

'I'm looking for a bed,' I say.

'Well, you've come to the right place.'

I wonder for a moment whether Brad is being facetious, but his smile seems genuine. We're standing in a showroom the size of several tennis courts, surrounded by mattresses, bases, ensembles and assorted bunks.

'What size are you looking for?' he asks. 'Single, small double, double, king-sized or super king-size?'

'Ah . . . right . . . maybe a single bed.'

'Is it for you, sir?'

'No.'

'A child?'

'A young woman.'

'And are you replacing an existing bed?'

'Yes.'

'And does the young lady have a small bedroom?'

'It's bigger than her last one.'

'Then perhaps she might prefer something larger – a double.'

'OK.'

I'm fascinated by Brad's hair, which sways in the opposite direction when he moves his head.

'What type do you have in mind?' he asks. 'We have platform, panel, sleigh, trundle, poster, canopy, futon, wooden, brass, wrought iron—'

'Just a regular bed. Something standard.'

'May I suggest a mattress and base combination – perhaps in our Slumberland range, which is on offer?'

He walks me across the showroom and we stop at a row of four beds.

'That one,' I say, pointing.

'Excellent. Now let's talk about the mattress.'

'Doesn't it come with a mattress?'

Brad laughs as though I'm being droll. 'You get to choose, sir. You can have open spring, pocket spring, memory foam, latex—'

'What do most people buy?'

'Pocket spring is the more luxurious. It's made from small individual springs each housed in a pocket of fabric. This means the springs move independently, providing more support so that when you roll over, you're not disturbing your partner.'

'That's what I'll have.'

'Soft, medium or firm?'

Dear Mother of God!

'Perhaps you'd like to try the difference,' says Brad, pointing to the mattresses. 'Don't worry about your shoes – we have mattress protectors.'

I'm expected to lie down. I feel like a corpse in a coffin. Brad is still talking.

'Feel how it supports your hips and shoulders and lower back. It's particularly good when one partner is significantly heavier than the other.'

'We're not partners.'

'Oh. I see. Perhaps you should bring her along – let her choose. We're open seven days a week.'

'I don't collect her until Friday,' I say.

Brad's smile disappears like a light being switched off.

'I'm getting her room ready,' I say, trying to recover. 'She's getting out, I mean, she's coming to live with me.'

'I see,' says Brad, although I don't think he *sees* at all.

'I'll take a medium mattress. Can it be delivered?'

'You haven't asked the price.'

'How much is it?'

'Normally you'd pay well over a thousand pounds, but I can do it for six hundred and ninety-nine.'

The shock must register on my face.

'It's very good value, sir. People spend far more money on a sofa that gets used for a few hours a day, whereas a bed gives us a crucial eight hours.'

'Fine.'

'What about a mattress protector?'

'No, thank you.'

'You'll need linen. And a duvet.'

He takes me to another section of the showroom and begins to list the different cottons and thread counts. The information washes over me and I become aware of how many extra things I will have to buy before Evie arrives: soap and shower gel for her bathroom. Toilet paper. What about women's things? She'll need tampons or pads. I've never had to buy those. Will Evie bring some with her? I could ask someone; Caroline Fairfax perhaps. No, I've had enough embarrassment for one day.

I stop for takeaway on the drive home because I have nothing in the fridge except leftovers that are covered in a greenish fur. I'll need to cook proper meals when Evie arrives. The extra responsibility will be good for me. I'll make shopping lists and eat better food. Healthy shit. I'll drink less and won't put my feet on the furniture, or cut my toenails at the kitchen table. I'll have to share the TV remote and listen to her music. What if Evie wants my favourite chair?

Maybe I haven't thought this through. Then again, I'm too young to be set in my ways. I'll learn things about myself. We'll learn things together.

After rinsing my plate, I carry another beer to the library and search my desk drawer for a writing pad and a fountain pen. I can't remember the last time I wrote a proper letter, on paper, with an envelope. I don't know if this will ever reach Sacha Hopewell, but I have to try.

Dear Sacha,

I hope you don't mind me using first names. I'm Cyrus, by the way. We haven't met, but I asked your parents to pass this letter onto you. If you're reading it, then I thank them.

I trust I didn't frighten them when I visited. It wasn't intended. Your parents tried to explain to me why you left home and keep moving from place to place. I still don't fully understand what happened, but I saw the depth of their pain and how much they were missing you.

I'm a psychologist working in Nottinghamshire. Several weeks ago, I met a young woman in council care. I can't tell you her name because it's the subject of a court order, but you'll know exactly who I mean when I say that she was found hiding in a secret room in a house in north London six years ago. She is a remarkable young woman, but also a very troubled one. You appear to be one of the few people she has ever learned to trust, which is why I'm reaching out to you. I'm hoping you might talk to me about those early days with Angel Face. Did she mention having a family? Did she hint at memories of her childhood – a place, or a favourite toy, brothers or sisters?

I know you've been asked these questions dozens of times before, but I'm hoping with the clarity of hindsight, you might have remembered something else.

I don't have a phone number (it's a long story), but I'm including my address and my pager number. I don't need to know where you are, or what you're doing, or why you're staying away (unless you want to talk about those things).

Contact me. Please. I guarantee complete discretion.

Yours sincerely,

Cyrus Haven

25

Angel Face

'When are you leaving?' asks Davina, nudging my shoulder.

'Friday.'

'You excited?'

I don't know what I am.

We're setting up the tables for breakfast in the morning – one of my chores – putting out bowls and spoons and boxes of cereal; refilling sauce bottles and checking the salt and pepper shakers.

The dining room smells of chip fat, boiled cauliflower and, for some inexplicable reason, carpet shampoo, even though the floor is tiled.

'Why him?' asks Davina.

'Who?'

'Dr Haven. You ran away from all those other foster families, but this guy pops up and you say yes.'

'It's different.'

'How?'

'He understands,' I say, which sounds lame. I don't know the reason. Maybe I've grown up. Maybe I'm sick of this place. Maybe I'll run the first chance I get.

'We're going to miss you,' says Davina.

'Liar.'

'Don't do that.'

'What?'

'People are allowed to tell lies, especially when they're trying to be polite.'

I can see her point, but why change the habit of a lifetime?

I don't mind doing kitchen duty. Whenever I get anxious, I get these bouts of OCD – although Guthrie calls them CDO, which is 'just like OCD except in alphabetical order'. My compulsion is to clean and put things in order. I once broke into the pantry – not to steal food, but to check the use-by dates and arrange all the tins with their labels facing outwards. Nobody caught me. I did it again a few weeks later. I broke in, but the pantry was still so neat that I messed it up. I figured I could fix it the next night, but they caught me on the way out. Sod's law.

Davina doesn't mind my obsessions. She has a little boy at home. Oscar. He's four. She talks about him a lot and has pictures on her phone. His dad looks after him when she's working. I don't think they're rotten poor, but they don't have much money. I keep telling Davina she should get her teeth straightened, but she says she can't afford to look like a supermodel. That's her idea of a joke.

Her partner is called Snowdon and he sometimes does odd jobs around Langford Hall because he's good with his hands, particularly fixing motors, which is how he makes his living – doing up cars and flogging them. Every time they hire him, he makes sure the job last four hours, so he gets a full day rate.

Terry Boland liked motors. He used to drive a limousine – one of those posh white ones that are stretched out. In the beginning he let me ride up front with him, but later when he had his shitty old Ford Escort I had to hide in the boot when we travelled.

He'd make me curl up in a long zip-up bag, which he slung over his shoulder and carried to the car. I was allowed to undo the zipper when the boot lid was closed. I lay curled up above the spare tyre, smelling the diesel fumes and oil and hearing the sound of the road only inches from my face.

Terry sometimes took me out of an evening, but it was always in *the bag. We'd drive for miles and stop at one of those motorway service centres with a McDonalds or a KFC. He'd park in the darkest corner and let me out of the boot.*

'Remember our story,' he'd say. 'You're my daughter. We're driving to Liverpool to see your grandparents. Your name is Sarah. I'm Peter.'

'What's our last name?'

'Jones.'

'Where do I go to school?'

'It doesn't matter. Stay close to me. Don't make eye contact with anyone. Don't start a conversation.'

I nodded and took deep breaths, enjoying the fresh air. I remember looking up one night, but I couldn't see the stars. I thought they might have all fallen and other people had made wishes, but Terry told me that you don't see stars when you live in London because of all the other lights.

He held my hand as we walked into the brightly lit food hall, passing racks of glossy magazines, most of which had Kate Middleton on the cover. She'd married William by then and people were on 'baby watch'. Terry let me watch the wedding on TV because there 'was nothing else on'. When Kate said, 'I do' I wanted the camera to zoom up close on her face, so I'd know if she was lying or thinking, 'What am I doing?'

Normally, I ordered a cheeseburger because I ate meat back then and I liked the way the fat coated my tongue. I also had French fries and a chocolate shake. One night I threw up on the way home, which made Terry angry because he had to wash the mats and the bag. It wasn't my fault. It was the fumes.

He didn't take me out again for a long time. And the next time he gave me drugs to make me sleep. When I'm anxious or nervous, I think of that zip-up bag, because it was somewhere soft and secret and safe.

Davina touches my shoulder. I pull away.

'Penny for your thoughts,' she says, laughing.

'They'll cost you more than that.'

26

Slipping a new disc into a DVD player, I fast forward through the early minutes until Craig Farley appears on screen. He's sitting at a familiar table in the interview suite at West Bridgford Police Station. Anxious, yet eager to please, he sits up straight, occasionally sipping from a can of soft drink.

Two detectives are seated opposite him – Prime Time and Edgar. Edgar is closer in age to Farley and they soon discover a shared interest in football, discussing favourite players and Premiership results from the weekend. The conversation moves on to pubs and the best ones for 'pulling a bird'.

Farley begins to relax because he's not being asked about Jodie Sheehan. He even banters with the detectives, telling a blonde joke that is older than the Bible. The detectives laugh, letting him feel like he's not so different from them.

'You must meet a lot of women at the hospital,' says Edgar. 'All those nurses.'

'Yeah, nothing beats a woman in uniform, eh?' echoes Prime Time.

Farley grins and nods enthusiastically. 'Some of them are OK – the young ones, before they get too old and cranky.'

'Yeah, the young ones,' says Prime Time. 'You must get plenty of action.'

'A bit.'

'Only a bit?'

'Some of them are pretty stuck up, you know. All fur coat and no knickers.'

'What sort do you like, Craig?' asks Edgar, dropping his voice to a whisper, as though they're sharing a secret.

'I don't like 'em too fat,' says Farley. 'Some meat on the bone is OK, you know. And I don't like 'em to be too mouthy or loud.'

'How do you meet them?' asks Edgar.

Farley perks up. 'I got Clancy trained.'

'What?'

'My dog. I got her trained. She goes up to them in the street and they start patting her and we get chatting and next thing . . .'

'What?'

'You know.'

'Is that how you met Jodie?'

Farley hesitates.

'Come on, Craig, you must have seen her around. Everybody seemed to know Jodie. She was a champion skater.'

Again nothing.

'Where did you see her? Waiting at the tram stop? Walking to school? In the park?'

'I never met her.'

'We found your semen in her hair.'

Farley shakes his head, as though refusing to listen to what's being said.

'You know about DNA, don't you, Craig? You might as well have written your name and address on a Post-it note and stuck it on her forehead.'

'I didn't kill her.'

'Maybe it was an accident,' says Prime Time.

'How could it be an accident?' scoffs Edgar.

'Maybe she tripped over. Hit her head. Was it an accident?' asks Prime Time.

'It wasn't me.'

'Who then?'

'How would I know?'

'Maybe you and your mate decided to double-team Jodie and now you're in the shit,' says Prime Time.

'No.'

'It's only a matter of time before we catch your mate, Craig, and I'm betting he's going to sing like Susan Boyle, saying it was your idea to follow Jodie, to knock her unconscious and take off her clothes.'

Farley doesn't know what to say. He's leaning further away from the table, expanding the space between them, going all silent and choked.

Edgar and Prime Time ease off, letting him recover before starting again.

I move through the rest of the interviews, making myself coffee to stay awake. As the hours pass, I see a different man at the table. At first, Farley backtracks, refining his answers, adding extra details or discarding those that haven't served him well so far. But slowly, he is worn down and his attitude changes. I hear the tension in his voice and see how his lips narrow into bloodless lines when he's caught lying. Eventually, he stops striving to please his interrogators. He switches to defiance, remonstrating about the wrongness of his arrest or the unfairness of the questions.

The interview teams change regularly, taking Farley back over his answers, pointing out the discrepancies. They work together, but often sit apart, making Farley swing his head from side to side as though he's watching a tennis match. Questions are fired quickly, giving him less time to react. His body bends under the weight of the accusations, slouching lower in his chair as he grows more and more despondent.

'Come on, Craig. Don't treat us like idiots,' says Lenny.

'I'm not.'

'Sure you are. Your mate is going to say that you followed Jodie, that you knocked her unconscious, that you pulled down her jeans . . .'

'That's all I did.'

'What?'

'I pulled down her jeans.'

The detectives exchange a glance, trying not to reveal their excitement.

Lenny clarifies. 'So you're saying you followed Jodie along the footpath?'

'No.'

'Where did you first see her?'

'By the pond.'

'What was she doing?'

'She was lying on the ground next to the pond. I thought she might be drunk.'

'Where were you?'

'On the footpath.'

'What did you do?'

'I wanted to make sure she was OK, you know.'

'Did you talk to her?'

'No.'

'Why not?'

'She was coughing. I must have frightened her because she tried to run.'

'You chased her.'

'No. I mean, I was worried about her.'

'Who brought the condom?'

'What?'

'You used a condom.'

'No. I tried to help her.'

'By raping her?'

'By keeping her warm.'

'Your semen was found in her hair.'

Farley's face crumples and locks in a long grimace.

'You have to speak, Craig . . . for the tape.'

He mumbles.

'Speak up.'

'I didn't mean . . .'

'What didn't you mean?'

'To touch her,' he says in a hoarse whisper. 'I wanted to help her . . . I did . . . she was on the ground . . .'

'You pulled down her jeans?'

'I wish I could . . . I didn't mean to . . .'

His voice breaks and he sobs, rocking in his chair, snot bubbling in his nostrils.

As I watch his capitulation, a shape begins to form in my mind. Not a shape – a weight. No, not a weight – a shadow that emerges from the murkiness of the detail. It's as though Craig Farley has fallen into step beside me and I am seeing the world as he does, feeling the earth beneath his shoes – a lonely inept young man; the slow kid at school, the last one picked for teams, the butt of jokes, the one too stupid to realise he was being teased. Socially anxious, clumsy, tongue-tied, yet longing to be included.

Some boys like this grow more confident with age, or befriend other outsiders, or muddle through life as an after-thought. A few of them suffer depression, sliding into alcohol or drug abuse, hoping stimulants can conquer their low self-esteem. Occasionally, one will develop a pathological desire for perfectionism, losing weight, pumping iron and growing to hate their former selves for being weak and pathetic. If the rejections and isolation continue, they may grow angry, blaming others for their failures. It's not their fault if they don't have a girlfriend, or a good job, or a nice car, or are still living at home with their parents.

All of this I can see, yet I cannot see a killer. Jodie ran from someone but had no defence wounds. Most likely she was unconscious when Farley removed her jeans, yet she was conscious when she had intercourse. There were no signs of forced penetration.

The sequence of events is the key and I can't make the facts fit the timeline. Unless. Unless . . . Even as the thought occurs to me, I want to dismiss the idea as being too far-fetched. I know what Lenny Parvel will say. She'll laugh and refuse to listen. I have to at least try.

I punch out her number. She doesn't answer. It goes to her messages.

Beep!

'We need to talk.'

27

Lenny Parvel is walking uphill, going nowhere. Strands of hair are plastered on her forehead and sweat drips from her nose, landing on the treadmill. Mirrors are everywhere, reflecting her back to me from several different angles, in a room that looks more like a dance studio than a gymnasium.

Dressed in silver boxing trunks and an oversized T-shirt, Lenny isn't trying to fit in among the gym junkies in their Lycra leggings and brand-name tops. Maybe she doesn't care about fitting in, or what others see when they look at her. I wish I had that confidence. I've been stared at too often. Pointed out. Talked about.

'You're not serious,' says Lenny, looking at me incredulously.

'I know everything points to Farley, but what if Jodie was already dead or dying? What if she was semi-conscious when he stumbled across her body?'

Her face has turned to stone. 'No, no, no.'

'Hear me out, please. Normally in a case like this, we'd see signs of control and dominance. The perpetrator becomes sexually aroused. He follows a woman, he abducts her, he instils fear. He rapes. He silences. That's not the right order for this crime.'

Lenny presses the stop button and jumps off the ramp, striding away from me. I hurry to keep up.

'I know it sounds—'

'Far-fetched? Absurd?'

'Unusual.'

'Do you know the chances of a sexual predator happening to stumble across a dead or dying teenager?' she asks. 'The chief constable will laugh me out of his office.'

'Tell him about Violet Jessop.'

'Who?'

'In 1911 Violet Jessop was working as a stewardess on RMS *Olympic* when it collided with a British warship and almost sank in the Solent. She survived. A year later she was working on the *Titanic* when it sank in the Atlantic. Again, she survived.'

'Is there a point to this?'

'Four years later, Violet was working as a nurse on a hospital ship, the *Britannic*, when it hit a German mine and started sinking. She jumped overboard and was sucked under the ship's keel, only to be dragged out of the water with a fractured skull. Again, she survived.'

'What in God's name are you on about?'

'I'm saying that stranger things have happened. Bigger coincidences. I think Jodie was already dead or dying when Craig Farley found her. I think someone else fractured her skull and threw her off the footbridge.'

Lenny grunts scornfully. 'It's ridiculous. More to the point it's dangerous. Farley hit her on the head, raped her and he left her to die. He confessed, for God's sake.'

Turning her back, she climbs onto an exercise bike and begins pedalling, pushing buttons to set the level of difficulty. I hold onto the handlebars as though stopping her from moving. I argue, putting facts in a different order.

'Jodie was hit from behind and either fell or was pushed into the pond. The shock of the cold water brought her round and she dragged herself onto the bank. She was disorientated. Coughing. Cold. Freezing. She stumbled along the path, only to collapse, unable to clear water from her lungs. Her respiratory system failed. If that didn't kill her, it was the sub-zero temperatures.'

Lenny ignores me, but I know she's listening.

'Farley is fascinated by pornography and young girls. He has a history of exposing himself. What does someone like that do when he stumbles across an unconscious girl?'

'Any normal person calls for help.'

'Farley isn't normal. He undressed Jodie and masturbated over her. Afterwards he realised what he'd done and panicked. He tried to clean up. He covered her with branches. He went home and dumped his clothes.'

Lenny is up out of the saddle, pedalling hard. A towel is draped around her neck.

'Someone had sex with Jodie using a condom,' I say.

'Farley.'

'Why would a rapist use a condom and then masturbate into her hair?'

'He had an accomplice.'

'Farley doesn't have any friends.'

Lenny's mouth has tightened into a grim line. 'Are you seriously suggesting that two predators, independent of one another, defiled that girl on the same night? One hits her and tosses her off a footbridge; and the other just happens to wander by and say, "What luck – here's an unconscious girl I can masturbate over."'

'I'm trying to make the facts fit the evidence.'

'No, you're putting a bomb under my investigation.' She drops her voice to a harsh whisper. 'You have to stop it, Cyrus! No more!'

'You asked me to review the evidence.'

'And now I want you to shut up and forget everything. Put none of this in writing. We have a confession. We have his DNA. He's our man.'

'A minute ago, you suggested he had an accomplice.'

'He didn't.'

'I'll leave that to the jury.'

Getting off the bike, Lenny wipes her face on a towel and walks away, heading for the change rooms. I follow her inside. Several women are in various stages of undress. One of them lets out a cry of surprise and holds a towel across her nakedness.

'Are you trying to get arrested?' Lenny asks.

'What about the money we found in Jodie's locker? We don't know who picked her up that night, or how she got to the footpath.'

Lenny is packing her gym bag.

'I want to talk to Tasmin Whitaker,' I say.

'She's been interviewed.'

'By the police, not by me. Best friends tell each other things . . . stuff they hide from adults. Secrets. People keep saying that Jodie was a normal teenager, who loved dancing and music and ice-skating, but there's more to her than that.'

'How do you know?'

'There always is.'

28

'Are you hungry?' I ask.

Evie makes a *meh* sound.

'I could start dinner now.'

'Whatever.'

I begin pulling things out of the fridge. Filling a saucepan with water.

'You're a vegetarian, right?'

'So?'

'Any other dietary requirements?'

She shrugs again. That's been the story since Evie arrived; I've experienced the full range of her shrugs, grimaces and monosyllabic vocabulary.

I try again. 'What sort of things do you like to eat?'

'Food doesn't really interest me.'

'What were the meals like at Langford Hall?'

'Shit.'

Evie is sitting cross-legged on a stool like an Indian swami. I strike a match and light the burner, putting on the water to boil.

'You should learn how to cook while you're here.'

'Why?'

'You'll be able to look after yourself when you leave.'

'I can look after myself.'

There is another long silence. I dice onions and garlic, frying them in a heavy-based saucepan.

'If we're going to live together, we should get to know each other,' I say. 'Let's start with simple things. My favourite song is "Things Have Changed" by Bob Dylan. How about you?'

'"Goofy's Concern".'

'Who plays that?'

'The Butthole Surfers.'

'Is that a real band?'

'Yeah.'

I don't know if she's being serious.

'My favourite colour is dark blue,' I say. 'How about you?'

'Black.'

'Technically that's not a colour.'

'Bite me.'

'Favourite film: *The Shawshank Redemption*.'

'I've seen that one,' says Evie.

'Did you like it?'

'No.'

'Why not?'

'It gives you all the answers. Nothing is left to wonder about. There's no ambiguity. It ends with happy people hugging on a beach. When does that ever fucking happen?'

'You don't believe in happy endings?'

'Every ending is unhappy.'

'Why?'

'Because we die.'

'Ah, you're a fatalist?'

'A what?'

'You think we have no power to influence the future and that everything we do is predetermined, or pointless, because our fate has already been decided.'

'No. I just know we're going to die.'

I can't argue with that.

Opening a tin of peeled tomatoes, I empty the contents into the saucepan, breaking them with a wooden spoon, adding torn fresh basil leaves, salt and pepper. The water is boiling. I add the spaghetti and take a block of Parmesan from the fridge, setting it on a plate with a cheese grater.

'What's *your* favourite film?' I ask.

'*True Romance.*'

'You like Tarantino?'

'Who?'

'Quentin Tarantino. He wrote *True Romance.*'

Evie looks at me blankly.

I change the subject. 'What's your favourite food?'

'Margherita pizza.'

'Dream holiday destination?'

'I've never had a holiday.'

'But you must have somewhere you'd like to go? Greece? Tahiti? America?'

Her face is a mask.

'How about your first memory? Mine is getting chased by this big-ass swan when I was feeding ducks with my mother. We were in Henley, near where they have the rowing races.'

'They race rowboats?'

'They're a bit more sophisticated than rowboats.'

Evie looks past me. 'My father once took me sailing,' she says, as though we've found a common interest. 'He rented a boat and we sailed out past the pier and the bay, into the open sea. The wind picked up and so did the waves. I knew Dad was scared, but he didn't want to show it.'

Evie grows animated as she describes the waves and the wind and water breaking over the bow.

'What happened?'

'We were rescued by a fishing boat and towed back to the pier.'

'Did you do a lot of sailing?'

'I don't remember.'

This is progress, I think, as I drain the spaghetti in a colander and divide it into bowls. I start spooning sauce onto the pasta. It's then I glimpse a postcard on the fridge. It shows a sailing boat, heeling sideways in the wind, water breaking over the bow.

'Was any of that story true?'

Evie doesn't respond.

'You don't have to lie to me.'

'You don't have to keep asking me questions.'

We eat in silence. Evie watches me grate the cheese on my spaghetti. I push it towards her.

She sniffs the Parmesan. 'Smells like sick.'

'It tastes better than it smells.'

She grates a little on her sauce. I watch her take the fork, fill it with pasta and lift it to her mouth. She closes her eyes and chews, letting out a small moan.

'Good?'

She doesn't respond and eats quickly, with one arm on the table, protecting her food like an inmate in a prison canteen.

'I'm going for a run in the morning, would you like to come?'

'Fitness shit. No.'

'You could look for a job. I could help you put together a CV.'

'What would I put on a CV?'

She's right.

'Have you thought about going back to school?'

'It's too late – I've missed too much.'

'How is your reading?'

'OK. I try to learn a new word every day. Today's word is *curmudgeon*. It means grumpy fucker.'

'I know what it means.'

She smiles as though congratulating herself, before changing the subject.

'You said I could have a mobile phone.'

'That's not what I said.'

'Why don't you like them?'

'I have nothing against mobile phones. I choose not to have one because I prefer to talk to people face to face. As a psychologist, my job is to listen to people and to learn things about them, which I can't do as effectively by reading a text or tweet.'

'It doesn't seem very professional,' says Evie.

'I have a pager. People contact me. I call them back.'

'You vet your calls.'

'That's not the reason.'

Evie studies my face, searching for the lie, but cannot find one.

Having cleaned her plate, Evie gets up from the table and turns to leave. I remind her about helping with the chores. She looks around the kitchen. 'Where's the dishwasher?'

'I don't have one.'

'How do you wash stuff?'

'The old-fashioned way.' I pull out detergent, rubber gloves and a scouring pad.

Evie turns on the taps, squirting detergent into the running water.

'You should do the glasses first,' I say.

Ignoring me, she picks up a plate, which slips from her fingers. She attempts to catch it in mid-air, but it slips again and shatters on the tiled floor, sending shards in every direction. Evie glares at me, as though it was my fault and then I notice a different emotion. Despair. Loss.

'It's only a plate,' I say, getting a dustpan and brush. 'No harm done.'

Evie turns away, not wanting to show any sign of weakness. Eventually, she confronts me with a new allegation.

'Stop staring at me.'

'What?'

'You keep staring at me. You're like all the others – the shrinks and therapists and social workers – you want to reach inside my head and hook your fingers in the cracks and open me up, see what makes me tick.'

'That's not true.'

Evie snorts, recognising my lie.

'Have you ever considered the possibility that I don't need to relive my past or explore my feelings? I don't need to be fixed because I'm not fucking broken.'

29

Angel Face

The old house is speaking to me. With every creak and groan, I imagine Cyrus standing in the corridor outside, the soft noise of his breathing, his timid knock, the door opening, light falling across the floor.

I climb out of bed and brace my shoulder against the chest of drawers, pushing it across the bare wooden floorboards until it rests hard against the door.

Returning to the bed, I reach beneath the pillow, searching for the knife I took earlier when I was washing the dishes. At Langford Hall they count every utensil after mealtimes — even the potato peelers — but Cyrus didn't bother to check.

I close my eyes but cannot sleep. I'm not used to this. For years I have lived in places where the doors were locked and the lights were dimmed; where CCTV cameras monitored my waking hours and the heating was controlled by a central switch and the water could be cut in the showers if I tried to block the drains. At 7.45 each morning I would press a buzzer and ask to come out. Most mornings the doors unlocked immediately, but occasionally I was kept inside my room until whatever emergency had passed.

Cyrus hadn't locked any doors or demanded the lights be turned off. I'm not his prisoner. I can wander down to the kitchen to grab a bite. I can walk outside and dance under a street light and nobody would stop me. Maybe that's what's keeping me awake — the choices.

I get out of bed again, open my bag and take out the marbles and the pieces of coloured glass and the button belonging to my mother. Finally, I come to an envelope of cash. Smoothing out the duvet, I count out the notes, separating them into different piles: ten, twenties and fifties: £2,580 in total. My eyes come to rest on an old armchair in the corner. It's covered in a faded floral fabric that is worn smooth where countless arses have sat. Rolling the chair onto one side, I study the stapled upholstery and the stitching, before taking the knife and carefully picking apart a seam, working the blade back and forth, until I create a pocket big enough to hold the cash. Once I'm finished, I return the chair to the corner and go back to bed, lying still, breathing slowly.

That's when I hear the noise — the clang of metal on metal and a guttural groan as though an animal is caught in a trap.

Crossing the room, I lean over the drawers and press my ear against the door.

Clang! Clang! Clang!

It's coming from below me. Downstairs. The basement. I want to investigate. I want to stay in bed and cover my head with a pillow, blocking out the sound. I push aside the drawers and step onto the landing, clutching the knife. I pause for a moment and listen. There it is again — the moaning; metal striking metal.

Descending slowly, I follow the noise, running my fingers along the wall to feel my way forward. Every floorboard is like a tripwire, ready to give my presence away.

Light spills from a room. Creeping closer, I peer around the edge of a door and draw back suddenly. Then I look again, half in fear and half in fascination. An ink-stained figure is hunched beneath a metal bar that curves across his shoulders, bearing coloured plates the size of hubcaps at either end. The figure squats and rises, his thighs trembling and his breath coming in short bursts. He does it again and again, each lift slower and harder than the last, until he groans and drops the weight onto a cradle.

His chest and arms are covered in an aviary of swallows, sparrows, hummingbirds, doves, lorikeets and robins. The birds move as he moves, animated by the muscles beneath his skin and the beads of sweat that trickle in rivulets down his neck and chest.

Cyrus turns to pick up a bottle of water. I see his back, which is covered by an enormous set of folded wings that stretch from his upper arms, across his shoulders, down either side of his spine where they disappear beneath his shorts and reappear on his thighs. Each feather is so beautifully drawn and finely detailed that I can make out every barb and vane, so lifelike that I can imagine him arching his back, unfurling his wings and taking flight.

Cyrus adds more weight to the bar before ducking underneath and bracing it across his shoulders. He tries to straighten. Moans. Nothing happens. It's too heavy. He tries again, this time the bar rises a fraction of an inch, then more.

Veins bulge in his arms and his face darkens with blood. This is not exercise. This is self-abuse. This is punishment.

I'm willing him to stay upright but his knees are buckling. He staggers. Sways. I catch my breath, sure that he'll fall, but Cyrus steadies and lowers the bar with painful slowness. It hovers over the cradle for a moment before dropping and he collapses onto a bench, his head draped over his splayed knees.

I back away, feeling like a voyeur, or worse, a thief. Returning to the bedroom and my new bed, I don't bother pushing the chest of drawers against the door.

30

Felicity Whitaker answers my knock with such a flourish that I'm sure she's expecting someone else. Squeaking in surprise, she touches her face almost instinctively as though caught without her make-up. She's in old jeans and a sweatshirt, her hair tied up in a scarf.

'I was cleaning.'

'I'm sorry to interrupt.'

'Don't be. Any excuse.'

She pulls off her scarf and pushes a stray lock of hair behind her ear. She's someone who favours jewellery that dangles and clinks.

'Housework can be very therapeutic,' I say. 'It gives me a sense of achievement.'

'I thought you'd have a cleaner.'

'No.'

'A wife?'

'No.'

Felicity raises her eyebrows and I wonder if she's flirting. I'm still standing on the doorstep. Apologising, she steps back, pushing a vacuum cleaner away with her foot. I squeeze past, almost brushing against her. She could give me more room.

The kitchen table is covered in boxes of cereal and bowls of soggy flakes.

'We slept in this morning,' she explains, pointing to a chair. 'Can I get you a cup of tea?'

'Thank you.'

She fills the kettle. I notice an array of postcards magnetised to the fridge with plastic fruit; images from New Orleans, Sydney, Mexico City and Berlin.

'Have you been to all these places?'

'Heavens, no!' she laughs. 'They're from my pen friends. I've been writing to some of them since I was eleven. My primary school started a programme. We were matched up with children around the world.' She is clearing the table as she talks. 'One day, when I win the National Lottery, I'm going to visit them all – take a world tour. I know it's a silly dream.'

'It's not silly.'

Through the door, in the sitting room, I notice a gangly-looking youth with an electric guitar on his lap. He's wearing headphones and his fingers are flicking up and down a fretboard, making music that only he can hear.

A girl is lying with her head next to his thigh, peering at her phone.

'My eldest, Aiden,' says Felicity, smiling. 'I think the girl is Sophie, but I could be wrong. She's here to comfort him. My children have become more popular since Jodie's death.' She gives me a guilty look. 'That's probably a terrible thing to say.'

Aiden dips the guitar and drives to a head-rocking crescendo.

'Is he in a band?' I ask.

'God forbid! No!' she laughs. 'He's reading law at Cambridge next year. He won the Charter Scholarship. Fully funded.'

'That's brilliant.'

'Isn't it though. We're so proud of him.'

She's opening cupboards, searching for something. Finally,

she retrieves a packet of biscuits that is tucked behind cake tins and Tupperware boxes, hidden from her children.

'It isn't easy getting out of this place. A lot of Aiden's friends have gone straight from school onto the dole or get trapped in dead-end jobs at call centres or franchise stores. They get some girl pregnant or marry too young out of boredom, or go into the family business, having promised themselves they never would. Not my Aiden. He's going to be a lawyer in a big London firm with a house in Hampstead and a villa in Italy.'

'Sounds like you have it all planned out.'

Felicity laughs and her earrings sway.

'Where did you meet Bryan?' I ask.

'On the ice. I fell over. He picked me up. Cheesy, I know. It was my nineteenth birthday. I was with a group of girlfriends, but I forgot about them completely as Bryan held me around the waist and we skated. He made me feel like we could be Torvill and Dean.'

'Did he ever compete?'

'For a while but he didn't have the support to make it to the top. Instead he turned to coaching. He taught Jodie how to skate. She took to it like a . . .' She looks for the right phrase. 'Do penguins skate?'

'I don't know.'

'Well, she was a natural.'

Felicity opens the biscuits and arranges them on a plate. 'People think figure skating is graceful and gentle, but you have to be hard as nails to survive. The injuries. The falls. Jodie could be a proper little madam when she lost a competition, blaming everyone but herself – the judges . . . Bryan . . . her mum.'

She jiggles teabags in two mugs.

'My sister-in-law is a complete saint. I can't remember the last time she bought a new dress, or had a holiday, or got her hair done, but Jodie always had a new costume. Her skates cost a thousand quid a pair and she needed new ones every year.

And don't forget the ballet lessons, gymnastics, physio and choreography. Bryan was coaching her for free, but it still cost a fortune.'

Felicity tucks hair behind her ear. It falls across her cheek immediately.

Aiden yells from the living room. 'Hey, Mum, get us a Red Bull.'

'Get it yourself – I have company.'

Aiden mutters sullenly and appears in the kitchen. It's the first time I've seen him up close. He has an almost genderless face, full of straight lines and sharp angles, except for large eyes and long dark lashes that brush his cheeks when he blinks. It gives him a strangely androgynous beauty.

'This is Cyrus Haven,' says Felicity. 'He works with the police.'

'Are you a detective?'

'A psychologist.'

'Nice to meet you,' he says, without offering to shake my hand. Instead he takes a can of Red Bull from the fridge and goes back to the sofa and his guitar. The girl dangles her legs across his lap. Aiden pushes her feet away. She tries to nuzzle his neck, but he's not interested. Eventually, she picks up her phone and curls up on the opposite end of the sofa, looking bored.

Felicity settles again, curling her fingers around the mug and blowing gently across the top. 'I thought Jodie would be fine, you know. She was going to make something of her life. She'd skate to Olympic glory, become famous and cash in.'

'Is there money in skating?'

'Oh yes. She could have become a TV presenter or done *Disney on Ice* shows in Las Vegas or gone on *Strictly*. If I'd been given even a tenth of her talent . . .'

She doesn't finish the statement, but I catch the hint of regret in her voice.

'What was your ambition?' I ask.

She smiles wistfully. 'I'm not the ambitious type. I did once think of applying to British Airways to become a flight attendant, but then I met Bryan. We both wanted kids, but it proved harder than we hoped.'

'In what way?'

'I struggled to get pregnant. We used up all our savings on IVF. Maggie had Felix by then and I felt like such a failure. I didn't have a career and I couldn't have a baby.'

'What happened?'

She glances towards the sitting room. 'Aiden came along like a gift from God. I was so relieved. Sometimes at parties when women ask me what I do, I feel guilty about being a stay-at-home mum and not having had a career. But I'm good at this. It's all I ever wanted. It's enough.'

The fridge rattles to life, as though punctuating the statement.

'I was hoping to ask you about Jodie,' I say.

'I thought the police had arrested someone.'

'They still have to prepare a case.'

Felicity nods.

'You watched her grow up,' I say.

'I was like her second mum.'

'What was she like?'

'Precious.'

I struggle with terms like precious, or treasure, or princess, because they tell me nothing. I need more. Was she flirtatious, brash, self-assured, or was she quiet, withdrawn or self-conscious?

'She was very good to our Tasmin,' says Felicity.

'In what way?'

'Teenage girls can be very cruel. Tasmin has been bullied since Year Six. Don't ask me why? I know she's not the prettiest girl and she isn't sporty or coordinated – her dance teachers used to hide her in the back row whenever they did recitals – but my girl has a good heart.'

Her voice has grown thick and she looks at her tea as though she's forgotten whether she's sugared it or not.

'Jodie stood up to the bullies. She made sure Tasmin was included.'

'Can I talk to Tasmin?'

Felicity glances at the ceiling. 'She's upstairs now. Some girls from school dropped round. They brought flowers.' I notice a ragged bunch of carnations in a vase. 'It's ironic really.'

'What is?'

'The same girls who used to exclude Tasmin now want to be her best friend. I'm not stupid. I know they're up there now, pumping her for details, wanting to be involved.'

As if summoned by a bell, I hear running above my head and jostling on the stairs. Three teenage girls appear.

'We're hungry,' says Tasmin, reaching for the biscuits. Felicity slaps her hand away. 'They're for guests.'

'I got guests.'

'I could toast some crumpets.'

Tasmin looks at her friends hopefully, but the signals aren't good.

Felicity points to a fruit bowl. 'We have apples and a sad-looking banana.'

'It's brown,' says Tasmin.

'It tastes the same.'

The taller of her friends is wearing a clingy top and a short denim skirt. Loitering in the doorway, she's trying to catch Aiden's attention, but he doesn't look up.

'Hi, Aiden,' she says finally.

'Hi, Brianna,' he replies, glancing at her briefly before going back to his guitar.

The girl on the sofa glares at Brianna in response.

'This is Dr Haven,' says Felicity. 'He's working with the police. He wants to ask you some questions about Jodie.'

Brianna immediately forgets Aiden and focuses on me.

'Are you a detective?'

'A psychologist.'

'I'm Olive,' says the other girl, not wanting to be left out.

She has doll-like eyes and blond hair that curls in ringlets to her shoulders. They're both prettier than Tasmin and she's self-conscious around them.

'Did Jodie have lots of friends, or just a few close ones?' I ask.

'We were her best friends,' replies Brianna, who is clearly the queen bee.

'Was she a leader or a follower?' I ask.

The girls look perplexed. I haven't framed the question well. I try again. 'When the latest must-have fashion came out, who would get it first?'

'Me,' says Brianna.

'OK. And if someone dared you to do something crazy, who's most likely to take up the dare?'

'Jodie,' says Tasmin, speaking for the first time.

'And if you were deciding what to do on the weekend, who came up with the ideas?'

'Jodie,' she says again.

'What sort of things did she like to do?'

'She was a really good figure skater,' says Olive, wanting to add something.

'Duh! Everybody knows that,' says Brianna.

'What else?'

'She liked dancing,' says Olive, looking hurt.

'Yes, dancing,' says Brianna. 'She took classes, didn't she?' They look at Tasmin, who nods.

'What kind of foods did she like?' I ask.

'Pizza and chocolate brownies and fruit smoothies,' says Brianna, clearly making things up.

'She wasn't allowed to eat pizza,' says Felicity. 'Maggie kept her on a strict diet.'

'She ate pizza sometimes,' counters Tasmin. 'When Aunt Maggie wasn't around.'

'What else did she do in secret?' I ask.

They glance at each other, less sure of the conversation.

'Did she have a boyfriend?'

'Toby Leith,' replies Brianna. 'He's in Year Twelve.'

Tasmin shakes her head. 'Jodie thinks he's an F-boy.'

'A what?' Felicity asks.

Tasmin blushes and looks at the floor.

'A guy who only wants one thing,' explains Brianna, nudging Olive.

'Were Jodie and Toby seeing each other?'

'They used to hook up.'

'It was *one* time,' protests Tasmin.

'It was more than once . . . first at Shelley Pollard's party, then at the Goose Fair.'

'And at the movies,' adds Olive. 'That day we saw *Infinity War*.'

'Was Toby at the fireworks?' I ask.

All the girls nod.

'Did Jodie talk to him?'

Tasmin hesitates. 'Toby was teasing her. He snatched her tote bag and wouldn't give it back.'

'What did Jodie do?'

'She slapped him in the face, but he just laughed. That's when Father Patrick showed up.'

'Father Patrick?'

'Our parish priest,' explains Felicity.

'He made Toby give the bag back,' says Tasmin.

'Did Jodie talk to anyone else?'

'Loads of people. They were coming up to her all night.'

'Why?'

Tasmin shrugs.

Brianna grins at Olive and I sense an in-joke.

I focus on Tasmin. 'Why did Jodie leave the fireworks?'

'Someone sent her a text and she said she had to go.'

'Who?'

'I don't know.'

'Did you know that Jodie was carrying a second phone?'

'No.'

191

'You told the police that Jodie went to get fish and chips.'

'That's what she told me.'

'Did you know that she had a second mobile phone?'

Tasmin doesn't answer.

'Could she have arranged to meet someone?'

'I guess.'

'A new boyfriend?'

Tasmin looks at her mother with a hurt helplessness in her eyes. 'I put some pyjamas on her pillow. I thought she'd come back to ours, but she didn't.' Her bottom lip trembles.

'When you woke and saw the bed was empty, what did you think?'

Tasmin is about to say something but Felicity interrupts. 'We assumed she'd gone home.'

'Is that what you thought?' I ask Tasmin.

She nods.

'Did you look for her?'

'Yes.'

'Where did you go?'

Her mouth opens and closes. She swallows. She looks at her hands. 'I went to Toby's house. I thought Jodie might have gone there . . .'

'But you said she didn't like him.'

'She sort of didn't, but I knew she still did, you know.'

'Did you see Toby?'

She shrugs and mumbles. 'He was with someone else.'

'Fuckboy,' whispers Brianna, under her breath.

'Where would I find Toby Leith?' I ask.

'At the skate park. He's there all the time,' says Brianna.

Olive raises her hand as though we're in a classroom. 'Did someone rape Jodie? Is that why . . .?' She doesn't finish.

'What makes you ask?'

She shakes her head, losing confidence.

Felicity visibly stiffens. 'I'm not sure the girls need to know the details.'

'The police also found condoms in Jodie's school locker,' I say.

'I knew it!' says Brianna, grinning wickedly. 'You don't get a guy like Toby unless you're putting out.'

'Please don't talk about Jodie like that,' says Felicity.

'I'm only telling the truth,' whines Brianna.

'I think you girls should leave.'

'Nooo,' complains Tasmin.

'It's time the girls went home.'

Brianna tosses her hair. 'Come on, Olive. This place gives me the creeps.' They're in the hallway, but Brianna can't resist a parting shot, this one directed at me. 'People keep making Jodie out to be some sort of Disney princess, all pure and innocent. You should talk to her brother.'

'Why?'

Another laugh; another toss of her hair; and I feel like I'm fourteen again with braces on my teeth and a pimpled face that betrayed every humiliation like a Magic 8 Ball.

31

The girls have gone by the time I get outside. I wonder how much of their provocative posturing and the sly nudges were designed to shock me. When I was their age, I found girls intimidating because they seemed to be so much more self-aware and confident, capable of destroying me with a single shrug, or curl of a top lip, or toss of their hair.

One girl in particular, Karen Heinz, terrorised me more than the rest. Most of my schoolmates felt sorry for me after what had happened to my family, but Karen took it upon herself to belittle and humiliate me at every opportunity, as though she resented my tragic fame. I wish I could put it down to hormones, or a shitty home life, or a period that lasted until A levels, but Karen was simply a bitch and I hate the fact that I still hate her.

Retracing my steps to Silverdale Walk, I pass the footbridge and turn left at the fork, crossing the meadow and the tram tracks before emerging at the edge of Forsyth Academy. The asphalt path is crumbling in places and partially covered in fallen leaves.

Ten minutes later, I reach Clifton – a slightly more upmarket area with neater gardens, newer cars and fewer abandoned supermarket trolleys. Keeping the school grounds to my left, I follow Farnborough Road until I reach a sign for Clifton Skate Park. A dozen teenagers are riding the concrete ramps, curved walls and jumps. I catch a whiff of something herbal in the air. One of them looks at me petulantly as he drags on a soggy spliff. Like the others, he's wearing an unofficial 'uniform': baggy jeans, a sweatshirt and a baseball cap.

I approach the nearest group. One girl. Four boys.

'I'm looking for Toby Leith.'

'And who are you?' asks the girl, trying to show her street cred by taking the lead.

A boy makes an oinking sound. The others laugh, but one glances over his shoulder and I know that Toby Leith must be nearby. A second group is racing BMX bikes on a series of parallel tracks that rise and fall over concrete jumps.

'Which one is he?' I ask.

The girl whistles. Decks are kicked into fists and bikes are propped on one foot. I pick out Toby because he's helmet-less and hatless and cockier than the rest. Ignoring the signal, he rises on his pedals and drops almost vertically down a ramp, accelerating along the flat bottom and getting airborne as he takes each jump. When he reaches the far end, he rockets up a steep incline and spins in mid-air before landing with both wheels on the top of the ramp, fifty yards away.

'Can we talk?' I yell.

'You a reporter?'

'I'm a psychologist.'

'I don't need a shrink.'

'I work with the police.'

'I already talked to the pigs.'

'Then you know all the answers.' I look over the edge at the vertical drop. 'It's easier if you come to me.'

'I can hear you from here.'

'I hear Jodie was your girlfriend.'

'I don't have a girlfriend.'

'Your ex then.'

Toby looks at me blankly. 'Just because I finger-bang a girl at a party doesn't mean we're engaged.'

The others laugh. Toby runs his hand through his hair, pushing it behind his ears. Grinning.

'You're talking about a girl who was murdered,' I say, and I see his bravado fade away. 'She was also only fifteen. A minor.'

'She was sixteen.'

'Afraid not.'

Toby shrugs, less certain than before.

Rocking onto the pedals, he balances the bike on two wheels and leans his weight forward, dropping into the void, aiming his body at where I'm standing. Exploding off the edge, he catches the bike in mid-air, only inches from my face.

He's testing me. I don't flinch.

'What's this really about?' he mutters.

'You saw Jodie at the fireworks.'

'So?'

'You were teasing her. She slapped your face.'

'Woah! Whoever told you that is lying.'

'Did you arrange to meet her later?'

'No.'

'Did you send her a text?'

'No.'

'Did you pick her up in your car?'

'Are you deaf or something?'

'There are witnesses, Toby. You were seen with Jodie. You took her bag. She hit you.'

'OK, I saw her, so what?'

'I think you bumped into her again outside the fish and chip shop on Southchurch Drive. She knocked a can of beer from your hands.'

He doesn't respond.

'What did you say to Jodie that made her so angry?'

Toby leans hard on the handlebars, as though trying to crush the bike, or push it into the ground.

'I was drunk. I invited her back to my place. I guess, I was a little crude.' He blinks at me sadly. 'I didn't mean any of it, you know. I wish I could take it back.'

32

Angel Face

I'm standing at the bay window, peering through the curtains. People are coming and going along the road. Children being walked to school. A street-sweeper with a barrow and a broom. A postman with a trolley.

I'm on my third can of lemonade since breakfast and the sugar rush feels good. Why so many? Because I can. I could have had a beer if I wanted. I could pour myself a Scotch. I thought about it but gagged when I cracked the lid and took a sniff.

When Cyrus left this morning, I opened the front door and stepped outside. Twice.

Outside.

Inside.

Outside.

Inside.

Then I immediately locked the door, latched the chain and went through the rest of the house, securing every window. I drew the curtains and closed the blinds. I studied the eaves and cornices, making sure that Cyrus hadn't been lying when he told me there weren't any cameras.

Opening a packet of chocolate biscuits, I start exploring the house properly, starting in the basement, where Cyrus has his weight-room.

His towel is still damp from last night. I run my fingers along the bar and try to lift it from the cradle, using both hands, but it won't budge. I try raising one side. It still doesn't move.

In the sitting room, I turn on the TV and pick up the remote. Where are all the channels? Doesn't he have satellite or cable? The next room is the library. Why does anybody need so many books? Has he read them all? I pick out a heavy volume bound in brown leather, spelling out the word Britannica *on the spine. It has columns and drawings – like a dictionary with pictures.*

I open a page and read, sounding out the words.

Annie Oakley, original name Phoebe Ann Mosey (born Aug. 13, 1860, Darke county, Ohio, US—died Nov. 3, 1926, Greenville, Ohio), American markswoman who starred in Buffalo Bill's Wild West show, where she was often called 'Little Sure Shot'.

I turn to another page.

George M. Pullman, in full George Mortimer Pullman (born March 3, 1831, Brocton, New York, US—died October 19, 1897, Chicago), American industrialist and inventor of the Pullman sleeping car, a luxurious railroad coach designed for overnight travel.

There are so many volumes of the Britannica *that I wonder if everybody has something written about them. I look up other names: Cyrus Haven, Adam Guthrie, Terry Boland, but none of them are mentioned.*

The library has a polished wooden desk with drawers on either side and a lamp that curls over the top. The leather chair creaks under my weight. Picking up a pen, I click it open and closed with my thumb. There is a pile of invoices awaiting payment. Electricity. Gas. Internet. According to a bank statement, Cyrus has £1,262 in his current account. He also has a double-barrelled surname, Haven-Sykes, but only uses one of his names.

I pick up a padded envelope and shake the contents onto the desk. There are six DVDs in plastic cases, each of them stamped with the words Nottinghamshire Police. *Opening one of them, I read the label. It has a number, a date and a name: Craig Farley. I glance at the DVD player in the corner before putting everything back where I found it.*

Having searched the ground floor, I climb the stairs and go to the main bedroom, where the bedclothes are rumpled and thrown haphazardly back into place. I imagine Cyrus lying in the bed with one hand resting on his chest and the other shielding his eyes. I want to ask him about each of his tattoos. What they mean − did they hurt? − does he like pain?

I open his wardrobe. He has four pairs of jeans, half a dozen shirts, two jumpers, a vest, a blue blazer and a black suit in dry-cleaning plastic. One of the shirts is denim with studs for buttons. I put it on and roll up the sleeves. It looks good on me − almost like a jacket.

Cyrus has a drawer for his socks and another for T-shirts and running shorts. He has four pairs of shoes, including hiking boots. I put them on, feeling like a child wearing my father's shoes, although I can't remember if I ever did that. I have almost no memories of my father − a man in an armchair by the fire. Sitting on his knee. Listening to him read. 'Have you brushed your hair and combed your teeth?' he'd ask, making the same joke every night, rubbing his stubbly jaw against my cheek. My mother is clearer, but even those memories are beginning to fade, or fray at the edges, losing colour and detail like the old rug on Cyrus's floor.

I have one memento − a tortoiseshell button. It came from her favourite coat, which was bright red with a fur-lined collar and she wore it on special occasions. She was wearing it when I last saw her. I wouldn't let go. I clung to her and the button came away in my hand. I screamed for her then. I wish for her now. I hold that button in my fist, believing it might bring her back if I have enough faith.

Putting the room back in order, I go to the bathroom and search the cabinet above the sink. Opening jars and bottles, I sniff at the contents. There are no pills or medications, but Cyrus has condoms

– a whole box, unopened. I close the cabinet and look in the mirror. I hate what I see. I hate my lank hair. I hate my downturned mouth. I hate my fat bottom lip. I hate the freckles on my nose. I hate my sticky-out ears. I hate my skinny legs.

The doorbell rings. My heart jumps.

I go downstairs and wait in the hallway. The bell rings again. I look through the spyhole. There are two young men in cheap suits. They look no older than me. I open the door a few inches.

'Hello, how are you today?' one of them says brightly. 'What a lovely old house.' There's no hint of sarcasm. 'Do you believe in God?'

'No.'

'What do you believe in?'

'Nothing.'

'Do you know much about Jesus Christ?'

'Who are you?'

'We're from the Church of Jesus Christ of Latter-Day Saints and we're here to share the message of Jesus Christ. My name is Elder Grimshaw and this is Elder Green.'

'Doesn't that get confusing?' I ask. 'Both being called Elder.'

'We're missionaries.'

'I thought missionaries were supposed to work in poor countries.'

'No, we're everywhere. We share our experiences because we believe in helping others to find peace and fulfilment in the love of Jesus Christ. Would you like to learn more?'

'No.'

'We're here to share.'

'You want to change my mind, that's not sharing.'

The two Mormons look at each other. I have my foot braced against the door, ready to slam it closed. The quieter of the two is waiting for his partner to take the lead.

I look at him. 'Do you truly believe that God exists?'

'With all my heart.'

'No. I think your mate does, but you're not so sure. Come back when you are.'

I shut the door and go back upstairs, continuing my search of the *house. The upper-floor rooms are supposed to be off-limits, according to Cyrus. That was a mistake. Who is going to ignore a challenge like that?*

Most of the rooms are full of old furniture and rolled-up rugs and boxes of magazines and sheet music and photographs. I wonder how many generations of people have lived here. How many have died.

The loneliness of the house is seeping into me and I wish Cyrus would come home, even though he'll want to know what I've been thinking behind my mask or want to squeeze my skull and shake things out.

Having searched the turret room, I go to the small dirty window and peer out at the near-empty street and at the houses opposite and the parked cars and the rooftops beyond. A woman pushes a pram along the pavement. A cyclist sweeps past her.

From somewhere behind me, I hear Terry's warning.

'You must never tell anyone who you are.'

'I won't.'

'Promise me.'

'I promise.'

33

As I near the Sheehan house, a neighbour appears at his front gate sitting astride a mobility scooter. Rolls of fat cascade over his belt, making it hard to see where his legs begin.

'Are you with the police?' he asks aggressively.

'No.'

I don't stop. He follows, accelerating to my pace. I recognise him from his photograph: Kevin Stokes – the former swim instructor who served eight years for sexually abusing two boys at a local swimming centre.

'Yes, you are. I saw you the other night. When are they gonna clean this up?' He nods towards his house where the words 'pedo' and 'pervert' have been daubed in red paint across his front fence.

I don't stop.

'What about my rights?' he yells.

'What about the boys you abused?' I mutter under my breath.

A police officer answers the door at the Sheehan house. Female. Uniformed.

'Is anyone home?' I ask.

'Mrs Sheehan has gone to church.'

'And Mr Sheehan?'

'He left early this morning.'

The constable jots down the address of a nearby church and draws me a map on a scrap of paper. I follow her directions until I see the steeple from two streets away. The main doors are locked so I try a side entrance and enter a nave with a vaulted ceiling criss-crossed by white beams that join together and plunge down pink-tinted walls. Seats are arranged on three sides around an altar.

Maggie Sheehan is cutting flowers and arranging them into tall vases. She has a warm, open face with a high forehead and pale blue eyes. She's an introvert. I recognised that when I first saw her deferring to Dougal, letting him speak first, almost seeking permission with her eyes before she voiced an opinion. It was as though she had grown accustomed to being in the background and I could imagine how easily she could disappear, fading into the wallpaper, or evaporating without leaving so much as a spot.

'I'm sorry to bother you, Mrs Sheehan,' I say, clearing my throat. 'Do you remember me?'

'Dr Haven.'

'Cyrus.'

She goes back to trimming the flowers. 'We've been sent so many I thought I should bring some to the church,' she explains. 'People are very kind. I do the flowers every week . . . and clean the presbytery for Father Patrick.'

'I called on Felicity earlier,' I say. 'It must be a comfort having her living so close.'

'She's like a sister to me. People used to think Bryan and I were twins, but he's two years younger. I remember when he first brought Felicity home to meet our parents. He whispered to me, "I'm going to marry this one." And he did.'

She snips another stem.

'I was engaged to Dougal by then. We talked about a joint

wedding, but I fell pregnant and we had to rush up the altar. Does that shock you?'

'No.'

'I guess it doesn't matter so much any more. Sex before marriage. A pregnant bride. Felicity was my birth partner because Dougal didn't want to see the "nuts and bolts". That's what he called it. I promised that I'd do the same for Flip but she took ages to fall pregnant.'

'Flip?'

'That's my pet name for her. It almost drove her mad – the IVF and the heartbreak. Then a miracle – Aiden came along. Did you meet him? Isn't he gorgeous? So kind and gentle. He's going to Cambridge next year.'

'Felicity told me.'

She smiles. I smile. Our voices echo in the emptiness of the church. She picks up a carnation and uses secateurs to trim it to the desired length.

'I used to think having children was our way of cheating death,' she says reflectively. 'We wedge our foot in a closing door, you know, giving ourselves a glimmer of hope that we'll leave something behind – some part of us will endure.'

'But surely you believe in Heaven.'

'I do. Yes. Even more so now. A part of me can't wait to get there – to see my Jodie.' Maggie raises her eyes to the ceiling, as though she suspects that Jodie may be listening to us. 'Father Patrick says I'm allowed to be angry with God. He says anger is a natural human response to situations that are out of our control or beyond our ability to understand. But I still think it's wrong. Jodie deserved more. I deserved more. Father Patrick says that if ever I come to place where I can't run, I should walk. And if I can't walk, I should crawl. And if I can't crawl, I should turn on my back, look up to Heaven and ask Christ for help.'

Maggie snips another stem and arranges it in a vase.

'The police found six thousand pounds in Jodie's school locker.'

I leave the statement hanging. Maggie blinks at me, as though not comprehending.

I try again. 'Have you any idea where she'd get money like that?'

'No. I mean, we don't have that sort of cash. We live month to month.'

'Could she have been holding the money for someone else?'

'Who?'

'Felix?'

Maggie makes a *pfffffmmmph* sound, as though I'm talking rubbish.

'Could she have been involved in something dangerous?'

'Like what?'

'I don't know – that's why I'm asking.'

'Is everything all right, Maggie?' asks a voice that echoes from all around me. A priest appears from a vestry. In his early forties with a shock of dark hair that is swept back in a wave, he's dressed in black trousers and a white open-necked shirt with small gold crucifixes pinned to each collar.

'You must be Father Patrick,' I say, introducing myself. He has a warm firm handshake and an uncertain frown.

'Have we met before?'

'No. I was talking to Tasmin Whitaker. She remembered you were at the fireworks. You did Jodie a service by retrieving her tote bag.'

Maggie looks confused.

'Jodie had a problem with some boys,' I explain. 'Father Patrick saw them off.'

The sudden revelation appears to embarrass him.

'How long have you been at the parish?' I ask.

'Eight years.'

'You must have known Jodie quite well.'

'I try to know all of my parishioners.'

It's a nothing answer.

'They found money in Jodie's locker,' says Maggie. 'Six thousand pounds.'

'Where did it come from?' asks the priest.

She shakes her head.

'I have to ask you about something else the police found in Jodie's locker. Perhaps we should talk alone – outside.'

Maggie shakes her head. 'I want Father Patrick to be here.'

'Jodie had a box of condoms in her locker.'

Maggie's mouth drops open and her hand covers it instinctively as though a word might suddenly fly out.

'Our Jodie was a good girl,' she says, defensively.

'Yes, of course, but there is evidence that she had sex with someone on the night she died.'

'She was raped.'

'Rapists don't normally use condoms.'

Maggie's voice grows strident and tears prickle in her eyes. 'Why are you telling me this? You . . . you have no right!'

'I'm trying to understand—'

'My little girl was raped and murdered and now you're doing it all over again.'

'I promise you – that's not my intention.'

'I think you should leave,' says Father Patrick, stepping into my space, making himself large. The odour of him touches my face – a mixture of shampoo, aftershave and mouthwash. Foamy bits of spit are clinging to his lips.

He puts his arm around Maggie's shoulders. She leans against him, pressing her face to his chest.

The priest isn't finished with me. 'I have spent the past week telling Maggie she is not to blame for what happened to Jodie; that sometimes terrible things happen to good people. She thinks she's a bad mother. She thinks she could have saved her daughter. Her only respite has been to come here and talk to me . . . and to God.'

'I'm sorry. I didn't mean to—'

'I want you to leave.'

My shoes echo on the flagstones, as I follow the centre aisle to the main entrance. As I pull open the heavy door, I turn back and see Father Patrick and Maggie sitting together. He holds her face in his hands and uses a handkerchief to wipe the tears from her cheeks.

34

Angel Face

'Did you go out today?' Cyrus asks.

I nod and watch him unpacking the Chinese takeaway, setting out the cardboard cartons and plastic trays.

'Where did you go?'

'To the shops.'

'What did you buy?'

'Nothing.'

I'm wrestling with the chopsticks, unable to make my fingers wrap around them. A spring roll drops in the dipping sauce, making a mess.

'Would you like a fork?' he asks.

'No!' I snap, hating that I can't do something when he makes it look so easy.

'Did you catch the number 22 bus?' he asks.

'Something like that.'

Instantly, I realise my mistake. There won't be a no. 22 bus. He's caught me lying again, which means follow-up questions, or accusations. Instead, he acts like nothing is wrong.

'You should try the dumplings.'

I sniff at the container. 'What's in them?'

'They're vegetarian.'

'How do you know it's not dog? They eat dogs in China – and pandas.'

'I don't think they eat pandas.'

I spear a dumpling with a chopstick and chew one corner, before emptying the rest of the carton into my bowl.

Cyrus has poured himself a glass of wine.

'Can I have one?'

'You're not eighteen.'

'Are we really still arguing about that?'

'I have it on the authority of a High Court judge.'

I take the last spring roll. Cyrus pours me half a glass of wine. I sip it tentatively – not really liking the taste, but I don't want him to know that.

'What did you do today?' I ask, not really interested.

'I interviewed some people.'

'About the Jodie Sheehan murder?'

'How did you know that?'

'You shouldn't leave your shit lying around the house.'

'What shit?'

I shrug.

Cyrus suddenly realises what he left in the library – the police interviews with Craig Farley.

'Did you find the DVDs?' he asks.

I admit to nothing. My silence says enough.

'Christ, Evie! That's highly confidential material. It's the basis of court proceedings. Evidence in a criminal trial.'

'Who am I going to tell?'

'That's not the point.'

'You didn't tell me the library was off limits.'

'It should have been obvious.'

'Not to me,' I say. 'I need the rules written down and posted on the wall. Staff only. Lights out. Mealtimes. Chores. Lessons.'

Cyrus mutters something about putting a lock on the door, but I ignore him, spearing another dumpling with a single chopstick.

We eat in silence for a while.

'So, did he do it?' I ask.

'What do you think?'

I consider this for a moment. 'By the end, I think he would have confessed to bombing Pearl Harbour.'

'OK, but was he telling the truth?'

'I don't know.'

Cyrus looks perplexed and starts again. 'I thought maybe because of your . . . ability . . . you might have been able to tell. I don't know how it works – this thing you do, whether it comes and goes, or if it's triggered by something.'

I hesitate, not sure of what I want to say, or if I want to say anything at all. I can't explain what I see. It is something in the face: a false note, a flicker, an invisible light . . .

'I have to be up close,' I whisper.

'Pardon?'

'For me to tell if someone is lying – I have to be close to them – in the same room, looking at their face. I can't do it otherwise.'

'So not from a DVD?'

'Not unless it's up close. Not accurately. I get a sense, that's all.'

'What was your sense about Farley?'

'He knows what he did was wrong, but I'm not sure if what he did is what you think he did.'

Cyrus has stopped eating and is leaning forward. Why is he looking at me like that?

He seems to recognise my anxiety and pulls back, dropping the subject.

I clear the table and start washing the dishes, remembering to rinse the glasses in clean water to stop them streaking.

Cyrus picks up a tea towel. 'I know you hate questions, but can I ask you one?'

I don't respond.

'How long have you had this . . . this . . .?'

'I don't remember.'

'Was it before you became Evie Cormac?'

I nod.

'I know why it frightens you,' he says. 'It would frighten me.'

'I'd have thought you'd like to know if someone was lying. It would make your job easier.'

'I wouldn't have a job at all.'

35

Early morning. Lenny Parvel sends me a pager message. She wants to talk. I go to the library and open my laptop, waiting for her Skype call. Her image appears but only the top of her head. She curses and tilts the screen down, but it goes too far. I can see chin and the collar of her dressing gown. She adjusts it again, centring herself. Her husband Nick is in the background, making a cup of coffee. He's wearing a T-shirt and boxers, showing off his hairy thighs. Nick is the hairiest man I've ever met, which is why Lenny calls him 'Bear'.

'Hi, Cyrus,' he says, waving at the screen.

'Hi, Nick.'

'Will you put some clothes on,' says Lenny, covering the camera with her hand. I can hear them arguing, although not seriously. Nick sells medical equipment to doctors and clinics, but his hours are flexible. His two boys are at university or have graduated by now. They're good lads. A credit.

Lenny removes her hand from the camera.

'I had a call from Ness last night. The toxicology results are in. Jodie Sheehan had no drugs or alcohol in her system.'

I sense there's something more.

'Ness noticed that Jodie's hormone levels were high and ran a test. She was pregnant – eleven weeks. Ness might be able to get DNA from the foetal material, but the lab work has to be done in America and could take a week, or longer. Any foetal DNA will have half the father's genes, which may be enough to identify someone.'

'Would Jodie have known she was pregnant?' I ask.

'Most girls are pretty good at keeping track – particularly in the age of smart phones.'

I pause, processing the information. It could have no bearing on Jodie's murder. Then again, the degraded semen found on her thigh has added significance because it didn't belong to Farley. It's now more likely that Jodie had consensual sex earlier in the evening – with a boyfriend, or a hook-up. Five hours are still missing from her timeline.

I want to ask Lenny what she's thinking, but there's too much evidence against Farley for her to change her mind. And there's now even less likelihood of an accomplice.

This isn't about police ignoring new evidence. They are shoring up their case, ensuring the inconsistencies won't jeopardise the prosecution. Lenny is thorough and diligent. More importantly, she's honest. She doesn't plant evidence or frame suspects, but neither does she chase rabbits down rabbit holes, wasting time and resources.

Knocking pipes signal that Evie is in the shower. She comes downstairs with her hair in a towel and her face set in a scowl.

'There's no hot water?'

'Sorry. The pilot light went out. It's a storage system – so it might take a while for the boiler to heat up.'

She utters a curse under her breath and notices that I'm dressed.

'Where are you going?'

'I have some people to see.'

'Can I come?'

'No.'

'I won't get in the way. I'll wait in the car, or downstairs, or wherever . . .'

Evie looks at me hopefully. She doesn't want to spend another day on her own. Loneliness is not something I associate with Evie because she lives so completely in her head and makes no attempt to befriend people or socialise. Even so, I don't want her spending another day on her own. She should be outside, reintroducing herself to the world, not spending her time in a creepy old house.

'Can you be ready in fifteen minutes?' I ask.

'I can be ready in five.'

Evie comes downstairs dressed in jeans, cowboy boots, a long-sleeved top and a denim shirt that she's wearing like a jacket. I have a shirt like that, I think, although I don't wear it often.

I have to sweep fallen leaves off the windscreen of my red Fiat, which has faded to a mottled pink. Pigeons have crapped all over the bonnet and someone has stuck a flyer beneath the wiper blades advertising a clearance sale at a carpet showroom. Twice I've had towing notices from the local council because neighbours mistook my car for an abandoned vehicle.

'Nice,' says Evie, being facetious.

The engine doesn't start first time. I encourage it under my breath. It splutters and coughs like a consumptive smoker, before idling so roughly we sway from side to side. I give it a moment to warm up.

'Can you teach me to drive?' asks Evie.

'No.'

'Why not?'

'The bus stop is two minutes from the house.'

'It will make me more independent.'

'You don't have a car.'

'I could borrow this one.'

'That's *not* going to happen.'

215

She folds her arms and looks out the window as we head along Derby Road past Wollaton Park. It's early on a Sunday morning and the traffic is light.

'How did Jodie Sheehan die?' asks Evie.

'I can't talk about the case.'

'Is it a state secret?'

'No.'

'Well then?'

I don't respond.

'I've watched the interviews,' she says. 'I know she was hit from behind.'

'You *have* to stop going through my stuff.'

Evie doesn't reply. Instead she props her cowboy boots on the dashboard, above the glove compartment. We're heading along Abbey Street, past the Priory Church and onto Castle Boulevard, passing south of the city centre.

'Does the CD player work?'

'No.'

'What about the radio?'

'I have to hit the right pothole.'

She sighs in disgust.

'The post mortem wasn't definitive,' I say, answering her first question. 'The pathologist couldn't decide if she drowned or died of exposure.'

'Farley said he didn't rape her,' says Evie, 'but even if he whacked off into her hair it was a pretty sick act. A guy like that deserves to be locked up, you know, but I guess that doesn't prove he killed her.'

'An innocent man would have tried to help her.'

'Sometimes we don't have a choice.'

The statement rattles something inside me and I picture Terry Boland being strapped to a chair having acid poured into his ears, while Evie listened to his screams.

I find a metered parking spot in the entertainment quarter of Nottingham and tell Evie to wait in the car.

'It's cold. Can't I come with you?'

'OK. But stay out of trouble.'

She joins me on the pavement, pulling up her collar and pocketing her hands. As we reach the corner, two young backpackers cross our path – a girl and a boy in their early twenties, who are talking excitedly in a different language. The girl laughs and calls the boy a name. Evie stops and turns. For a moment I think she's going to respond, but instead she watches the couple walk away.

'What made you turn around?' I ask.

'Nothing.'

'Was it something she said?'

'No.'

'She sounded Russian or Polish. Did you understand her?'

'No.'

'What then?'

'She looked familiar,' says Evie, and I don't know whether to believe her. That's the trouble with Evie. I risk reading clues into everything she does. Actions. Inactions. Silences. Shrugs.

We're crossing Bolero Square to the National Ice Centre, a twin stadium building made of metal and glass. Pushing through the revolving doors, we step into a cavernous foyer dominated by a forty-foot-high poster montage celebrating British skating champions past and present.

A woman at the information desk barely glances up from her screen. She hands Evie a form. 'Fill this out for the academy trials. The changing rooms are through those doors. Don't put your skates on until you're on the ice.'

'She's not a skater,' I explain. 'I'm here to see Bryan Whitaker.'

'He's coaching.'

'I can wait.'

Evie and I follow signs to an amphitheatre the size of a concert hall with tiered seating on all sides, rising into darkness at the higher levels. The rink itself seems to glow from within, taking on a bluish tinge. A dozen skaters are warming up, gliding across the ice in graceful movements that look so effortless that a mere flick of their fingers sends them pirouetting or skating backwards. One of them accelerates, leaps and spins, landing on a single blade, arms outstretched and back arched.

Most are dressed in tight black leggings and fitted tops. Training wear. I recognise Bryan Whitaker. He's wearing an official-looking tracksuit and yelling instructions to a couple of the girls, who look to be thirteen or fourteen. Other coaches are working with their own students.

Whitaker claps his hands, signalling the girls to the side of the rink. He issues instructions. One of them shakes her head. He puts his hand on the back of her neck, pulling her face to his, touching foreheads, whispering, his eyes bright, a gold bracelet winking on his wrist.

The girl nods and skates away, pulling up at the far end of the rink. After taking a few deep breaths she sets off, swinging her arms as she builds up speed. She switches direction, skating backwards and then switches again, leaping off one foot and spinning twice through the air with her arms across her chest before landing on her opposite foot and gliding in a graceful circle, unfurling her arms like wings.

Whitaker claps. The girl beams. He nods to the next skater, who sets off across the ice, accelerating with less confidence. Stiff. Nervous. I can see her steeling herself, telling herself to jump, but at the last moment she pulls out of the attempt and circles back, hitting her thigh angrily. She collects herself and tries again, her face a mask of determination, ice flicking from her skates, but she doesn't have the speed when she leaps and spins. Her arms don't cross. Her legs tangle. Balance lost, she lands heavily and shoots across the ice, thudding into the hoardings.

Whitaker goes to her. He picks her up. She's crying. Hurt. He wipes her tears away and strokes her back like he's petting an animal.

'Do you want to try again?'

She nods.

'You don't have to.'

'I know.'

She brushes ice from her knees and hips before skating back to her position. She tries again, looking even more determined. I don't want her to fall. Neither does Evie.

'She should do one spin,' she whispers. 'Two is too much.'

The girl launches herself forward, caught in a truncated twirl, before crashing and sliding across the ice. She gets up, ready to try again. Whitaker stops her.

'That's enough for today, Lara. You'll get it tomorrow.'

The girls glide towards the gate, chatting to each other. Whitaker goes to the side of the rink where he picks up a clipboard and makes a note.

'You stay here,' I tell Evie, who seems fascinated by the display.

Walking around the rink, I approach Bryan Whitaker. He's a small man, with delicate hands and the posture of a ballet dancer.

'Dr Haven,' he says, glancing up at me quickly and going back to the clipboard. 'Bear with me.' He scribbles a further note. 'Felicity said you'd dropped by. I heard that some of Tasmin's friends were there.'

He steps through a gate and sits down to unlace his skates.

'A tough session,' I say.

'Not really. If Lara can't land a double axel, she'll never land a triple. And without a triple she'll never compete at the top level.' He moves to his other boot. 'Figure skating may look graceful, but the falls are brutal on body and soul.'

'Was it like that for Jodie?'

He seems to relish the question.

'Some skaters take two years to master a double axel. Jodie took a month. It's a rare thing to find someone who can take the most difficult jump and within days make it look routine – like she could do it in her sleep.'

'Did you know Jodie was pregnant?'

Shock registers on his face. Perhaps Evie could tell if his reaction was genuine.

'She didn't tell you?'

'No.'

'What would you have done?'

'Arranged an abortion.'

'Without telling her parents?'

Whitaker pauses for a moment, glancing past me at the ice-resurfacing machine that is moving back and forth across the rink. 'Maggie is very Catholic. She wouldn't have agreed.'

'What about Dougal?'

'He would have found the bastard who got her pregnant and broken him in half.'

Several ice dancers are circling the rink, waiting for the machine to finish. Whitaker watches them move in tandem, arm in arm, kicking and gliding.

'Eight years ago one of your students made an allegation that you photographed her while she was in the shower.'

'There were no photographs. I didn't think anyone was in the changing room.'

'Why were you even there?'

'One of the girls phoned me. She thought she'd left her wallet in the changing room. I went to check. I knocked. I thought it was empty. I apologised to the girl in question.'

'Why did she say you took photographs?'

'That was her father. He thought he could get money out of me.'

'Where is the girl now?'

'The family moved to Leeds.'

'Another rink?'

'Just so.' He pauses. 'Why are you asking me about her?'

'The pathologist thinks he can get a DNA profile from Jodie's unborn child. They'll be able to identify the father.'

He shrugs ambivalently.

'Aren't you interested?'

'Not particularly.'

'May I ask why?'

'It won't bring Jodie back.'

Something about his attitude annoys me. I can't tell if he's mourning the loss of his niece or the loss of a future champion; his ticket to reflected glory.

'It must be a very close relationship – a coach and his student. Working together, travelling to events, staying overnight . . .'

His body tenses and his eyes are fixed on mine.

'What exactly are you suggesting?'

'Did you have separate rooms?'

Whitaker's face goes through a transformation from amazement to anger, as the red mist descends. His features become tighter and smaller, rushing to the centre of his face.

'How dare you suggest – how dare you think . . .'

'It's a question that has to be asked.'

'It's a question that could destroy my career,' he says angrily. 'Even the merest hint of something like that and I'd never coach again. You have no right. You . . . you . . .' He can't finish. 'The suggestion that I slept with my niece is obscene. You have a sick mind. A sick, sick mind.'

36

Angel Face

I've been watching them talking, but I'm too far away to hear what they're saying or decide if they're lying. Neither would be very good at poker. Too many 'tells'. Cyrus is holding his emotions in check, but the coach is all over the place.

When people swear on the Bible, promising to tell the truth, the whole truth and nothing but the truth, that's bullshit. Everybody lies. Lawyers. Social workers. Counsellors. Doctors. Foster carers. Teenagers. Children. It is what people do: they breathe, they eat, they drink, and they lie.

I once did a survey at Langford Hall, keeping count of how many porkies I heard in a single day and I came up with an average of eighteen per person . . . before lunch. These were only the obvious lies, not the small fictions that people tell to keep others happy. I love your new haircut. What a cute outfit. I didn't take your yoghurt. Others were lies they told themselves. I'm not so fat. I'm not too old. I know what I'm doing. If I had more time I would . . .

The obvious lies are the easiest to pick. Others are better hidden or so close to the truth that the dividing line is blurred. Some lies are selfish. Some inflate, or conflate, or mitigate, or simply omit. Some are told for good reason. People lie because they think it doesn't matter.

They lie because telling the truth would mean giving up control or the truth is inconvenient, or they don't want to disappoint; or they desperately want it to be true. I've heard them all. I've told them all.

Walking between the tiered seats, I follow the passage to the changing rooms. The two skaters I saw on the ice are putting on their street clothes. One of them is in a hurry to leave, angry with herself, slamming the door of her locker and limping out. The other is still unlacing her skates.

'You were very good,' I say. 'That's the first time I've ever seen anyone skate, up close I mean. When you see it on TV, you don't realise the speed, or hear the sound of the skates on the ice.'

I sit down on the bench opposite her. 'I'm Evie, by the way.'

'Alice.'

'How long have you been skating, Alice?'

'Since I was five.'

'Have I left it too late?'

'Anyone can skate. Most people just do it for fun.'

'Is it fun for you?'

'Today, yeah. Ask me tomorrow.'

Alice pulls a heavy fleece over her head, lifting her hair out from the collar.

'Did you know Jodie Sheehan?' I ask.

'Sure. We trained together.'

'With the same coach?'

Alice nods. 'Mr Whitaker.'

'Was Jodie his favourite?'

A cloud of uncertainty passes across her face. 'He pushed her harder than the rest of us.'

'Why?'

'Because she was so good.'

'I wish I could have seen her skate,' I say, running my finger over one of the blades. 'Can we play a game, Alice?'

She glances up nervously. 'My mum is picking me up.'

'This won't take long. It's a bluffing game called two truths and a lie. I tell you three things about me and you pick which one is a lie.'

'OK.'

'My real name isn't Evie. I'm a twin. And I can fit four boiled eggs in my mouth all at once.'

'That's a lie.' Alice laughs.

'You mean about the eggs? No, that's true. I could prove it to you if we had four boiled eggs. Now it's your turn. You tell me three things about Jodie — two truths and a lie.'

'Why Jodie?'

'It makes things harder.'

Alice begins thinking. 'OK. Jodie wanted to quit skating; she had a secret boyfriend; and she once screamed so loudly at a horror film that the girl next to her peed her pants.'

'That's hilarious,' I say. 'Were you the girl?'

Alice nods, blushing. 'How did you know?'

'I guessed. Why did Jodie want to quit skating?'

Alice looks over her shoulder and back again, whispering, 'The headaches. She had three concussions in a row.'

'From falling?'

Alice nods. 'She was trying to learn to triple axel.'

'Did Mr Whitaker force her to keep trying?'

'Jodie didn't want to disappoint him.'

'What about her boyfriend?'

'That was supposed to be a lie,' says Alice. 'I couldn't think of one.'

'It's hard to think of a lie when you need one,' I tell her. 'Do you know his name?'

'No.'

'Why was he a secret?'

'I think he was older.'

'What makes you say that?'

'I mean, she wouldn't talk about him, so I thought . . .' Alice's phone is beeping. She glances at the screen. 'I have to go.'

She puts her skates away, forcing them into a crammed locker.

'Did Jodie have one of those?' I ask.

Alice nods and leads me around the corner where she points to a locker with blue and white police tape criss-crossed on the diagonals.

'They searched that one,' says Alice, 'but missed the other one.'

'What other one?'

'Jodie managed to get two. Natascha quit during the summer and she gave her key to Jodie, who never gave it back.'

Alice takes me along the row and points to an unlabelled metal door.

Her phone beeps again. She's late. Slipping her arms through the straps of a small backpack, she raises her fingers in a wave. 'If you really want to learn to skate you should come back when the rink is open to the public.'

'I will,' I say, still looking at the locker.

I'm alone in the changing rooms. The muffled sound of classical music permeates from the rink. Leaning my back against the metal door, I pull at the handle, testing the strength of the padlock. Reaching into my hair, I slide a kirby grip free from against my scalp. Bending it back and forth until it breaks, I bite off the plastic tips, exposing the metal ends. Sliding the sharpest point into the barrel of the padlock, I feel it bumping over the internal mechanism, forcing down the sequence of pins.

A kid called Forager taught me how to open locks. We called him Forager because he used to break into the kitchens at Langford Hall and steal packets of biscuits, juice boxes and the chef's private supply of chocolate. Forager could open almost anything. He began teaching me, but I gave up after mastering padlocks because I kept getting caught and punished.

This one is easy. I hear a tell-tale click and the shackle releases, falling open in my hands. Inside the locker I find ballet shoes, leggings, socks and a fleece-lined jacket with a badge saying, 'British Junior Figure Skating Team'. I check the jacket pockets and up-end the shoes. On the lowest shelf, pushed to the back, I discover a padded yellow envelope with a torn flap. Inside is Jodie's passport and a handful of SIM cards, still in their packaging, as well as a cheap mobile phone. Tipping the envelope upside down, I discover a pen-shaped object with writing on one side and a small circular window with two pink vertical lines. I know what this is — a pregnancy test.

A door opens somewhere out of sight and I feel the slight change in the air temperature. I close the locker and lean against it, slipping my hand behind my back and securing the padlock. The envelope is tucked under my right arm, beneath Cyrus's loose-fitting denim shirt.

'What are you doing in here?' asks a woman. She's one of the coaches I saw on the rink.

'I needed the bathroom.'

'This is for academy students only.'

'I was busting.'

The woman eyes me sceptically but I try to match her stare, opening my palms, as if to say, 'Nothing to see here.'

'I think you should leave.'

'Don't get all shitty on me.'

'What did you say?'

'I said don't get shirty. I made a mistake. I'm sorry.'

I flounce confidently between the benches, turning right through the door, cradling the envelope under my arm. Along the tunnel, up the stairs, through the exit doors, I don't look back until I reach Cyrus, who is waiting in the foyer.

'Where have you been?' he asks, sounding relieved.

'Loo.'

'You shouldn't just wander off.'

'Why? Am I a prisoner? Did you want to follow me to the ladies? You could watch me. Some men get a kick out of that.'

He doesn't answer.

Side by side, we cross Bolero Square. I have to lengthen my stride to keep up with him.

'Jodie Sheehan wanted to quit skating,' I say, making it sound like a revelation.

'Who told you that?'

'Alice. She's one of the other skaters.'

Cyrus stops and turns. 'How do you know Alice?'

'I talked to her when she came off the rink. Alice said Jodie had a boyfriend. He was older, she said, but didn't know his name.'

Cyrus is staring at me, unsure how to react.

I pull the envelope from inside my shirt. 'You didn't tell me that Jodie was pregnant.'

'How could you possibly know that?'

'I found this in her locker.'

37

Yelling at Evie is like shouting at a TV, or at a car that won't start. I can hear myself getting more and more worked up, while she regards me with utter ambivalence or worse, complete disdain.

'Have you any idea of how many laws you've broken? The position you've put me in? That was someone's private locker. You stole possible evidence. You could be charged. I could lose my job. Bad show, Evie! Bad show!'

She gives me a dull stare. No regrets. No remorse. Whatever warmth or connection may have existed has gone, replaced by an icy wasteland that I might never cross again.

I order her into the car. She doesn't react. Pedestrians are watching us, drawn by my raised voice. I'm clutching the yellow envelope as though it's going to explode in my hands.

The wind lifts hair from Evie's forehead and makes her eyes water, but she doesn't blink. It's as though she is closing down her mind, going somewhere else. I stop myself and swallow my anger. Evie isn't ambivalent or unmoved. She is doing what she's always done when under attack – she's escaping to a safe place. This is how she survived years of sexual abuse.

'Please get in the car,' I say, softening my voice.

Evie looks at the open door.

'I shouldn't have shouted at you. I'm sorry.'

She doesn't say anything.

'Do you want to go back to Langford Hall?'

'Is that what you want?' she whispers.

The question thumps into my chest. I should say something to reassure her but I'm too angry. What am I to do with this girl? I know practically nothing about her, despite having read her files. She is surly, ungrateful, stubborn, and her presence in my life makes it seem impossibly overcrowded. I want to yell, 'Don't be a child! Grow up!' but Evie had no childhood. This is it.

We drive through steady traffic and spitting rain to the sound of my wiper blades slapping against the side of the windscreen. When we reach the house, Evie goes upstairs to her room. An hour later I stand outside her door, unsure of whether to knock. I press my ear against the panels of wood. Nothing.

Retreating to the library, I empty the contents of the envelope onto my desk – the pregnancy test and the SIM cards and the cheap mobile phone – an old-fashioned Nokia with a flip screen, most likely second-hand.

I should give the envelope to the police. How would I explain it? If I tell them that Evie broke into Jodie's locker they'll send her back to Langford Hall and I'll likely be investigated and lose my job.

Perhaps I could post the envelope anonymously; or leave it on Lenny's doorstep. Evie's fingerprints will be on the contents. So will mine. Shit!

The police already know that Jodie was carrying a second phone on the night she died because she kept receiving messages after her own handset was turned off. Now we have proof of a third cell phone and multiple SIM cards. Why would a fifteen-year-old girl need different phone numbers? And what was she doing with six thousand pounds?

Yesterday at the Whitakers' house, Brianna hinted that Jodie wasn't as innocent as everybody made her out to be and said I should talk to her brother. It sounded like teenage bitchiness but hinted at more. Felix Sheehan could be the key to this.

In the meantime, I have to do something about the envelope. Opening my laptop, I put a Skype-call in to Lenny. She answers on her mobile. I hear laughter in the background.

'Am I interrupting?'

'Sunday lunch. It's like feeding time at the zoo.'

'I have a package that belonged to Jodie Sheehan. You can't ask me how I came upon it.'

'I can, and I will,' says Lenny, not in the mood for games.

'Someone left it on my doorstep.'

'Don't fuck with me, Cyrus.'

'I need this favour.'

Seconds tick by. I can hear her breathing.

'Where is this mystery package?'

'You should send a car.'

38

Angel Face

I'm sitting in the lee of a bus shelter, head down, hood up, listening to the traffic swish past on the wet road. My anger is so hard against my front teeth that I can taste it in my mouth. Cyrus had no right to shout at me. I was trying to help him, to do something nice. I don't need his lectures, or his charity, or his sad eyes or his psychoanalysis. Fuck him!

A bus pulls up and the doors fold open. I hesitate for a moment.

'Are you getting in?' asks the driver in a thick accent. I step on board and hand him money.

'No cash,' he says irritably. 'Card only.'

I remember Cyrus gave me some sort of travel pass. I search my pockets and hand it over.

'Tap. On reader. Box. Here.'

'How should I know?' I mutter, as the bus pulls away. I sway down the aisle and choose a seat where I can't see my reflection in the mirror. Beneath my overcoat, I'm wearing the dress that Caroline Fairfax chose for my court appearance, but I've unpicked the high collar and undone the top buttons, making it look sexier. Mascara and eye-shadow have made my eyes look bigger and my lashes thicker.

Chloe Pringle once told me that lipstick was supposed to emphasise a woman's sexuality by echoing the colour of her labia. I thought this was disgusting and stopped wearing lipstick for a month.

Reaching into my coat pocket, my fingers close around my roll of banknotes — my stash, my stake. Soon I won't need charity, or Cyrus or anyone else.

The old brick warehouse is squeezed between a minicab office and used-car yard, close enough to the railway line for the whole building to shake when the freight trains roar past. Opposite is a vacant lot where a handful of cars are parked amid mounds of rubble and patches of weeds.

The bouncer on the door is wearing a neck brace that makes him bend from the waist when he looks down at me.

'What do you want?'

'I'm looking for a cash game?'

'How old are you?'

'Eighteen.'

'You got proof?'

I shrug off my coat, revealing my dress and boots. I've bundled my hair on top of my head, trying to look older.

'Nice try,' he says. 'Piss off!'

I peel off two twenties and slide the notes into his trouser pocket, letting my hand brush over his groin.

'How old do I look now?' I whisper.

When he flinches, I duck under his arm, through the doorway and up a set of stairs before he can stop me. The cashier is a large woman with peroxide blonde hair that seems to glow in the dark. She's sitting in a wooden booth behind a glass window. I hand her the roll of banknotes and watch her count out stacks of coloured chips that she takes from a drawer. Cupping my hand over each stack, I pick up the chips and let them drop through my fingertips, counting by touch.

'You've shorted me.'

'The house takes five per cent,' says the cashier. 'You're in the Aces High Room. Third door on your right. Toilets are out back. Drinks are extra. You want to nap during games, find a couch. They can't be reserved.'

I take my chips and move along the corridor, not bothering to knock before entering. Nobody looks up. Four men are sitting at a green baize table in a circle of bright light and a haze of cigarette smoke. Each has a pile of chips in front of him and tumblers of various spirits. The dealer is a young woman, perched on a stool.

I clear my throat.

The dealer eyes me curiously. 'Hello, Sunshine, you're new. Are you waiting for someone?'

'No, I'm here to play.'

One of the men laughs. 'Go home and watch Sesame Street.'

The dealer kicks him under the table. 'Where are your manners?'

The fat man rubs his shin and fetches a chair from against the wall, positioning it next to him.

'You sit right here, young lady,' he says, pretending to dust the seat. 'You're going to bring me luck.'

'You need more than luck – you need divine intervention,' says a large black man with tight curly hair and a small emerald stud in his left ear.

A third man is wearing sunglasses that seem to swallow half his face and a T-shirt that says: I COULD GIVE UP GAMBLING, BUT I'M NO QUITTER. *He continues the conversation. 'You're so unlucky – if you fell in a sack full of tits, you'd come up sucking your thumb.'*

A fourth man interrupts, his voice shaking the room. 'Why don't you all shut up and play the fucking game!'

His face is drooping on one side as though collapsing in on itself, while the other side is so animated that one eye sparks dangerously.

'What are you staring at?'

I look away, wishing I could un-see the image.

The dealer leans closer. 'Don't you worry about Barnum – he's all bark and no bite.'

'All jacks and no aces,' says the fat man, who blows his nose on a tissue and shoves it into the pocket of a shapeless jacket.

The dealer is in her late twenties, dressed in black trousers and a white blouse. 'I'm Katelyn,' she says. 'You want something to drink?'

'No, thank you.'

233

'Come on, have a drink,' says the black man, holding up a bottle of Scotch. 'I'm Livingstone.'

'Don't force her,' says the fat man, whose paunch is like a pregnancy.

'Deal the fucking cards,' says Barnum, drumming his manicured fingers on the baize.

'We're playing Texas hold 'em,' says Katelyn. 'No limit. The buy-in is two thousand. The blinds are ten and twenty.'

I arrange my chips on the table in order of value, so that I can see at a glance exactly how much money I've won or lost. The first hands are playing quickly as I feel my way into the game. Even when I draw strong hole cards, I fold quickly, letting others fight for the pot.

The fat man is easy to read. He talks too much and fidgets, constantly counting and re-counting his chips. Shades is also an open book because he procrastinates before making each bet and always checks on the river. Livingstone reveals himself through his superstitions, betting from a different pile of chips depending on the strength of his hand. Barnum is the wildcard because of his drooping face and his impatience, constantly trying to speed up the game. He's the kind of player who waits until he has good hole cards before committing himself to a hand, but reacts carefully, often betting or raising before the flop, but folding quickly if it threatens him in any way.

Two hours later, I'm five hundred pounds to the good, having won regularly but never too much. Each of them has tried to bluff at some point. I let them go. Folded. Watched.

Midnight comes. The game is down to four because the fat man has gone home. I've doubled my initial stake. More. 'That's it for me,' I say, getting up from the table.

'What's wrong, girlie? Past your bedtime?' says Barnum.

'Let her go,' says Livingstone.

'She's taken all our money, so she can stay for one more hand – what's the harm?'

'Don't let him bully you,' says Katelyn.

I know I should quit while I'm ahead, but I'm well ahead. Retaking my seat, I watch the hole cards being dealt. I get a pair: two nines. Barnum pushes a stack of chips into the centre without counting them.

He's making a play, keeping his eyes fixed on mine, challenging me, but he's got nothing. Zilch. A clumsy bluff.

I match his wager and wait for the flop cards, which give me another nine.

Barnum isn't looking at me now. Instead, he lifts and drops a stack of chips, counting them between his fingers. He pushes one stack into the centre . . . then another. Three thousand pounds.

I hear Katelyn's intake of breath. A voice inside my head tells me to fold, to walk away, to pocket my winnings. Don't play this game. Don't trust this man. I look at the pot. I could run a long way with that much money. I could set myself up.

'Come on, girlie, show us what you're made of,' Barnum brays.

I don't like him, but I can't let that influence me.

His head is down. His hands are covering his cards. I want him to look at me. I need to see his face.

'Are you going to grow a pair, or fold?' he says, tilting his head. His good eye catches the light.

I push my chips into the centre of the table, all of them.

The mood in the room has changed. This is no longer a game. It's combat.

The river card is dealt — the jack of spades. Barnum throws back his head and laughs. Something is wrong.

'All jacks and no aces, eh?' he says, sliding his hands away from his cards and flipping them over. He has three jacks.

I don't bother turning my cards. I get up from the table and take my coat from my chair.

'You played a good game, but you got schooled,' says Barnum.

I turn slowly and whisper, 'You cheated.'

Air leaves the room like a lung collapsing.

Barnum gets to his feet, growling, 'What did you say?'

I lean across the table and turn the jacks. 'These are newer cards. You swapped them in.'

I know I'm right. It's written all over his face. The lie.

Shades holds up the cards, comparing them to the rest of the deck. Two of them look newer.

'She's a liar!' says Barnum.

'Empty your pockets,' mutters Shades.

'Fuck off!'

Barnum holds the bottom of his shirt, creating a basket, and scoops poker chips from the table. Livingstone grabs him by the wrist. Barnum swings a punch with his other hand, but the black man is bigger, quicker and stronger. Poker chips spill across the floor, rolling and rattling under the table and chairs.

Barnum is pushed face-first against the wall with his right arm twisted behind his back. Playing cards fall from his other sleeve – two queens and two kings, along with a seven of clubs and a six of hearts. He's been holding picture cards, waiting for his chance to swap them in.

The bouncer's boots are heavy on the stairs and his shoulders threaten to widen the door.

Katelyn pulls me away, shepherding me into another room.

'But my money!'

'I'll fix it.'

She locks the door and we listen to the blonde cashier yelling at Barnum, telling him he's barred. Barnum threatens to call the police and 'have you all arrested!'

'And I'll tell your wife how much money you owe me,' yells the cashier.

Katelyn pulls a packet of cigarettes from the strap of her bra. 'Christ, you were cool in there. How did you know he was cheating?'

I gesture with a lift of my shoulders.

'I've never seen anyone play poker like you – the way you stare people down. You're fearless.'

She offers me a cigarette. I accept, wishing I could stop my hands from shaking. The lighter flames. Smoke is exhaled in a cloud.

'You should play professionally,' says Katelyn. 'You'd be a rock star.'

I don't answer. I want to get away from this place.

'You could join the poker tour,' says Katelyn. 'There are big tournaments all over the world, televised events. With your looks and your skill, you'd be top table in no time.'

'I don't want to be on TV.'

'We're talking millions. All you need is a decent stake. I could help you. We could be partners.'

'I don't need a partner.'

'I could get you sponsorships and brand deals.'

Why isn't she listening?

'I want my money.'

'OK, OK, I'll talk to the boss.'

I follow Katelyn out of the room. The cashier is on her hands and knees picking up the fallen poker chips.

'They're hers,' says Shades, motioning to me.

'Can she prove that?' asks the cashier.

'I'm her proof.'

'And me,' says Katelyn.

Back in her booth, the cashier opens a safe, taking out bricks of cash, which she begins counting.

'If you like I could mind this for you — keep it in the safe. You can pick it up tomorrow, or the next time you play.'

'I'm not coming back,' I say.

The cashier looks annoyed. She hands me my money — more than seven grand. I shove it deep into my coat pocket and descend the stairs.

The bouncer has gone, along with Shades, Livingstone and Barnum. The street lights barely touch on the darkness and the air is damp with mist.

Katelyn has followed me outside. 'Do you want a lift?' she asks. 'My car is just there.' She points to the vacant lot where two cars are parked amid mounds of rubble. I can't see her face.

'Good luck finding a cab at this hour,' she adds, lifting the collar of her coat. 'Not around here.'

'How far is the station?' I ask.

'Trains won't be running.'

I sniff at the silence.

'You could come back to mine,' says Katelyn. 'I got a sofa. My boyfriend won't mind.'

The quiet descends again.

'Make up your mind. I'm freezing my tits off out here,' says Katelyn. She sets off. Halfway across the road, she yells, 'Hope you don't run into that arsehole Barnum.'

I glance up and down the empty street, wondering if she's right. She's almost at her car. I run to catch up. She opens the passenger door and leans inside to sweep envelopes and fast food wrappers onto the floor. She straightens and holds the door for me.

'Mind your head.'

I duck. In that split second I realise my mistake as Katelyn takes hold of my hair and drives my forehead into the frame of the door. It bounces off and she does it again. My legs fold and a knee rises up to meet me on the way down, snapping my head sideways. And then darkness.

39

The night feels tilted.

I'm cradling my pager in my hands, staring at the screen, willing Evie to send me a message . . . any message. She can abuse me for all I care. I just want to know she's safe.

When we first met at Langford Hall Evie told me that people wanted her dead. I thought she was exaggerating or turning every setback into a catastrophe. What threat could she possibly pose, a teenage girl who has spent a third her life in care?

Sacha Hopewell's parents were the same − convinced their daughter had been hounded out of her home and forced to hide by some nefarious, nameless conspiracy.

I shouldn't have shouted at Evie for stealing the envelope. I should have remained calm and let her explain. It should have been a discussion, not a confrontation, but I fucked up. Despite my training, I'm unequipped for this. Floundering.

I've searched Evie's room. She didn't take a rucksack with her clothes or her make-up. I think she's wearing the dress and boots that Caroline Fairfax bought her for the court hearing.

The other thing I noticed was that she'd decorated her bedroom, painting the walls with vertical green and white stripes. She must have found some old paint in the laundry, or garden shed. I wonder how she managed to get the lines so straight.

Again, I've misjudged her. All this time I thought she was skulking around the place and poking through my stuff, but she was doing something useful. Apart from painting, she re-organised the pantry and the laundry, lining up cans and bottles in alphabetical order and according to size, the labels always facing out.

I don't know what to do next. What if she's jumped off a bridge or thrown herself under a train? She could be unconscious or have amnesia. I've called the city's hospitals, asking about admissions. The obvious next step is to contact the police, but I know the ramifications of that. Evie will be classed as a runaway and returned to Langford Hall where Guthrie and the others will make sure she stays. I don't mind being proved wrong. I didn't force Evie to stay with me. I gave her a choice. I bought her clothes, a new bed, vegetarian food and sugary breakfast cereal. I promised her a phone. I've offered her normality, a home, freedom . . . In the same breath I chide myself for being so stupid. Evie is damaged. Broken. Wild.

Victims of childhood abuse don't associate kindness with trust. There is no fairness, or balance. I am everything Evie has learned to mistrust. Men. Authority figures. Experts. Just being here – alone with me in this house – must have worried her, possibly frightened her.

The last time she lived in a house with a man she was sexually abused and kept in a secret room. She became so reliant on her abuser and traumatised by her ordeal that she didn't run when she had the chance. She hid from his killers and the police and the tradesmen who renovated the house.

Even as I rationalise this, another thought occurs to me. I look around the room again – at the freshly painted walls and the ageing furniture and the bed that still smells of plastic. On the landing, I glance up the stairs and begin climbing to the top floor. This part of the house is closed up, with the rooms used for storage or awaiting a purpose. I enter each of them, turning on the lights. Not all of them work.

The remotest of the rooms is in the attic, reachable by a narrow, uncarpeted set of stairs that creak under my weight. The small recessed window is grey with cobwebs and dust. Boxes of my grandparents' things are stacked beneath beams that follow the sloping roofline to the eaves. Everything seems to be made on a miniature scale, so that I feel huge.

There are signs of disturbance: fingermarks on the dusty flaps of cardboard boxes and smudges on the floor where a trunk has been moved and pushed back into place. Subtle alterations. I picture Evie finding this place, going softly through the stillness and shadows. What was she looking for?

As I turn to leave, I notice how some of the boxes have been stacked to form a partition with a small gap in between. Crouching and peering into the space, I discover a nest, of sorts. Evie has spread a dust sheet over the floorboards perhaps as protection against splinters. She has added blankets and throw pillows, two bottles of water, a packet of dry biscuits, a volume of *Encyclopaedia Britannica*, letters G to H; and a collection of marbles and pieces of coloured glass.

Is this where she sleeps, I wonder. Do I frighten her that much?

The doorbell rings. My heart lifts.

I'm all the way at the top of the house and it takes an age to reach the front door. I pull it open, expecting to find Evie, but the man on my doorstep is an old family friend – or perhaps a friend for someone who has no family.

Jimmy Verbic pulls me into a bear hug and holds me for a beat longer than is comfortable. I can feel his breath on my ear and the smoothness of his unshaven cheek.

He lets me go.

'Dr Haven.'

'Councillor Verbic.'

'I hope you don't mind.'

'Not at all,' I say, unsure of why he's here.

Behind him I see two bulked-up minders whose bodies are shaped like port-a-loos and make their expensive suits look like sacks. Most politicians travel with PR types or chiefs of staff. Jimmy has muscle.

'I saw the light on.'

'Because you happened to be passing.'

'I know you're a night owl.'

He looks past me along the hallway.

'I like what you've done to the place. Shabby chic.'

'No, just shabby.'

With a nod of his head, he tells his minders to wait outside and wipes his expensive Italian shoes on my doormat. He's dressed in pleated trousers, an open neck shirt and blazer, each item matched to the other. I doubt if Jimmy has anything in his wardrobe that isn't stylish and colour coordinated, or perfect for the occasion.

Rich beyond counting, he has twice been mayor of Nottingham and otherwise served on numerous committees, boards and charitable foundations. He is Nottingham's man for all seasons, a churchgoer, philanthropist, politician, yachtsman, pilot and entrepreneur, with a finger in every pie and a toe in every jacuzzi.

Jimmy often boasts about his humble roots, growing up in a soot-stained pit village and losing his father to black lung disease, but there is nothing working class left about his lifestyle or his business interests, which include nightclubs, child care centres and a five-star hotel. Yet he possesses the common man's touch, able to chat to football fans on the terraces or hobnob with opera lovers at the Theatre Royal. I've seen him goal a slap shot from just over the blue line in a charity ice-hockey game; and hit a two-hundred-yard five-iron to within three feet at a golfing pro-am.

People say he's handsome, although I've always found him

to be slightly androgynous with his smooth egg-white skin and wet brown eyes. Now in his early sixties, he has escorted a string of beauties over the years, filling the society pages and gossip columns while remaining stubbornly single.

When my parents and sisters were killed, it was Jimmy who paid for the funerals and set up a trust fund for my education. He didn't know my family or me. He did it anyway. Perhaps he felt sorry for me, but so did everybody else. It was Jimmy who stepped up. As the caskets were wheeled from the cathedral, he put his arm around my skinny shoulders and said, 'If you ever need anything, Cyrus, you come to me. Understand?'

In the years that followed, he matched his words with actions, showing up at school speech days and my graduation from university, never acknowledging the fact, or seeking publicity. Most people say he's a good man and I have no reason to doubt that but having followed the fortunes of Nottingham over the years I have learned that Jimmy swings like a weathervane when it comes to having his convictions. He always follows the prevailing wind.

Although no longer the lord mayor, Jimmy is still a city councillor and the sheriff of Nottingham, a ceremonial position rather than a keeper of law and order. He greets tourists, poses for photographs and promotes the Robin Hood legend.

'How can I help you, Councillor?' I ask.

'Jimmy, please.'

We're in the kitchen. I offer him a drink. He refuses and examines the chair before sitting.

'It's been too long,' he says. 'I was trying to think. I last saw you at Easter.'

'The Parkinson's fundraiser.'

'That's the one. You're looking well. Working out, I see.'

Jimmy is an expert at small talk and I let him carry on, knowing this isn't a social call – not at this hour.

'One of my employees came to see me yesterday. He was rather upset by something you'd done.'

'Me?'

'I didn't want to believe him. It sounded so out of character.'

'Who are we talking about?'

'Dougal Sheehan.'

'I didn't know he worked for you.'

'He's my part-time driver and a valued employee. He's in shock, obviously. We all are. Jodie was such a lovely girl. Passionate. Pretty.'

'You knew her?' I say, keeping the surprise out of my voice.

'Didn't everyone?' he replies before realising how smart-alecky it sounds. 'Dougal introduced me,' he explains. 'Occasionally, we'd drop Jodie off at school in the Rolls. She thought that was great fun.'

'Did you see her skate?'

'Of course. I was one of her sponsors.'

'You gave her money?'

He shrugs. 'I paid some of her bills. Dougal and Maggie were very appreciative.' He looks at me askance. 'As you'll recall, I did the same for you after your family died. It's what I do, Cyrus. I help where I can.'

Jimmy lets the statement linger, as though wanting me to feel guilty for questioning his motives. I can't hold his gaze.

'Dougal is a broken man,' he explains. 'I don't know what to say to him, or how to ease his pain. But you can imagine my concern when he told me that Maggie came home from church in tears after a conversation with you. He said you were dragging Jodie's name through the mud.'

'That's not my intention.'

'What is your intention – if you don't mind me asking? A man has confessed to the crime. He's awaiting trial.'

'There is a question mark over whether Craig Farley acted alone.'

'You're saying he had an accomplice.'

'DNA evidence has raised the possibility.'

Jimmy smooths back his hair and his mouth narrows to a

tight pucker. I sense that he wants to frown, but his smooth white forehead refuses to buckle.

'Obviously, you have a job to do, Cyrus, but perhaps you could use a little more tact around Jodie's family.'

'Of course.'

Jimmy nods and smiles, as if his work here is done. Then he looks around the kitchen, noting the general state of disrepair.

'I heard a whisper about you the other day,' he says, catching a glimpse of his reflection in the window. 'You know I'm not one for gossip.'

I almost laugh. Jimmy sees the funny side as well.

'Somebody told me you had fostered a child.'

'Yes.'

'What made you do that?'

'She needed somewhere.'

He looks past me. 'Is she here?'

'She's asleep.'

'Well, that's very noble of you, Cyrus. I hope you haven't given up on the idea of having your own family some day. Are you seeing anyone?'

'No. Are you?'

Jimmy laughs properly, showing his white, perfectly aligned teeth. 'OK, OK, it's none of my business. I care about you, Cyrus. You're like a son to me.'

One of many, I want to say, but hold my tongue. I owe Jimmy a lot and he's never given me a reason to doubt him.

'Have you been to see Elias?' he asks.

'Not for a while.'

'You should keep in touch with him. He's family.'

All I have left, is what he means to say, but I don't need reminding. Not a day goes by when I don't relive some moment of that night. What I lost. What he took from me.

I follow Jimmy along the hallway to the front door, where his minders are standing like sentries on either side of the steps.

'Was Dougal Sheehan working for you on the night of the fireworks?' I ask.

'Yes, as a matter of fact. I had my annual Guy Fawkes soirée. Dougal was on hand to drive people home.'

'He didn't mention that to the police.'

Jimmy flashes me another smile. 'I expect my employees to be discreet.'

'What time did Dougal start work?'

'Around nine, I suppose.'

'Did you see him?'

'No.'

'Was he driving the Rolls?'

'Heavens no! I told him to use the Range Rover. I don't want drunken freeloaders throwing up on white calfskin seats.'

Jimmy opens his arms and hugs me again. 'We should have lunch. I'll call you.'

'I don't have a phone.'

'Of course you don't. You are an odd duck, Cyrus.'

One of the minders jogs ahead, checking the street before opening the door of a Rolls-Royce Silver Shadow. Jimmy slips inside. The door closes. As the car ghosts away, I remember the famous advertising slogan written in the fifties.

'At sixty miles an hour, the loudest noise in this new Rolls-Royce comes from the electric clock.'

40

Angel Face

I open my eyes. Clamped tightly in a foetal ball, I remain completely still, trying to place myself in the universe. I wiggle my fingers, stiff with the cold, then my toes. I flex my legs and arms. I move my tongue, tasting iron. Blood. I put my hand between my legs, touching my knickers. Relieved.

Raising my head, I bump something hard and cry out. My fingers brush against greasy metal. I'm lying beneath the chassis of a car, where I half remember crawling. Gasping shallowly, I pull myself along the ground until I'm clear of the vehicle and can see the sky. Bracing my hands on the gravel and broken concrete, I attempt to stand, but the pain finds parts of me that I didn't know existed. I stop. Lie still. Breathe.

I remember leaving the game with Katelyn and walking across the road, I picture her opening the car door . . . my head bouncing off the roof. Reaching into my coat pockets, I search for my winnings. Every pocket. Nothing.

Shit! Fuck!

I crawl back beneath the abandoned car, hoping I might have dropped the money, but I know the answer already.

A bile-like wretchedness fills my chest, rising up my throat, making me want to gag, but I cannot find enough saliva to spit it out. The feeling is familiar, this sense of desolation and helplessness. During all the weeks in the house with Terry's body and afterwards, I had always expected to die. I made plans to kill myself, taking a knife from the kitchen and choosing a spot on my chest that corresponded with the organ I could feel beating inside. Twice I held the knife in my hands when I heard them getting close to finding me. Even as I doubted my strength, I told myself I could do it. I promised. But when the time came, I couldn't bring myself to push the knife into my chest. Coward! Weakling!

I get slowly to my feet and stumble across the vacant lot until I reach a wire fence that has collapsed under the weight of a vine. Leaning against the mesh, I take ragged breaths and wonder if my ribs are broken. Could I be bleeding inside? The bump on my forehead feels like an egg beneath my skin.

I have no money, no phone, nowhere to go. I think about Cyrus. He'll have searched my room by now. He'll have knocked on my door and waited for permission to enter, worried that I might be half-dressed or that I wouldn't hear his knock because I was plugged into my music. He'll have searched my things, looking for clues. How long will he wait before he calls the police?

Straightening again, I walk gingerly along the road towards a railway bridge. Street lights are burning palely, floating in air the colour of dirty water. A truck rumbles past. A taxi slows. I feel like a figure from an earlier time – a street urchin, or waif, destined for the poor house, or a prostitute forced to walk the streets. I often picture myself like this – in other guises, living other possible lives. Sometimes I'm famous like Meghan Markle or Taylor Swift but more often I'm famously tragic like Amy Winehouse or Marilyn Monroe.

Halfway across the bridge, I place my palms on the stained brick wall and watch a freight train pass beneath me, louder then softer, shaking the world. I have fucked up big time. I have no money or means of escape. Nowhere to go. How much will it cost to get to London? Maybe I could steal the money or beg for loose change.

The bus station is in York Street near the Victoria Centre, which is an indoor shopping mall, full of department stores, boutiques, cafés and food halls, none of which are open at this hour of the morning. The station concourse is brightly lit and dotted with the sleeping bodies of backpackers resting on rucksacks, and the homeless, whose possessions are stuffed into plastic bags or piled in trolleys. A bus for London leaves at four-thirty and another at five. I could be in London by nine o'clock . . . if I had ten pounds.

I go to the ladies and examine myself in the mirror. Apart from the bump on my head, my face avoided the worst of the beating. I can hide the bruise with my fringe.

A woman enters. Our eyes meet in the mirror. She's middle-aged, wearing jeans and canvas shoes and a bulky sweater. Her lank hair has been dyed so often that her natural colour is a distant memory. She enters a cubicle and locks the door.

'Excuse me,' I say. 'Can you lend us a tenner? My mum is real sick and I need to get to London.'

The woman doesn't answer.

'I lost my purse. I think someone stole it.'

'I can't help you,' the woman says.

'It's only ten quid.'

'How do I know you're not a junkie?'

'I'm not.'

'Yeah, but I don't know that.'

'Junkies don't normally dress like me.'

'You could be a hooker.'

'If I was a hooker I wouldn't need to borrow money.'

'Oh, so you're borrowing now.'

'I'll pay you back.'

'Yeah, sure.'

She flushes the toilet. The cubicle door opens. This time she's holding a can of something in her fist, pointing it at my face. 'Come anywhere near me and you'll get this,' she says, waving the aerosol.

'That's deodorant,' I say.

'No, it's pepper spray.'

'I can read the brand name. It says Dove.'

Clutching a tote bag to her chest, the woman skirts the sinks, keeping her eyes on me. The zip of her jeans is still undone.

'Are you going to wash your hands?' I yell, but the woman has gone.

Back on the concourse, I approach the ticket office where a middle-aged man is putting new paper in a printer.

'Won't be a second, love,' he says, snapping the lid shut and pressing a button to make the paper feed through a slot.

Short and thickset, he's wearing a uniform that is so tight across his stomach that the fabric gapes between the buttons, showing his white singlet.

'How can I help you?'

'I need a ticket to London.'

'Return?'

'One way.'

He looks up at the screen. 'There's one leaving in ten minutes. I have three seats left.'

'I'll take one.'

He rings up the register. 'That'll be nine-fifty.'

'I don't have any money.'

He sighs rather than frowns.

'I'm really good at telling when someone is lying,' I say.

'That's a coincidence – so am I.'

'No, I'm being serious. Test me.'

'Get lost.'

'Tell me something true or false and I'll tell you if you're lying.'

'I'm not here to play games.'

I notice the drawer of the cash register is open. 'Look at a banknote. Don't show me. Tell me the last digit of the serial number. I'll say if you're lying or not.'

The clerk looks past me, wondering if this is some sort of scam. He picks up a ten-pound note.

'What's the last number?' I ask.

'Seven.'

'That's true. Try another.'

'The first number is a zero.'

'No.'

I grow more confident. 'If I get the next two right – will you give me a ticket to London?'

The clerk doesn't reply. He examines the note more carefully. 'The fourth digit is a nine.'

'Can you look at me when you say that?'

'What?'

'I need to see your face.'

'What difference does that make?'

'It's not a nine,' I say, feeling my chance slipping away.

He sighs heavily down his nostrils. 'Step back from the window.'

'What! No! I'm right.'

'I think you had a friend come in earlier who gave me that tenner after you'd memorised the serial number.'

'I don't have a friend. Pick another note. Test me.'

'Step away or I'll call the police.' He reaches for the phone.

I retreat angrily, as if robbed all over again. Finding an empty row of seats, I hug my knees, feeling the pain in my back where a boot must have landed. Cyrus will have called the police by now. They'll be looking for me. I'll be sent back to Langford Hall or some worse place. I should get away from the bus station. It's one of the first places they'll look.

'Hello there,' says a voice.

I brace myself, ready to run. A young man is grinning at me. He's holding two cans of Coca-Cola. 'I thought you looked thirsty.' He holds one out to me.

I eye him warily, as he pops the lid of his can and drinks. His Adam's apple bobs as he swallows and looks like a tiny animal trapped in his throat. Tall and thin, he has mutton-chop sideburns that crawl down his cheeks but seem to run out of energy before they reach his chin.

'I'm Felix,' he says, belching quietly. 'What's your name?'

'Does it matter?'

'Not to me.' He laughs, showing a chipped front tooth. 'You could be Queen Nefertiti for all I care.'

'Who?'

'She was one of the most beautiful women who's ever lived. An Egyptian queen. Married to a Pharaoh. That's what Nefertiti means – a beautiful woman to come.'

'How come you know so much about Egypt?'

'A past life,' Felix laughs. 'Hey, you hungry? I know this place down the road that opens early for breakfast. They make proper French pastries, you know, pain aux raisins and pain au chocolat. One sniff and you'll swear you were in Paris.'

'I've never been to Paris.'

'All the more reason . . .'

I open the can of drink. The cold liquid feels good sliding down my throat and the sugar charges through my veins, shaking exhaustion away. I spend a fraction too long gazing at Felix, wondering why he doesn't look in the mirror and see the absurdity of his facial hair.

'Can you lend me ten pounds? I need to get to London.'

'Going to meet your boyfriend?'

'No.'

'Family?'

'I don't have any.'

This answer seems to please Felix. 'I can't just give you the money,' he says thoughtfully. 'But you could earn it.'

I look at him warily. 'I'm not fucking you.'

'Keep it down,' he whispers, glancing over his shoulder. 'Nobody said anything about fucking anyone.'

'What do I have to do?'

'Let's discuss it over breakfast.'

'I can't afford breakfast.'

'That's OK. I'm buying.'

41

At some point I tumble into an exhausted sleep, full of shadowy dreams and images of Jodie Sheehan floating in a pond or lying half-naked in a clearing, surrounded by trees. My mind's eye moves closer, zooming in from above, down through the branches, coming into focus until it settles on a face that belongs to a different girl.

I sit bolt upright, unable to draw breath; a scream is stuck in my throat. But I'm not awake. I'm dreaming of being in a dream. Evie is standing in front of me, by the side of the bed. I can almost touch her. She is holding a pack of cards, shuffling them, asking me to play a game.

'If you win you get to ask me a question.'

'What's your real name?'

'Not that one.'

'Are you coming home?'

'Where's home?'

My pager buzzes on the bedside table. Reaching for it too quickly, I send it clattering to the floor and the battery dislodges. I go searching on my hands and knees, collecting the pieces, putting it back together.

Robert Ness has left me his number. I get dressed and put on my coat, before walking to the corner shop. The front door jangles and Mrs Patel smiles from behind the counter. Her long grey hair is plaited down the back of her bright green and gold sari.

'Good morning, Dr Haven.'

'Please call me Cyrus.'

'Sorry. I keep forgetting.'

'I think you do it on purpose.'

She smiles again, before handing me a cordless phone.

Mrs Patel, a widow, has two daughters, one studying medicine at Edinburgh University and the other doing her A levels. In all the years I've known the family, I've never seen Sonny and Bittu playing in the street like other kids. They were always at school, or studying, or working behind the counter of the shop, which opens at seven every morning and doesn't close until late. Mr Patel, an alcoholic, died of a heart attack a decade ago and it took four paramedics to carry his body down the narrow stairs. I never saw him behind the counter.

I make the call. Robert Ness picks up on the first ring.

'When are you going to get a phone?'

'Why, do you want to sext me?'

'Very droll,' says Ness. I can hear him sipping a coffee. 'The lab in America has managed to pull DNA from foetal matter in Jodie Sheehan's womb. The results will take another few days, but they can rule out Farley.'

'He's not really boyfriend material. What does Lenny say?'

'She can't look past the confession,' says Ness. 'And I can see her point. I mean, the idea of a second perpetrator makes it harder to get a conviction.'

'Jodie could have had consensual sex earlier in the evening.'

'Yes.'

'We should be looking for a boyfriend.'

'Or leaving it well alone.'

'What if I'm right?'

'You'll still be wrong.' He laughs and keeps talking. 'The condoms you found in Jodie's locker. We pulled a full thumb print. The computer found a match – her uncle, Bryan Whitaker.'

'What did Lenny make of that?'

'She wants to put all men in a sack and drown them. Apart from you, of course – her golden boy.'

'Get lost!'

'Happy to.'

Ness hangs up and I hand the phone to Mrs Patel. I offer to pay but she waves me away. I buy a carton of milk instead.

'I met your cousin the other day,' she says, with an inflection in her voice.

'Who?'

'Evie. She seemed very nice. She said she was visiting.'

'Oh.'

'She came in to buy turpentine to clean her paint brushes. Is she going to be staying long?'

'I don't think so.'

'Shame. You should fill that big house. Find a wife. Start a family.'

I smile and nod, aware that she's only half-teasing me.

Lenny is sitting outside the house, with her car door open, listening to the radio and tilting her face up to the weak sunshine filtering through the branches.

'Nobody answered,' she says. 'I thought I might meet your new house guest.'

'She's sleeping,' I reply, amazed at how easily the lie rolls off my tongue.

'How is she settling in?'

'Good. Fine.'

I should tell Lenny. Perhaps she could make some discreet enquiries. That way I'd know if Evie was lying unconscious in a hospital bed, or languishing in a police cell, or worse. But I can't ask Lenny to keep a secret like this – it wouldn't be fair

255

or professional. And there's still time for Evie to come home. Once I report her missing, it will be out of my hands.

Lenny is watching me, puzzled by my silence. 'Are you OK?'

'Yeah. I just need a coffee.' I hold up the carton of milk.

'No time,' she says, unlocking the passenger side door.

'Where are we going?'

'We enhanced the CCTV footage of Jodie Sheehan when she was outside the fish and chip shop in Southchurch Drive. A reflection in the shop window gave us a partial plate and model of the car that picked her up: a Peugeot 207. Turns out a teacher at her school has that same model and plate. Her form tutor – Ian Hendricks.'

'Why didn't he say anything?'

'Exactly.'

Lenny pulls out, accelerating between each gear change. A second unmarked police car, three-up with plain-clothed detectives, slots in behind us.

'What do we know about Hendricks?' I ask.

'Married. Three kids. Wife pregnant with a fourth. No priors, not even a speeding ticket. According to the school trustees he's a rising star. Popular with his students and his colleagues.'

A school bus pulls out in front of us and chugs gently forward until the next stop. Schoolkids jostle to get on board, some staring at mobile phones, or plugged into earbuds.

Lenny is still talking.

'Hendricks graduated from Leeds University in 2011 and transitioned to teaching two years later. He's been at Forsyth Academy since 2014 working in the English department and taking religious education classes.'

'The righteous ones are the biggest hypocrites.'

'What about the liars?'

'Them too.'

The two-storey bungalow looks like a cookie-cutter version of every other dwelling in the cul-de-sac. Signs urge motorists to slow down because children are ahead. This is also evident from the turning circle, which has become a playground full of ramps, hopscotch grids and an obstacle course made from orange traffic cones and garbage bins.

At least a dozen youngsters are playing outside, some waiting to be taken to school and others too young to be institutionalised. They're riding an assortment of bicycles and tricycles and scooters, beneath a large, laminated 'Neighbourhood Watch' sign.

Lenny presses the door buzzer and glances at her feet where the doormat reads, THIS HOUSE RUNS ON COFFEE AND JESUS.

A woman answers. She's holding a toddler on her right hip and has a familiar bulge beneath her sweater. Her curly hair is cut too short for hair clips so that stray locks have fallen across her eyes. She puffs her cheeks and blows them away.

'Can I help you?'

'I'm Detective Chief Inspector Parvel, this is Dr Cyrus Haven. Is your husband at home?'

Her forehead creases just above the bridge of her nose. Two young boys sprint up the front path, pushing past us and grabbing at her thighs, afraid of missing out. Both are dressed in school uniforms and have their hair neatly combed, parted on the left.

'Ian is about to leave for work,' she says, glancing above her. 'Can this wait?'

'No, I'm sorry,' says Lenny, apologetically.

The sound of an electric keyboard reverberates from upstairs, thumping out chords to a rock beat.

'I'm Cathy, by the way,' she says, showing us to a front room while her oldest boy is sent to fetch his father. He sprints up the stairs. Moments later, the music stops.

'Ian plays in a band at the church,' she explains.

'What church is that?' I ask.

'Trent Vineyard.'

I know the place. It's one of those newer churches where

Christianity comes with a light show and pumping rock music in a cavernous warehouse on an industrial estate in Lenton. Thousands of people show up every Sunday, praising the Lord and opening their wallets because salvation is available on a weekly payment plan – all credit cards accepted.

Ian Hendricks appears behind her, looking concerned, yet greeting us warmly.

'I'll take the boys to school,' Cathy says, shooing them into the hallway where she wrestles them into coats and scarves. We can hear her talking. 'Daddy is busy. Yes, the police . . . No, nothing is wrong.'

Hendricks smiles tiredly.

'Do you remember us?' asks Lenny.

'Yes, of course. You're DCI Parvel and . . .?' He clicks his fingers, trying to remember me.

'Cyrus Haven,' I say.

'Yes, that's right. The psychologist.'

Lenny unbuttons her overcoat, letting it flare out as she settles into an armchair.

'What car do you drive, Mr Hendricks?'

'We have a Honda Odyssey – a seven-seater.'

'Do you also own a Peugeot 207?'

'That's my wife's car.'

'Were you driving a Peugeot 207 on the night of the fireworks?'

Hendricks hesitates. 'To be honest I can't remember.'

'You went to the fireworks.'

'Yes, but we left early. Tristan had a temperature. We brought him home.'

'But you went out again.'

Hendricks's tongue pokes out, looking to moisten his top lip, but can't find the spit. I can see him trying to work out how much Lenny knows.

'I went to get fish and chips for dinner.'

'In Southchurch Drive?'

'Yes.'

Lenny waits.

Hendricks breaks. 'I bumped into Jodie Sheehan. She was outside on the footpath. I offered her a lift home. There were lots of young lads roaming about. Some of them were drunk. Rowdy. I thought it wasn't safe.'

'Why didn't you tell us this earlier?' asks Lenny.

Hendricks seems to gaze past us helplessly. 'I didn't think it was important. I mean, you'd already arrested someone, so I knew . . . I didn't want to . . .'

'Get involved.'

He nods, searching for understanding.

'We hadn't arrested Craig Farley when we spoke to you,' says Lenny.

'I knew it wouldn't look good. Teachers aren't supposed to fraternise with students outside of school.'

'By fraternise you mean . . .?'

'Be alone with them.'

'But you ignored the rules.'

'We were only talking.'

'Alone in your car.'

'I know it's frowned upon, but Jodie was different. She'd come along to our church a few times.'

'At your invitation?'

'Yes.'

'Why?'

He takes a moment to collect his thoughts. 'I knew Jodie was struggling with things. She was exhausted, what with her training, travelling and competing. She wasn't allowed to go to parties or to have a boyfriend.'

'She told you this?'

Hendricks nods. 'I thought that maybe she might find some answers, if she talked to Jesus.'

'You were trying to convert her.'

'We don't convert people – we embrace them.'

'Did you *embrace* Jodie Sheehan?'

'Not like that. I don't appreciate what you're insinuating.'

'Did Jodie ever write notes to you?' I ask, remembering the valentine card we discovered in her school locker.

'No.'

'Did she send you a valentine?'

He falls silent.

'Did you give her one?'

'No, of course not.'

'I can see how these schoolgirl crushes can happen. It must have been flattering.'

'Nothing happened!'

'You're young and good-looking. You're took an interest in her. You listened.'

'I was tutoring her.'

'Because she fell behind?'

'Yes.'

'You gave her more attention in class – called on her first.'

Hendricks is shaking his head.

'Soon you were sharing private jokes and secret smiles and stray touches. You told her she was special. You found excuses to be alone with her. If only you were ten years younger, you said.'

'Stop it!' the teacher whispers. 'I'm a Christian.'

'So was Myra Hindley,' Lenny says, 'and Peter Sutcliffe.'

'I can't help it if she had a crush on me,' says Hendricks. 'I gave her spiritual advice, that's all. As God is my witness.'

'Do you need God as a witness?' I ask.

'It's a figure of speech.'

He drops his head into his hands. I can see the top of his scalp, where faint traces of dandruff cling to the parting in his hair.

'Were you sleeping with her?'

'Never! I wouldn't.' His voice has risen in pitch.

'Did Jodie tell you she was pregnant?'

The teacher's head snaps up and fear sparks in his eyes. 'What? No!'

Lenny reaches into her jacket pocket and retrieves a small sealed plastic tube with a cotton bud inside. At the same time, she takes out a pair of latex gloves.

'Have you ever heard of Locard's Exchange Principle, Mr Hendricks?'

Hendricks shakes his head.

'It holds that every perpetrator of a crime will leave something at the crime scene and take something away from it. It could be soil, fibres, semen, skin cells or a single strand of hair. Wherever they step, or whatever they touch, they cross-contaminate.'

Lenny unscrews the lid of the plastic container.

'What are you doing?' asks Hendricks.

'Collecting a DNA sample. Science is going to put Jodie in your car. Science may also find your semen on her body and your baby in her womb.'

'That's crazy! I'm a happily married man. A father. I would never . . . I didn't . . . We talked, is all. Nothing happened.' His voice has a pathetic wheedling quality.

'Open your mouth.'

'No.'

'Are you refusing to co-operate?'

'I want a lawyer.'

Lenny sighs in disgust. 'In my experience, conscientious teachers don't ask for lawyers and refuse DNA tests. Conscientious teachers rarely lose their jobs – unless they're sleeping with a student.'

Hendricks takes a moment to weigh up his choices, before allowing Lenny to swab the inside of his mouth.

His wife has returned from the school drop-off. Her toddler is rugged up in a colourful coat that makes her look like a beach ball with limbs. Outside two men in overalls are winching a rust-streaked Peugeot 207 up the sloping ramp of a truck with a police insignia on the doors.

'That's my car!' she exclaims.

'It's all right, Cathy, they have a warrant,' says Hendricks.

'It's that girl, isn't it?' she says.

'Did you know Jodie Sheehan?' I ask.

'She came to our church.'

'Did you see her at the fireworks?'

'No.'

'Your husband has told us that he borrowed your car that night and picked up Jodie Sheehan,' says Lenny.

Cathy Hendricks glances coldly at her husband and something passes between them.

'What time did he get home?' asks Lenny.

'I can't remember.'

'I thought he was getting fish and chips for dinner.'

She struggles to find an answer. 'Tristan had a temperature. I put him into our bed and fell asleep.'

'Where did your husband sleep?'

'In the boys' room.' She fixes her husband with a stare that doesn't need translation.

'I gave her a lift, that's all,' says Hendricks. 'It was a mistake, but nothing happened. I didn't . . . I wouldn't . . .'

Cathy hoists the toddler higher on her right hip and turns away, carrying the child deeper into the house. With that last gesture, I recognise a woman who favours castrating her husband rather than giving him an alibi.

Unless . . .

Unless . . .

The Peugeot is Cathy's car. What if she went looking for Jodie that night and her husband is covering for her? A mother of three, pregnant with a fourth, has a powerful reason to protect her family, particularly from a pretty teenage girl with a crush on her teacher. One rumour, one allegation, and Jodie Sheehan could unpick the seams of Cathy's perfect life and leave her marriage in tatters.

Ian Hendricks is standing on the front path watching the wheels of the Peugeot being chocked and chained.

'You didn't just talk to Jodie. You gave her a lift,' says Lenny.

Hendricks doesn't answer.

'Where did you take her?'

'She got a message on her phone and asked me if I could drop her off.'

'Where?'

'An address in the city – a house in The Ropewalk.'

Lenny and I exchange glances.

'Could you find the house again?' she asks.

'I think so.'

Lenny points to her car. 'Get in.'

'But I have to be at work.'

'You can be late.'

42

Angel Face

The café smells of sugar and cinnamon. I finish two pains aux raisins and two milky coffees, trying to ignore Felix, who is watching me eat and smiling like it gives him pleasure. Maybe he's a feeder and he's looking for some fat chick to stuff like a foie gras goose. Well, that's not me.

He talks constantly without saying anything – making observations about people, or the weather, or the traffic beginning to build up outside, or the homeless guy washing windscreens with an old Evian bottle and a squeegee.

'What's your name?' he asks, having cleaned up my crumbs.

'Does it matter?'

'I have to call you something.'

'Evie.'

I notice the scars on his knuckles and the heavy silver necklace dangling against his hairless chest.

'OK, that's a start. Now what do you want, Evie?'

'I want to go to London.'

'OK. And then what?'

'That's my business.'

'Yeah, of course.' He leans back and lifts his foot onto a chair

between us. 'But without money — you won't get very far. Ten quid is a bus ticket — then what? How will you live? You can't sleep in a park. It's not safe — not for a girl. Not for anyone.'

'I'll find a job.'

'You don't have any work clothes. No phone. No plan. The police will find you and send you back home. I'm assuming you don't want to go home.'

I don't say anything. Felix scratches his cheek.

'Most people want something, Evie. A nice house. A flash car. Holidays in the sun. Love. Money.' He is watching my face, as though waiting for the wheels on a fruit machine to stop spinning and tell him if he's hit the jackpot. 'Sometimes they just want to be safe. Me? I want respect. Independence. I want to make more of myself than my old man did.'

'What does he do?' I ask.

'That doesn't matter. You have nowhere to stay, am I right?'

Again, no answer.

'That bruise on your forehead says that someone messed you up. I won't let that happen to you.'

'I don't need your protection.'

'I think you do. I think you should stay with me. You'll have your own room, your own bed, somewhere warm. And two weeks from now I'll give you a bus ticket to London and a thousand quid.'

'What do I have to do?'

'Work for me.'

'Doing what?'

'Running errands.'

'Drugs?'

'No. I supply dietary supplements, steroids, vitamins and other pick-me-ups.'

The lie just trips off his tongue.

'You're a drug dealer,' I say.

'Why get bogged down in semantics?' he replies. 'Let's just say that not all of my product is available over the counter, which is why I require discretion.'

'What's discretion?'

'Secrecy. I deal with a lot of professional people – solicitors, bankers, architects, even politicians. They pay on time and they keep their mouths shut.'

'What do I have to do?'

'Deliver the stuff. I pay your cab fares and provide you with a phone. How old are you?'

'Seventeen.'

'Good.'

'Why?'

'You're still a minor, which means if the police pick you up, you won't get charged, or the judge will likely set you free because you're just a kid.'

'I don't want to be arrested.'

'And you won't be, I promise.'

Another lie.

'You don't have to make your mind up now. Come back to my place. See your room. Clean up. Get some sleep. If you decide tomorrow that you're not interested, I'll give you the ten quid. No hard feelings.'

Does he ever tell the truth?

Felix talks as we walk, escorting me to the multi-storey parking garage where he unlocks a four-wheel-drive Lexus that is parked in a space set aside for disabled drivers. He opens the passenger door, but I refuse to get in until he moves away. Parking tickets are balled up on the floor next to empty soft drink cans, fast food wrappers and advertising flyers.

'The seats are heated. You can adjust the temperature,' says Felix, reaching across to show me. I rear away, balling my fists.

'OK, OK. I get the message. So, who beat you up?'

'I don't want to talk about it.'

'Suit yourself.'

Felix drives to impress me, swerving in and out of traffic, jumping lights and tailgating slower cars.

'Do you often pick up girls at the bus station?' I ask.

'It's a good place to recruit.'

'I'm not a volunteer.'

'Course not. You're an employee. But you were lucky I found you first. It could have been the Pakis or Bangladeshis. They look for strays and runaways. White girls mainly. First, they give you a burger, then it's drugs and alcohol. Next thing you're strapped to a bed, fucking every cousin and uncle from here to Birmingham!'

He's not lying this time.

The car pulls up outside a derelict-looking building with a broken sign that says COACH HOUSE INN. A tattered flag flaps from a flagpole and a sign on the cyclone fence warns, 'Trespassers Will Be Prosecuted'.

'I know it doesn't look like much,' says Felix, 'but you can't judge a book by its cover, you know.'

That's the only way I judge books, I think.

He ducks through a gap in the fence and pulls back a sheet of corrugated iron, revealing a door with a keypad entrance that looks out of place given the state of the building.

Felix punches in the code, trying to shield the keypad with his body, but I clock the number anyway: 4.9.5.2.

'Is this where you live?'

'Nah, I got my own place.'

'Who lives here?'

'People like you.'

We enter a lobby area littered with broken furniture and smashed ceiling tiles. The walls have been tagged with graffiti or spray-painted with pictures of male and female anatomy. Someone or something has defecated in the corner, creating a smell that makes me want to gag. Corridors run off in three different directions. Felix leads me along one of them until the stench starts to fade. He nudges open a door with his foot.

'This can be your gaff.'

I peer inside. The low-wattage bulb barely casts a shadow. The room is shabby and neat, with a bed, a nightstand, a table and chair. The carpet is scarred by cigarette burns and the bedspread is a faded green with a yellow fleck; at least I hope it's a fleck. In my imagination, I picture how many thousands of people have stayed here, and the acts of desperation that have been performed on the mattress; the humping bodies, warm corpses, lonely travellers, tourists, cheating spouses, sales reps and battered wives who have cried themselves to sleep holding their children.

The adjoining bathroom has a toilet, sink and shower. Pulling open the rear curtains, I look out onto a wrecker's yard full of rusting car bodies and piles of twisted metal. Beyond another fence is a factory full of metal shipping containers stacked in rows.

I glance down at a pile of clothes on the bathroom floor: ripped jeans and cheap blouses and a Mickey Mouse jacket with silver spangles threaded around Mickey's ears.

'Whose room is this?'

'She's gone.'

'Why did she leave her stuff?'

Felix shrugs. 'Maybe I gave her too much money. Maybe she stole from me.' He looks at the pile. 'You're welcome to her gear.'

I shake my head.

'Suit yourself.' Felix scoops up the clothes and tosses them into the hallway.

'Is that you, baby?' asks a high-pitched voice, before an emaciated girl-woman dashes into the room and throws herself at Felix, who catches her and takes a step backwards, carried by her momentum. Her legs wrap around his waist, her arms around his neck. She's dressed in jeans and a bra. She tries to kiss him. Felix turns his face away. 'Your breath reeks.'

'I been sleeping.'

The girl-woman notices me for the first time. 'What's she doing here?'

'This is Evie.'

'You said we didn't need nobody else.'

'Anybody,' says Felix, correcting her.

The girl-woman frowns with eyes that are black rimmed and hollow, as if her skull were collapsing. She could be anywhere from twelve to thirty, with sharp hipbones sticking out from above the waist of her jeans and no discernible breasts.

'This is Keeley,' says Felix.

'We're together,' says Keeley, holding onto Felix. There are bruises along her arms and more on her neck.

'Did you bring me something?' she asks in a pleading voice. 'Baby wants her medicine.'

'Later,' he says dismissively. 'We have company.'

'But you promised.'

'I said later!'

Keeley drops off him like he's raised a fist. Instead he reaches into his pocket and pulls out a wad of cash, peeling off several twenties. 'Go buy some food. And get Evie a toothbrush.'

'Why me?'

'Because I asked you nicely.'

Keeley doesn't want to leave. Felix gives her a look and she grudgingly obeys, shooting me daggers on her way out. I'm still thinking about the money Felix had in his pocket.

He turns in a slow circle. 'Home sweet home. I know it's not much, but it beats lying in the gutter. The shower works if you want to freshen up. There's no kitchen, but Keeley has a microwave in her room. Either that, or you can get takeaway.'

'Where are you going?' I ask.

'To see my dear old mum.'

'You said I could earn some money.'

'Yeah, sure, but it's too early in the day. Deliveries are mostly at night.'

'What do I do until then?'

'Sleep. You look like shit.'

I want to a make a smartarse comment back at him, but I can't think of one because I'm too tired.

Not everything Felix has told me has been the truth, but that makes him like everybody else – not to be trusted. Right now, I don't have many choices. I need somewhere to stay, and money to start again and this is the only game in town.

43

Lenny is on speakerphone with DS Edgar asking about Jodie Sheehan's burner phone.

'There were thousands of people at the fireworks and most of them were carrying phones,' says Edgar. 'It's like looking for a needle in a haystack.'

'This might help,' says Lenny. 'Jodie was picked up by Ian Hendricks from outside the fish and chip shop that Monday evening. He claims he dropped her at a house on The Ropewalk at nine-thirty. If we isolate signals from those locations, we should be able to identify which phone Jodie was using.'

'What was she doing at The Ropewalk?' asks Edgar.

'Ask me later. We're heading there now.'

The call ends and Lenny follows signs towards the city centre. Ian Hendricks has been quiet in the back seat but grows more animated as we get closer to The Ropewalk – an upmarket area full of grand Victorian houses, many of which have been converted into flats or turned into offices for accountants and solicitors. A few private houses remain, lovingly restored and harking back to a time when horse-drawn carriages clip-clopped over cobblestones carrying women in whalebone corsets and men in frock coats.

'That's the place,' says Hendricks, leaning between the seats.

We've stopped outside an imposing cream-coloured house that looks like an iced wedding cake.

'Are you sure?' Lenny asks.

'Yeah. I dropped her at the gates and she walked up the driveway to the side door. The place was all lit up – like they were having a party. Cars were parked up and down the road.'

'I know this house,' I say, surprising both of them. 'It belongs to Jimmy Verbic.'

'The mayor!' says Lenny.

'He's the sheriff of Nottingham now.'

Her forehead creases as though an invisible hand is squeezing her skin. 'Why would Jodie Sheehan come here?'

'Her father works for Jimmy as a driver.'

'He didn't mention that in his statement.'

Lenny gets out of the car and signals to the detectives who have been following in a second vehicle.

'Take Mr Hendricks to his place of work.'

The schoolteacher gets out of one police car and into another. Lenny isn't finished.

'Don't think you're off the hook, Mr Hendricks. You could still be charged with withholding information from a murder investigation.'

'All I did was drop her off. I promise.'

The second vehicle pulls away. Lenny and I are standing on the footpath. She turns and gazes through the iron gates at the grand house, muttering, 'Jimmy Verbic.'

'We're only talking to him,' I say, sensing her disquiet.

'Councillor Verbic and the chief constable are best mates. They go on golfing tours together and salmon-fishing weekends. For all I know they swap wives.'

'Jimmy isn't married.'

'You know what I mean.'

As if someone has been eavesdropping, the gates suddenly begin to move, sliding open on a chain. A Mercedes sports car turns the corner and approaches, pulling into the driveway. I catch a glimpse of a young woman behind the wheel, wearing oversized sunglasses and a scarf tied loosely around her neck.

We follow the Mercedes through the closing gates and watch it pull up at the front of the house. One elegant white-linen clad leg emerges, then another, both sporting high heels. She bends back into the car to collect polished paper shopping bags. Louis Vuitton and Cartier. Hearing our approach, she straightens and props her sunglasses on her forehead. She's in her mid-twenties, tall and slim, with a proud countenance. She smiles.

'You're Cyrus Haven.'

'How did you know?'

'Jimmy talks about you all the time. He has a photograph of you in his study.'

'And you are?'

'Scarlet.' She holds out her hand as though I might want to kiss it. Her face is almost impossible to read. Beautiful yes, but somehow bland, as though she's been photoshopped or airbrushed in a glossy magazine.

'Is the councillor home?' I ask.

'He should be.'

As if summoned, Jimmy appears, jogging down marble steps beneath an arched porte cochère.

He embraces me, smiling. 'Cyrus! What an unexpected surprise.'

There is a subtext to his use of the words 'unexpected' and 'surprise', meaning unbidden, or without warning.

I introduce Jimmy to Lenny.

'Yes, of course, DCI Parvel. You were in charge of the Jodie Sheehan investigation. Job well done – making such a quick arrest. I rang the chief constable personally to pass on my congratulations.'

Was that a name drop?

Jimmy slips his arm around Scarlet's waist and gives her a squeeze. 'Have you been spending my money again?'

'It's your mother's birthday next week. You would have forgotten.'

'She's right,' says Jimmy, laughing. 'Scarlet is my PA, my Girl Friday, my walking Filofax.'

'What's a Filofax?' she asks.

Jimmy laughs again and says, 'old technology', which annoys her. I can see it in her hips when she marches into the house, her heels clicking up the steps.

'Where did you find Scarlet?' I ask.

'My sister sent her along. Have you met Genevieve?'

'No.'

'She runs an employment agency in Manchester.'

'Are you sure it's not a modelling agency?'

'Yes, she is rather easy on the eyes.' Jimmy smiles mischievously. 'I know I mentioned getting together, Cyrus, but you could have given me some warning.'

'It's a business call,' says Lenny. 'We've received information that Jodie Sheehan visited this house on the night she was killed.'

'Here!'

'Yes.'

'Who told you that?'

'I'm not in a position to reveal that information.'

Jimmy looks at me, hoping I might help him. His smile has slowly been dismantled in a series of adjustments to his facial muscles. He still comes across as affable, but in a more menacing way.

'Pardon my scepticism, DCI Parvel, but this sounds like a crude attempt to smear me. In politics you grow accustomed to cheap shots and malicious gossip. I hope that Nottinghamshire Police haven't fallen into a trap like that.'

All hint of warmth has gone.

'You had a celebration that night,' I say, trying to ease the tension.

'My Guy Fawkes party. I have one every year. I can assure you that Jodie Sheehan wasn't on the guest list.'

'How many people were here?' asks Lenny.

'Two hundred, although it felt like more.'

'Did you know everyone at the party?'

'Dear me, no. The hangers-on and freeloaders come out when there's an open bar.'

'But you have a guest list.'

Jimmy smiles wryly. 'Some of the attendees were very prominent people who might not appreciate being questioned by the police on some frivolous fishing expedition.'

'A girl was raped and murdered.'

'And someone has confessed.' Jimmy turns out his palms. 'Why are you here, detective? You've made an arrest. Held the press conference. Received the kudos.'

'There are some gaps in Jodie's timeline.'

'Gaps. I see. Well, if politics has taught me anything, it is how easily gaps can be filled with misinformation, particularly by the media, who seem to love conflating random harmless details and smearing innocent people in the process.'

I half expect him to use the term 'fake news', but mercifully he stops talking. Lenny glances at me, understanding the inference.

'What's through those doors?' I ask, pointing to the side of the house.

'The kitchens.'

'Who looks after them?'

'Rowena, our housekeeper, but we had caterers that night. A local firm.'

Scarlet emerges from inside, having changed into faded jeans and a loose-fitting top. She's holding some sort of fruit smoothie in a tall glass and still wearing her sunglasses.

'Did you see Jodie Sheehan on the night of the party?' I ask.

'Who?'

'The girl who was murdered,' Jimmy says.

'Dougal's daughter.'

Jimmy's face seems to register the information as though he's solved a problem that has vexed him for hours. 'That's right! Dougal was working. Jodie must have been looking for him.' He glances from Lenny's face to mine, waiting for us to agree.

'Any idea why?' I ask.

'Maybe she wanted a lift home.'

I'm concentrating on Scarlet, who seems to be dredging up memories from wherever she stores them.

'There was someone who turned up at the kitchen door. One of the caterers came and found me. He said a girl was looking for someone at the party. She wouldn't give a name. She wanted to wait for a text message. I told her to leave.'

'You *saw* her?'

'No. I told the caterers to tell her.'

Jimmy makes an exasperated sound, suddenly less certain than before. 'Who is this witness?' he asks, sceptically.

'The person who drove Jodie here and watched her walk through the gates,' replies Lenny, studying Jimmy's reaction. 'For the record, when did you last see Jodie Sheehan?'

'Not that night.'

'When?'

'A few weeks ago. Dougal asked me to be Jodie's sponsor. I covered some of her travel expenses; a few grand here and there.'

'How did you pay the money?' asks Lenny.

'Directly to Dougal. But I told Jodie that if she ever needed anything she should come and see me.'

The statement resonates deep within me. Jimmy made the same promise as we watched the caskets of my parents and my sisters being wheeled from the cathedral. He had no ulterior motive. It's what he does.

'Is Dougal Sheehan working today?' asks Lenny.

Jimmy glances towards a four-car garage where two of the doors are open.

'Please don't harass a grieving father.'

'Thank you for your co-operation, councillor,' says Lenny.

Jimmy tries to match her politeness but hasn't taken his eyes off me. He thinks I'm responsible for bringing the police to his doorstep, for failing to warn him.

'You should have called,' he mutters when Lenny is out of earshot.

'I don't have a phone.'

Dougal is polishing the Range Rover as we step into the dark cool of the garage, which smells of wax and window cleaner. He shakes out a cloth and dabs his brow before tucking it into the pocket of a vinyl apron that is protecting his clothes.

Lenny isn't as polite as the last time she spoke to him.

'Why didn't you tell us you were working for Councillor Verbic on the night Jodie disappeared?'

'I said I was driving a cab – same difference. I picked people up. I dropped them off.'

'Did you see Jodie that night?'

'No.'

'But she was here,' I say.

Dougal looks genuinely surprised.

'Jodie was dropped outside the gate just after nine o'clock.'

'Why would she come here?' asks Dougal.

'We're hoping you can tell us that.'

He looks from Lenny to me and back again. 'Did Jimmy see her?'

'Councillor Verbic doesn't recall seeing Jodie that night.'

I notice a faint tremor in Dougal's left hand, which isn't a sign of infirmity. He doesn't know how to react, or what to say.

'Did Jodie know where you were working?' asks Lenny.

'I don't know. Maybe.'

'Has she been here before?'

'Once or twice. I can't be sure.'

'If we have forensic officers look at these vehicles, are they going to find Jodie's DNA inside?'

Dougal's gaze drops to his feet as though he's standing on the edge of a cliff, unsure of whether he should jump. 'She's been in the Silver Shadow.'

'With Jimmy?'

'Yeah. We picked her up from skating practice and drove her to school.'

Lenny is walking around the Rolls-Royce. She cups her hands to peer into each window, deliberately leaving smudges on the glass.

'What else do you do for Councillor Verbic?' she asks.

'What do you mean?'

'Ever run errands?'

'Yeah, sometimes.'

'Pick people up?'

'Sure.'

'Drugs?'

'I don't know what you're talking about.'

'Why would Jodie have a burner phone?'

'A what?'

'A cheap disposable phone,' says Lenny. 'We also found spare SIM cards and hidden cash in her locker – all the trappings of a spy, or a terrorist or a drug dealer.'

A light seems to trigger behind Dougal's eyes, something red and bright, which flares and remains burning. For a moment I think he might tell us something important, but instead his voice drops to a harsh whisper.

'Our Jodie was raped and murdered. She was left to die alone in a dark cold place. I thought nothing could be more horrible than seeing my baby girl in the morgue, but I was wrong. This is worse. You're the real monsters.'

44

'What did you make of that?' asks Lenny, shaking Tic Tacs into the palm of her hand. She rattles the container, offering me some. I refuse.

We're still parked outside Jimmy Verbic's house, sitting in her unmarked police car. An elderly couple shuffles past. The husband rocks forward on a Zimmer frame and his wife pauses at each intersection to wait for him.

'Jodie didn't come here looking for her father,' I say.

'Agreed.'

'She came to deliver something or pick something up.'

'I'm listening.'

'How much do you know about Felix Sheehan?'

'He has an alibi.'

'A partial one. You still haven't confirmed where he spent the night.'

Lenny rubs her eyes with the heels of each hand.

'Does Felix have a criminal record?'

'Not as an adult.'

'Before?'

'Juvenile records are sealed.'

'I'll take that as a yes.'

Clearly, Lenny could tell me more but chooses not to. It's another reminder that I may work for the police, but I'm not part of the club. I don't have the unambiguous, unerring certainty needed by someone like her, a crusader who divides the world into good and evil.

She reaches for the ignition, but something moves in the periphery of her vision. The electronic gates are opening. Moments later, a black cab pulls out and accelerates past us. Dougal Sheehan is behind the wheel, in a hurry.

Lenny doesn't hesitate before pulling out and following. She's better at this than I am – tailing someone – keeping at the optimum distance to avoid being caught by red lights or clocked in the cab's mirrors.

We drive in silence, but my question about Felix is on her mind.

'Do you know why juvenile records are sealed?' she asks.

'To assist with rehabilitation and treatment,' I reply.

'Exactly. We don't want youngsters stigmatised or labelled as career criminals. They deserve a second chance.'

'I agree.'

'Felix was picked up at a summer music festival in Sherwood Forest. A sniffer dog found him carrying small amounts of crystal meth and ecstasy. He was fourteen – too young to be charged – but he was most likely a runner for a local gang.'

'Could he be still involved?'

'If he's stupid. We've had three stabbings since January, all of them unsolved. The Moss Side Bloods are moving in from Manchester and those guys are seriously dangerous. Most of the gangs operate away from home because they're less likely to draw attention from the competition or be known to the local coppers. When they move into an area, they look for a base – normally a squat, or a derelict building, or sometimes they target the vulnerable, like an addict, or someone with mental health problems, befriending them and moving into their house. They call it cuckooing. Once they establish there is a market, they begin recruiting runners. Usually they trawl the train stations, amusement arcades and skate parks, looking for strays or kids on the margins, from dysfunctional families or failing at school. They might offer them alcohol or cigarettes or computer games. Some get turned into junkies; or the girls are groomed for sex.'

I remember following Felix to the train station and the Jobcentre. If he's still involved with drug dealing it could explain the mobile phones and the money in Jodie's locker. Would he risk using her as a runner?

We're heading along Maid Marian Way, past the Broadmarsh Shopping Centre and along Canal Street towards the A612. As we reach the outskirts of Nottingham, the cab takes the exit on a roundabout signposted to Nottingham Racecourse. Another right turn and we're almost at the river, approaching a newly minted high-rise development called Trent Basin. Cranes dot the skyline and a huge billboard advertises LUXURY RIVERSIDE APARTMENTS.

The cab stops suddenly in a loading bay. Dougal Sheehan leaps out, heading for the entrance where he stabs impatiently at the button of an intercom. The glass door unlocks. Dougal takes the stairs. Lenny shoves her foot in the closing door and follows him, climbing quickly. I'm a dozen steps behind her, losing track of the floors.

We reach an open door and enter an apartment with a large open-plan living area dominated by floor to ceiling windows overlooking the river. I hear raised voices.

'What did you do?' yells Dougal.

'Nothing. Get off me!'

'Don't hurt him! Don't hurt him!' pleads a woman.

They're in the bathroom.

'Why was Jodie there?' demands Dougal.

'I don't know what you're talking about.'

'Police!' yells Lenny, spinning through the door.

Dougal Sheehan is crouching over his son, gripping Felix by the hair and forcing his head into the bowl of a toilet. He presses the flush lever, draining the cistern. Water sloshes over Felix's head, spilling onto the floor.

'You're killing him! You're killing him!' yells Maggie Sheehan, begging him to stop.

Dougal presses the button again. Felix can't breathe. His legs are twitching.

Lenny kicks Dougal hard in the back of his knees, making his legs buckle. She twists his arm behind his back and forces his face against the white tiles. Felix rolls away from the toilet, opening and closing his mouth like a stranded fish. His teeth are stained pink by blood and water drips from his hair.

Maggie drops to her knees and hugs him, wetting her blouse. He pushes her away and manages to sit up, leaning against the bath. Shirtless and concave-chested, he's dressed in baggy jeans that hang low off his hips, showing the crack of his arse.

'What's this about?' asks Lenny.

Felix wipes his wide, slack mouth. 'Ask him.'

Dougal's face is still pressed hard against the tiles, twisting his mouth out of shape. 'It's family business,' he mutters.

'Does it involve Jodie?'

Neither man answers. Lenny looks at Maggie. 'Are you going to tell me?'

She's too frightened or clueless to respond.

As the silence stretches out, Lenny realises that she can't force the issue.

'I should charge all of you,' she says disgustedly, releasing Dougal, who rubs his shoulder and glares at her belligerently. 'You can both leave. I want to talk to Felix,' she says.

'You can't talk to him without us being here,' replies Dougal.

'Sure, I can. He's over eighteen.' Lenny looks at Felix. 'Do you need Daddy or Mummy to hold your hand?'

'I want a fucking lawyer.'

'By all means,' says Lenny. 'You can wait for him at the station. Our holding cells are just like this place – well-appointed, fully furnished, with hot and cold running junkies and scumbags. You'll be right at home.' She pauses and wipes her hands on a towel. 'Your other option is to talk to me now – a novel approach, I know, but you're not under arrest . . . not yet.'

Lenny looks up at Dougal. 'You're still here.'

'He's my son.'

'You tried to drown him.'

'What's he done?' asks Maggie. 'Is this about Jodie?'

'Leave now, Mrs Sheehan. I won't ask again.'

I can hear husband and wife whispering harshly as they wait for the lift.

'But what's he done?'

'Nothing.'

'It must be something.'

'Shut up, woman!'

Felix uses a towel to dry his hair. Still shirtless, he walks into the living room, where he opens the sliding glass doors and takes a packet of cigarettes from the balcony table. He takes one and taps both ends against his wrist – an affectation that pre-dates filters on cigarettes.

The view sweeps across the south of the city and as far west as Lady Bay Bridge.

'Nice place,' I say, glancing around the room, noting the flat-screen TV, gaming consoles and expensive sound system. 'Yours?'

'I'm looking after it for a friend.'

'What's your friend's name?'

'John Smith.'

Felix lights up, swallowing smoke. He slumps onto a leather sofa, knees spread, convinced he knows exactly what happens next.

Lenny takes an armchair. 'Why was your old man so pissed at you?'

'Whites and coloureds.'

'What?'

Felix grins. 'I put a pair of red socks in a white wash. Spoiled Mum's favourite blouse.'

Lenny's gaze is absolutely neutral. 'I've had smarter bowel movements than you.'

I'm standing at the open glass doors looking across the river at a nature reserve called 'The Hook' where acres of woodland are fringed by wildflower meadows and orchards.

'Do you know Councillor Verbic?' I ask.

'Isn't he the mayor?'

'Used to be.'

'What about him?'

'Is he one of your customers?'

'Never met the guy.'

'Your father works for him as a driver,' says Lenny.

Felix wrinkles his nose as though some unpleasant smell has reached him.

'If we ask Councillor Verbic – will he say he knows you?'

This time Felix takes a moment, considering his options.

'I might have met him. I meet a lot of people in my line of work.'

'What exactly do you do?' I ask.

'I told you – I buy and sell stuff.'

'Anything in particular?'

'Antiques mainly.'

'I can't see any antiques around this place,' says Lenny.

'Not fond of them, myself,' says Felix, 'but a lot of folks like old shit. Your old man must tell you that all the time.'

Lenny doesn't rise to the bait. 'Business must be good.'

'I do OK.'

'The police found six thousand pounds in Jodie's school locker. Do you know how she got it?'

'No idea.'

'Can we look around?'

'Do you have a warrant?'

'With your permission.'

Felix spreads his arms. 'Knock yourselves out.'

Clearly, he's too experienced to keep anything incriminating in his apartment, but I still wouldn't mind seeing more of the place – learning things about him. I notice a BlackBerry phone on the glass coffee table. It's a brand favoured by criminal gangs because it can use military-grade encryption, making it almost impossible for police to access the data, or intercept messages.

'Jodie was using a mobile phone the night she disappeared,' I say, still looking at the BlackBerry. 'Not her usual one, but another handset, a cheap disposable most likely. It's only a matter of time before the police identify her new phone. They'll be able to read her text messages and look at her call logs.'

'Maybe even trace her movements,' says Lenny, picking up on the theme. 'You think you're safe, Felix, because your data is encrypted, but you can't hide the signal. Every phone has a unique signature that pings the nearest mobile phone towers, which means we can see where you've been – every house, pub, car park . . . every girlfriend. Every business meeting.'

Felix has gone quiet. He draws on his cigarette and exhales, blinking into the smoke. His eyes drift lower, focusing on the BlackBerry. He lunges, grabs the phone, pulls back his arm, and hurls it towards the balcony door and the river beyond. In the same breath, I shove the sliding glass door. It closes on smooth runners and the phone clatters against the double-glazing, landing at my feet. I pick it up.

'Give it back,' says Felix.

'It's a criminal offence to dispose of evidence,' replies Lenny, taking the phone from me and sliding it into her pocket.

Felix is less certain than before. 'You need a warrant.'

'We'll get one.'

I watch how the young man changes. He wants to be menacing, but like a lot of weedy men he's all push and self-possession, whereas someone like his father, a shambling shaggy heavyweight, wears the crown more easily.

'Was Jodie a runner?' asks Lenny.

'No comment,' he replies.

'Did you know she was pregnant?'

This time Felix hesitates and tosses us a bone. 'She came to me a few weeks ago, said she was up the duff.'

'Who was the father?'

'She didn't say.'

'Did you ask?'

Another shrug.

'What did Jodie tell you?'

'She didn't want Mum and Dad finding out. Mum would have thrown a wobbly, you know. Crying and praying.'

'Jodie must have wanted something.'

'Cash.'

'Why?'

'The scrape, I guess.'

'Terminations are free – why would she need money?'

'She wouldn't get it done in Nottingham. Too many people know her. She said she was going to London.'

'And you gave her six thousand pounds – that's very generous of you.'

'She stole that from me. I keep a bit of cash around the place, you know, in case of an emergency.'

'Why didn't you get it back?'

Felix doesn't answer.

'She was blackmailing you,' I say.

Again, silence. Felix puts his thumbnail between his teeth and bites at the edges.

'Did you send her to a house on The Ropewalk on the night she disappeared?'

'No comment.'

'I'll take that as a yes. Who was she delivering to?'

Felix laughs. 'You must think I'm an idiot.'

'That's a given,' says Lenny. 'The question is – how big an idiot.'

I want to get back to Jodie. 'When was she going to London?' I ask.

'She didn't say. She brought an overnight bag around here and put it in the spare room. Said she'd come by and pick it up when she was leaving.'

'Where is the bag now?' asks Lenny.

Felix nods towards one of the bedrooms.

'Can we take a look?' I ask.

Felix's expression changes, his features pushing outwards in a calculating smile. 'Do I get my phone back?'

I see Lenny weighing her options.

'If everything you've told us is true, I'll return your phone, but if you've been lying to me, Felix, I'll be all over you like a drunk aunt on a dance floor.'

He smirks.

In the bedroom, I open the wardrobe and pull out a small suitcase with a stencilled insignia for the British Ice-Skating Team. Lenny tosses me a pair disposable gloves and dons her own. The main zipper slides open, revealing clothes – knickers, tops, a sweater, two skirts and pair of jeans, as well as a woollen hat with ear muffs. There are separate pouches for Jodie's toiletries and make-up. Lower down, I find soft toy, a floppy-eared rabbit with a missing eye and a chewed ear. She was taking folic acid tablets and reading a book called *How to Grow a Baby and Push It Out*.

'Why pack a suitcase?' I ask, without realising I've said it out loud.

'She was going to London,' says Lenny.

'Which is only two hours away by train. She didn't have to stay overnight. According to Ness, Jodie was eleven weeks pregnant, which was still early enough for her to have a medical abortion. She could have taken a pill and come back a few days later for a second one.'

I look again at the contents of the bag – the clothes, the make-up, the vitamins and the much-loved childhood toy. Suddenly, the answer is clear to me.

'Jodie wasn't terminating a pregnancy – she was running away.'

45

Tasmin Whitaker is still dressed in her school uniform when she answers the door. She opens it far enough to peer over the chain, squinting as though the sun is in her eyes. A dusting of icing sugar covers her top lip.

'Mum and Dad aren't home.'

'It's you I wanted to see.'

A shadow passes across her face.

'I want to talk about Jodie.'

Tasmin looks over her left shoulder, holding the door with both hands.

'Who is it, Tas?' asks a voice from inside.

'The police,' she replies.

'I'm not the police.'

Aiden pushes Tasmin out of the way, opening the door wider. He's wearing track pants and a football jumper that hangs loosely on his slim frame. They don't look like brother or sister. It's as though Aiden was given first dibs at the beauty buffet, getting the eyelashes, cheekbones and clear skin, while Tasmin had to make do with the leftovers.

'What do you want?' he asks.

'I was hoping I could talk to Tasmin.'

'I thought you did that already.'

'I have a few more questions.'

Aiden seems to pounce on the statement. 'You can't talk to her without an adult present.'

'It's not a formal interview,' I reply, 'but you seem to know the rules.'

'I'm reading law at Cambridge.'

'I thought that was next year.'

'Yeah, well, I know my shit,' he says defiantly.

'Yes, you do,' I say. 'You'll make a great lawyer.'

Aiden isn't sure if I'm teasing him. Tasmin steps in between us. 'I don't need a babysitter.'

'I could talk to both of you,' I say.

Aiden agrees grudgingly and the door shuts behind me with a ragged click. We choose the sitting room because the kitchen table is covered in scraps of yellow fabric and a sewing machine.

'Mum is decorating my coat for the memorial service,' explains Tasmin. 'Yellow was Jodie's favourite colour.'

'When is the memorial?'

'The day after tomorrow. Do you want a cup of tea?' She sounds like her mother.

'No, I'm fine.'

Aiden checks his phone before sitting next to his sister, who is perched on the edge of the sofa, as though I'm interviewing her for a job. She's holding a small stuffed monkey in her lap that makes her look younger.

'Is that one special?' I ask.

'Jodie won it for me at the Goose Fair. You had to get five balls through the hoop. I couldn't get one.'

'You two were friends for a long time?'

'We went to the same primary school and to Forsyth Academy and dance classes and skating and we went on holidays together and other stuff.'

'Do you skate?'

'No. Daddy says I skate like a baby hippo.' There's no hint of regret in her voice.

'How often did Jodie come here?' I ask, motioning around me.

'All the time. We were like sisters.' Again it's her mother talking.

'After school?'

'Yeah. Aiden used to help her with her homework.'

I glance at Aiden for confirmation. 'She was missing a lot of school,' he explains, not bothering to look up from his phone. 'I helped her with her maths.'

'How often?'

'Twice a week.'

'Who arranged that?'

'Aunt Maggie asked Mum and she asked me.'

'Were you paid?'

'What?'

'Were . . . you . . . paid?'

'Yeah.'

Another silence. Tasmin is growing bored because it's not about her. She's playing with the monkey in her lap, twisting its arms into a knot and undoing them again.

'I talked to some of Jodie's skating friends who mentioned that she wanted to quit figure skating because of her injuries and headaches. Did she ever say anything to you?'

'Dad would have had a fit,' says Aiden.

I'm waiting for Tasmin who is looking at the scuffed toes of her school shoes, swinging them back and forth.

'No,' she whispers, but I suspect she's lying.

'Did you ever feel jealous of Jodie?'

The question seems to surprise her but she doesn't hesitate. 'All the time.'

'Why?'

'It was always Jodie this and Jodie that. Every time she sneezed or sniffled or fell over, people would be fussing over her, calling the doctor, handing her tissues. Isn't she wonderful, isn't she beautiful, isn't she talented . . .'

'It wasn't like that,' says Aiden.

'How would you know?' snaps Tasmin. 'They said the same things about you. You're the golden child and I'm the golden retriever.'

'Shut up, Tas.'

'You shut up!'

I interrupt. 'Did Jodie have a secret boyfriend? Someone older.'

'What difference does that make?' asks Aiden.

'I'm just trying to understand her.'

Tasmin scratches at the bridge of her nose but her eyes betray something other than jealousy or boredom.

'Sometimes she'd tell Aunt Maggie that she was staying with me, but then she'd go off and do other stuff.'

'What other stuff?'

'You shouldn't be telling tales,' says Aiden.

'They're not tales. Jodie used to sneak out at night and come back before we all woke up. I used to worry that she'd be late for practice, but she never got caught.'

'Do you know where she went?' I ask.

Tasmin shakes her head.

'When did this start?'

'During the summer holidays.'

I turn to Aiden. 'Did you know?'

'I'm her cousin, not her babysitter.'

'You didn't notice her coming and going?'

'I'm not here,' he replies, pointing into the garden where a small egg-shaped caravan is parked against the back fence. A power cable snakes across the lawn to the house.

'How did Jodie get in and out?' I ask.

'I'd leave the sliding door unlocked on the patio,' replies Tasmin.

'What about the night she disappeared – did you leave it unlocked?'

She lowers her head and bites her bottom lip, leaving white marks in the indentations.

'Did you forget?'

'No.' A teardrop hangs on her lower lashes, growing fatter before it falls. 'I wanted to punish her for leaving me alone at the fireworks . . . not taking me along.'

'You weren't to know,' says Aiden, putting his arm around her shoulders.

'If I'd left the door unlocked, she wouldn't have tried to walk home. She wouldn't . . .'

Tasmin can't finish and Aiden doesn't know how to comfort her.

A door key slides into a lock and the front door swings open. Bryan and Felicity Whitaker carry bags of groceries into the hallway, still arguing about something that must have started in the car. They stop abruptly.

'What are you doing here?' asks Bryan, his eyes sparking with anger.

'I'm talking to Aiden and Tasmin.'

'Without our permission.'

'Aiden is an adult.'

The groceries are dumped without ceremony on the floor. 'I don't want you talking to my children without us being here. I don't want you putting words in their mouths.'

'That's not what I'm doing.'

Everybody is on their feet and the sitting room feels small. Felicity has gone to Aiden, putting her arm around his waist. She went to him first, not Tasmin, who is clearly more upset.

'Jodie was pregnant and planning to run away,' I explain. 'I thought she might have talked to Tasmin.'

'You think our daughter deliberately withheld information,' says Bryan.

'No.'

'That's what you're inferring.'

'It's all right, Bryan,' says Felicity. 'Let it go.'

'He accused me of molesting Jodie.'

Tasmin makes a gagging sound and Aiden laughs sarcastically. I don't know what makes Bryan Whitaker angrier – my presence or the reactions of his children. He's not a big man, but he makes himself larger, lunging at me.

Felicity intercepts and pushes him back, warning me to leave.

I take a business card from my jacket pocket and give it to Aiden and Tasmin.

'This is my address and my pager number. If you think of anything – get in touch.'

'You're not welcome here,' yells Bryan. 'Don't come back.'

Felicity catches up with me before I reach the footpath. She pushes hair from her eyes, blinking wetly.

'You have the wrong impression of this family, Dr Haven, if you think we'd do anything to hurt Jodie.'

46

Angel Face

The pizza is cold by the time it arrives. I have a slice and leave the rest to Keeley, who eats noisily, letting cheese hang from her lips. In between mouthfuls, she guzzles glasses of pink wine from a box, treating it like cordial. Where does the food go? There's nothing of her.

During the afternoon, an Uber driver had delivered two plastic bags containing clothes for me − a short suede skirt, red tights, knickers, socks and a fitted white blouse with a Peter Pan collar − all of them new. The knickers are black and lacy and a size too small. I have never worn a thong before. At Langford Hall they issue the girls with grandma knickers from Marks & Spencer and sports bras that never fit properly.

Keeley wrinkles her nose as she examines each new piece of clothing, holding it between her thumb and forefinger as though she might catch something. The only thing she seems to covet is the patent leather ankle boots.

She's sitting on the bed, waiting for me to finish showering.

'Where are you from?' I ask, over the spitting water.

'Why do you care?'

'I don't.'

There is a pause. 'Sheffield.'

'Do you have family?'

'There's me and Mum and two half-brothers. They must be two and four by now.'

'You ever see them?'

'Nah.'

'Why not?'

'My stepdad.'

The answer doesn't need elaboration. I've known at least a dozen girls from Langford Hall whose parents had split up and a new partner pushed them to leave. It's like when a new lion takes over the pride. He kills the cubs or forces them out, clearing the way for his own progeny. That's one of my daily words: 'progeny'. It means descendants or children. Blood is thicker than sentimentality.

Turning off the shower, I reach for a towel and catch a hated glimpse of myself in the mirror. The bruises on my ribs are yellowing at the edges and turning a deep purple at the centre. They only hurt when I touch them.

Emerging from the bathroom with a towel around my chest, I use another to dry my hair.

'Where does Felix live?'

Keeley shrugs.

'Have you been there?'

'No.'

'But you're his girlfriend.'

Her eyes flare. 'What's that supposed to mean?'

'Nothing.'

'You should keep your opinions to yourself and your hands off him.'

I begin getting dressed. Keeley spies my tuft of pubic hair and snorts with derision.

'What?'

'Your bush.'

Embarrassed, I turn my back to her and slide the skirt over my thighs. Once I'm dressed, I risk looking in the mirror, surprised at the transformation. They used to bring me new clothes all the time when

I was young: dresses and pinafores and leotards and gowns. Some made me look younger, others made me look older, but none of them felt like they belonged to me.

A door opens somewhere and voices echo through the derelict building.

'They're here,' says Keeley.

'Who?'

'You'll see.'

The visitors are in the lounge – two black men in their twenties and a skinny middle-aged woman wearing a sarong and sandals like she's holidaying somewhere warm.

One of the black men, Tuba, has his hair shaved in rings around his head like crop circles in a wheat field. His friend is lighter-skinned but morbidly obese. He wants me to call him Rambo, but Tuba says, 'Nice one, Kev.'

'I can call myself Rambo,' complains Kev, who has multiple chins and rolls of fat that fill out a huge shiny orange tracksuit that must be visible from outer space.

'You should call yourself Star-Lord,' says Tuba. 'Or the Hulk.'

'Fuck off!'

The middle-aged woman ignores their banter and lights a cigarette. She hasn't acknowledged me, concentrating instead on her phone and chewing at the edges of her fingernails like she's trying to sharpen them.

I introduce myself. The woman ignores me.

'Don't mind Carla,' says Tuba. 'She's not a people person.'

'She's a voodoo priestess,' says Kev, who starts singing 'I Put a Spell on You' and waving his arms around like he's Harry Potter.

Felix arrives, carrying two six-packs of beer. He's showered and changed, dressed up for a night out, in expensive jeans and a designer shirt. He greets Tuba and Kev with a choreographed 'handshake' involving bumped shoulders and dabbed fists. Keeley drapes herself over him, purring into his ear.

Carla stops staring at her phone and says, 'Sorry about your sister.' Her voice is coarsened by cigarettes or alcohol or both.

'Yeah, brah,' echoes Tuba. 'Fucking intense.'

'It was all over the TV,' says Kev. 'Pictures of Jodie and your folks.'

Felix doesn't answer.

'What happened to your sister?' I ask, more alert than before.

'Nothing,' says Felix.

'Is she the girl who got killed?'

'Not up for discussion.'

The statement is so savage that I bottle up my curiosity.

Kev sits down and splays his legs, taking up the whole sofa. Tuba keeps moving in a loose-limbed sort of swagger like he's playing a pimp on TV. Carla has lit up another cigarette, sucking so hard that the filter compresses between her lips.

'What's she doing here?' she says, thrusting a bleeding fingernail at me.

'She's a new recruit.'

'How do we know she's not a narc?'

'Does she look like a narc?' replies Felix.

'Where did you find her?'

'At the bus station.'

'Oh, great! Yeah, she's definitely not a narc.'

Her sarcasm annoys Felix. 'I found you at an AA meeting. Maybe you're the narc?'

Carla backs off but isn't happy. Felix tells me to wait outside.

I don't mind. I didn't like the vibe in the room, or the direction of the conversation. Nobody had been lying, but I sensed how quickly the mood changed when Jodie Sheehan's name was dropped.

Cyrus didn't mention that Jodie had a brother. And his name didn't come up in any of the police interviews with Craig Farley. Yet here he is, organising deliveries of vitamins, or steroids, or whatever shit he deals in. It surprises me. I don't know why. It's not as if murder victims have to come from a squeaky-clean family. Surely the opposite is sometimes true.

Standing in the poorly lit hallway, I press my ear to the door, listening to the muffled voices, which become clearer when they relax and open the beers.

'You got to stop picking up strays,' says Carla. 'It's too risky.'

'She's a juvie. A runaway. Someone beat her up,' replies Felix.

'She knows our names and what we look like.'

'She won't be here long.'

'Good,' says Keeley. 'I don't like her.'

'All of you shut up,' Felix says angrily. 'I'll check her out before she does a run, OK?'

'Are we working tonight,' says Tuba, 'or gasbagging?'

'No. I'm putting deliveries on hold for a while,' replies Felix. 'I had a visit from the pigs today. They know fuck all, but we're going to lay low for a spell.'

'For how long?' asks Kev.

'Until the heat dies down.'

'I got bills to pay,' complains Carla.

'More like a habit to feed,' replies Kev.

Carla must react because Kev says, 'You're such a classy lady.'

'And you're a fat bastard,' she replies.

'I thought they caught the guy,' says Tuba.

'Yeah, but they're still sniffing around. We'll give it a week – ten days tops.'

'And what are we supposed to do?'

'Take a holiday. Go somewhere warm. You're dressed for it.'

'What about our customers?' asks Tuba.

'When we get back on track, we'll offer them a discount.'

I step back from the door and wrap my arms around my chest, shivering but not from the cold. I don't trust any of these people. I should have stolen the pizza money from Keeley and caught a bus to London. I should have gone back to Cyrus. Even if he sent me to Langford Hall, it wouldn't be for ever. What am I afraid of? I've spent most of my life in one box or another. Waiting.

The meeting is breaking up. Tuba and Kev leave together, filling the corridor with their laughter and bulk. Carla ignores me as she passes, disappearing in a cloud of cigarette smoke.

Keeley is wrapped around Felix, almost dry-humping his leg. He pushes her away and reaches into his pocket, removing a tiny plastic bag, which he shakes against his thigh and gives to her.

'Now piss off. I'm busy.'

Keeley looks at me with a mixture of disgust and loathing, but also a strange emptiness behind her eyes, like she's already left the building.

I hover in the open doorway until Felix tells me to sit down. He gets another beer from a chest fridge, removing the top by hooking the cap on the edge of the counter and thumping the bottle with his fist.

'You want one?'

I shake my head. 'I thought I was delivering stuff.'

'Not tonight.'

'But my money.'

'Chill. You'll get it.'

He turns on a stereo and cranks up the volume on an electro-pop track with so much bass it shakes my insides.

'What sort of music do you like?' he asks.

'Not this.'

He grins and sits on the stained sofa whose fabric has been worn thin by squirming arses. Beer at his fingertips, he takes a small glass pipe from his pocket, which has a bulb on one end like a pregnant test tube. It reminds me of the science lessons at Langford Hall where we distilled salt water into fresh water using a Bunsen burner and two flasks.

Felix takes another clear plastic bag from his thigh pocket and holds it up in front of his eyes, examining the contents that look like tiny granules of rock salt. He pinches some of the crystals between his fingers and drops them into the glass pipe where they settle at the base of the bulb. Taking a cheap lighter from his pocket, he triggers the flame and holds it under the glass, filling the room with a soft crackling sound. Smoke, as white as cotton wool, appears in the pipe. Felix draws it deep into his lungs, puffing out his cheeks and letting his head loll back. The same smoke slowly leaks from his lips, lifting the corners of his mouth into an odd smile. It's like a chemical reaction – cause and effect – flooding his eyes with bliss.

He hands the pipe to me. I shake my head.

'Relax. Lighten up.'

'I'll have a beer.'

Felix collects one from the fridge, turning his back as he removes the top. I'm still staring at the glass pipe and the darkened crystals in the bulb. I have smoked weed before, but nothing like this. Maybe I should try it. What harm could it do? It's not as though my life has been a picnic up until now. The opposite is true. All questions and no answers; a real shit show.

Counsellors and therapists have always told me to accept my reality, but none of them has ever explained why. In a world full of suffering and sadness, why should anybody 'accept their reality' when they could change it? That's why those makeover TV shows are so popular – they feed on people's compulsive desire to be someone else; to swap their boring, shitty life for something better. To avoid, to deny, to forget . . .

Felix hands me the open beer. I wipe the top with my sleeve and take a drink, filling my mouth, cooling my throat. I don't stop until the last drop falls on my tongue. Another beer is pulled from the cooler. This time I hold it between my knees, telling myself to drink more slowly.

Felix picks up the pipe and thumbs the flame. Smoke curls along the glass tube as he inhales.

He holds the pipe towards me and turns the lighter upside down.

'Don't be afraid. Relax. Let it happen.'

I lean forward, opening my lips.

'It's like riding a dragon,' he says. 'It's like drinking in clouds.'

My stomach spasms and the walls of the room suddenly bulge and suck away.

He gave me something. He spiked my drink. I know about such things – roofies and date rape drugs – but I didn't think . . . should have thought . . . Stupid girl! Foolish girl!

Felix is talking. His features seem to morph and transform into Halloween masks and monstrous creatures, all lips and teeth and multiple eyes.

'What did you give me?' I slur, not recognising my own voice. When did the music change?

He pulls me up. I stumble. He catches me, putting his arm around *my waist. I try to speak, telling him I want to lie down, but my words are garbled and make no sense. He's leading me along the hallway, holding me up as he fishes for the keys. The door opens to reveal a bedroom, a bed, a camera, a tripod . . .*

He lets me fall backwards onto the mattress, where I curl up, wanting to sleep, but a bright light blasts through my closed eyelids. He puts his hands on either side of my face and kisses me; his tongue pushing into my mouth, ammonia on his breath. I gag, turning my face away and grabbing his shoulders, trying to push him off, but he has wedged his knee between my thighs, forcing them open. Fingernails scratch at my skin, pulling elastic aside, rummaging like he's searching for a lost pound. I beg him to stop, but my voice won't make the sounds.

In slow motion, Felix leans back and unbuckles his trousers. He grabs my head, pressing his thumbs into the soft flesh beneath my ears, guiding me towards him. I understand. I fight. I pull at his fingers, pleading for forgiveness or for mercy, although I don't know what mercy means. This is my life. Who I am. What I've been. That person. Used. Abused. Unloved. Unlovable.

My stomach spasms and guts erupt.

Felix rears back uttering a sharp cry.

'Bitch!'

He's holding his arms out, looking at the masticated mush of cheese and pizza dough clinging to his shirt.

'This cost me a hundred quid.'

He goes to the bathroom and takes off his shirt, scrubbing it under the running water.

I know I have to run. I try to stand but topple over. I crawl on my hands and knees until I reach the corridor and heave the remaining contents of my stomach onto the carpet.

Getting to my feet, I stumble down the passageway, swaying from side to side, bouncing off the walls. I take in gulps of air, trying to focus.

Somewhere behind me the tap is turned off and light spills past me.

'Hey! Where are you going?'

I've reached an unlit exit sign. I push down on the horizontal bar, shouldering the door open and lurch across a landing to a short flight of stairs. Felix is close behind, reaching for me, clawing at my face to stop me screaming. He slams me against a brick wall, but his thumb has found my mouth. I bite down hard, feeling his skin break, reaching bone. He curses and releases his grip. I lash out with a boot, finding his shin.

'Psycho bitch!' he yells.

I'm free. Running. Revived by the cold air. Aware that my skirt is partially undone. I'm through the fence and onto the road, stumbling towards a light. A car swerves, braking hard, wheels locking. I spin away, turning the corner, not looking back. A bus, brightly lit, sounds a horn. I don't stop . . . I won't stop . . . because he is somewhere behind me.

Suddenly, my head fills with the blast of a police siren and a spotlight turns everything white. Momentarily blinded, I bounce off the side of a parked car and fall to the bitumen. A police officer is crouching next to me. He's saying something, but I can't make out the words.

I'm a child again, fuddled by sleep and feverish dreams, conscious of a door opening, a figure backlit, whispering my name, pulling back the bedclothes, saying, 'You know I love you. You know I won't hurt you.'

A hand touches my arm, telling me to lie still.

I would cry if I weren't so tired, so desperately tired.

47

'Her ribs are bruised, but nothing is broken,' says a triage doctor wearing crumpled blue scrubs and a cotton surgical cap cocked at a jaunty angle. A rust-coloured rosette of toilet paper is stuck to his neck that must have been there since this morning. He'll soon need to shave again.

'Evie said her drink was spiked, so I've organised a tox-screen and given her drugs to counteract whatever she might have taken. I've also prescribed her some painkillers. Raising her arms above her head is going to hurt, so she might need help getting dressed.'

'Was she . . .?' I don't finish the question.

'Sexually assaulted? I have no idea. She refuses to let anyone examine her internally.'

The waiting room of A&E is dotted with the broken, wounded, grazed and bleeding, all with jaundiced-looking faces from the fluorescent lights. I've been here since just after midnight, when the police messaged my pager. Evie gave them the number before she fell asleep in an ambulance on the way to the hospital.

She's awake now, talking to the police officers that found

her. I take a seat and watch a man with fuzzy hair and a food-stained shirt arguing with a triage nurse, demanding pain-killers. She uses his first name and tells him to sit down or she'll call security. The man retreats to his shopping trolley, which is parked outside the automatic doors, laden with filthy blankets and folded cardboard.

Two officers emerge from the consulting room and have a conversation, heads together, before summoning me. The more senior one looks at me with a sullen animosity, as if I'm person-ally to blame for his working nights and never seeing his family.

'I'm PC Burton,' he says. 'This is PC Huntley. How do you know Evie Cormac, sir?'

'I'm her guardian.'

'Do you have any ID?'

I show him my driver's licence.

'What was she doing out last night?'

'What did she tell you?'

'She said she went out to meet friends and her drink was spiked. She says she can't remember what happened after that . . . where she's been, or who she was with. She doesn't want to give us the names of her friends because most of them were underage. Can you help?'

'Not really.'

'When did you last see Evie?'

'Yesterday afternoon,' I lie.

'Do you have any idea where she was last night?'

'No.'

The officer is taking notes in a small flip-top notebook.

'Listen, Cyrus. Can I call you Cyrus?'

He's going to do it anyway.

'Evie was found with no money, or phone, or ID. The state of her clothing and her bruises indicate that she was attacked, robbed and possibly sexually assaulted. It may be that she's too scared to reveal the identity of her attacker. You should talk to her. Tell her it's in her own best interests.'

Is it, though?

'Of course,' I say, trying to sound genuine, when I have no idea what to tell Evie. I have treated dozens of victims of sexual assault – some of whom reported their attacker to the police and others who kept it secret. I can't say for sure which of them made the right choice. For every perpetrator who was punished, three walked away without being charged, or were cleared by a jury. Right now, all I can think about is Evie – what she's been through, how to make her whole.

Finally, they let me see her. She's sitting on the edge of an examination table with her head down, letting a curtain of hair cover her eyes. She doesn't acknowledge my arrival, or the sound of my voice.

'How are you feeling?'

'Like shit.'

'Are you in pain?'

'No.'

The officers are watching how she reacts to me – reading her body language. No doubt my name will be run through the Sex Offenders Register and they'll contact Social Services, checking on my status as a foster carer.

'I need the bathroom,' Evie says, pushing past me. We still haven't made eye contact. A nurse escorts her to the ladies and waits outside. The officers are talking on their phones. Occasionally, one or both of them glance at me.

'Can I take her home?' I ask the doctor.

'Unless you want me to refer her to the psych ward.'

'I'm a psychologist.'

It raises an eyebrow.

Minutes pass. Evie has been gone too long. There could be another exit. She could be trying to run again. I have to stop myself grabbing a nurse and getting her to check inside the cubicle, but suddenly Evie appears. She has slicked down her hair with water and rubbed and washed her face. A nurse must have given her lipstick and eyeshadow.

For the first time I notice her clothes – the suede skirt, torn blouse and ankle boots – and wonder how and where she got them.

'Put this on,' I say, giving her my coat. 'It's cold outside.'

PC Burton stops us before we reach the main doors. He gives Evie his card, telling her to call him if she remembers anything. She nods in a non-committal way.

The younger officer escorts her outside, while his partner puts a hand on my shoulder, leaning close until his mouth brushes my ear.

'If I discover you've touched her, I'm going to break your jaw and shit down your throat.'

48

Reaching for her seatbelt Evie flinches and turns her face away, staring into the lightening sky. I start the engine and we pull out of the parking area, driving along near-deserted roads wet from the rain.

'Where did you go?' I ask eventually.

'I found a poker game.'

'For two days!'

She doesn't answer.

A bus pulls out ahead of us. I overtake, catching a glimpse of the brightly lit interior, where a handful of bleary-eyed shift workers rest their heads against the glass.

'I won,' whispers Evie.

'The police said you had no money.'

'I was robbed.'

'Who robbed you?'

'I didn't take down their names.'

Normally a line like that would be delivered with sarcasm, but Evie doesn't seem to have the energy or the anger.

'Why didn't you go to the police?'

'Why do you think?'

'You could have sent me a message.'

Evie looks at me with unexpected coldness, laying waste to something within me. Not for the first time, I recognise something missing inside her – a deficit or arrears. I have never met such a pure nihilist. She is like a new species of human, raised in almost total annihilating self-hatred that has destroyed any self-regard she may once have had. In her mind and heart she is an insult to the ground that she walks upon and the air that she breathes. All her strength, all her mental faculties are telling her that she must hate the world; that she must smash it to pieces before it destroys her.

Yet all my experience tells me that that she *wants* to be normal. She *wants* to be included. She's like a child who has never been invited to a party, but who presses her face against the glass, listening to the laughter and watching the games being played, hoping to be asked to join in, yet willing to burn the house down without a second thought.

'Are you sending me back?' she asks, biting on the inside of her cheek.

'I haven't decided.'

'What? I'm on probation?'

'You've *always* been on probation.'

My fingers grip the wheel too tightly and I realise – not for the first time – that I'm afraid of Evie. I fear her physical proximity and her darkness and the damage she could inflict upon me when she senses her power.

She gazes out of the window, no doubt aware that we're not heading home, or towards Langford Hall, but she doesn't say anything. I'm taking us east, across the river, past Trent Bridge Cricket Ground and through the outskirts of Nottingham where the houses give way to patchwork fields stitched together with hedgerows.

The Radcliffe Animal Shelter has a small shop attached to a series of kennels and prefabricated buildings that look like miniature aircraft hangars.

'Come on,' I say, getting out of the car. Evie is still wearing my overcoat. She follows me into the front office where a woman behind a desk is chewing on a triangle of Marmite-covered toast.

She licks her fingers. 'You're up early.'

'We're looking for a dog,' I say.

Spinning her chair, she pulls out a form. 'Adopting or fostering?'

'Fostering,' I reply. 'For the moment.'

I pass the form straight to Evie. She blinks at me, lost for words.

'You put your name and address at the top.'

There are questions on the page, wanting to know the size of our yard and whether we want an inside or an outside dog, what breed and gender. Evie keeps glancing at me, unsure of how to answer.

'You choose,' I say.

'You can meet a few,' says the woman, picking up a walkie-talkie and summoning someone she calls Raptor. Moments later a young man appears dressed in a green uniform with heavy work boots. His hair is dyed blond at the ends and pulled back into a ponytail. We follow him along a cement path to a series of low kennels and wire enclosures. The dogs have heard us coming and set off barking, spurring each other on.

'I got just the one for you,' Raptor says. 'She's my favourite. She loves being around people and doesn't cope with being on her own, you know. Separation anxiety.'

He tells us to wait in the yard. Evie watches him leave. Her hands are deep in her pockets. She seems to be holding her breath, anxious that I might change my mind.

'Is this a trick?' she whispers.

'No.'

'Why are you being so nice to me?'

'That's the thing, Evie. You shouldn't be surprised when people treat you with respect. It's how it should be.'

'Does this mean you want me to stay?'

'I've *always* wanted you to stay.'

She turns away, hiding her face. 'I went to the bus station, hoping I could get to London, but I didn't have any money. This guy came and talked to me. He offered me somewhere to stay.' Evie hesitates. 'It was Felix Sheehan – the brother of that girl.'

'Are you sure?'

'Yeah.'

I take a deep breath. 'Did he . . .? Were you . . .?'

'No.'

'The doctor said you were drugged.'

She doesn't answer. 'Felix is a dealer. He doesn't deliver the stuff himself – he has people do it for him.'

'Is that what he wanted you to do?'

Evie nods.

'We have to tell the police.'

'No!'

'He attacked you.'

She looks at me pleadingly. 'They'll send me back to Langford Hall.'

'Not necessarily.'

'I ran away. I gambled. I hung out with drug dealers . . .' Evie sucks in a breath and starts again. 'I think he took pictures of me.'

'What sort of pictures?'

She shakes her head. 'Please don't tell the police.'

I want to argue, to change her mind, but at that moment a door opens and a Labrador bounds into view, pulling on a lead and wagging her tail so furiously that her whole body is shaking. Raptor tries to hold her back, but she wants to sniff everything and everyone

'Her name is Poppy,' says Raptor. 'We reckon she's about eighteen months old. Still a puppy really, but she's been neutered and microchipped and had all her jabs.'

Evie has dropped to her knees and grabbed Poppy by the head, rubbing behind her ears and under her chin. Poppy's tongue lolls out, wanting to lick Evie's face. Evie laughs and wrestles with her – every movement practised and assured. She's more comfortable around animals than people. That's why she wasn't frightened of Sid and Nancy in the kennels – why she stole food for them.

Raptor is still talking.

'She's very intelligent, although a little neurotic. We had to call the vet last week cos Poppy chewed up some of her toys and swallowed the plastic.' He looks back at the kennel. 'You want to see some of our other rescues?'

'No,' says Evie. 'Poppy is perfect.'

'If she were mine, I'd walk her at least twice a day – maybe more. She needs lots of stimulation.'

'I will.' Evie looks up at me. 'You want to pat her? She's really friendly. She has golden flecks in her eyes. See?'

As I kneel down, Poppy tries to jump into my arms, knocking me backwards. I finish up on my backside on the damp grass.

'She doesn't know her own strength,' says Raptor. 'You should train her. Get her used to socialising with people and other dogs.'

Evie nods, draping herself across Poppy.

Paperwork has to be filled out. Forms signed. I buy a bag of dried dogfood from the shop, as well as a harness and lead, and bowls for the kibble and water.

'Where is she going to sleep?' asks Evie.

'I thought maybe the laundry.'

'That's too cold. Can she stay in my room?'

'We'll see how it goes tonight.'

Evie sits in the back seat with Poppy, cracking a window so the Labrador can sniff the air outside. I get behind the wheel and reach for my seatbelt. Suddenly, Evie wraps her arms around my neck and presses her cheek against my ear. It is a stiff hug. Unpractised. Uncertain.

'Thank you,' she whispers, her voice breaking. 'Thank you.'

49

Angel Face

I want to tell Cyrus what happened. I want to tell him nothing.

Confiding in him would go against everything I was ever taught. Trust nobody. Believe in nothing. Terry told me that. He proved it.

'You think you can rely on someone,' he said. 'You think you know their name, you think you've seen their worst side, but that is a blindness. You haven't looked closely enough.'

Sitting at the kitchen table, I shuffle the cards and deal a hand, playing them in my head, before shuffling again. Cyrus is at the sink using a sharp knife to divide slabs of chuck steak into portions that he'll freeze for Poppy. The Labrador is sitting on her haunches, hoping a morsel might fall to the floor.

'Don't you dare feed her from the table,' says Cyrus.

I let my hand slip from my pocket and drop a piece of meat under the chair. Poppy sniffs it out and guzzles it greedily.

'Labs are notorious overeaters,' says Cyrus. 'You don't want her getting fat.'

Poppy is licking my fingers.

Cyrus is talking about building 'a run' for Poppy in the back garden.

'She can't stay inside all day. She's too destructive.'

I glance towards the laundry, where one of his Nike runners has been chewed into a scattering of rubber, mesh and synthetic leather.

'I'm sorry about your shoe,' I say, for the umpteenth time. 'I'll pay for new ones.'

'What with?'

'When I get a job.'

Cyrus doesn't comment.

The Labrador seems to be listening. Her paws make clicking sounds on the floor as she crosses the kitchen, wagging her tail and shoving her nose into Cyrus's crotch. He pushes her away. 'We should teach her not to do that.'

'She's saying sorry.'

'She's begging.'

I laugh and produce a phone from the pocket of my smock dress. It was on my pillow this afternoon, along with a note saying, 'I know it's second-hand, but I can't afford a new one.'

As I tap the phone, the screen lights up, showing the different icons and apps. I don't have anyone to call, but that's OK.

'I've programmed my pager number into the contacts,' says Cyrus. 'Next time if you get into trouble—'

'I won't get into trouble.'

'I know, but just in case . . .'

A piece of meat drops from the chopping board and is quickly gobbled up by Poppy.

'Hey! You said not to feed her.'

'That was an accident,' says Cyrus, winking at me.

'You have a bathtub,' I say, in a mildly enquiring tone.

'Yes.'

'I've never had a bath. At least I don't think I have. I don't remember.'

'You can borrow mine,' he says.

'When?'

'Whenever you like.'

'Now?'

'Sure.'

I go upstairs and collect a towel. In Cyrus's bathroom, I adjust the taps and begin filling a deep, claw-footed tub. Spying a bottle that says 'bath crystals', I pour half the contents into the running water. Pillows of foam erupt from beneath the taps, getting higher and higher. Maybe that was too much.

Slipping out of my clothes, I avoid looking in the mirror, because my bruises look like the ink-blot tests that Guthrie used to give me.

'What does this remind you of, Evie?' he'd ask.

'A vagina.'

'And this?'

'Another vagina.'

It did his head in.

Having run the bath, I slide into the tub, sending a tsunami of foam spilling over the sides onto the floor. I'm not sure what to do next. In a shower you wash yourself, but in a bath – going by the films I've seen – people read magazines or drink champagne or go to sleep. I rest my head on a folded hand-towel and close my eyes, letting the warm water soak into my muscles and bruises.

I can see the point of baths now. I'm going to stay in this tub for ever.

Cyrus knocks. Immediately, I cover up, before remembering the door is locked.

'Are you OK?' he asks.

'Yeah.'

'I thought you might have drowned.'

'No.'

'OK.'

'Hey, Cyrus?'

'Yeah.'

'How do you get scurvy?'

'By not eating enough fruit.'

'Oh.'

'Why?'

'My fingers have gone all white and wrinkly.' I wait. 'Why are you laughing?'

'No reason.'

50

I hear the news on the radio the next morning.

'*The alleged killer of schoolgirl Jodie Sheehan is under police guard in hospital after a failed suicide attempt. Twenty-six-year-old Craig Farley was found hanging from a torn bedsheet in his cell at HMP Nottingham and was revived by a prison medical team.*

'*Farley was charged two weeks ago with the rape and murder of Nottingham schoolgirl, Jodie Sheehan, whose body was discovered near a popular footpath . . .*'

My pager is vibrating, showing Lenny's number. Opening my laptop, I Skype her.

Her face appears on screen. 'You heard the news?'

'Just now.'

'It's another sign of his guilt.'

'If you say so.'

Lenny doesn't take the opportunity to gloat. 'Farley's lawyer has given you permission to talk to him.'

'Why now?'

'The guy is suicidal. You're a psychologist.' She makes it sound like a simple sum.

'The hospital has a psych department.'

'Yeah, but he asked for you.'

A police officer is dozing on a chair in the corridor, his hat resting over his eyes. Nobody has told him I'm coming. He grumbles and mutters darkly under his breath before making the necessary calls to confirm my visit. Half an hour is wasted.

Farley is out of intensive care and in a private room. I knock. Enter. He's lying on a bed, facing the window where the blinds have been left open and the sky outside is the colour of cigarette ash in a white bowl.

'Hello, Craig,' I say.

He turns his head and I notice the bruising around his neck. He looks at me with interest, frowning, as though he's expecting someone older, or someone else, or salvation in general. The future is a scary place when you've been charged with raping and murdering a child. Prison is not an end point. Paedophiles and child killers are the lowest form of life behind bars, normally segregated, or held in solitary, for their own protection. Farley might not be the brightest bulb on the Christmas tree, but he knows what awaits him – the beatings, insults and hurled bodily waste; until the inevitable moment when a crude shank finds its mark and, if he's lucky, he's condemned to pissing into a bag for the rest of his days.

He has lost weight since I last saw him in the interview room at West Bridgford Police Station. His face has thinned out and his eyes seem to be submerged in pools of shadow.

'My name is Cyrus,' I say. 'Do you mind if I sit down?'

He doesn't answer, but I take a chair and pull it closer to the bed. Settling.

'How are you feeling?'

No response.

'Do you mind if I turn the light on?' I don't wait for him to answer. I can see the blue of his eyes and the dry patches of skin on his forehead.

'You can always try again,' I say.

'What?'

'If you really want to die – you can always try again.'

He frowns, unsure if I'm being serious.

'How old are you, Craig? Mid-twenties. Still a young man. You could live to be ninety. You could choose any one of those days to die. What's the rush?'

I wait for an answer. Each second without sound creates tension, like a rubber band being stretched out.

'Aren't you supposed to talk me out of dying?' he croaks, his vocal chords bruised by his near hanging.

'Everybody dies, Craig.'

'Yeah, but that's different.'

'You mean they wait for old age, or disease, or some tragic, unexpected accident.'

'Yeah.'

I lean forward and rest my elbows on my knees.

'You're not special, Craig. Most people contemplate suicide at some point, even if it's only to imagine who might show up at the funeral and what they might say. Living isn't evolutionary. We can pull a trigger at any time – step off a cliff or walk in front of a train or wrap a torn sheet around our necks. Most of us don't. We wait and see what happens.'

Farley pretends not to be listening. He reaches for a cup with a straw and takes a sip, staring at me over the rim.

'I don't think you killed Jodie Sheehan,' I say.

He blinks at me.

'Maybe you played a part. Maybe you could have saved her, but I don't think you killed her.'

The silence in the room magnifies the humming of the air conditioning.

'I can understand why you were charged – and why you'll be convicted. You pulled down her jeans and her underwear. You masturbated into her hair. That's pretty damning stuff. Most people would happily put you away for a long stretch. Some

317

would pull the trapdoor. But while I have you, I want to ask a question. Why? Jodie was right there in front of you. She was everything you desired – young, pretty, unconscious. You could have done anything to her, but you didn't.'

'You're sick.'

'Did you lose your erection when you tried to penetrate her? Maybe you wanted to humiliate her.'

Farley's fist rattles on the side of the bed where he's been handcuffed to the frame.

'I know you put branches on her body, but it's not as though you covered your tracks. You left footprints at the scene. You tied your dog to a nearby tree. You bragged to a schoolgirl that the police had found Jodie. You couldn't have made it any more obvious if you'd hung a sign around your neck saying, "Arrest me".'

'I'm not dumb.'

'Prove it to me.'

Farley goes quiet. I let the silence build until it fills every corner of the room. It leaks into his ears and his chest and his bladder and his bowels and every dark place in his mind. Very few people are comfortable with silence. It's one thing to be on a plane, or in a train carriage, or in a waiting room and to ignore those around you, but not when you know someone is expecting you to answer.

'How?' he mutters.

'Tell me what happened – the whole story. I'm not the police. There are no cameras, or recorders, no notebook, no witnesses. I'm not a priest. I can't take your confession. I don't care if you're guilty. I don't care if you *feel* guilty. I only want the truth.'

Farley turns to face the window and I wonder if he's chosen to stonewall me.

'I didn't chicken out,' he whispers.

'What were you doing on the footpath?'

'When I can't sleep, I walk my dog.'

'Why did you choose that path?'

'It's close to home.'

'There are parks that are nearer.'

Farley raises his shoulders. Drops them. It might be a shrug. It might be resignation.

'I got a dog yesterday,' I say. 'A Labrador called Poppy. She's not really mine. She belongs to a friend of mine who's staying with me, but we're going to take turns to walk her. I do the night walks, because I don't like my friend going out alone.'

Farley is listening.

'Our nearest park gets locked up at dusk, so last night I took Poppy around the block a few times. It's a different world at that hour. You think the roads would be deserted, but all sorts of people are out walking their dogs. Some stop and chat, talking about the weather or the stars. Last night, I was two streets from home when I looked up and saw a woman getting ready for bed. She'd left her curtains opens.'

'Was she naked?' asks Farley, facing me again, more animated now.

'She was wearing a dressing gown and drying her hair.'

'How much could you see?'

'She was studying herself in the mirror, turning her face left and right, as though she was searching for something she'd lost.'

'What?'

'Youth.'

Farley doesn't understand.

'I felt sorry for her. She looked lonely. I wondered if that's why she left the curtains open – to be noticed.'

'Lots of them do,' he says.

'Really?'

'Oh, yeah.'

'Is that why you go walking at night?'

He goes quiet.

'Is that what you were doing on the night you saw Jodie – looking in windows?'

Again nothing.

'Did you see Jodie on the footpath?'

'No.'

'What about on the footpath?'

He shakes his head.

'Where was she?'

'In the water.'

'You first saw her in the water?'

'I heard her.'

'What did you hear?'

He looks at me plaintively. 'Splashing.'

I make him go over it again, describing how he left home with his dog, and went along certain roads where he'd been lucky in the past. At some point, he decided to take Silverdale Walk, past the school and across the tramlines. As he approached the footbridge he heard someone cry out and then a splash.

'I thought it was an animal, you know.'

'What did you do?'

'When I got to the footbridge, I peered over the side. That's when I saw her.'

'Jodie?'

He nods. 'I didn't know it was her. I thought somebody had dumped some rubbish into the pond. I went to check it out – in case it was something valuable, you know – but I saw her moving. She was crawling through the reeds.'

He swivels his head slowly, eyes wide, wanting me to believe him. I can smell the sweat rising from his body and the faint hint of urine.

'Then what?'

'I scrambled down the bank. I thought she might need some help. She was coughing. Wet. Cold. I wanted to keep her warm. I offered her my jacket.'

'What did she say?'

'Nothing.'

He lifts his eyes, blinking miserably, unable to make his mouth form the words.

'She ran away. You chased her.'

'I didn't mean to hurt her. I wanted to make her warm.'

'But you didn't. You tied your dog to a tree. You undressed her. You were going to rape her.'

His head rocks from side to side.

'You tried to have sex with a dead or dying girl.'

'Please don't say that.'

'That's why you couldn't penetrate her.'

'No. No.' The handcuffs rattle against the frame.

'You could have called an ambulance. You could have kept her alive. You could have saved her.'

Snot is running from his nostrils, over his upper lip to his mouth.

'Tell them I'm sorry.'

'Who?'

'Her parents.'

51

Angel Face

The weeds reach as high as my knees: nettles and creeping thistles, daisies and dandelions. My feet seem to be taking root like I'm just another unwatered plant, caught between cracks in the broken concrete.

Nobody has gone in or out of the Coach House Inn for the past two hours. Skirting the fence, I duck through a broken gate and approach the main doors. I'm holding a two-foot length of steel pipe, which is hollow yet heavy, keeping it tucked under my arm. The keypad is covered by a plastic milk bottle, cut to form a rain shield. My fingers punch out the code and I nudge the door open, listening.

I cross the foyer and follow the corridor, retracing my steps from the other night, feeling the stickiness of the carpet beneath my feet. The door to the lounge is open. There are beer bottles spread across the table and cigarettes crushed into ashtrays. I try to remember which room belonged to Felix. I look for a padlock. Find it.

Kneeling before the door, I slip a kirby grip from my hair and bend it back and forth until it breaks. This one is harder to pick than Jodie's locker. My fingers grow sore and sticky with sweat. I wipe my hands and begin again, listening as I hold down the pins, being directed by the clicks. One more . . . one more . . .

The lock falls open. The door swings inwards. The room is as I remember — the bed, the rumpled sheets, the soiled mattress, the camera on a tripod. Clothes are strewn across the floor. It reminds me of another room, in another house, where I lived with Terry's body watching it bloat and discolour and leak.

Swinging the metal pipe, I shatter the camera, sending shards of broken plastic and glass pinging off the walls like fists full of thrown gravel. The tripod buckles. I tear at the sheets and punch holes in the mattress and rip at the clothes. Breathing hard, I pause, looking at the destruction, feeling dissatisfied. How does this hurt him?

Emptying my mind, I study the room, searching for hiding places. I'm good at this. Nobody is better. Dragging the mattress to the floor, I lever the metal pipe between the narrow horizontal slats, tearing out nails and splintering the wood, exposing the floor beneath. Crawling inside the bed base, I tap at the skirting board, listening for a hollow echo. Silverfish, dead and living, tumble or scurry as I search the carpet for signs of wear, or concealment. Nothing.

I start again, walking up and down the room, taking small steps. The floor creaks under my right foot. Dropping to my knees, I peel back the carpet, revealing a loose sheet of plywood that covers a gap between the beams. Lifting the board away, I discover a shoebox. Inside the shoebox is a package, double wrapped in tape. I tear open one corner with my teeth and recognise the contents. Crystals. Ice. Meth. There's something else wrapped in an oily black rag, heavy in my hand: a pistol with a long narrow barrel and brown polymer handle. It looks old, like it should be in a museum.

I test a button and a compartment slides from the handle into my other palm. Bullets are pressed inside, one on top of the other.

I've held a gun before. Terry had one. He used to clean it on the kitchen table, taking it apart like a puzzle and wiping down each part with solvent and oil, using a cut-up T-shirt and a brass rod for the barrel.

One day he grabbed my wrist and made me pick it up. I didn't want to touch it.

'Go on,' he said. 'Feel how heavy it is.'

I took the gun in both hands.

'Put your finger on the trigger.'

I did as he asked.

'Point it at me.'

'No.'

'Aim it just here.' He tapped the centre of his chest.

'No.'

'Point the fucking gun. I'm a bad man, remember.'

I shook my head.

'Do it! Now. Pull the trigger.'

My hands were trembling.

Terry sighed in disgust and took the pistol from me. 'There's no bullet in the chamber, you idiot.' He showed me how to release the magazine and rack the slide and clear the chamber.

'Next time I tell you to shoot, you better follow my fucking orders.'

I re-wrap the pistol in the rag and tuck the bundle into the waistband of my jeans, where it rests against the small of my back. Then I replace the empty shoebox and the plywood and the carpet, before taking the package of drugs to the bathroom, where I rip it open, spilling crystals into the toilet bowl. Most of them sink, while others float on top like soapy scum. I flush. Water swirls and disappears. I flush again. 'Bye bye.'

Voices! They're here!

Edging across the floor, I press my cheek against the door. Keeley. Tuba. Felix. They're in the hallway, getting closer.

'What time is the memorial?' asks Tuba.

'Three o'clock.'

I left the padlock lying on the floor. What if Felix looks down . . .? If he sees . . .?

They're passing, turning into the lounge. Edging the door open a crack, I look across the hallway and sees Tuba unpacking beers and putting them in the cooler box. Felix is wearing a coat and tie. His hair is oiled. I want to stay hidden. I want to curl up and wait them out. But if Felix sees the padlock, I'm going to die.

You have a gun.

He'll take it from me.

Not if you shoot him first.

Felix lights a cigarette and tosses the lighter onto the table, resting the ashtray on his stomach and tilting his head back. Tuba puts on some music. They're arguing over whether British rap is better than American rap. This is my chance.

Unwrapping the pistol, I hold it against my chest and slip out of the room into the empty corridor. Quickly, quietly, I pass in front of the lounge, momentarily glimpsing Felix lounging on the sofa. He doesn't see me. I keep moving. Eyes ahead.

The floor creaks and Keeley steps out of a room, looking at the screen of her phone. I freeze, holding the pose as though we're playing a game of musical statues.

She lifts her eyes and opens her mouth. I lunge and grab her hair, yanking her to the ground and covering her mouth with my other hand.

'Not a word!' I whisper. 'Not a word!'

I close my teeth around her earlobe, feeling the back of a silver stud scratching at my tongue. Keeley whimpers.

I show her the gun, pressing the muzzle against her forehead and holding one finger upright against her lips. 'Not a fucking word.'

Keeley cowers.

I get to my feet and walk backwards until I reach the foyer, then the main doors and the steps and the parking area and the road outside. Finally, I run, holding the gun inside my sweatshirt.

52

The incident room is slowly being dismantled. Shredded paper spills from bins and the whiteboards have been picked clean of photographs and maps. The bulk of the task force has been reassigned, but a few remaining souls are typing out statements and tying up loose ends.

Lenny's office is full of half-packed boxes and empty filing cabinets. I haven't had a chance to talk to her about her transfer and whether she's seriously considering retirement. She's too good at her job to walk away; but too poor at the politics to change direction.

'I have another week to wrap up the Jodie Sheehan investigation,' she says, putting another box file in a carton. 'Once I turn over the brief to the CPS, the lawyers take over.'

'What if Farley's confession is disallowed?'

'Won't matter. We have DNA, fibres and dog hairs. Those things are better than a signed confession. People might not believe in God, or ghosts or man-made climate change, but they believe in forensic evidence.'

I move a box from a chair and sit down. 'I talked to Farley. He heard Jodie being thrown off the footbridge.'

'Let it go, Cyrus.'

'Tasmin didn't leave the patio door unlocked. Jodie couldn't get inside. That's why she walked home.'

Lenny reads another label on a file. Behind her, Antonia appears in the doorway. 'Dr Ness wants a word.'

'Patch him through,' says Lenny.

'He's waiting outside.'

Lenny glances at me, raising an eyebrow. The chief pathologist rarely ventures outside the morgue unless it's to a crime scene, or the golf course. Stepping around Antonia, Ness smiles apologetically, his eyes bright and his tightly curled hair looking like a furry helmet. He gives Lenny's office a quick once over, as though he might be in the market for one just like it, before taking a seat next to me and pulling off his soft leather gloves, one finger at a time.

'There's been a development,' he says. 'The DNA report on Jodie Sheehan's unborn child was emailed through from the lab in Boston this morning. It closely matches the traces of semen found on her thigh and indicates that the father was someone close to her.'

Lenny frowns. 'When you say, "close to her"?'

'He shares "runs of homozygosity".'

'Runs of what?'

'He's family,' I say, understanding a little more of the science. Lenny looks from Ness to me. 'Which one?'

Ness gives us both a quick lesson on chromosomes and DNA.

'When children are born from incest their genomes show an absence of heterozygosity because their DNA contains large chunks where the mother and father's contribution are identical because they already share much of the same genetic code. These are called "runs of homozygosity". The more chunks of the child's DNA where the mother and father's contribution are identical, the more likely it is that they're first-degree relatives.'

'OK, so who are we looking for?' asks Lenny.

Ness won't be rushed. 'A brother and sister share fifty per cent DNA. If they had a baby it would likely share roughly twenty-five per cent. It's the same if father and daughter incest leads to pregnancy.

'An uncle and niece share twenty-five per cent DNA and their offspring would have twelve point five per cent. The figures are the same for half-siblings. First cousins share about twelve point five per cent, but any offspring would have less than this. These figures aren't absolutes, but a Y-chromosome match with the blood relative can confirm the incest.'

Lenny is growing impatient. 'Who impregnated Jodie?'

Ness blinks at her before realising that he's only told us half of the story. 'The foetal sample showed a commonality of twelve point five per cent – so you're looking at the uncle, Bryan Whitaker. Like I said – you'll need to test him to be absolutely sure, but unless she has another uncle . . .'

I glance at Lenny. Her fists are clenched. Bloodless.

'He was home that night,' I say. 'Jodie could have confronted him – threatened him with blackmail.'

Lenny grabs her coat from a hook on the wall and opens the door, yelling, 'Antonia, I want a car. Now!'

We're moving. Lenny projects her voice across the incident room. 'Edgar, you're with me. Monroe. Get me a search warrant for the Whitaker house and car. I want everything we have on Bryan Whitaker. Sexual complaints. Rumours. Whispers. We need his phone records and Internet search history.'

I'm in the corridor with Lenny ahead of me. Ness has been left behind. Lenny looks over her shoulder.

'Where do I find Whitaker?'

'He'll be at the memorial service.'

53

Bryan Whitaker is arrested in the parking area of the Corpus Christi Catholic Church as the memorial service ends. Mourners are slowly filtering through the doors, many of them dressed in yellow hats and scarves or carrying yellow balloons.

Lenny dispenses with the handcuffs and offers Whitaker a phone call, which he uses to call his wife rather than a lawyer, a poor decision. Felicity is still inside, comforting Maggie, or shielding her from sympathisers and reporters.

'I don't understand what this is about,' Whitaker says from the rear seat of the police car. 'What am I supposed to have done?'

'You've been read your rights,' replies Lenny.

'What am I being charged with? Aren't you supposed to tell me?'

'You've been arrested on suspicion of murder.'

'That's ridiculous.'

Lenny ignores his subsequent questions and protests, but lets him keep talking, enjoying his frustration.

We're nearing the police station, when she turns and looks over her shoulder from the front seat. 'Are you a religious man, Bryan?'

He doesn't answer.

'There's a passage in the Bible. The Gospel of Matthew if memory serves. "If anyone causes one of these little ones, those who believe in me, to stumble, it would be better for them to have a large millstone hung around their neck and to be drowned in the depths of the sea."'

'I would never hurt a child.'

'You love them, I know, all the nonces say that.'

Whitaker's face alters, twisting out of shape, and his fists clench and unclench.

Lenny doesn't press the issue. Instead, she puts him in an interview room at West Bridgford Police Station and lets him marinate for a few hours in a toxic slurry of fear and uncertainty.

In the meantime, a search warrant is issued for his house where laptops, tablets and mobile phones are seized. Felicity Whitaker is brought to the station, entering through a rear door. Although she's not under arrest, everything about her body language seems to be weighted down like she's a deep-sea diver wearing leaden boots, walking along the ocean floor.

'Can I get you something?' I ask, as she waits to be questioned in a 'comfort room' normally set aside for sexual assault victims.

'No, thank you.'

I bring her a cup of tea anyway. She leaves the teabag dangling inside as she holds it with both hands to keep it steady.

'How long will this take?' she asks.

'I don't know.'

She's nursing a leather handbag, touching it occasionally like she's petting a cat.

'Do you want to be left alone?' I ask.

'No. Stay.' She sips her tea. 'I've never been to a police station. I mean, I've seen them on TV. I used to love *The Bill* and *Inspector George Gently*. Crime dramas, you know. I like a good detective story.'

'Are you very good at picking the villain?'

'Hopeless. Half the time they don't give us a chance, do

they? They make it someone so unlikely.' Her hands are shaking.
'I'm sorry Bryan shouted at you. He didn't mean to be rude.
What's this about?'

'Jodie was pregnant.'

'Yes, I know, but what's that got to do with Bryan?'

'On the night she went missing, did Bryan go to the
fireworks with you?'

'No. He had an AA meeting at the Methodist church in
Sherwood. He goes every week. He's been sober for nearly
nine years.'

'Was he a bad drunk?'

'He never took it out on the kids.'

'What about you?'

She sighs. 'We've been married a long time. Some arguments
are worse than others.'

'What time did you get home that night?'

'Nine-thirty. I was a bit tipsy. Maggie kept filling my glass
with champagne.'

'Did you see Bryan?'

'I heard him come home. I was in bed.'

'What did you hear?'

'The front door. Keys on the table. The shower running.'

'Did he get up during the night?'

Felicity looks at the teabag, which is solidifying in the bottom
of her mug. 'We don't sleep in the same room . . . not for . . .
not since.' She shakes her head. 'You can't really believe that
Bryan had sex with Jodie.'

'The DNA tests on her unborn child show she was carrying
his baby.'

Felicity stares at me, as though waiting for a different punch
line. Then she shakes her head from side to side, gasping. 'Oh,
God, what will Maggie say? She'll never forgive me.'

'It's not your fault.'

'He's *my* husband.'

* * *

Lenny carries a pile of printouts and folders into the interview room, putting them on the table in front of Bryan Whitaker. It's part of the theatre – a prop to unnerve the suspect. Right now he's wondering how he could have generated so much paperwork in such a short time.

Opening a folder, Lenny turns several pages, silently reading the contents while Edgar pulls up a seat and checks the recording equipment, announcing their names, along with the time, date and location.

'How long have you been married, Bryan?' asks Lenny.

'Twenty-two years.'

'That's a fair innings. Do you still look into your wife's eyes when you tell her that you love her?'

'Leave my wife out of this.'

'I'll take that as a no,' says Lenny. 'I doubt if there's a single drop of passion left after that long, although I'm sure you can pretend. You can close your eyes. You can imagine you're with someone else. Tell us about Bonnie Dowling?'

Understanding seems to blossom behind Whitaker's eyes. 'She made a vexatious complaint.'

'Vexatious. That's a big word – a lawyer's word. You took photographs of her in the showers.'

'No.'

'You walked in on her.'

'That was an accident.'

'Why would she lie?'

'Her father owed me coaching fees. Four hundred pounds. He wouldn't pay up. I threatened to sue him. Next thing, he's accusing me of being a pervert.'

'But you ended up paying him.'

'I waived his fees. I should have sued him for slander.'

'That sounds plausible,' says Lenny, 'but it seems odd that your phone was stolen before the police could investigate the complaint. I can't work out if that's convenient or unfortunate.'

'There were no photographs,' says Whitaker. 'It was bullshit.'

Watching him through the observation window, I can see him fortifying himself, but he's less confident than before.

'When did you start coaching Jodie?' asks Edgar.

'I've always coached her.'

'When did you start grooming her?'

'That's a lie.'

'Your fingerprints were found on condoms in her school locker,' says Lenny.

The statement rattles his composure. 'I bought them for her when I discovered she was sexually active. I didn't want her falling pregnant.'

'That's very avuncular of you. Did Jodie's parents know you were buying her condoms?'

'Of course not.'

'Did Jodie ask you to?'

'No.'

'How did you discover she was sexually active?'

'I guessed . . . I feared . . . I've had it happen before. Young skaters reach a certain age. They think they're missing out or they go boy crazy . . .'

'You must see how it looks, Bryan. You're her uncle – her skating coach – and you're buying her condoms. You're facilitating her having underage sex. Did you take her virginity?'

'Don't be ridiculous!'

'I can see how it could happen. You're travelling together to competitions – sharing a room to save money, separate beds to begin with. Then one night . . .'

Whitaker is breathing heavily through his nostrils, while his eyes are screwing a hole through Lenny's forehead.

'You're wrong!'

'You got her pregnant, Bryan.'

'No.'

'We've found the search history on your laptop – you were looking up abortion clinics.'

'I wanted to help her.'

'By lying to us.'

'No! I mean. Jodie came to me. She told me she was pregnant. I thought, because of her skating career and her age . . . I mean, she was too young to have a baby. Jodie couldn't talk to her parents. Maggie is so devoutly Catholic and Dougal would have gone to war. I thought if we could do it quietly, without anyone knowing . . .'

'It was *your* suggestion.'

'Jodie agreed.'

'But she changed her mind.'

Whitaker doesn't answer.

'We've done the DNA tests, Bryan. We know you're the father.'

'What! No!'

'It doesn't matter if Jodie consented. You were in a position of trust and she was a minor. In a few hours from now, technicians will have triangulated the signals from Jodie's phone, pinpointing her movements in her last hours. They're going to put you and Jodie together on the night she died. I think you had sex with her and afterwards you followed her. You begged her to have an abortion, but she wouldn't listen. She threatened everything – your career, your marriage, your reputation. You hit her from behind and dumped her off the bridge. You left Jodie for dead – and that's what happened, she died cold and alone in that clearing.'

'No,' he moans. His chest is bent forward towards his knees and his forehead almost touches the table.

Opening a different folder, Lenny begins pulling out crime-scene photographs, laying them down one by one. 'Don't look away, Bryan. See what you did.'

Whitaker blinks at her wordlessly. The deep lines around his eyes are etched in misery.

'I didn't . . . I wouldn't . . . Ask Felicity.'

'We've spoken to your wife. She didn't see you come in that night.'

'I was there. I came home. I had a shower. I went to bed.'

'You sleep in different rooms.'

'I didn't go out again.'

Lenny sighs and collects the photographs. 'You can keep telling that story all the way to your trial, but eventually a jury is going to see right through your fabrications and bluster.'

'You caught the guy. You charged him.'

'Craig Farley is guilty of many things, but he didn't get Jodie pregnant; he didn't hit her from behind or push her off a bridge.'

Dropping his head into his hands, Whitaker groans.

'This is wrong! A mistake! Let me talk to Felicity. Let me explain.'

54

Three words appear on my pager: *Poppy has gone.*

I call Evie's mobile and she answers breathlessly, unable to get the words out quickly enough.

'There's a hole under the fence . . . near the gate. I found her collar hanging on the chain. I've looked everywhere.'

I tell her to calm down. 'She won't go far.'

'What if she gets run over? What if someone took her?'

'We'll find her.'

Minutes later, I'm behind the wheel. Each time I catch myself driving too quickly, I reluctantly touch the brakes, cursing the amount of traffic. Why is every Sunday driver out today? Every little old lady, slow truck, Belgian, Audi owner and lawn bowler.

I don't want to imagine losing Poppy – not because I've grown attached to her, but because of Evie. I should never have got her a dog. The downside risk was too great. She hasn't loved anything or anyone in so long and now I've opened her up to being hurt again. Abandoned.

Pulling up outside the house, I see Evie standing on the

brick wall, yelling Poppy's name. Her arms are wrapped around her body, hugging her chest, shaking.

She tells me again about the collar and the fence and how she's knocked on doors and talked to neighbours. I know how hard that must be for Evie – meeting strangers and interacting with people.

'We should make posters,' I say, wanting to keep her occupied. 'Do you have a photograph?'

She holds up her phone.

'OK. Download them onto my laptop and make a poster and flyers. We'll put them up on lampposts and in mailboxes.'

Upstairs, I begin getting changed, pulling on a T-shirt, compression leggings and a fleece-lined top. I have to wear my old running shoes, which are almost worn through.

'Where are you going?' Evie asks.

'I can cover more ground.'

'What will I do?'

'You put up the posters.'

She shows me an A4 page with a photograph of Poppy taken in the garden and the headline: MISSING DOG. Underneath is a description of Poppy and Evie's phone number, along with the words: REWARD OFFERED.

'What reward?' I ask.

'We'll think of something,' she says hopefully.

We decide on a plan. I'll cover the park and run along Wollaton Road, while Evie knocks on doors and distributes the flyers. Setting off, I jog my usual route, along Parkside, before turning through the entrance to Wollaton Park. I soon grow breathless, trying to run and call Poppy's name at the same time. Occasionally, I stop and ask people if they've seen her, showing them Evie's poster, which is damp with my sweat. I carry on running . . . calling . . . asking.

Having circled the park, I cross Derby Road and search the grounds of the university, past the boating lake and the faculty buildings. Nottingham is suddenly a maze. Poppy could be anywhere, sleeping under a hedge or in someone's garden. She could be miles away by now, or I could run right past her and never know.

They say there are only four human emotions and sadness is one of them, but there are different types of sadness. Loss. Failure. Abandonment. Depression. Some of these are unavoidable. Some are necessary. Some make us human and whole. I remember seeing a Michael Leunig cartoon showing a tiny sad-eyed man with a noose around his neck. The rope was curled over a beam with a large bucket tied to the other end. As the man cried, his tears filled the bucket and lifted him higher and higher off the ground. Evie is that figure, standing on her tiptoes, filling a bucket with her tears. If only she could stop crying . . .

It's growing dark. I'm exhausted. I cannot run or stumble any further. With dread in every step, I turn for home, trying to fashion words for Evie.

As I turn the corner, I see her waving from the gate. Yelling. 'She's home! She's home!'

A wave of relief breaks over me, rushing over the shingles with a soft rattling hush that whispers, 'Thank God!'

55

Angel Face

'I knew you'd come,' the woman had announced.

I had been about to put a flyer through the mailbox when the door swung open and she said, 'Labrador. Golden coloured. What's her name?'

'Poppy.'

'Come! Come! She's in the garden.'

She ushered me along the hallway and through patio doors to a small neat garden with paving stones and raised flower beds. Poppy was tethered to a wheelbarrow full of ornamental plants.

'She didn't have a collar, but I knew she belonged to someone. She's such a beautiful girl.'

Short and dumpy with a pudding-bowl haircut, the woman had a yappy dog in her arms and two cocker spaniels leaping around her legs.

I threw myself at Poppy, burying my face in her neck, squeezing her so hard that she whimpered, but she kept wagging her tail.

'We were in the park and Poppy came bounding over and started playing with Ajax and John Brown,' the woman said. 'They were having such fun. I kept looking for her owner, but nobody showed up. Poppy followed us home and sat at the front door. Eventually, I brought her inside. I knew you'd come looking.'

The lump in my throat made it hard for me to answer. It's still there now as I tell the story to Cyrus, who is unlacing his running shoes and looking at a blister on his heel. Meanwhile, Poppy is curled up on a rug in the laundry, oblivious to the trouble she's caused.

'I promised her a reward,' I say.

'Do you think she expects money?'

'We could take her flowers.'

'Good idea.'

'I saw a nice garden a few doors down.'

'We're not stealing flowers.'

'OK. Right.' *The blister looks really nasty.* 'I've tightened Poppy's collar, so it won't slip off, but there's still a hole under the back fence, so we can't let her go outside.'

'I'll fix it,' *says Cyrus, retying his runners.*

'You don't have to do it now.'

'I should.'

Cyrus collects a metal toolbox from beneath the stairs and walks outside to the garden shed. After a few minutes, he emerges with a sawhorse under his right arm and several wooden planks balanced on his opposite shoulder.

He kneels and examines the hole beneath the fence. Some of the palings have rotted where they were partially buried in the ground, breaking easily in his fingers. He kneels and begins scooping out soil.

'Can I help?' *I ask.*

Cyrus hands me a torch and peels off his sweaty T-shirt, tossing it onto the steps. Then he takes out a tape measure and calculates the dimensions of the gap.

I notice his tattoos. The inked birds on his torso and arms look like mythical creatures that shimmer in the torchlight, transforming into new shapes as he moves his arms and bends his body, measuring wood and marking it up. He tucks the pencil behind his ear and picks up a handsaw, which he draws back and forth along the line with a strong easy rhythm, creating puffs of sawdust that fall onto the grass like tiny flakes of snow.

'Where did you learn to do that?' *I ask.*

'My father taught me. These were his tools.'

I look at the folding drawers of the toolbox; full of chisels and screwdrivers with worn wooden handles. There is a small axe. Momentarily, I contemplate what happened to Cyrus's family, before pushing the thought away.

Cyrus kneels again and measures the piece of wood against the hole. I try not to look at the cabled veins and muscles on his back. The tattooed wings are so beautifully drawn, I have to fight the urge to reach out and touch them with my fingertips, to stroke the feathers, feeling their softness.

'Light, please.'

'Huh?'

'The torch.'

'Oh, sorry.'

I focus the light on Cyrus's hands as he measures another length of wood and begins sawing. When he straightens, I notice the downy line of dark hair beneath his navel and the slight shadow where the waistband of his running leggings is stretched across his hipbones.

'Are you cold?' I ask. 'I can get you a sweater.'

'I'm OK,' he replies.

'What about a cup of tea?'

'I'd prefer a beer.'

I go inside and glimpse him through the kitchen window, telling myself to stop being so foolish. Getting two bottles of Heineken from the fridge, I open them and return to the garden.

Cyrus takes the beer and empties it in one long series of swallows. He notices that I have one too.

'Is that for me?' he asks.

I mumble and thrust the bottle towards him.

He smiles and says, 'No. You have it,' before turning back to the repairs.

I'm aiming the torch, but my eyes stray again. This time I'm looking at his mouth and wondering what it would be like to kiss those lips, the upper one thinner and shaped like a cupid's bow, the lower one fuller and pinker. How would it feel to touch his teeth with my tongue?

Don't be stupid!

Foolish girl!

I am not a sexual being, or a sensual one. I don't crave physical contact or need sexual release. Yet I feel strange around Cyrus. Different.

Light spills across the grass from the open door, a golden glow with slashes of purple where the shadows are deepest. Cyrus has stopped speaking. He's looking up, waiting for me to say something, but I haven't been paying attention. Has he asked me a question?

He brushes dirt from his knees. 'Are you OK, Evie?'

'What?'

'I asked what you wanted for dinner?'

'Oh.'

'The pub on the corner does a good steak. The fillet is this thick.' He holds his thumb and forefinger an inch apart.

'I'm a vegetarian.'

'They have other things.'

'That'd be nice,' I whisper.

56

Evie has pinned back her hair, letting a few, carefully arranged locks fall across her cheeks, framing her face. She's wearing mascara and eyeshadow, making her eyes look enormous and her skin impossibly pale. I prefer it when she's scrubbed clean of blandishments and I can see her freckles; when she looks her age.

We find a table in the restaurant area, away from the busy front bar where people are watching a European Cup match on the TV, groaning or cheering at the ebb and flow of the action.

Evie is mirroring my movements – unfolding her serviette, putting it on her lap, reading the menu. At times like this she doesn't seem like a damaged teenager. She is confident and articulate and trying to be normal. Practising.

Our relationship has already crossed boundaries in professional terms because of the emotion that comes with therapy. When you hire a lawyer, it doesn't matter if he or she believes in your innocence, or if you like spending time with them. The same is true of a surgeon. As long as they do a good job, your personal feelings don't matter. With a psychologist it's different because it involves observation and trust and engagement and empathy. I am walking a tightrope when it comes to Evie because I'm not sure if I can be everything she needs – a guardian, a therapist, a friend and a confidante.

She has a gift. She calls it a curse. Perhaps she's right. Perhaps she'll never lead a normal life, but I can try to protect her. If others discover what Evie can do, they'll never let her go. Guthrie was right about that much. The questions, experiments and clinical trials will never stop. Evie will become a guinea pig, a lab rat, a freak, a weapon. I will not let that happen.

The restaurant is short-staffed and the lone waitress is chatting to two young guys at the bar. I wave. She ignores me. One of the young men glances at Evie, trying to make eye contact. She seems oblivious. I signal to the waitress again. Nothing.

Evie gets up and weaves between tables, interposing herself between the waitress and the two men.

'Sorry if I'm interrupting your planning for tonight's threesome, but we're waiting to order.'

Heads turn. The waitress looks horrified. The men laugh. Evie jabs one of them in the chest with the knuckle of her forefinger. 'If you don't stop staring at me I'll shove that glass in your face.'

His smile evaporates and he steps back, no longer certain of anything.

Returning to the table, Evie sips from her glass of water, acting as though nothing has happened.

'You didn't have to do that,' I say.

'Do what?'

'Embarrass people.'

'He was staring at me.'

'He was admiring you.'

'What?'

'You look nice tonight.'

Evie screws up her nose, embarrassed by the compliment.

She doesn't understand praise because it heightens expectations. She thinks I don't mean it or that I should be praising someone else.

The waitress arrives, glancing at Evie nervously.

'I'll have a rum and Coke,' says Evie. 'And the mushroom risotto.'

I order the fillet steak, medium rare, with a peppercorn sauce on the side. We share a salad.

Waiting for our meals to arrive, Evie picks up her drink and leans back in her chair. She holds the glass to her lips, studying me over the rim.

'Any thoughts on what you might like to do?' I say, making conversation.

Evie considers this for a bit, giving the question a sense of gravity.

'I could work with animals.'

'You mean like a veterinary assistant?'

'Or a dog walker. I saw one today. She had six dogs in the park and a van with the company logo on the side.'

'You don't have a driving licence.'

'I know.'

'We could apply for a provisional one.'

Her face brightens. 'Really?'

'All we need is a birth certificate or a passport.'

'I don't have anything like that.'

'But the court gave you a new identity.'

'Without papers.'

This information surprises me, but Evie seems resigned to the fact. It's another reminder that she has no official past beyond a secret room in a murder house. Most people belong somewhere. They have a family, a school, a neighbourhood and a country. They share interests, join groups, support teams, vote for parties and form tribes. Evie has none of this.

'I'll see what I can do about getting you a licence,' I say, not sure of who I can call. Maybe Caroline Fairfax can help.

We've almost finished eating when my pager beeps and Lenny's number appears on screen. I call her from a payphone near the cigarette machine.

'Bryan Whitaker didn't break,' she says, 'but we'll have another crack at him in the morning. Sex with a minor is worth two years, but I want him for more than that.'

I hear loud music in the background. She pauses for a moment, telling someone to turn the volume down. She's back.

'The boffins managed to isolate Jodie Sheehan's burner phone. It was purchased a month ago as a job lot of six phones from an eBay seller. The signal puts Jodie at the fireworks and the fish and chip shop and at Jimmy Verbic's party.'

'How long did she stay?'

'Fifteen minutes, give or take. Most likely she was delivering drugs for Felix, but I'm leaving that out of my report.'

'Does Verbic frighten you that much?'

'Yes,' she says bluntly. 'There were two hundred guests and, for all we know, one of them was the chief constable.'

I can see her point. 'Where did Jodie go when she left Verbic's place?'

'The signal shows she walked to Old Market Square and caught the ten o'clock tram towards Clifton South. She got off the tram at Ruddington Lane, probably heading for the Whitaker house, which is ten minutes away. She used the pedestrian underpass beneath the A52 and walked along Somerton Avenue.'

'What time was that?'

'A quarter to eleven.'

'Tasmin Whitaker said Jodie didn't arrive.'

'According to the signal, Jodie spent nearly three hours at the house, which puts Bryan Whitaker on the hook. Her phone stopped transmitting just before two a.m.'

'Where?'

'Best approximation – on the footbridge.'

The facts are starting to fit the timeline. Whitaker came home from his AA meeting and found Jodie at the house or had arranged to meet her there. They had sex. Maybe she tried to blackmail him. They argued. He followed her. She finished up dead.

Evie is waiting for me at the table where the bill is sitting on a saucer with a single mint. Evie is sucking on the other one. I open my wallet and take out my card.

'Thank you,' she says, rubbing a lock of hair between her forefinger and thumb.

'My pleasure.'

'I'll find a way to repay you.'

'You don't have to.'

We take our coats from hooks beside the stairs and get a blast of frigid air as we step outside. A clear day means a cold night. Evie puts her arm through mine. It feels self-conscious, as though she's unsure how I'll react. Our hips and shoulders bump together as we walk.

'What is Claire like?'

'Nice,' I say, feeling the tameness of the word.

'Is she pretty?'

'Yes.'

'She must be very smart to be a lawyer.'

'Yes, she is.'

'Do you miss her?'

'Sometimes.'

'Do you think you'll get married?'

'I don't know if we're still together.'

'Not to her, necessarily . . . to someone else.'

'Maybe.'

Evie tries to walk on her toes, putting one foot in front of the other, like a catwalk model.

Reaching the house, I unlock the front door, standing back to let her pass me. Suddenly, she pushes herself against me in a reckless hug. My whole body stiffens. Undeterred, Evie kisses me. It's not so much a kiss, as a wrestling hold, or a spin-the-bottle attempt by someone who has practised for hours on the back of her hand.

I push her away. She tries again. This time I'm firmer, shoving her hard, holding her at arm's length.

'Don't do that!' I snap. The colour drains from her face. 'What's got into you?'

'You think I'm ugly.'

'No.'

'I'm damaged goods.'

'Of course not.'

'Bullshit!'

'Look at me, Evie. Ask the question again.'

'Do you think I'm damaged goods?'

'No.'

'Do you think I'm ugly?'

'No.'

She believes me now.

'Why then?' she asks.

'It's unprofessional.'

'You're not my shrink.'

'I'm your guardian.'

'I won't tell anyone.'

'It can't happen, Evie.'

'How long do I have to wait?'

'It's not a matter of time. It's *never* going to happen. Ever.'

Evie studies my face and sees that I'm telling the truth. It makes her angry. Embarrassed. Humiliated.

I should have seen this coming. I did. I feared her physical proximity and how my actions could be misinterpreted or misconstrued. Evie has been lost in the system for years, labelled 'a management problem' to be controlled, not listened to. Then I come along; someone who doesn't make demands or rush to judgement or punish her for mistakes. If anything, I've rewarded her worst behaviour because I know where it comes from. This must be enormously attractive to someone like Evie.

We're still on the doorstep. Every fibre of her seems ready to flee, or fight, or have the ground swallow her up. She slaps me hard across the face.

'What was that for?'

'Nothing. I'm sorry. You can hit me back.' She braces herself.

'No.'

'Please.'

'No.'

57

Angel Face

Foolish girl!

Stupid girl!

My hand is stinging from the slap and Cyrus has fingermarks on his cheek, outlined in white, as if my hand had been covered in chalk dust when I hit him.

I rock from foot to foot, unable to look in his eyes, frightened of what I might see. He turned cold the moment I kissed him. He didn't want to touch me, not my face, not my mouth, not my body. Of course not. Other men have touched me and kissed me and done things that didn't feel right. I thought that if I did it with someone like Cyrus it would feel different. It wouldn't be wicked. It wouldn't be wrong.

'I'll get you some ice,' I say.

'No. I'm fine.'

'I keep messing things up.'

'We won't mention it again.'

Why doesn't he get angry? Why won't he hit me?

He hasn't shut the door.

'Are you leaving?' I ask.

'Just for a while.'

'Because of me?'

'No. The police have tracked Jodie Sheehan's last movements. I thought I might retrace her steps.'

'Can I come?'

'It's a tram ride — nothing exciting.'

'I want to.'

Cyrus hesitates.

Please let me come! Please let me come!

He nods. I breathe again and say, 'I'm sorry about before.'

'Before?'

'The kiss.'

'What kiss?'

An Uber drops us in central Nottingham, opposite a grand Victorian house that looks like it's made from white marzipan. Mist has turned the street lights into fuzzy yellow balls that seem to be suspended from invisible strings.

I've been quiet on the journey, still angry with myself. What was I thinking! He's not handsome. He's one of them — the white coats. A shrink. Ugh!

We're standing on the side of the road, wrapped up against the cold.

'What was Jodie doing here?' I ask.

Cyrus nods into the darkness. 'She went to a party up the road.'

I recognise a half-truth.

'Was she delivering for Felix?'

He doesn't answer. He doesn't have to.

We're walking down Regent Street, retracing Jodie's steps. Occasionally I have to skip or add an extra step to keep up with him.

As we near the centre of the city there are more people, spilling out of pubs, bars, restaurants and fast food places that smell of piri piri chicken, hamburgers, pizzas and kebabs. We pass the city library and cross Old Market Square to the tram stop in the shadow of the Council House. A dozen people are waiting, some of them drunk, others kissing, a few studying their phones.

'She caught the next one,' says Cyrus, checking the time. He buys tickets from a machine.

Five minutes pass and a modern-looking tram ghosts quietly into view, pulling up at the platform. We sit near the front, side by side. I'm not sure if I should talk, or if Cyrus needs quiet to concentrate. When he's thinking his brow furrows and his eyes take on the colour of green sea glass as though he's searching for an idea, or listening to a distant, unseen object that is broadcasting information to him.

The tram heads east along Cheapside and turns south when it reaches Weekday Cross. I know some of these places from daytrips away from Langford Hall.

'They have cameras,' I say, pointing above the driver's head. 'Do you think someone followed her?'

'Maybe.'

I pull my feet up and wrap my arms around my shins.

'Did you know your brother was sick?' I ask. 'When he killed your family, I mean.'

'He'd been on medication since he was sixteen.'

'Do you blame him for what happened?'

'No.'

'Mmmmmm,' I say, making it clear I don't believe him. 'Where is Elias now?'

'A place called Rampton. It's a secure psychiatric hospital about an hour north of here.'

'Do you ever visit him?'

'Yes.'

He's lying, but not completely.

'The last time I visited, Elias caused a scene because I didn't bring him any jelly babies.'

'Jelly babies?'

'They're his favourite, but visitors aren't allowed to bring in food.'

'What happened to him after the murders?'

'He pleaded guilty to manslaughter on the grounds of diminished responsibility.'

'Does that mean he can get out one day?'

'I suppose it does.'

'Is that why you became a psychologist?'

'People assume that.'

'What do you say?'

'I avoid self-analysis.'

That's another lie.

'My grandparents wanted me to be a surgeon, but I chose psychology because it was the most difficult thing I could imagine doing.'

'Why?'

'Surgery has rules. The problems are tangible and technical, whereas psychology relies more on instinct and empathy. A surgeon can see his or her results and knows all the answers after the operation. He can declare a decision right or wrong, looking forwards and understanding backwards, which is how we all live. A psychologist has no such certainty. I cannot reach inside a brain and rearrange things. I cannot search for holes with my fingertips, or repair damage with sutures and clamps. Yet that's what I have to do — fix holes, paper over cracks, mend and compensate. I have to repair what's broken using words and ideas and thoughts.'

'You want to heal the world,' I say.

'Or to save myself.'

The answer it too glib. Too neat.

'I think you don't want to visit your brother,' I say. 'You don't want to look into his eyes and remember what he did. And it doesn't matter how many times you remind yourself that he's your brother and you should love him, it doesn't change how you feel.'

Cyrus looks sad rather than angry. 'I wish you wouldn't do that.'

'What?'

'That.'

The tram has been moving quietly between stops and the carriage has slowly emptied. It crossed a river and skirted a pond before the tracks straightened for a long stretch.

'This is us,' says Cyrus, as it slows again.

Ruddington Lane has an uncovered platform bathed in a pale yellow glow from trackside lights.

'This way,' says Cyrus.

We follow a concrete footpath, past rows of neat semi-detached houses and cottages, most of which are dark except for security lights that trigger as we pass, or the occasional grey flickering of a TV behind the curtains.

'Do you know who got Jodie pregnant?' I ask.

'Her uncle.'

'Did he rape her?'

'We don't know.'

'What about Craig Farley?'

'I think he found Jodie's body.'

'Alive?'

'Close to death.'

I make a mmmpph sound through my nostrils. 'And people say I'm screwed up.'

58

The Whitakers' house is dark except for a light upstairs behind a glowing square blind. I know the layout of these post-war bungalows. Three bedrooms and one bathroom on the upper floor with a narrow staircase that partially doubles back on itself. The ground floor has an entrance hall, sitting room, kitchen, laundry and a dining area overlooking a patio and rear garden.

I try to picture Jodie arriving here that night. Smoke from bonfires and the smell of gunpowder must have lingered in the air.

'Jodie didn't have a key,' I say out loud. 'Tasmin had promised to leave the patio door unlocked.'

'Did she?' asks Evie.

'No. She wanted to punish Jodie for keeping secrets.'

'Is that why she walked home?'

According to the phone signals, Jodie spent three hours here. She must have knocked on the door or found another way inside. Perhaps Bryan Whitaker let her into the house.

I glance along the side path to the small silver caravan. Aiden told the police he was home that night, but that he didn't see Jodie. Surely, he'd have a key to the house.

Headlights swing around the corner towards us, bleaching our faces white. Evie instinctively raises her hand to shield her eyes. I recognise the distinctive silhouette of a black cab. Dougal Sheehan doesn't seem to notice us as he brakes hard and flings open the driver's door. Moments later, he's hammering his fist on the front door and holding down a plastic button that chimes through the house.

Nobody answers. He grunts disgustedly and leaps over the low hedge before jogging down the side path towards the caravan.

'Aiden,' he yells. 'Are you in there?'

He tries the handle. It's locked. He tries to break it off but fails. Dipping his head, he drives his shoulder into the side of the van, making it rock violently on rusty springs.

'Come out, you coward!'

'Stay here,' I say to Evie, before sprinting across the road and down the path.

Dougal Sheehan has picked up a shovel and is trying to smash the back window of the caravan. He succeeds on his third attempt, sending glass exploding inwards. Stepping to the right, he starts on another window.

'Did you touch her?' he bellows. 'Was it you?'

Aiden is trapped inside, calling for help. Felicity Whitaker appears from inside the house wearing a dressing gown and slippers. She throws herself at Dougal, grabbing at his arms, trying to wrestle the shovel from his hands. He pushes her away, sending her sprawling onto the grass. Up again, she hammers her fists on his back, yelling at him to leave Aiden alone.

'It was Bryan!' she sobs, breaking down. 'It was Bryan.'

Dougal hurls the shovel at the caravan. It bounces off the door leaving a dent in the aluminium.

'I promise you. Please. Don't blame Aiden.' Felicity has pulled him down to his knees, where she cradles his head against her chest, like a mother comforting a hurt child. Dougal wants to argue, but she puts a finger to his lips, saying, 'Leave it be. It's better that way.'

Another voice. Tasmin is standing on the patio in her pyjamas. 'Mummy? Is everything all right?'

'Go back to bed,' says Felicity, wiping her cheeks. She notices me for the first time. There is a beat of silence and a sharp light enters her eyes.

'What are you doing here?' she says accusingly. 'Have you been spying on us?'

'No.'

Dougal has climbed to his feet. 'Did you follow me?'

'I was tracing Jodie's last movements.'

Felicity's voice has changed to a harsh whisper. 'You're trespassing!'

I glance at Dougal, hoping for an explanation. 'What has Aiden done?'

'Get off this property!' yells Felicity. 'Leave my family alone.'

Her face is twisted in fury and her fists are tightly bunched. She is half Dougal's size, but I fear her more because she doesn't seem rational.

Behind her, the caravan door bursts open and Aiden leaps from inside, almost spinning his legs in mid-air before he lands on the grass and takes off, sprinting down the side path and out onto the road, past the black cab and Evie Cormac. A small dark knapsack bounces loosely on his back.

Felicity yells for him to stop. 'It's all right, love. You've done nothing wrong.'

Dougal tries to take off in pursuit, but Felicity pulls him back, begging him to stop. The big man can't hope to catch Aiden, who has gone by the time I reach the road.

'He went that way,' says Evie pointing towards Silverdale Walk.

I listen and imagine I can still hear his footsteps on the asphalt path, crossing the bridge and skirting the meadow, but the only sound is Felicity tearfully calling his name, telling him to come home.

59

Angel Face

I fall into step beside Cyrus as we walk along the footpath as far the footbridge and glance over the railing at the pond.

'Why did Jodie come this way?' I ask.

'It's the shortest route home.'

Silently, I mouth the word 'home'. It should be a simple concept, but I've never understood what it means. Is home a place, or a language, or a culture, or a climate or geography? People run away from home and get homesick and become homeless. Does home mean something different to each person? Do we make our own? Does it make us whole?

I wipe my nose on my sleeve. 'Why did that boy run?'

'I don't know.'

'He looked frightened.'

'Yes.'

Cyrus pauses and raises his face to the treetops, as though sniffing something on the breeze. Without warning, he turns off the path.

'Where are we going?'

'There's a place just beyond those trees — an old hunting lodge. I want to check it out.'

He takes my hand, leading me along a muddy path that narrows in places and is soft beneath my boots. A cobweb brushes and breaks against my cheek. Faint night sounds are audible between our footsteps.

I can see the building now. The roof has partially collapsed, like a house of cards that has fallen on one side; and vines have grown up into the rafters, trying to wrestle the remaining walls to the ground.

'Wait here,' he says.

'Don't go.'

'Do you have your phone?'

I nod.

'If I'm not back in fifteen minutes, I want you to call the police.'

'Ten minutes.'

'OK.'

I lose sight of his silhouette in the deeper shadows but hear the creak of weight being placed on wooden steps.

I hear his voice – 'Aiden?' – but no reply.

The trees lean towards me, closing over my head, blacker than the sky, although some are edged by faint traces of silver from cobwebs and beads of dew. I'm used to understanding night sounds. Not the insects or the birds, but the creak of floorboards and the groan of branches and someone breathing in the darkness.

Time passes. I look at my phone. The brightness of the screen blinds me for a few seconds. I don't know how many minutes have passed. I didn't make a note of the time when Cyrus left. It must be ten by now. Longer. I softly call his name. Louder.

'Don't leave me,' I want to say.

Is he playing a game? Is he hiding? Is he hurt?

Moments later, I hear voices. Cyrus appears. The boy is with him. Aiden keeps his eyes down, not acknowledging me. His hair is uncombed and wild. He scuffs his shoes in the fallen leaves.

'This is Evie,' says Cyrus. No hands are shaken. No looks are exchanged.

'Can we go home now?' I ask.

'Yeah.'

*　　*　　*

After midnight. The kettle is cooling. Tea has brewed. Aiden is sitting at the table with his bag between his feet, occasionally running his hands through his hair. He looks like a girl, I think. Prettier than most. Prettier than me.

Cyrus asks him if he's hungry. A shake of the head.

'Do you have any cigarettes?'

I offer him one of mine from the packet I keep in the laundry, on a shelf above the dryer. Poppy lifts her head from the oversized wicker basket that has become her bed.

'We'll have to smoke in the garden,' *I say.* 'Cyrus has a thing about second-hand smoke.'

'I'll make an exception for tonight,' *Cyrus says.*

I give him a raised eyebrow.

'Maybe you should go to bed, Evie.'

'I'm fine.'

He jerks his head towards the door, but I reach for a cigarette and light up, positioning an ashtray between Aiden and me. Cyrus opens a window. Settles again.

'What was all that about — the fight with your uncle?'

Aiden shrugs. Eyes down. Faltering.

Cyrus tries again. 'Jodie came to your house on the night she died. I think she knocked on the door of the caravan.'

Aiden doesn't have to say anything. He's an open book. He's a whole library of open books.

'How long had you two been . . . ?'

'Five months,' *says Aiden, filling his lungs with smoke.*

'Who knew?'

'Nobody.'

'Are you sure?'

Aiden is staring at his reflection in the window.

'We couldn't tell anyone. Aunt Maggie would have freaked out. She's so Catholic, you know. Jodie and me have known each other since we were kids. Most of that time, I thought she was just another annoying brat like Tasmin, but then . . .' *He stops and starts again.* 'Tasmin had a sleepover party for her sixteenth birthday. It was all girls, dressed in pyjamas, playing games and dancing around the house to crappy pop songs. They were sneaking vodka into their lemonade. I was supposed to be the responsible adult, but I let it go, you know. I paid for the pizzas and then made myself scarce, hanging out in my van.

'Tasmin wanted to play hide-and-seek. I could hear the girls finding hiding places in the garden and upstairs. Next thing, Jodie burst into the caravan and pleaded with me to hide her. I told her to find somewhere else. I mean – you've seen my van – there are no hidey holes or crawlspaces. She could hear Tasmin counting; calling out, "Ready or not!" Jodie burrowed under the duvet next to me and lay still with her head on my chest and her arms and legs wrapped around me.'

Aiden looks up at Cyrus imploringly.

'I know what you're thinking, but it wasn't like that. Up until that night, Jodie was just Jodie, you know. We grew up together. We splashed in wading pools and played Monopoly and wrestled for the TV remote. She was my cousin. Not even a girl. But now she was wrapped around me, her head on my chest. I could feel her warm breath and smell her shampoo. Tasmin came bursting through the door, asking if I'd seen Jodie. I told her no. She left. Jodie didn't move. For minutes she lay there, holding me, her face invisible, her body warm. Eventually, she pushed back the duvet and looked up at me. Her eyes were shining. We'd never kissed before, not even on the cheek, but this was a proper kiss, an on-screen kiss, you know, like in the movies. She had a wad of chewing gum in her mouth. It finished in mine. It felt like we were trying to breathe for each other.'

'Did you have sex that night?'

'Not then. Later.'

'Was Jodie a virgin?'

He nods.

'Did you know she was pregnant?'

'Uh-huh.'

Cyrus glances at me, wordlessly asking the question. I nod. Aiden is telling the truth.

He continues. 'We took precautions most of the time. Jodie wanted to go on the pill, but we knew what Aunt Maggie would say if she found out.'

'Who did you tell?'

'Nobody, at first, but when Jodie got pregnant she told my dad because she didn't want to keep practising the difficult jumps. He wanted her to land the triple axel, but she knew that any fall could hurt the baby.'

'Did he know about you?'

'No. Jodie refused to say. Dad wanted her to get an abortion. He said nobody had to know if they did it quietly; and that Jodie could keep skating and stay at school.'

'But she wanted to keep the baby,' says Cyrus.

Aiden nods, stubbing out his cigarette. He reaches for another.

'It's not illegal – you know. First cousins get married all the time – and have babies. I checked. Charles Darwin married his first cousin and so did Albert Einstein. Queen Victoria and Prince Albert were cousins. It's not taboo, or anything like that. The baby would have been fine.'

'You planned to run away,' says Cyrus. 'Where to?'

'We figured we'd go to London and rent a place.'

'What about your law degree – the scholarship?'

'I don't want to be a lawyer. Never have. I only applied because of Mum. It was her dream – not mine.'

'What's your dream?'

'I want to write songs and produce them. People think that's pie-in-the-sky stuff, but I'm good. You should listen to my stuff. I got a CD.' He rummages in the bag at his feet and hands Cyrus a USB stick with the words 'Bedroom Recordings' handwritten on the side. 'I should be able to try, right?' asks Aiden. 'If it doesn't work out, I can go to university.'

He's looking from face to face, wanting us to agree. He must have had this argument a thousand times in his head, convincing himself before he risked talking to his parents.

'They took DNA from Jodie's unborn child,' says Cyrus. 'You're not the father.'

'No! You're wrong. Dad would never . . . she would never.'

Again, Cyrus looks at me. Again, I nod. Aiden believes what he's saying, but that doesn't make it true.

'Who knew that you were sleeping with Jodie?' asks Cyrus.

'Nobody.'

'What about your mother?'

'No, I mean, she almost caught us one day and went batshit crazy. I lied to her. I told her we were just fooling around. She read me the riot act, telling me that Jodie was underage and that she was my cousin and that Dougal and Maggie would be heartbroken if they knew and that I couldn't touch her like that again. I told her nothing had happened and promised her that nothing would.'

'When was this?'

Aiden pauses, trying to remember. 'Early September, maybe.'

'Before you knew that Jodie was pregnant?'

'Yeah.'

Cyrus seems to be calculating the dates and rearranging the timelines. 'On the night Jodie came to the caravan, what happened?'

'Nothing. I mean. She was cold and tired. Some old letch at a party had groped her and offered her money for sex, but she ran away.'

'What did you do?'

'I made her a cup of tea. We talked . . .'

'You slept together.'

Aiden nods.

'Why use a condom?'

'Force of habit,' he says, without irony.

'What made Jodie go home that night?' asks Cyrus.

Aiden shakes his head, unable to explain 'When she left the caravan, I thought she was going to sneak into the house and sleep in Tasmin's room. It's what she always did. I gave her my key.'

'What time was that?'

'Early hours. Jodie had to be up for training at six.'

Cyrus looks at the clock above the sink. It's almost two a.m.

'You can sleep here tonight. We'll talk to the police in the morning.' He turns to me. 'Can you help me make up a bed for Aiden?'

I nod and empty the ashtray and put the mugs in the sink.

'You should call your mother and tell her you're OK,' says Cyrus.

Aiden baulks. 'I don't want to speak to her.'

'It can wait until morning.'

Upstairs, Cyrus shows me where he keeps the spare sheets and blankets. We make the bed together, although he's pretty useless. I'm an expert at making beds with nurse's corners. They used to check mine every day at Langford Hall.

'He was telling the truth,' I say.

'Or what he believes to be the truth,' Cyrus replies.

'What are you going to do?'

'Let the police decide.'

I hold a pillow under my chin and shake it into a slip.

'Do you know who killed Jodie Sheehan?' I ask.

'Not yet.'

'Mmmmmmm.'

Cyrus frowns. 'You always make that sound when you don't believe me.'

'Mmmmmmm.'

60

The sun is almost liquid, angled so low that it slants through the blinds, reflecting from computer screens and empty white-boards in the incident room. Aiden is sitting next to me wearing yesterday's clothes, but he's showered and combed his hair.

Lenny is in a meeting. I can hear raised voices behind her closed office door. One of them I recognise.

Antonia glances up from her desk.

I whisper, 'Who is it?'

She mouths the words, 'Timothy Heller-Smith and Jimmy Verbic.'

'Why?'

She motions me to move closer, cupping her hand over my ear.

'I'm not sure but it could have something to do with Felix Sheehan. He's in hospital with a broken jaw and internal bleeding.'

'What happened?'

'Lenny thinks he ripped off his supplier and copped a beating. Apparently, he started off asking for police protection, but then changed his mind.'

The office door opens suddenly. Antonia jumps up as though it has triggered a motor inside her. She bustles around collecting coats and hats and scarves.

Heller-Smith recognises me and smiles mockingly.

'Ah, it's Dr Haven. The shrink who won't shrink.'

'Have we met?' I ask.

'No, but I've heard all about you. DCI Parvel seems very enamoured. Maybe it's a gender thing.'

This he finds funny. I glimpse the loathing in Lenny's eyes but know she won't say anything.

'I assume you two know each other,' says Heller-Smith, gesturing towards Jimmy.

We nod but don't shake hands.

'Councillor Verbic has asked for and received a formal apology from Nottinghamshire Police for any hurt and inconvenience we have caused him. The chief constable feels that it has bordered on harassment.'

'The chief inspector was only doing her job,' says Jimmy. 'I'm sure it wasn't personal.'

'It wasn't,' says Lenny.

Heller-Smith ignores the comment. 'I have also received a complaint from the Sheehan family accusing the police of being insensitive and heavy-handed.'

'I'll draft a response,' says Lenny.

'Yes, you do that.'

Heller-Smith notices Aiden.

'Let me guess – another suspect. Who is it this time?'

Aiden doesn't move. I glance at Lenny wanting to talk to her privately, but this isn't the time or the place.

'This is Aiden Whitaker,' I say. 'He wants to make a statement.'

'Did he kill Jodie Sheehan?'

'No. He claims to have got her pregnant.'

'Another one! Should we start compiling a list?'

'She was *murdered*,' I say through clenched teeth.

'That case is closed,' replies Heller-Smith.

'With all due respect, sir, that's not your decision,' says Lenny, stepping forward. 'This is still *my* investigation and I decide when it's closed.'

Heller-Smith smiles crookedly and scratches his cheek. It's like he's marking up an unseen ledger, keeping a list of whatever slights and abuses he will avenge later.

'Another example of why you're being transferred,' he says to nobody in particular.

'Maybe, but not until Monday.'

The men leave. Heller-Smith makes a barking sound all the way along the corridor, growing louder as he passes the incident room, letting everyone know what he thinks of Lenny.

She gives me a lazy sideways glance but doesn't hold my eyes.

'Your timing is shit,' she mutters, addressing me, but studying Aiden.

'He was with Jodie that night,' I explain. 'They were together in the caravan. He claims the baby is his.'

'He's wrong. Cousins don't match the DNA profile.'

Aiden shakes his head. 'No. I'm the father.'

'How do I know you're not saying this to protect your old man?'

'I'm not. I loved her.'

Lenny sighs and yells to Antonia. 'Get me Ness.'

'On the phone?'

'No, here. Now!'

61

Angel Face

Poppy is barking at a squirrel in the garden.

'Be quiet,' I tell her, worried the neighbours might complain about the noise. The Labrador spins and lopes across the soggy grass, pausing to look back at the squirrel, as if to say, 'I'll get you next time.'

I'm sitting on the back steps, barefoot and in my pyjamas, wrapped in a blanket. Poppy's tail thumps against my thigh as I scratch her behind the ears. Is this how happiness is meant to feel?

I miss Cyrus. I miss hearing his footsteps, and the creak of the plumbing when he turns on the taps, and the clang of his weights dropping into the cradle. The house feels empty when he's not here.

Wandering back inside, I think about reading some of his books, or beading my hair, or watching TV. I flick through the channels where people are buying houses in the country, or showing off kitchen gadgets, or yelling at each other in a courtroom.

The mail-flap echoes along the hallway. The newspapers are lying on the doormat, wrapped in plastic, along with the morning mail: two letters and a postcard with an Irish stamp. It shows a picture of a rocky coastline in the Aran Islands. Four words are scrawled beside the address: 'Leave my parents alone.'

I have no idea what it means, but leave it on the desk for Cyrus.

Unwrapping the newspaper, I read about Bryan Whitaker's arrest. The photograph shows him sitting in the back of a police car with a coat over his head, which means it could be anyone. The story gives details of his skating career and how he'd coached Jodie Sheehan since she could walk.

The doorbell starts ringing and doesn't stop. Someone is holding his or her finger on the button. I answer, ready to complain, but a woman pushes past me, knocking me off balance.

'Where is he?'

'Cyrus isn't here.'

She's moving from room to room. Searching.

'Where's Aiden?'

'They've gone to the police station.'

'Get them back!'

'What?'

'I said get them back.'

'I can't.'

'GET THEM BACK!' she screams. Frantic. Desperate.

I flinch, backing away. 'Cyrus doesn't have a phone.'

She swallows a deep breath and apologises. 'Please. I have to talk to Aiden.'

This must be Felicity Whitaker, Aiden's mother. She was at the house last night, but I didn't meet her.

'I can send him a message.'

Mrs Whitaker steps closer as I type on my phone.

'He has to bring Aiden. Nobody else. No police.'

I press send. The message disappears.

Poppy has come to the back door, whining and scratching, wanting to come inside.

'Who's that?'

'My dog.'

'Where are you going?'

'To let her inside.' I say. 'She won't hurt you.'

'No! Leave her.'

The blanket has dropped from my shoulders. She looks at my pyjamas.

'Are you his daughter?'

'What?'

She speaks slowly as though I'm retarded. 'Are . . . you . . . his . . . daughter?'

'No. He's . . . I'm . . . I'm a foster child.'

'Where is your mother?'

'Dead.'

The bluntness of my answer surprises her.

'What happened to her?'

'It doesn't matter. Would you like a cup of tea?'

'No.'

'I could make coffee.'

'No.'

She's pacing back and forth, knocking her fist repeatedly against her head, as though trying to dislodge a thought. She's mumbling. Poppy barks. I glance at the clock above the sink. Why hasn't Cyrus called?

'Call him?' *she says, pointing to my phone.*

'I told you – he doesn't have a mobile. I know it's weird. He doesn't have a landline either.'

'Don't bullshit me, girlie. Call him.'

'I'm not lying.'

I realise that she's going to hit me before it happens but can't stop the blow. She backhands me across the face, knocking me sideways so that my head strikes the doorjamb. I slide down the wall, seeing sparks when I blink.

She takes hold of my ponytail and jerks my face around.

'Call him! Tell him not to bring the police. I want Aiden. Nobody else.'

62

I glance at my pager and see Evie's number.

You have to bring Aiden home, says the message. A moment later, a second one arrives: *No police.*

I glance at Lenny.

'What's wrong?' she asks.

'Can I use your phone?'

I call Evie's number, listening to it ring. She answers.

'Cyrus?'

'Is everything OK?'

'Bring him back! Now!' snarls Felicity Whitaker.

'Felicity?'

'I want Aiden.'

'He's talking to the detectives.'

'Stop him!'

'Why? What's wrong?'

'Tell him to shut up!'

'He's at West Bridgford Police Station. Why don't you come here and talk to him?'

'Bring him here.'

'I can't do that.'

Silence for a long time, but I can hear her breathing.

'Are you there, Felicity? Let me talk to Evie.'

'Aiden's done nothing wrong,' she blurts.

'I know.'

'Tell the police.'

'I will. Put Evie on the phone.'

'No! You're not listening. Bring Aiden now.'

'He'll be home soon.'

'Bring him, or she gets hurt . . . I'll do it. I'll kill her. I'll kill myself. Bring Aiden, or she dies.'

The line goes dead. My heart is suddenly where my brain should be, the blood pounding behind my temples. Vaguely I'm aware of Lenny yelling orders across the near empty incident room, calling for a tactical response team. No sirens. Radio silence.

In between firing off commands, she is asking me questions about Felicity Whitaker and the layout of the house. How many entrances or access points? Are the windows locked or unlocked? Could she be armed? How did she seem?

'Upset,' I say.

'Irrational?'

'Yes.'

'What about the girl, Evie – is she likely to panic?'

I hesitate, trying to think. I remember the incident at Langford Hall when Evie disarmed Brodie. Back then she had been so calm it had bordered on serenity.

'She'll look to escape,' I say.

We're talking and moving, descending the stairs, into the parking area, where three unmarked police cars are waiting. Lenny pulls body armour from the boot of the first car and throws a black vest in my direction.

'It that really necessary?'

'You wear it, or you stay here.'

There are more questions on the journey, most of them about Felicity's state of mind.

372

'Does she have any history of mental illness?'

'I don't know.'

'Why take a hostage?'

'She doesn't want Aiden talking to the police.'

'Why?'

'Maybe she's worried this will jeopardise his future. He's been offered a place at Cambridge to study law. A full scholarship.'

'Sleeping with his cousin won't jeopardise anything.'

'Jodie was underage.'

'And he's not much older.'

Lenny takes a call. I can only hear one side of the conversation.

'No helicopters . . . A drone? How noisy is it? . . . OK. Yeah . . . Evacuate whoever you can without alerting Mrs Whitaker. Do it quietly.'

Lenny turns to me: 'Do any of the neighbouring properties overlook the front or back of the house?'

'The front, yes.'

'OK. We need a floor plan. You might have to sketch one. What room are they likely to be in?'

'The kitchen, maybe. It's at the back.

We're getting closer to Wollaton Park. My pager beeps. It's another message from Evie.

Where are you?

63

Angel Face

'I'm sorry. I'm sorry. I didn't mean to hit you.'

Mrs Whitaker is fussing over me, looking for frozen peas in the freezer.

'I don't normally, I mean, I never hit Aiden or Tasmin. I don't know what came over me.'

Her eyes are jittering from side to side as she paces the kitchen. I've seen someone overdose before. And I've seen loads of kids suddenly kick off because they're angry, or high, or hearing voices, but nothing like this.

'I'll wait upstairs,' I say.

'No.'

'I should get dressed.'

'Stay here.'

'But I need the loo.' I cross my legs as though I'm busting.

'There must be one downstairs.'

I reach for my phone, but she takes it from me.

'What if he calls?' I ask.

'I'll answer it.'

The loo is off the laundry. I lock the door and glance at the window. It's too small for me to crawl out. Maybe I can stay here until Cyrus arrives.

'I can't hear anything happening,' she says from the far side of the door. 'You're making me nervous.'

'Piss or get off the pot.'

My phone is ringing. She answers, asking, 'Where's Aiden?'

I don't hear the reply, but it must be Cyrus.

After another pause, she knocks.

'He wants to talk to you. You have to tell him you're OK.'

I unlock the door and step out. Cyrus is on speakerphone.

'Hey,' I say.

'Are you all right?'

'Yeah.'

'Has she threatened you?' asks Cyrus.

Mrs Whitaker interrupts. 'She's fine. Where's Aiden?'

'You can come out and see him.'

'No!'

'He didn't hurt Jodie. You don't have to protect him. He's giving the police a statement, that's all.'

She curses under her breath. 'No statements!'

'You can't make demands.'

'I WANT MY SON!' she screams, grabbing a knife from the wooden block beside the stove.

'Please, stay calm,' says Cyrus.

'DON'T TELL ME TO BE CALM!'

'She has a knife!' I yell, ducking under her arm and bolting for the door. She grabs my hair and hauls me back. I cry out in pain.

Cyrus has heard it all.

'Don't hurt her,' he pleads. 'Evie? Evie? Can you hear me?'

Mrs Whitaker holds the knife to my neck. 'Answer him.'

'I'm here.'

'Are you hurt?'

'No.'

'Are you sure?'

'Yeah.'

He exhales with relief, but doesn't say anything for a while. It's like he's lost for words. Finally, he says, 'Let me come inside, Felicity.'

'Not without Aiden.'

'How about we do a swap? Take me instead of Evie.'

'No.'

'She's just a kid.'

'So is Aiden.'

'The police aren't going to let him walk into a house where you've threatened someone – not when you're holding a knife. Talk to me.'

'Get me Aiden. Then we'll talk.'

64

Police cars have been parked diagonally across the road to create a staggered series of checkpoints, each one closer than the next. The outer ring is a hundred yards from the house where uniformed officers are keeping spectators behind barricades. Most of them are neighbours, who are no doubt filling the vacuum of uncertainty with breathless rumours of terrorism or a domestic siege.

'The hostage negotiator is still forty minutes away,' says Lenny.

'I'm trained,' I say.

'You're personally involved.'

'I know the layout of the house. I know Felicity Whitaker.'

'I'm not giving her a second hostage.'

'What if she agrees to release Evie?'

'She just refused.'

More police are arriving. Men dressed in black wearing body armour and helmets, carrying rifles, battering rams and shields. The head of the tactical response team is straight out of Hollywood casting, with chiselled features and a Clooneyesque haircut.

'We'll be ready in fifteen,' he tells Lenny, who remains in overall command until negotiations are deemed to have failed.

'Do we have eyes?' she asks.

'We had a sighting in the kitchen, before the blinds were lowered,' says Edgar.

'What about ears?'

'The directional microphones aren't picking up much.'

Lenny looks at me. 'Phone her again.'

I dial Evie's mobile. It goes to her voicemail. I try again. Nothing.

'Can we get Aiden here?' I ask.

'He's on his way.'

Lenny motions towards the tactical response officers who are taking up positions behind hedges and parked cars and in neighbouring properties with windows that overlook the house.

'What would you do?' she asks.

'Give her more time. She's a middle-aged mother of two, not a wanted terrorist.'

Lenny gazes at the house as though contemplating tomorrow's headlines. 'OK, but first I want confirmation that Evie Cormac is unharmed.'

Grabbing a loudhailer from the front seat of her car, she signals for me to follow.

The birds have gone quiet and traffic noise drops away, leaving a soundtrack of our shoes crushing seedpods on the footpath. We reach the front gate. Lenny raises the megaphone.

'Mrs Whitaker? I know you can hear me. I'm DCI Parvel. We met a few weeks ago.'

We wait. Watching. Nothing moves behind the curtains.

'Your son is on his way, but I can't help you unless you help me. I need proof that Evie Cormac is safe and unharmed.'

The front door opens a crack. Felicity yells, 'She's safe.'

'I'll need more than your word for it.'

The door opens wider and this time Evie emerges, dressed in her red flannelette pyjamas, printed with penguins. She's barefoot and looks younger than eighteen. Younger than fourteen. Too young.

Felicity Whitaker has her arm wrapped around Evie's neck, crooked at the elbow, using her has a human shield. She's holding a bottle of clear liquid in her right hand. She holds it aloft and begins emptying it over Evie. Fluid splashes across her head and shoulders . . . into her eyes. Evie screams, trying to cover her face. What is it? Paint thinners? Gasoline? Turpentine?

Evie tries to drop and roll, but Felicity holds her upright and tosses the empty bottle away. It bounces down the steps and rolls onto the grass. She pulls a cigarette lighter from her pocket and holds it against Evie's cheek.

'You know what I want.'

The door closes.

65

Angel Face

My eyes are burning. My mouth, my nostrils, my ears, every hair follicle is on fire. It's like red-hot wires have been driven through my pupils straight into my brain. I use my pyjama sleeves to wipe at my eyes, but the liquid is all over me, soaking the fabric, clinging to my skin.

Dragged backwards along the hallway, I'm dumped in the library, where I curl up on the floor. More liquid is splashed across the desk and book shelves, the fumes scalding my throat, making me gag.

'Why are you doing this?' I scream.

'They aren't listening.'

'That's not my fault.'

She grabs my hair again.

'How many entrances?'

'Two. Front and back.'

She pulls me from room to room where she closes the blinds and curtains, checking the windows are locked.

'Water,' I plead. 'My eyes.'

We're in the kitchen. She holds my head over the sink and turns on the tap. I splash water onto my face, but still can't see properly. Bottles and cans are scattered across the floor. She has emptied the shelves in the laundry and kitchen, examining the labels, keeping some bottles and discarding others. I spent hours tidying those shelves, putting paints on one side and cleaning products on the other, with the labels facing out.

She makes me sit down and unspools a roll of masking tape, wrapping it around my wrists and up my forearms.

'You don't have to do this.'

'Shut up!'

'I'm not Dr Haven's daughter. We're not related.'

'You're living here.'

'I'm visiting.'

'You must mean something to him.'

The statement jangles something inside me. Does Cyrus care about me? He must do. He didn't send me back to Langford Hall. He let me have Poppy. Darling Poppy. Poor Poppy. She's whining from the back steps, wondering why she's being ignored.

In a different life, in a different house, I listened to dogs barking as Terry was tortured to death. He stopped begging after a while. Then he stopped talking, which infuriated them even more. He groaned and cried and I wished they would hurry. I wished they would finish. I wished his suffering would end.

I've heard people die before. Some hardly made a squeak, while others fought like drowning cats in a sack. My father. My mother. My sister. They left me alone with the nameless men and the faceless men. Only they do have names and they do have faces. And I remember every one of them. Next time I will pull the trigger. Next time I won't hesitate.

66

Lenny is yelling orders over the two-way, wanting fire crews in place and the gas and electricity turned off to the house. The nearest hospital burns unit is on standby. Her eyes spark with a fresh energy, as though she's operating on a different level to everybody else, seeing several moves ahead.

'Where is Aiden Whitaker?'

'Ten minutes away,' replies Edgar.

'No sirens,' says Lenny. She glances at me. 'Tell me something I don't know.'

'She's desperate.'

'That's obvious. Come on!'

'She's delusional.'

'Why?'

'This is about Aiden. She's protecting him.'

'Why?'

'Maybe she thinks he killed Jodie.'

'Did he? The kid could be playing us.'

'He's not lying.'

'How can you be so sure?'

I can't tell her about Evie and what she can do. Last night

she asked me if I knew the killer's name. She didn't believe me when I said no. I thought she'd made a mistake and that she wasn't infallible after all.

An idea rises from the depths of my unconscious mind, becoming clearer as it nears the surface. When I chatted to Maggie Sheehan at the church, she said that Felicity had struggled to get pregnant. It took her years of IVF – one failure after another. She almost went mad, Maggie said. Then Aiden arrived, her miracle child, and she projected onto him all her dreams and unfulfilled ambitions. A mother's job is to protect her children, to keep them safe? There must be more.

Suddenly I see it. Aiden. Jodie. Bryan. Dougal. Felicity. They are like cards in a poker hand, a full house. That's what Evie saw last night – some shard of light from my subconscious mind. The 'tell'.

'Let me go in,' I say. 'I know why she's doing this.'

Lenny hesitates and glances at the tactical response group. She hands me a radio device that clips to my belt.

'Give us the word and we're going in. If that happens, keep your head down.'

Moments later, I'm walking alone past parked cars, cutting across the grass verge to the front gate. I press the doorbell, smelling the turpentine that has been splashed on the threshold.

A voice from inside. 'Aiden?'

'No. It's Cyrus.'

'Where's Aiden?'

'He's on his way.'

'I'll torch this place! I'll burn her first!'

'I promise you he's coming.'

Felicity is talking to me from the hallway with only the door separating us.

'I'm just going to sit here,' I say, lowering myself onto the step and leaning against the brickwork. I pluck a flower from the overgrown garden and begin picking off the petals one by one. The silence is filled with quiet breathing.

'I had a pen friend when I was at school,' I say, remembering the postcards that were stuck on Felicity's fridge. 'Her name was Camille. She lived in Manila, in the Philippines. We wrote to each other every month for about ten years. Letters at first, then emails. We promised that one day we'd meet up.'

'Did you ever do it?'

'We came close. We were both turning twenty-five and we planned to celebrate our birthdays in Singapore.'

'What happened?'

'She had a baby – a little boy.'

I pluck another petal from the flower.

'You could still make your world tour – see all your friends,' I say.

Felicity makes a mocking sound. She's closer now, only inches away from me. I imagine her leaning her back against mine, with only the door separating us.

'I've heard some of Aiden's music. He's very good.'

'Music is just a hobby. He's going to Cambridge. He won a scholarship.'

'Did he apply for that, or did you?'

Felicity ignores me. 'He was a straight-A student. His teachers said he was the best and brightest. He's going to be a lawyer. He's going to make a difference.'

'A difference for who?' I ask.

Felicity goes quiet. The pause stretches out for so long I wonder if she's still leaning against the door.

'What does Aiden want?' I ask. 'Have you asked him?'

Nothing.

'I know it feel goods good basking in Aiden's successes, but if children are pushed into fulfilling parental expectations, they can fail to explore other opportunities. They can feel stifled. Trapped.'

'I know my son.'

'I'm sure you do, but Aiden is scared of disappointing you. He wants you to listen. I've treated kids who feel pressured to fulfil some sort of destiny. Some achieve great things, but others suffer anxiety and depression, which feeds addictions. Some even sabotage themselves rather than risk disappointing those who expect too much.'

'That's not me,' she says savagely.

'I talked to Aiden. He was sleeping with Jodie. He got her pregnant.'

'No! It was Bryan!'

'You've known all along, haven't you?'

Silence. I can hear her breathing.

She seems to swallow her answer. Glancing along the front path, I see Lenny moving into place. Aiden is with her. They're both wearing body armour. Firemen have unspooled hoses and hooked them to the nearest hydrants, positioning them just in case.

'I know what you did, Felicity. I know why you did it. You couldn't fall pregnant. It wasn't your fault. You did everything the doctors suggested – the vitamins and diets. Rounds of IVF. How many times did you try?'

'Four,' she whispers.

'That must have been expensive.'

'It almost broke us. Bryan didn't want to keep paying. "If it happens, it happens," he said.'

'That must have been hard. Being around Maggie made it worse because she had Felix. Every day you were being reminded of what you couldn't have . . .'

She gives a hiccupping sob.

'In your desperation to have a child, you slept with your brother-in-law. Dougal is Aiden's father, not Bryan.'

Felicity groans.

'Nobody could ever find out – not Maggie, or Aiden, or your husband. That's why you couldn't let Aiden fall in love with Jodie. You couldn't let them sleep together or have a baby.'

'It was incest. It was wrong,' she whispers.

'When Bryan told you that Jodie was pregnant, you didn't know that Aiden was the father until you overheard them together in the caravan that night. You confronted Jodie. You begged her to have an abortion.'

'I wanted her to understand,' says Felicity. 'Why wouldn't she listen?'

'You followed her.'

'She was being foolish. She was risking Aiden's future and her own. He's going to Cambridge. She's going to the Olympics.'

'Did you tell her that Aiden was her half-brother?'

I hear another stifled sob. 'She wouldn't have believed me.'

'What happened?'

'I wanted her to hear what I was saying . . . to listen. She was ruining everything.'

'You tried to stop her.'

'I didn't hit her hard.'

'What did you use?'

'A piece of iron – a fence post. It was lying on the ground . . . near the bridge. I only hit her once. I thought she was pretending, you know. I shook her. I said her name. I put my hand on her chest . . .'

'You pushed her body into the water.'

'I thought she was dead. I thought I'd killed her.'

'She was still alive.'

Felicity moans.

Lenny is signalling me from the road. Aiden is with him.

'He's here,' I say. 'The police have brought Aiden.'

I hear the floorboards creak as Felicity stands. Moments later, the library curtains twitch and open a crack.

'I want to talk to him,' she says. 'I need to explain.'

'Come out and you can talk to him.'

'No! Send him in.'

'That's not going to happen.'

Her voice changes: 'SEND HIM IN, OR I'LL KILL HER!'

'Please stay calm,' I say. 'If you lose your temper the police will storm this place.'

'Let them try.'

'You don't want that. Let me come inside. Swap me for Evie. I can make them understand. I can get Aiden for you.'

There is a long pause before the lock turns. The door swings inwards. Felicity has her arm around Evie's neck.

'Let her go.'

'Not until you're inside.'

'Don't believe her,' yells Evie. Her eyes are swollen and almost closed, and vomit stains the front of her pyjamas. I slip past them into the hallway, which reeks of turpentine, gas and alcohol.

Felicity keeps her distance, holding the cheap plastic cigarette lighter to Evie's cheek.

'Put your hands through the railings,' she says, pointing towards the stairs.

Felicity kicks a roll of packing tape across the floor and tells Evie to bind my wrists. Evie struggles to unspool the tape because her own wrists are bound, but manages to secure my hands while Felicity stands over her.

'Turn off the gas and open the windows,' I say. 'We have to air the house.'

Felicity ignores me, jerking her thumb towards the door, telling Evie to get out.

'I'm not going without Cyrus.'

'Please, Evie, just go,' I say.

'She's going to set the house on fire. She's poured stuff all over your books.'

Felicity waves the lighter in front of Evie's face, threatening to flick at the flint-wheel. 'Last chance.'

Evie seems to react instinctively, spinning around and scrambling up the stairs. Blindly, she collides with a wall and bounces off, but keeps going, disappearing into the upper floors. This is madness. She has to get out.

'Stupid little cow,' curses Felicity, climbing past me on the stairs.

'Leave her,' I say. 'You have other things to worry about.'

Lenny's voice interrupts me, projected through a loudhailer.

'Mrs Whitaker . . . we have your son.'

67

Angel Face

I squeeze between boxes in the turret room, navigating by touch. I slide my hand beneath a pillow until my fingers close around the oily rag. The pistol. I rack the slide, putting a bullet in the chamber, pointing it towards the door. There are no footsteps on the stairs. No blurry shadows in the doorway.

I put down the handgun and pick up the knife. Jamming the handle inside a closed drawer, I lean my hip against the front panel to keep the blade steady. I run my wrists back and forth against the sharpest edge, cutting the masking tape before ripping it with my teeth, spitting out bits of torn plastic.

I can hear Cyrus yelling my name, telling me to get out, until another voice drowns him out. Coming from outside.

Feeling my way between boxes, I stand on tiptoes at the window. Through watery eyes, I see two figures standing near the front gate.

I recognise Aiden's voice. 'Mum? It's me.'

Mrs Whitaker answers, repeating his name, as though wanting to be sure.

'What are you doing, Mum?' yells Aiden.

'I'm so sorry, baby. I didn't mean . . . I need to explain.'

'OK. Are you coming out?'

'Listen, baby.' Her voice seems to break. 'You're going to hear some things about me, but you have to believe that everything I did was for you.'

'What did you do?'

'I tried to protect you. I wanted you to be happy.'

'I was happy.'

'You and Jodie . . . it was wrong. You couldn't be with her — not like you were.'

'Why?'

The question brings silence. Aiden asks again. 'Mum? Why couldn't I be with Jodie?'

Felicity answers in a wheedling, sorrowful voice. 'She was your half-sister.'

'You mean my cousin,' says Aiden, less certain now.

'No.'

'How can she be my half-sister?'

'I couldn't get pregnant . . . not with your Dad.'

'So, who is my father?'

Felicity answers hoarsely. 'Your Uncle Dougal.'

Aiden doesn't respond.

'Are you there, baby? I know it's a shock. I know I should have told you.'

Aiden's voice changes. 'Did you hurt Jodie?'

Another pause followed by a defeated moan. 'It was an accident. I didn't mean it. You have to forgive me.'

He says nothing.

'Aiden?'

Without a word, he turns and brushes past the shoulders of the detective, walking past the police cars and the barricades and the watching crowd. Mrs Whitaker is calling after him. Begging him. He doesn't stop.

390

68

'It's over, Felicity. Put down the lighter.'

She's kneeling on the hallway rug, hunched over, breathing raggedly. Words get caught in her throat. She tries again.

'What have I done? What have I done?'

'Listen to me. You have to open the windows. The house is full of gas.'

Rocking on her knees, she holds her stomach, moaning.

'You can get Aiden back. Explain things to him. It's not too late. Right now, we have to get out of here.'

She's not listening to me.

I hear Lenny on the loudhailer: 'Mrs Whitaker, can you hear me? You talked to your son. I want you to come outside.'

She's doesn't respond.

I can picture the SWAT team outside ready to break down the doors. The smallest spark will light this place up.

'Give us a minute,' I yell to Lenny.

I concentrate on Felicity, who can't see beyond her misery.

'It was an accident,' I say. 'I don't think you meant to hurt Jodie. But what you're doing now is making things worse.'

'I've ruined everything,' she sobs. 'He'll never forgive me.'

'You made some bad decisions. Don't make another one. Open the windows. Let's walk out of here together.'

'It's too late.'

'It's only too late if you give up,' I say. 'If something happens to you, it won't end the pain. You'll be passing it on to Aiden and Tasmin.'

'They'll be better off if I'm dead.'

'You'll stain their lives. You'll be betraying them. Rejecting them.'

She is staring at the cigarette lighter, which is cupped in her hands like an offering. An answer. A key.

'I lost my parents and my sisters. You know the story. Not a day goes by when I don't wonder if I could have saved them. If I'd come straight home from football practice; if I hadn't stopped for chips; if I hadn't ridden my bike past Ailsa Piper's house. What if? Maybe? If only. Don't let the same thing happen to Aiden. Come on. Let's get out of here.'

I yell up the stairs. 'Evie, it's time to go!'

She doesn't answer.

'Can you hear me, Evie? We're leaving.'

69

Angel Face

'I can hear you.'

I'm on the landing, peering through the wooden railings. My eyes are swollen shut and the shapes below me are vague and indistinct like I'm watching them from the bottom of a swimming pool.

Cyrus is sitting on a lower step with his hands taped around the wooden spindles. Mrs Whitaker is kneeling in the hallway.

'You have to open the doors and windows. Then go outside. Get away from the house.'

I descend, touching the wall with my right hand. I'm holding the pistol behind my back. As I get closer, I can see Mrs Whitaker more clearly, but not her face. I want to see her face.

'Open the windows, Evie. Then leave.'

'What about you?'

'The police will cut me free.'

'Stay where you are!' Mrs Whitaker gets to her feet. Swaying. Sweating.

I am between steps. The gun is heavy in my hand. I pull it out, aiming at the centre of her chest. Cyrus takes a sharp breath. He utters my name and the word 'no'.

She turns to face me, holding the cigarette lighter in her hand, her thumb on the flint-wheel.

'Don't do it!' says Cyrus. 'The gas!'

I realise my mistake, but I don't lower the gun.

'She's not going to let us go,' I say.

'Yes, she is. We're all getting out.'

'Are you letting us go?' I ask.

She doesn't answer.

The gas and fumes are making me light-headed. Rocking forward, I catch myself before I fall, and slide down onto a step, holding the gun in my lap, no longer aiming.

Cyrus looks up at me. 'We're getting out of here.'

Mrs Whitaker hasn't spoken. I give her the evil eye. It's the look I used on Guthrie and Miss McCredie and kids who pissed me off at Langton Hall.

'You're too selfish to let us go,' I say. 'It's always been about you. You wanted a baby so badly, you cheated on your husband. You wanted Aiden to go to Cambridge because it made you look good. You wanted Jodie to get rid of the baby because it threatened your secret. You're such a coward you can't even die alone.'

Anger flares in her eyes.

'You asked me about my mother. You see this?' I open the palm of my left hand and show her a tortoiseshell button the size of a fifty-pence piece. 'It's all I have left of her. She had this bright red coat with a fur-lined collar that she said made her feel like a Russian tsarina. I think that means princess. She was wearing it when they found her body. I hugged her for as long as I could, until they had to bend back my fingers to make me let go. When she'd gone, I found this button in my fist.'

I close my fingers and hold it against my cheek.

'She gave up – just like you're doing. She abandoned me. She pushed me away. For years I told myself that I didn't blame her, but I'll never forgive her because she can't tell me why.'

There is a beat of silence and I wonder if anyone is listening.

Slowly, Mrs Whitaker gets up from her knees. She glances into the kitchen.

'I'll turn off the gas. You open the door,' she says.

I slide down the stairs until I reach Cyrus. I don't have the knife.

'Open the front door,' he says, nodding along the hallway.

I'm a step below him when I hear a surprised cry or half a curse. In that same instant, the house seems to breathe in and then out, as though someone has suddenly opened the window of a moving car, lifting dust and litter from the floor. The world explodes around us, filling the air with wood, plaster, dust and debris. Flames shoot out of the kitchen doorway and suck back again as the walls buckle.

Mrs Whitaker appears, her face blackened, eyes white and wide with shock. She touches her smoking head, as though seeking physical proof, and looks at me curiously before collapsing forwards. The entire back of her head has disappeared, and her clothes have burnt off like a plastic doll held too close to the fire.

The whooshing sound returns and fire rolls across the hallway ceiling to the library. I look at my pyjamas and know I can't survive.

Cyrus grabs my arm, yelling for me to get out. How? There's no escape. The kitchen ceiling has collapsed, leaving the claw-footed bath where the table used to be. Flames have reached the front rooms, blocking the hallway. I hear the sound of smashing glass. Hoses are blasting water through the windows, turning spray to steam.

'Get out, Evie! Get out!'

I pull at the tape around his wrists and run my fingers down the lathe-turned spindle. Bending my leg, I kick hard, but I'm barefoot and don't have the strength to break the wood. I scramble up the stairs and retrieve the pistol. Holding the barrel against the spindle, I unlock the safety and pull the trigger. The noise is louder than I expect; louder than the guns on TV and in films. Cyrus pulls free, scrambling to his feet, taking me with him.

'This way,' he says, tugging at my sleeve, wanting me to follow.

'What about her?'

'She's dead.'

70

Christ, Evie! Where in God's name did you get a gun?

We've reached the landing. Thick black smoke has filled the stairwell. Evie is coughing so hard she doubles over, curling up on the floor.

'Stay with me,' I yell, making her focus. I put her hands on the back of my belt and close her fingers. 'Don't let go.'

I crawl blindly across the landing, leading Evie. Feeling my way, I find her bedroom door and then her bed. My head bumps against the far wall. I reach for the sash window, I pull it up and lean outside, taking deep gulps of air.

Evie?

She's let go of me. I drop to my knees and feel for her, touching her hair. At that moment, flames sweep past the bedroom door, feeding on the oxygen from the open window.

I drag her to her feet and lean her body outside, telling her to breathe. Poppy is below us in the garden, barking and leaping up the wall, planting her paws on the bricks as though wanting to climb.

I lift Evie onto the window ledge with her feet dangling out. The garden is twenty feet below us. A jump like that will break her legs. Where are the ladders? The firemen? On the wrong side of the house.

I take Evie's wrists and lower her down so that she's dangling above Poppy, but it's still too high.

'Let go,' she yells, as a window blows out beneath us and glass scatters through the shrubbery.

I notice a downpipe to my right, but it's too far for Evie to reach. Four feet. More. I begin to move my shoulders, swinging her back and forth, building up momentum. She gets the idea and kicks with her legs, swinging out further, but I can't hold her much longer.

Her fingertips touch the downpipe, but she's unable to hold on and slides away. I swing her one more time and let go. She wraps her hands around the black-painted metal and clings on. Slipping down. Safe. It's my turn. I can't make a jump like that. I doubt if the pipe can take my weight.

These old houses know how to burn with their dry timbers and draughty rooms. My history is in flames. Family photographs. Books. Heirlooms. Memories.

Smoke billows past me and I can't see the pipe any more. I can't see Evie or Poppy. I can't breathe.

I hear her voice, yelling at me, but not the words. I lower myself out of the window, clinging by my fingertips, my shoes scrabbling for a toehold in the mortared bricks. I'm ready for the fall . . . for whatever comes. But as I let go, strong hands find my feet, directing me onto the rungs of a ladder, helping me down one step at a time through the smoke. My feet touch soft earth and I wheel around, stumbling a dozen paces before falling to my knees, coughing as though my lungs might slither out of my throat and convulse on the grass.

Evie has her arms around me, her head buried in my neck. The girl without tears is crying. Her wet cheeks are smeared with soot that clings to her like a second skin, except for around her eyes, giving her the appearance of an emaciated cartoon panda.

I wrap my arms around her. Holding her. Feeling her sob.

Meanwhile jets of water arc over the rooftop, falling onto our heads like rain.

'Where did you get the gun?'

'I stole it from Felix.'

'Why?'

'In case they come.'

71

Angel Face

I'm sitting on my bed, sticking pictures in a scrapbook. Cyrus will be here soon. He tries to come every day, when he can, bringing me cigarettes and chocolate fingers and pictures of Poppy. Poppy in the park. Poppy chasing squirrels. Poppy drinking from the bird bath. Poppy wading in the pond.

Langford Hall is the same. The food. The routines. The staff. I'm used to it now. I feel safe here.

I once read a story about how inmates sometimes get so used to being behind bars they don't want to leave. I can't imagine myself ever getting to be like that, but I can survive this. I've lived through worse.

Other girls my age are going to parties, or getting a job, or hanging out with friends, but I don't want any of those things. I wouldn't know what to do with that sort of life. That's why I don't have a calendar on the wall or a clock in my room. I don't want to see time passing. Instead, I've become an expert at existing and letting each day play out like the one before.

I miss Poppy. I miss Cyrus. I wish he didn't blame himself for what happened.

'It was nobody's fault,' I told him. 'Bad luck follows me around.'

'You don't believe in luck,' he replied, and I knew that he understood.

Cyrus can't foster me again. They say he put me in danger and involved me in a murder investigation. The gun would have sealed the deal. I was ready to take the blame, but Cyrus wouldn't let me. He said they'd keep me locked up for longer or send me to an adult prison or a general psych hospital. Guthrie would love that. So I told the police that Felicity had the gun and nobody could prove otherwise.

Davina knocks on the door. 'Your boyfriend's here.'

'He's not my boyfriend.'

'Well, why are you smiling?'

'Fuck off!'

'I love you, too.' She laughs as she disappears down the corridor, tossing her dreads and swinging her hips.

Cyrus pokes his head around the corner.

'Hi!'

'Hello.'

He hugs me. I stiffen. I wonder if I'll ever get used to someone touching me like that.

'I have a surprise,' he says.

'More photographs.'

'Better.'

He wants me to close my eyes. I look at him suspiciously, but obey, letting him lead me out of my room and along the hallway. He tells me to mind my step when he opens the sliding door to the courtyard.

Poppy is tied to a baby tree, trying to rip it out of the ground. Let loose, she leaps all over me, pushing me backwards onto the grass, licking my face and hands.

Cyrus sits on a concrete bench and watches while we chase, wrestle and run. Later, exhausted, I sit beside him. Normally, I'd light a cigarette but I'm trying to quit.

'How have you been?' he asks.

'Fine.'

'Are you sleeping?'

'Yeah.'

He always starts this way – with the simple questions – before he begins asking me about my dreams and earliest memories; my fears and regrets.

'Victims of childhood abuse often dissociate,' he says, talking like a textbook. 'They block out cognitive links and emotions. Sometimes they do it so completely, it's as if they never consciously experienced trauma. That could be why you have so few memories.'

'It could be,' I say.

'Whatever was done to you as a child, it wasn't your fault.'

'I know.'

'You don't have to blame yourself.'

'I don't.'

I know what Cyrus wants. Details. Facts. He wants to climb down into the same sewer that I escaped from. He wants to join me in the filth and lead me out again. He wants to know what went through my mind during all those hours, days and weeks. What I heard. Why I stayed hidden. How I managed to stay alive.

I remember it all. I remember nothing important.

'I can understand you wanting to forget some things,' he says. 'But don't you want to know who you are, or if you have family?'

'I have no family.'

'You mentioned your mother.'

'I won't talk about her.'

'What about your childhood?'

'It doesn't matter.'

'It does to me,' says Cyrus. 'And it will to you, if you let it.'

I sigh and close my eyes. 'You want to go where I have been.'

'Yes.'

'To see what I have seen.'

'I think I'm owed.'

'I can't go back there.'

'I'm not asking you to go back.'

'Yes, you are. You want to open up my mind and peer inside, but I am not a plaything. I am not an experiment.'

'I know what he did to you – what he took.'

I feel myself getting angry. 'You know nothing.'

'Where did he find you?'

'He didn't find me.'

'Come on, Evie, help me. Don't let this monster win.'

'He's not a monster.'

'He kidnapped you. He locked you up.'

'No.'

'He deserved to die.'

'Don't you dare say that!'

'Hostages often grow attached to their captors, but that's not love, Evie. Kidnapping a child. Imprisoning her. Abusing her. You can't think that's love.'

'You don't understand.'

'Explain it to me.'

My eyes are fractured with tears that refuse to fall. 'You want to know about love,' *I whisper.* 'Love is allowing yourself to be tortured to death rather than tell people where someone is hiding. Love is dying slowly and horribly, rather than betraying them. You think Terry was a monster. You think he locked me in a room and abused me. You're wrong. He died rather than tell them where I was hiding. He saved me.'

'Saved you from who?'

'I can't tell you.'

'Why?'

'He made me promise.'

'That's not a promise, Evie. It's a threat.'

I give him a pitying stare and shake my head.

'Just tell me your real name,' *he says.* 'Surely I deserve that much.'

'I can't.'

'Why?'

'Everybody I love dies. I can't let that happen to you.'

72

My nightmares no longer involve my family. Evie inhabits my dreams, calling my name, hiding in a dark place as chaos unfolds around her. I cannot save her. I can never run fast enough, or jump high enough, or reach far enough, to grab her fingertips as she falls past me into the void. I wake screaming, damp with sweat, my heart hammering and her name dying on my lips.

I don't know what triggered the explosion that killed Felicity Whitaker and destroyed part of my house. It could have been the central heating kicking in, or static electricity, or maybe Felicity changed her mind. Evie doesn't believe that. She saw the truth.

I was wrong about many things. Terry Boland didn't abduct Evie and lock her in a secret room. He didn't sexually abuse her or force her to live off scraps and dog food. I don't know what is more disturbing – the notion of his innocence, or the knowledge that he died protecting her.

One thing is worse – the realisation that she heard it happen. She listened to him screaming as the acid was poured into his ears and hot pokers burnt away his eyelids. She heard them calling her name, ripping up carpets, toppling furniture, punching holes through walls.

How many days did they search for her? How many nights? *Come out, come out, wherever you are.*

Evie stayed hidden. She's still hiding. It's why she took the gun. It's why she slept with a knife beneath her pillow. It's why she constantly looks over her shoulder, searching for figures in the shadows; people watching her from doorways, or parked cars, or white vans.

Sometimes late at night, when I hear a car door slam or footsteps on the pavement, or the scaffolding rattle, I imagine someone is climbing towards Evie's old room, trying to find her. I get up and navigate around the paint tins and bags of plaster, wishing the builders would finish soon. I check the windows are locked and go back to bed, but I won't sleep again.

Evie will stay at Langford Hall, at least until next September when she turns eighteen. I won't be allowed to foster her again, but Caroline Fairfax is quietly hopeful that Evie's release date will be honoured. After that, I don't know what will happen. Maybe they'll send her to a secure psych unit like Arnold Lodge in Leicester or she'll begin a programme of day release. I'm hoping for the latter.

Will Evie ever be free? I wish I knew. It's like that old story of the man who falls into the river and is dragged downstream towards the waterfall. A fisherman holds out a rod and says, 'Grab hold, I'll pull you in,' but the man replies, 'It's OK, God will save me.' Then a hiker leans from a fallen log and says, 'Grab my hand, I'll lift you out,' but the man waves to him and says, 'God will save me.' Finally, a helicopter hovers overhead and a crewman throws down a rope ladder. The drowning man ignores the offer, saying, 'Don't worry, God will save me.' Moments later he crashes over the waterfall and perishes on the rocks below. Later, at the gates of Heaven, he says to God, 'Hey, didn't you see me down there? Why didn't you save me?' And God replies, 'I tried three times, but you turned me away.'

I'm the last person who should be telling religious jokes,

heathen that I am, but Evie Cormac cannot do this on her own.

Many years ago, a university lecturer of mine, Joe O'Loughlin, told me that a truly effective psychologist is someone who commits; who goes into the darkness to bring someone out. 'When a person is drowning, someone has to get wet,' he said.

I'm ready to get wet, Evie. Hold on.

ACKNOWLEDGEMENTS

Writing is a solitary profession, but publishing is a team effort. I am supported by a wonderful group of editors, agents, designers, marketing reps and publishers who release my stories into the world. Without them I'd be the proverbial tree falling in an empty forest.

I do want to acknowledge Colin Harrison, Lucy Malagoni, Rebecca Saunders, Alex Craig, Mark Lucas and Richard Pine, who read the early manuscript and gave me their fearless and considered advice.

This book introduces a new character, Evie Cormac, a brilliant, engaging, damaged and self-destructive teenager. I have helped raise three daughters, who are nothing like Evie, yet are responsible for her parts. Thank you Alex, Charlotte and Bella.

My partner in life, if not crime, deserves equal praise. Vivien is the glue that holds us together and that beacon that brings us home. She is our family.

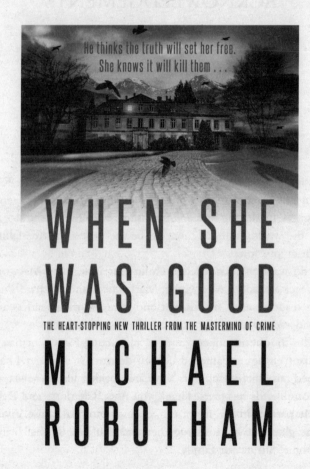

He thinks the truth will set her free.
She knows it will kill them . . .

WHEN SHE WAS GOOD

THE HEART-STOPPING NEW THRILLER FROM THE MASTERMIND OF CRIME

MICHAEL ROBOTHAM

1

Cyrus

May 2020

Late spring. Morning cold. A small wooden boat emerges from the mist, sliding forward with each pull on the oars. The inner harbour is so mirror smooth it shows each ripple as it radiates outwards before stretching and breaking against the bow.

The rowing boat follows the grey rock wall, past the fishing trawlers and yachts, until it reaches a narrow shingle beach. The lone occupant jumps out and drags the boat higher up the stones where it cants drunkenly sideways, looking clumsy on land. Elegance lost.

The hood of an anorak is pushed back and hair explodes from inside. True red hair. Red as flame. Red as the daybreak. She takes a hairband from her wrist, looping the tresses into a single bundle that falls down the centre of her back.

My breath has fogged up the window of my room. Tugging my sleeve over my fist, I wipe the small square pane of glass to get a better view. She's finally here. I have been waiting six days. I have walked the footpaths, visited the lighthouse, and exhausted the menu at O'Neill's Bar & Restaurant. I have read the morning newspapers and three discounted novels and listened to the local drunks tell me their life stories. Fishermen mostly, with hands as gnarled as knobs of ginger and eyes that squint into brightness when there is no sun.

Leaning into the rowing boat, she pulls back a tarpaulin revealing plastic crates and cardboard boxes. This is her fort-nightly shopping trip for supplies. With her hands full of boxes, she climbs the steps from the beach and crosses the cobble-stones. My eyes follow her progress as she walks along the promenade, past shuttered kiosks and tourist shops towards a small supermarket with a light burning inside. Stepping over a bundle of newspapers, she knocks on the door. A middle-aged man, red-nosed and rosy-cheeked, raises a blind and nods in recognition. He turns the deadlock and ushers her inside, pausing to scan the street, looking for me perhaps. He knows I've been waiting.

Dressing quickly in jeans and a sweatshirt, I pull on my boots and descend the pub stairs to a side entrance. The air outside smells of drying seaweed and woodsmoke; and the distant hills are edged in orange where God has opened the furnace door and stoked the coals for a new day.

The bell jangles on a metal arm. The shopkeeper and the woman turn towards me. They're each holding matching mugs of steam. She braces herself, as if ready to fight or flee, but holds her ground. She looks different from her photographs. Smaller. Her face is windburned and her hands are callused and her left thumbnail is blackened where she has jammed it between two hard objects.

'Sacha Hopewell?' I ask.

She reaches into the pocket of her anorak. For a moment, I imagine a weapon. A fishing knife or a can of mace.

'My name is Cyrus Haven. I'm a psychologist. I wrote to you.'

'That's him,' says the shopkeeper. 'The one who's been asking after you. Should I sic Roddy on to him?'

I don't know if Roddy is a dog or a person.

Sacha pushes past me and begins collecting groceries from the shelves, loading a trolley, choosing sacks of rice and flour; tins of vegetables and stewed fruit. I follow her down the aisle. Strawberry jam. Long-life milk. Peanut butter.

'Seven years ago, you found a child in a house in north London. She was hiding in a secret room.'

'You have me mistaken for someone else,' she says brusquely.

I pull a photograph from my jacket pocket. 'This is you.'

She gives the image a cursory glance and continues collecting dry goods.

The picture shows a young special constable dressed in black leggings and a dark top. She's carrying a filthy, feral child through the doors of a hospital. The young girl's face is obscured by wild, matted hair, as she clings to Sacha like a koala to a tree.

I pull another photograph from my pocket.

'This is what she looks like now.'

Sacha stops suddenly. She can't help but look at the picture. She wants to know what became of that little girl: Angel Face. The girl in the box. A child then, a teenager now, the photograph shows her sitting on a concrete bench, wearing torn jeans and a baggy jumper with a hole in one elbow. Her hair is longer and dyed blonde. She scowls rather than smiles at the camera.

'I have others,' I say.

Sacha looks away, reaching past me and plucking a box of macaroni from the shelf.

'Her name is Evie Cormac. She's living in a secure children's home.'

She grips the trolley and keeps moving.

'I could go to prison for telling you any of this. There's a Section 39 Order that forbids anybody from revealing her identity, or location, or taking pictures of her.'

I block her path. She steps around me. I match her movements. It's like we're dancing in the aisle.

'Evie has never spoken about what happened to her in that house. That's why I'm here. I want to hear your story.'

Sacha pushes past me. 'Read the police reports.'

'I need more.'

She has reached the cold section, where she slides opens a chest freezer and begins rummaging inside.

'How did you find me?' she asks.

'It wasn't easy.'

'Did my parents help you?'

'They're worried about you.'

'You've put them in danger.'

'How?'

Sacha doesn't reply. She parks her trolley near the cash register and gets another. The red-nosed man is no longer at the counter, but I hear his footsteps on the floor above.

'You can't keep running,' I say.

'Who says I'm running?'

'You're hiding. I want to help.'

'You can't.'

'Then let me help Evie. She's different. Special.'

Boots on the stairs. Another man appears in the doorway at the rear of the supermarket. Younger. Stronger. Bare-chested. He's wearing sweatpants that hang so low on his hips I can see the top of his pubic hair. This must be Roddy.

'That's him,' says the red-nosed man. 'He's been snooping around the village all week.'

Roddy reaches beneath the counter and retrieves a speargun with a polyamide handle and a stainless-steel harpoon. My first reaction is to almost laugh because the weapon is so unnecessary and out-of-place.

Roddy scowls. 'Is he bothering you, Sacha?'

'I can handle this,' she replies.

Roddy rests the speargun against his shoulder like a soldier on parade.

'Is he your ex?'

412

'No.'

'Want me to dump him off the dock?'

'That won't be necessary.'

Roddy clearly has eyes for Sacha. Puppy love. She's out of his league.

'I'll buy you breakfast,' I say.

'I can afford my own breakfast,' she replies.

'I know. I didn't mean . . . Give me half an hour. Let me convince you.'

She takes toothpaste and mouthwash from the shelf. 'If I tell you what happened, will you leave me alone?'

'Yes.'

'No phone calls. No letters. No visits. And you'll leave me and my family be.'

'Agreed.'

Sacha leaves her shopping at the supermarket and tells the shopkeeper she won't be long.

'Want me to go with you?' asks Roddy, scratching his navel.

'No. It's OK.'

The café is next to the post office in the same squat stone building, which overlooks a bridge and the tidal channel. Tables and chairs are arranged on the footpath, beneath a striped awning that is fringed with fairy lights. The menu is handwritten on a chalkboard.

A woman wearing an apron is righting upturned chairs and dusting them off.

'Kitchen doesn't open till seven,' she says in a Cornish accent. 'I can make you tea.'

'Thank you,' replies Sacha, who chooses a long, padded bench, facing the door, where she can scan the footpath and parking area. Old habits.

'I'm alone,' I say.

She regards me silently, sitting with her knees together and her hands on her lap.

'It's a pretty village,' I say, glancing at the fishing boats and yachts. The first rays of sunshine are touching the tops of the masts. 'How long have you lived here?'

'That's not relevant,' she replies, reaching into her pocket where she finds a small tube of lip-balm, which she smears on her lips.

'Show me the pictures.'

I take out another four photographs and slide them across the table. The pictures show Evie as she is now, almost eighteen.

'She dyes her hair a lot,' I explain. 'Different colours.'

'Her eyes haven't changed,' says Sacha, running her thumb over Evie's face, as though tracing the contours.

'Her freckles come out in the summer,' I say. 'She hates them.'

'I'd kill for her eyelashes.'

Sacha arranges the photographs side by side, changing the order to suit her eye, or some unspoken design. 'Did they find her parents?'

'No.'

'What about DNA? Missing persons?'

'They searched the world.'

'What happened to her?'

'She became a ward of court and was given a new name because nobody knew her real one.'

'I thought for sure that someone would claim her.'

'That's why I'm here. I'm hoping Evie might have said something to you – given you some clue.'

'You're wasting your time.'

'But you found her.'

'That's all.'

The next silence is longer. Sacha puts her hands in her pockets to stop them moving.

'How much do you know?' she asks.

'I've read your statement. It's two pages long.'

The swing doors open from the kitchen and two pots of tea are delivered. Sacha flips the hinged lid and jiggles her teabag up and down.

'Have you been to the house?' she asks.

'Yes.'

'And read the police reports?'

I nod.

Sacha pours tea into her cup.

'They found Terry Boland in the front bedroom upstairs. Bound to a chair. Gagged. He'd been tortured to death. Acid dripped in his ears. His eyelids burned away.' She shudders. 'It was the biggest murder investigation in years in north London. I was a special constable working out of Barnet Police Station. The incident room was on the first floor.

'Boland had been dead for two months, which is why they took so long to identify his body. They released an artist's impression of his face and his ex-wife called the hotline. Everybody was surprised when Boland's name came up because he was so small-time – a rung above petty criminal, with a history of assault and burglary. Everybody was expecting some gangland connection.'

'Were you involved in the investigation?'

'God, no. A special constable is a general dogsbody, doing shit jobs and community liaison. I used to pass the homicide detectives on the stairs, or overhear them talking in the pub. When they couldn't come up with any leads, they began suggesting Boland was a drug dealer who double-crossed the wrong people. The locals could rest easy because the bad guys were killing each other.'

'What did you think?'

'I wasn't paid to think.'

'Why were you sent to the murder house?'

'Not the house – the road. The neighbours were complaining about stuff going missing. Bits and pieces stolen from garages and garden sheds. My sergeant sent me out to interview them as a public relations exercise. He called it "bread and circuses": keeping the masses happy.

'I remember standing outside number seventy-nine, thinking

how ordinary it appeared to be, you know. Neglected. Unloved. But it didn't look like a house where a man had been tortured to death. The downpipes were streaked with rust and the windows needed painting and the garden was overgrown. Wisteria had gone wild during the summer, twisting and coiling up the front wall, creating a curtain of mauve flowers over the entrance.'

'You have an artist's eye,' I say.

Sacha smiles at me for the first time. 'An art teacher once told me that. She said I could experience beauty mentally, as well as visually, seeing colour, depth and shadow where other people saw things in two dimensions.'

'Did you want to be an artist?'

'A long time ago.'

She empties a sachet of sugar into her cup. Stirs.

'I went up and down the road, knocking on doors, asking about the robberies, but all anyone wanted to talk about was the murder. They had the same questions: "Have you found the killer? Should we be worried?" They all had their theories, but none of them actually knew Terry Boland. He had lived in the house since February, but didn't make their acquaintance. He waved. He walked his dogs. He kept to himself.

'People cared more about those dogs than Boland. All those weeks he was dead upstairs, his two Alsatians were starving in a kennel in the back garden. Only they weren't starving. Someone had to be feeding them. People said the killers must have come back, which means they cared more about the dogs than a human being.'

The waitress emerges again from the kitchen. This time she brings a chalkboard and props it on a chair.

'What about the robberies?' I ask.

'The most valuable thing stolen was a cashmere sweater, which a woman used to line her cat's bed.'

'What else?'

'Apples, biscuits, scissors, breakfast cereal, candles, barley sugar, matches, magazines, dog food, socks, playing cards, liquorice allsorts . . . oh, yeah, and a snowdome of the Eiffel Tower. I remember that one because it belonged to a young boy who lived over the road.'

'George.'

'You've talked to him.'

I nod.

Sacha seems impressed with my research.

'George was the only person who saw Angel Face. He thought he saw a boy in an upstairs window. George waved, but the child didn't wave back.'

Sacha orders porridge and berries, orange juice and more tea. I choose the full English breakfast and a double espresso.

She is relaxed enough to take off her coat; I notice how her inner layers hug her body. She brushes stray strands of hair behind her ears. I'm trying to think who she reminds me of. An actress. Not a new one. Katharine Hepburn. My mother loved watching old movies.

Sacha continues. 'None of the neighbours could explain how the thief was getting in, but I suspected they were leaving their windows open or the doors unlocked. I rang my sergeant and gave him the list. He said it was kids and I should go home.'

'But you didn't.'

Sacha shakes her head. Her hair catches the lights. 'I was walking back to my car when I noticed two painters packing up their van. Number 79 was being renovated and put up for sale. I got talking to a young bloke and his boss. The house was a mess when they arrived, they said. There were holes in the walls, broken pipes, ripped-up carpets. The smell was the worst thing.

'The young guy, Toby, said the house was haunted because stuff had gone missing – a digital radio and a half-eaten sand-wich. His boss laughed and said Toby could eat for England and had probably forgotten the sandwich.

'"What about the marks on the ceiling?" said Toby. "We've

painted the upstairs bathroom three times, but the ceiling keeps getting these black smudges, like someone is burning candles."

"'That's because ghosts like holding séances," joked his boss.

'I asked them if I could look around. They gave me a guided tour. The floorboards had been sanded and varnished, including the stairs. I climbed to the upper floor and wandered from room to room. I looked at the bathroom ceiling.' Sacha pivots and asks, 'Why do people have double sinks? Do couples actually brush their teeth side by side?'

'It's so they don't have arguments over who left the top off the toothpaste,' I suggest.

She smiles for the second time.

'It was Friday afternoon and the painters were packing up for the weekend. I asked if I could borrow their keys and stay a while longer.'

"'Is that a direct order from the police?" Toby asked, making fun of me.

"'I can't really make orders," I said. "It's more of a request."

"'No wild parties."

"'I'm a police officer."

"'You can still have wild parties."

"'You haven't met my friends."

'Toby's boss gave me the keys and the van pulled away. I went upstairs and walked from room to room. I remember wondering why Terry Boland would rent such a big house. Four bedrooms in north London doesn't come cheap. He paid six months in advance, in cash, using a fake name on the tenancy agreement.

'I sat on the stairs for a few hours and then made a make-shift bed from the dust sheets, trying to stay warm. By midnight, I wished I'd gone home, or I had a pillow or a sleeping bag. I felt foolish. If someone at the station discovered I'd spent all night staking out an empty house, I'd have been the office punchline.'

'What happened?'

Sacha shrugs. 'I fell asleep. I dreamed of Terry Boland with belts around his neck and forehead; acid being dripped into his ears. Do you think it feels cold at first – before the burning starts? Could he hear his own screams?'

Sacha shivers and I notice the goose bumps on her arms.

'I remember waking up, bashing my fist against my head trying to get acid out of my ears. That's when I sensed that someone was watching me.'

'In the house?'

'Yeah. I called out. Nobody answered. I turned on the lights and searched the house from top to bottom. Nothing had changed except for a window above the kitchen sink. It was unlatched.'

'And you'd left it locked.'

'I couldn't be completely sure.'

The waitress interrupts, bringing our meals. Sacha blows on each spoonful of porridge and watches as I arrange my triangles of toast so that the baked beans don't contaminate the eggs and the mushrooms don't touch the bacon. It's a military operation – marshalling food around my plate.

'What are you, five?' she asks.

'I never grew out of it,' I explain, embarrassed. 'It's an obsessive-compulsive disorder – a mild one.'

'Does it have a name?'

'*Brumotactillophobia*.'

'You're making that up.'

'No.'

'How are you with Chinese food?'

'I'm OK if meals are pre-mixed, like stir-fry and pasta. Breakfast is different.'

'What happens if your baked beans touch your eggs? Is it bad luck, or something worse?'

'I don't know.'

'Then what's the point?'

'I wish I could tell you.'

Sacha looks baffled and laughs. She is lightening up; lowering her defences.

'What happened at the house?' I ask.

'In the morning I drove home, showered and fell into bed, sleeping until early afternoon. My parents wanted to know where I'd spent the night. I told them I'd been on a stakeout, making it sound like I was doing important police work. Lying to them.

'It was Saturday and I was due to go out with friends that night. Instead, I drove to a supermarket and picked up containers of talcum powder, extra batteries for my torch, orange juice and a family-sized chocolate bar. Near midnight, I went back to Hotham Road and quietly unlocked the door. I was wearing my gym gear – black leggings and a zip-up jacket and my trainers.

'Starting upstairs, I sprinkled talcum across the floor, down the stairs, along the hallway to the kitchen. I went from room to room, covering the bare floorboards in a fine coat of powder that was invisible when the lights were turned off. Afterwards, I locked up the house and went to my car, where I crawled into a sleeping bag, reclined the seat and nodded off.

'A milkman woke me just after dawn – the rattle of bottles in crates. I let myself into the house and shone my torch over the floor. There were footprints leading in both directions, up and down the stairs, along the hallway to the kitchen. They stopped at the sink, below the window I found unlatched the night before. I followed the footprints, tracking them up the stairs and across the landing and into the main bedroom. They ended suddenly beneath the hanging rails of the walk-in wardrobe. It was like someone had vanished into thin air or been beamed up by Scotty.

'I studied the wardrobe, pushing aside hangers and running my fingers over the skirting boards. When I tapped on the plasterboard it made a hollow sound, so I wedged the blade of my pocketknife under the edge of the panel, levering it back and forth, making it move a little each time. I put my weight against the panel, but something seemed to be pushing against me. Eventually, I hooked fingers through the widening gap and pulled hard. The plasterboard slid sideways, revealing a crawlspace behind the wardrobe. It was about eight feet long and five feet wide with a sloping ceiling that narrowed at the far end.

I shone the torch across the floor and saw food wrappers, empty bottles of water, magazines, books, playing cards, a snow-dome of the Eiffel Tower. "I'm not going to hurt you," I said. "I'm a police officer."

'Nobody answered, so I put the torch between my teeth and crawled through the hole on my hands and knees. The room seemed empty, except for a wooden box that was wedged between the ceiling and the floor. I moved closer, saying, "Don't be scared. I won't hurt you."

'When I reached the box, I shone my torch inside on to a bundle of rags, which began to move. The slowness became a rush and suddenly, this thing burst past me. I reached out and grabbed at the rags, which fell away in my fingers. Before I could react, the creature was gone. I had to backtrack through the panel into the bedroom. By that time, I could hear door handles being rattled and small fists hammering on the windows downstairs. I looked over the banister and saw a dark shape scuttling along the hallway to the sitting room. I followed the figure and saw legs poking from the fireplace, like a chimney sweep was trying to climb up.

'"Hey!" I said and the figure spun around and snarled at me. I thought it was a boy at first, only it wasn't a boy, it was a girl. She had a knife pressed to her chest, over her heart.

'The sight of her . . . I'll never forget. Her skin was so pale that the smudges of dirt on her cheeks looked like bruises; and her eyelashes and eyebrows were dark and doll-like. She was wearing a pair of faded jeans with a hole in one knee, and a woollen jumper with a polar bear woven on to the chest. I thought she was seven, maybe eight, possibly younger.

'I was shocked by the state of her and by the knife. What sort of child threatens to stab herself?'

I don't answer. Sacha's eyes are closed, as though she's replaying the scene in her mind.

"'I'm not going to hurt you," I said. "My name is Sacha. What's yours?" She didn't answer. When I reached into my pocket, she dug the point of the knife harder into her chest.'

"'No, please don't," I said. "Are you hungry?" I pulled out the half-eaten chocolate bar. She didn't move. I broke off a piece and popped it into my mouth.

"'I love chocolate. It's the only thing in the world I could never give up. Every Lent my mother makes me give up one of my favourite things as a sacrifice, you know. I'd happily choose Facebook or caffeine or gossiping, but my mother says it has to be chocolate. She's very religious."

'We were ten feet apart. She was crouched in the fireplace. I was kneeling on the floor. I asked her if I could get up because my knees were hurting. I eased backwards and sat against the wall. Then I broke off another piece of chocolate before wrapping the bar and sliding it towards her across the floor. We stared at each for a while before she edged out her right foot and dragged the chocolate bar closer. She tore open the wrapping and stuffed so much chocolate into her mouth all at once, I thought she might choke.

'I had so many questions. How long had she been there? Did she witness the murder? Did she hide from it? I remember making a sign of the cross and she mimicked me. I thought maybe she was raised a Catholic.'

'That wasn't in the file,' I say.

'What?'

'There's no mention of her making a sign of the cross.'

'Is that important?'

'It's new information.'

I ask her to go on. Sacha glances out of the window. The sun is fully up, and fishing boats are returning to the bay, trailing seagulls behind them like white kites.

'We must have sat there for more than an hour. I did all the

422

talking. I told her about the talcum powder and the latch on the kitchen window. She gave me nothing. I took out my warrant card and held it up. I said it proved I was a special constable, which was almost the same as being a trainee police officer. I said I could protect her.'

Sacha looks up from her empty bowl. 'Do you know what she did?'

I shake my head.

'She gave me this look that laid me to waste inside. It was so full of despair, so bereft of hope. It was like dropping a stone into a dark well, waiting for it to hit the bottom, but it never does, it just keeps falling. That's what frightened me. That and her voice, which came out all raspy and hoarse. She said, "Nobody can protect me."'